THE SECRETS OF GHOSTS

SARAH PAINTER

Siskin
Press

This is a work of fiction. Names, characters, organisations, places, events, and incidents are either products of the author's imagination or are used fictitiously. Any resemblance to actual persons, living or dead, or actual events, is purely coincidental.

This (print) edition published by Siskin Press Limited (2020)

First published in ebook format (2014)

by Carina, an imprint of Harlequin (UK) Limited, Eton House, 18-24 Paradise Road, Richmond, Surrey TW9 1SR

For Dave, with love.

CHAPTER 1

$\mathcal{K}$atie Harper closed her eyes as the last lines of 'happy birthday' finished and blew out the candles on her cake. She concentrated with every ounce of her being, and wished more fervently than she'd ever wished before. More fervently than when she'd been in the middle of her horse phase and been hoping for a pony. More strongly, even, than when she'd thought she'd been in love with Luke Taylor and had tried her first real spell. She squeezed her nails into her palms and bit the inside of her cheek to provide a spark of necessary pain, biting hard enough to draw blood. Wishes could come true. There was magic in thought and intention. Katie knew this and when she opened her eyes, she expected the world to have changed.

It hadn't.

The disappointment thumped through her. She saw a flicker of concern on her aunt Gwen's face and hastily slapped a smile in place.

She kept the smile while the cake was cut, while her

uncle Cam gave her a hug and a cheque, and while she thanked everyone in the little group for coming.

Her face was beginning to ache by the time her mum and dad were saying goodbye. Her mum kissed her on both cheeks and apologised for the millionth time for rushing away. 'It's an early start tomorrow,' she said. 'And you know I get travel sick.'

'I know, it's fine.' Ruby and David were going on a cruise, their third in two years. They were taking their duties as empty nesters seriously and, honestly, Katie couldn't blame them. She hadn't been the easiest teenager to live with. She hugged them both, inhaling the scent of Ruby's perfume and moisturiser. 'I'm not staying late, either. I'm working tomorrow.'

'If you're sure,' Ruby said, but she was already halfway out of the door.

'Positive.' Katie was picking up every extra shift going at The Grange and, truthfully, didn't really feel like celebrating her twenty-first at all. Coming into her power. Now, that would be a day worth shouting about.

Katie followed her parents to the door, waving as they walked down the garden path and got into their silver Audi. Gwen had lined the path with candles in jam jars and strung tiny lights through the trees and hedges in the garden.

'You're working too hard. I don't like it,' Gwen said, coming up behind Katie and handing her a plate.

Gwen's tradition when it came to birthday cakes was to produce different flavour combinations and you had to guess what they were. Katie had caught a whiff of lime when she blew out the candles and she was expecting something sweet to counteract the acidity so the honey wasn't a surprise. There was something spicy in there, too, but she wasn't sure what. She took another bite and let it dissolve in her mouth.

Gwen was looking at her expectantly.

'Cardamon?' Katie said.

'Close.' Gwen shook her head. 'Cumin.'

Katie struggled to keep her face neutral. She was rubbish at the herbal stuff. What kind of witch was rubbish with herbs? A crap one, that was what.

Gwen was still talking about her birthday plans. 'You only turn twenty-one once. At least tell me you're going out for a wild night with your friends later. Clubbing or something.'

'It's almost ten already,' Katie said, then felt embarrassed. Lots of people went clubbing at ten o'clock at night. Maybe not in Pendleford, but still.

Later, picking her way through the candle-strewn path, she tried to rationalise. Her birthday was an arbitrary deadline, a day like any other. There was no real reason to expect her powers to come in on her twenty-first, any more than there had been on her sixteenth or eighteenth, either. She'd held real hope for her nineteenth — her final teenage year — but, truly, there was no reason to believe that it wouldn't happen tomorrow or next month or on a random rainy Thursday in October. She sat on the wooden bench at the bottom of Gwen's garden. There was no need to panic.

'What are you doing?' Anna had snuck up behind Katie. She was carrying a glass of sparkling wine and a concerned expression.

'Panicking,' Katie said. What if she didn't take after Gwen after all? What if she was actually just like her mother, Ruby? While her grandmother could read fortunes and Gwen could find lost things, Ruby was about as magical as a bowl of cereal.

'I'm having a mid-life crisis,' Katie said, shifting over to make room for Anna.

'You're too young for that.' Anna sat down. 'Quarter-life, maybe. Although, personally, I'm planning to live to one hundred and fifty.'

Katie forced a smile. It was nice of Anna to try and cheer her up. 'Have you tried the cake, yet?'

'Twice. I still have no idea. So, what's the crisis about?' Anna said. 'You don't want to work at The Grange for the rest of your natural born life?'

'God, no.'

Anna laughed. 'Me, neither. I'm going to open my own place. One day.'

'Are you?' Katie was surprised. Anna was a brilliant waitress: competent and quick and always smiling. She never seemed dissatisfied but then, Katie knew, she didn't know her all that well. And, of course, you never knew what was really going on inside people.

'What?' Anna looked at her sideways. 'You think I can't do it?'

'You'd be brilliant. You're so organised.' Katie nudged her. 'Unlike say, for instance, me.'

'That's true. I might not even hire you as a server. You're a bit rubbish.'

'Charming,' Katie said, mock offended. 'And on my birthday, too.'

Cam had followed Gwen into the garden and Katie watched as he put his arms around her. Gwen leaned back against him, twisting her neck so that they could kiss.

'Your aunt and uncle are really loved up, aren't they?' Anna said, noticing the floor show.

'Sorry,' Katie said, although she didn't know why she was apologising.

'At least someone is getting some,' Anna said. 'I'm in my prime, here. It's a crime not to be using this.' She indicated her body.

'I think women hit their prime really late. Like in their thirties or something.'

'I'm not waiting that long to have sex.'

Katie laughed. Katie had been really touched when Anna had asked to come to her party. They worked together at The Grange, and had only known each other for a few months. Most of Katie's friends had dispersed. They'd gone to university or London or on year-long round-the-world trips. A couple might still have been in Bath, but Katie had moved to Pendleford and, truthfully, not made all that much effort to keep up with anyone from school. As a result, Anna was probably her closest friend, but Katie assumed Anna had a battalion of other mates who, rightfully, came above Katie in ranking for time and energy.

Gwen said she had trust issues, but, as Katie liked to reply, she'd earned them.

She watched her party. Figures moved in the shadows at the edges of the garden, away from the lights. Gorillaz came on and Shari began dancing on her own in the middle of the lawn. She was the kind of person who could get away with things like that. The kind of person who got called a 'free spirit' and who always knew where the parties were happening and had exotic boyfriends who made films.

'Is that your flatmate?' Anna said, gesturing to Shari.

'Ex-flatmate,' Katie said. Shari was nice, but Katie had discovered that 'free spirit' translated to 'no boundaries' and she'd been relieved when Shari had decided to go and live with her latest boyfriend, Liam.

'Oh, sorry,' Anna said.

'Don't be,' Katie said, deadpan. 'If she hadn't moved out, I might've killed her.'

Anna frowned and Katie wondered if her tone hadn't been jokey enough. She opened her mouth to explain, but Anna had already moved on.

'This place is amazing,' Anna said. She gestured to Gwen's enormous vegetable patch, which spanned the side of the house. 'Have you seen what your aunt is growing? Aubergines, peppers, chillies. How does she——?'

'It's been really hot this year,' Katie said. She believed in honesty and never tried to hide her family's peculiarities, but, equally, sometimes it was nice not to endure a double take, a disbelieving look. She usually went with saying as little as possible. As long as it wasn't an outright lie, she wasn't breaking her vow of honesty.

'Another of her special abilities?' Anna said. 'That is so cool.'

Of course, this was Pendleford. It was common knowledge that the Harper family had certain abilities. If you needed to find something that couldn't be found, if you needed good advice, or a herbal remedy that would work when nothing from the GP had helped, you went to see Gwen. Katie wanted to follow in Gwen's footsteps; she just needed to find her own power, her raison d'être. She put down the empty cake plate and tried to look happy for the party guests, for Anna, for Gwen. It wasn't their fault she was a massive failure.

THE NEXT DAY, Katie still felt out of sorts and the flat was cold and empty. She almost wished Shari were still there, walking around in her underwear while talking full volume into her mobile. Or, maybe not. What the place really needed was a cat, but the lease didn't allow pets. Not even when Katie had explained that it was vital for her work. Every witch needed a familiar.

She lay on the sofa and tried to relax, but she couldn't stop thinking about her last failed spell and the way she couldn't even identify cumin in her birthday cake. She was supposedly in training with Gwen, but she seemed to be getting worse, not better. And the harder she tried, the worse she seemed to get. This was supposed to be her purpose in life. Her role. She hadn't gone to university or backpacking with her friends; she'd committed to training with Gwen. Gwen had run away, spent thirteen years denying her gifts and Katie wasn't going to make the same mistake. So why did it feel as if she'd taken a wrong turning?

Katie heaved herself from the sofa, mustering just enough energy to get the biscuit tin from the kitchen and shove a DVD into the player. Back on the sofa she prepared to comfort watch *His Girl Friday* for the thousandth time and eat chocolate digestives.

The phone rang just as Rosalind Russell was calling Cary Grant a snake. It was Anna, complaining about how Horrible Frank had been made Head Waiter. 'It's a travesty of justice,' she said, 'and he's messed up the staff rota for the week. I need you to save me. Come in early?'

Katie stared at the paused image on the television screen while she deliberated. What would Hildy do? Hildy had a proper career, the answer came back. But she'd work. 'Okay,' she said into the phone. 'Tell Frank that I'm keeping my tips this time.'

'You make many of those?' Anna said.

'I'm an excellent waitress,' Katie said, ignoring the pinch on her left ear that meant she was lying and that she knew it.

Anna laughed and hung up.

'Rude,' Katie said out loud and went to get ready.

She tied her hair into a high ponytail, smoothing back a stubborn wing of fringe. It fell into her face again, so she twisted it and used nail scissors to snip an inch away at an angle. When she let go the wing looked more asymmetrical and was now poking her in the eye. Fabulous. She put on her waitress uniform: — fitted black shirt, short black skirt, opaque black tights, and platform shoes — and tucked her revolver necklace inside the neck so that it was hidden. She was going to roast in tights, it was a warm day, but she knew from experience that a skirt meant better tips than trousers. It was icky, but true and, as Gwen would say; there was no such thing as a free lunch.

At The Grange Katie checked the staff rota and walked through the kitchen. 'Here comes trouble,' Jo said over her shoulder. She was frying what looked like ten different things at once, so Katie didn't pause to chat. Jo was tiny, four foot something, and the head chef. She also had the loudest shouting voice Katie had ever heard, as if to compensate for her stature. She'd terrified Katie when she'd first started at the hotel, but now she knew that Jo played that role. As long as you weren't completely inept. Katie cringed as she walked past a new kitchen assistant who appeared to be ladling coulis around an individual cheesecake with all the finesse of a Labrador. Sure enough, she heard Jo yelling before the door had swung shut.

Katie picked up a spare apron and tied it around her waist, slipped a pen and pad into the front pocket and headed into the restaurant. 'What are you doing here?' Frank, puffed up with his new position as Head Waiter, greeted her with his customary lack of charm. Katie was not in the mood so she just raised an eyebrow and said nothing.

'You're supposed to be in the function room. Wedding. Go. Go.' Frank made little shooing gestures with his hands, as if Katie were a naughty puppy.

When I get my power, I'm never waitressing again, Katie promised herself. She plastered on her professional smile and pushed open the door to the private dining room. A thin man dressed in waiting-staff black zoomed up. 'Are you Katie? Thank Christ. You've done silver service before, right? Brilliant.' He practically dragged her to the side of the room where buffet tables were laid out. Platters of cold meat and bowls of salad gave way to gigantic metal trays of chicken wings and pork escalopes crusted with a topping that Katie feared would slide off the moment she tried to haul them onto a plate. She tried to manoeuvre herself to the cold end, thinking that if she threw some salad down a punter at least she wouldn't give them third-degree burns.

The people who had been seated at round tables around the room decided, as one, that it was chow time and a queue formed. It was a polite queue; no pushing or shoving, just lots of chatter punctuated by braying laughter. Katie picked up the oversized serving tongs and prepared to fling food at the guests.

The waiter next to her smiled hello. 'I hope the MOPs are hungry — they might not notice the food is lukewarm.'

Katie smiled back. MOP stood for member of public and had been one of the first bits of insider lingo she'd learned at The Grange. It was something she loved about the job, the feeling of belonging to a team, of knowing a secret language. Perhaps more so because of being an only child. Katie had always longed for a sibling — ideally a twin sister — who she could share secrets with.

'Excuse me?' A youngish guy was holding out a half-full plate of food. 'Would you mind giving me some of that—' he frowned momentarily at the tray of chicken parcels '—stuff?'

Katie glanced at the far end of the buffet where the first guests were just beginning to be served. 'You're supposed to queue that way.' She waved her tongs.

He grinned at her and she thought: good looking and he knows it. 'I'm a rule-breaker. A maverick. And what's a MOP?'

'You'll be a hungry maverick if you don't join that queue.'

'Oh, go on, I know you're not nearly that mean.' He put a hand to his stomach and Katie tried not to notice how nice his torso looked, how well he was wearing his shirt and buttoned-up waistcoat.

'You have no idea,' Katie said, narrowing her eyes.

'Fine, I shall simply have to fill up on carbs. But I'm blaming you when I feel all bloated and lethargic later.' He grabbed a bread roll from the basket and stuffed it into his pocket, then piled two more onto the side of his plate.

By now one of the legitimately queuing people had reached Katie so she turned resolutely away from the cheeky good-looking guy and said: 'Would you like a chicken and Parma ham parcel, madam?' The woman at the front of the queue opened her mouth to answer but didn't get a chance.

'That sounds heavenly. You know, I've changed my

mind and I will.' Cheeky guy had his plate out again and was smiling at Katie, his dark eyes shining with barely suppressed humour. Katie wanted nothing more than to slap the plate out of his hands but Frank was hovering nearby, eyeballing her with an intensity that suggested guests ought to be walking away with chicken parcels, not engaging in a Mexican stand-off with the staff.

Katie knew when she was beaten. She successfully manoeuvred the chicken parcel onto the plate and gave him a fake smile. 'Enjoy!' Then she turned back to the woman who was waiting.

While Katie concentrated on her silver-service tongs, she couldn't help watching the chicken thief. He looked quite boyish, but with a scruffy bit of stubble that contrasted rather pleasantly with his smart clothes. She wondered, for the thousandth time, why suit-wearing had gone out of fashion for men. Cary Grant, James Stewart, Henry Fonda, all bona fide hotties in their day, and all unlikely to look quite so delicious in hipster jeans and an over-sized knitted beanie.

There was something a bit off, though. Katie almost dropped a chicken parcel down a customer's dress as she contemplated him. He had taken his plate of food and eaten standing up. He chatted to people, looked as if he was always on his way to a table, but never actually landed anywhere. It was almost as if he didn't have a seat to go to.

The chicken thief had a slim build and light brown hair that was kind of curly and wild as if he'd just rolled out of a particularly enjoyable bed. He smiled easily whenever anybody looked his way, but in between he was watching the crowd with an unnerving purpose. After studying him for a while, Katie realised that he looked like a predator in a herd of gazelle. Something was telling her that he was up to no good, although God knew what she could do about it, when she was distracted by an over-excited pageboy having the sugar rush of his life. When she next looked for him, he'd disappeared. It was none of her concern, anyway. Wasn't her wedding. Wasn't her problem.

Later on, after the dining tables had been moved and the disco cranked up, Katie was pushing the last bits of buffet food around on the serving plates, trying to make them look a little less sad and leftover, when Frank hustled up and barked orders: 'It's winding down here. Go and help with room service.'

She fetched the tray from the kitchen and checked the room number. Mr Cole in The Yellow Room had ordered a late-night snack of cheese and biscuits and a glass of port. Katie had been upstairs in The Grange many times before but, in her depressed state of mind, the grand staircase seemed oppressive. There was too much oak panelling everywhere and the brass stair rods just made her wince in sympathy with whoever had to polish the damn things. She had a sudden, horrifying vision of that person being her. What if she never worked out what she wanted to do? What if she ended up working at The Grange for ever and ever?

The Yellow Room was on the top floor. Katie walked down one grand hallway to a narrower staircase and up two flights to a plainer corridor. The walls were papered in cream with a thick embossed damask pattern but the ceiling was lower and the decorative mouldings less fancy. The old servants' quarters, most likely. The corridor was very clean and very quiet. The fire door whispered shut on the stairwell and, at once, the light seemed to dim.

Katie didn't know why she suddenly felt so uneasy. She told herself she was tired and a bit miserable, but it didn't help. She felt a blast of cold air on her back and turned to see who had opened the door. It was shut.

Katie readjusted her grip on her tray and forced herself to walk down the hallway. There were muffled voices from behind one of the closed doors, the muted sounds of a television from another. Katie willed her heart to stop beating quite so fast and tried to laugh at herself. She was being ridiculous. She was Katie Harper and a little cold breeze wasn't going to make her twitchy.

The Yellow Room was the last door and she wedged the tray against her body so that she could hold it with one hand and knock with the other.

No answer.

She knocked again, and called out in a chirpy, 'I'm here to help!' voice: 'Room service.' The door wasn't locked properly and it swung open.

Katie edged into the room, keeping her gaze lowered in case something private was happening. 'Hello? Is everything all right? Shall I just leave the tray—?'

She caught sight of something in her peripheral vision. A man was lying on the polished hardwood floor. His tie askew.

'Sir? Are you all right, sir? Mr Cole?'

There was something about the way the man was lying. His absolute stillness. Katie knew without touching him that his skin would be cold. In fact, cool air seemed to be spreading outwards so that Katie could feel it even where she was standing. She put the tray down on the floor with a clatter and stepped over it to kneel down next to the man. 'Mr Cole? Can you hear me? Are you all right?'

She touched his arm then, remembering first-aid lessons at school, pressed two fingers to the side of his neck. He was cold. Really cold. Just-come-out-of-the-freezer cold. His eyes were wide open and his expression fixed in a way that Katie knew that she would never, ever forget.

The coolness travelled up her fingers from where she'd pressed them against the man's skin and she just had time to think that he shouldn't be that cold, that it wasn't right, when she felt an icy stillness spread up her arm and across her chest, making her breathing suddenly slow. Soon, every part of her body was chilled and her scalp was prickling. She tried to move away, but her strength had gone. One moment she was kneeling upright next to the dead man, her hand at his neck, and the next instant she was slumped sideways and unable to move. Mr Cole's head was uncomfortably close. Through the horrible numbing cold, she felt revulsion and fear. She wanted to move away, but couldn't. She wanted to shut her eyes, to stop seeing his face, but she couldn't do that either. She felt as if her eyelids were frozen in place. From her angle on the floor, Mr Cole's face was in profile, and the terror and panic just as obvious. He looked as if his worst nightmare had risen up in front of him.

Katie felt a surge of panic. She still couldn't move and the cold was bringing back terrible memories. Not again, she thought. *Not again.* There had been a time. One very bad time when she'd felt a similar draining of control. A time when she'd stumbled out in the snow, drunk and crying and something else besides. She had felt herself dissolve, her will liquid and useless, and she'd vowed never again. As the cold slowed her thoughts further, she fought against it. Imagined pinching herself, imagined the pain she'd feel, and willed it to keep her conscious and rational. She stared at the pores on Mr Cole's face and tried to remember. She hadn't done any magic; she was sure of that. Hadn't tried any for months, now. The weakness was spreading. She wanted to sleep so badly, to stop thinking, and now her vision was fading. She heard a voice say, 'Oh, Christ,' and she thought, It's okay, someone's come, and the last of her strength disappeared and the world went black.

atie opened her eyes and light flooded in. A blurred circle of white gradually resolved into a face. Brown hair flopping forwards over unfamiliar features. After a moment, the nose stopped dancing, three eyes became two and the mouth pulled into a worried line. At once, she realised who was leaning over her: the good-looking wedding guest. The one she'd thought didn't belong.

'Oh, thank Christ,' he said, sitting back on his heels. 'You're alive.'

Katie moved her head and saw that she was still lying next to the dead man. She struggled to sit up and the young guy lunged forwards. 'You shouldn't do that. You might have hurt your back or neck or something.'

'I didn't fall,' Katie managed. Her voice hurt her head, which was already pounding. It made it difficult to think clearly. She could move, though. She stretched out an arm, flexed her fingers.

'Look…' he was standing up, now '…I've got to go. I'll send someone up here.'

Katie was trying to unscramble her thoughts. She'd

come in and seen the man and then she'd passed out. No, she'd knelt down and touched the man and then she'd felt very weak. She looked up, wincing as the pendant light shone too brightly into her eyes.

The good-looking man was at the door, hesitating. 'You're okay, now,' he said, as if reassuring himself.

'He isn't,' Katie said pointing at the man. They had to call an ambulance. He was past that, of course, but still. Suddenly, she realised she was going to be sick. She got to her feet and, the room spinning wildly, made it into the en suite to throw up in the sink.

When she came out the man had gone, but she heard footsteps in the corridor.

LATER, she sat in the public lounge with a sweet cup of tea and a female police officer. Either an autopilot setting had kicked in, or she was still spaced from fainting, but she was calm and methodical as she told the officer what she'd seen. A second track of her mind was running its own commentary. Katie expected it to be shocked and sad and all the things she imagined to be normal human reactions, but instead it thought: *Well, at least my birthday will be memorable for something.*

Katie closed her eyes. She was a bad, bad person.

Jo came out of the kitchen, still in her chef's whites, and gave her a hug. Jo nodded to the police officer, then looked into Katie's face. 'You okay?'

Katie nodded. 'Just a bit of a shock. I'm fine.'

Jo squeezed her shoulder. 'You should be at home.' She glanced at the officer whose name Katie had already managed to forget. 'Don't keep her hanging about, will you? It's not right.'

The female officer had a monotone voice, as if she were reading from an autocue and wasn't very good at it. 'There is a procedure that we have to follow.'

'I'm fine,' Katie said, before Jo could tell the police what she thought of their procedure. She rustled up a smile for Jo, who gave the officer one last long look before walking away.

'So,' the officer said, seemingly unaffected by Jo's display of concern. 'Do you remember seeing anything out of the ordinary tonight?'

'No, nothing,' Katie said. 'I mean, apart from the man. Mr Cole.'

'We're talking to all the members of the wedding party and the staff, but is there anybody else who may have had contact with Mr or Mrs Cole this evening?'

The chicken thief. Oh, bugger. If her hunch was correct and he'd crashed the wedding, he wouldn't be listed as a guest. Did that matter, though? She hadn't seen him talking to Mr Cole, although he had been upstairs in the hotel, where he'd had no business to be. On the other hand, bringing him into the conversation would delay the interview and she really wanted to go home.

While she dithered, the police officer continued her list of questions. 'Any loud disagreements, anybody acting strangely?'

'It was a wedding,' Katie said, wondering if her face had betrayed her. 'Define "strange".'

Patrick Allen strode into the room and straight up to the senior policeman who was conducting an interview at a nearby sofa. 'I came as soon as I could. I own The Grange.'

The detective stood up and they shook hands. Katie had inherited a less-than-positive opinion of Patrick

Allen from her aunt Gwen, but at that moment she felt sorry for the man. His hair was sticking up at the back as if he'd got out of bed to come to the hotel and he looked grey with concern. Maybe he wasn't the heartless suit Gwen had always described him as.

'We're not a chain,' Patrick was saying. 'We can't take this kind of publicity, and in this financial climate...' He seemed under the impression that the detective was a journalist. 'I don't want a circus.'

'There is no reason for alarm, sir,' the detective said. He started to say something about it looking 'very routine' but they moved away as they were speaking and Katie didn't catch it properly.

'Miss Harper.' The police lady opposite was leaning forward, her notebook balanced on one knee. 'Can I ask you again to think if you saw the deceased argue with anybody this evening?'

Katie snapped back to the conversation. 'Wasn't it a heart attack or something? Why are you asking that?'

'We don't know the cause of death at this time and we need to get as complete a picture as possible of Mr Cole's last few hours.'

Those words — 'last few hours' — flipped a switch inside Katie and, at once, she felt incredibly sad. That man, Oliver Cole, ate his salmon starter and drank the over-priced fizzy wine and chatted to people with no idea that he was enjoying the very last few hours of his existence. She reached into her shirt and touched her necklace as another thought hit her: with the Harper family intuition, would she be as clueless? Iris certainly seemed very prepared for her passing: she'd sorted out her journals, left notes for Gwen... But was that better? Preferable? How did it feel when you knew exactly how many more seconds there were to go on the clock?

Suddenly, Katie really wanted to get out of the overly warm living room. She wanted to go back to her flat and sleep for a day. Maybe two. She focused on the policewoman, who was looking a bit irritated. 'That's everything I can tell you. It's time to wrap this up.'

The woman's eyes slid over Katie's face as if searching for purchase. Then she said: 'It's probably about time to wrap this up. If you think of anything else, anything at all—' She held out a business card.

'I'll call you,' Katie said, getting up. She walked swiftly out of the room before the policewoman regained her senses and went to the staff room to collect her denim jacket and bag. Katie felt shaky. For a horrible moment she'd thought the policewoman had been going to ignore her suggestion. Light distraction or suggestion was one of the basic skills of the Harper women, as natural and easy as telling a white lie or reading cards to help a friend make a decision. It was one of the first hints that she was a Harper, turning up when she was just fourteen, and as much a part of her as the colour of her hair. What if each skill were stripped away until there was nothing left? What if, rather than coming into her true power, she was experiencing the disintegration of the abilities she already had?

The staff entrance was behind the kitchen so she said goodbye to Jo on her way through.

'You sure you're all right?' Jo frowned at her, her pixie-cropped hair sticking up at odd angles where she'd had her hat pinned all evening. 'Here.' Jo disappeared inside her walk-in fridge and returned with half a cheesecake on a cling-filmed plate.

'Thank you.' Katie was touched by Jo's kindness and it made her want to cry. She got out of the kitchen before Jo could see her eyes filling up, but it was a close-run thing.

The hot weather was holding and the night air was freakishly warm, even though it was past eleven o'clock. The curtains in the hotel were drawn and blocks of red-tinged light hit the gravel that circled the house, but the driveway was a pitch-black tunnel. She'd told Patrick last year that he needed to put more of the solar ground lights along it but he clearly hadn't been listening. As soon as she stepped away from the lights of the main building the shape of the low garden walls and clipped hedges took on a grey and menacing appearance, becoming strange and other in the half-light.

As a result she didn't notice the figure sitting on the top step of until the very last moment and she nearly kicked him in the back.

She recovered her balance without falling over him. 'Jesus! You scared me.'

'Sorry.' The chicken thief stood up. He was too close for comfort. Especially in the dark, deserted garden. Katie took a step back.

He stepped away, too, as if aware of her discomfort, giving her more space. 'I'm sorry I startled you.'

'Why are you loitering out here?' She didn't mean to sound so abrupt, but it hadn't been the best evening.

He held up an unlit cigarette. 'I'm wrestling with my demon.'

'Ah,' Katie said. 'I've heard it's harder to give up nicotine than heroin. Or is it cocaine?'

He shrugged.

'Why aren't you in there?' Katie gestured to the hotel. 'The police want to speak to you.'

'To everyone, surely. Not me specifically.' He tilted his head back. 'You look better. Are you feeling better?'

'You did find the deceased,' Katie said. 'I think that makes you a key witness or something.'

'You found him first.'

'And I've spoken to them,' Katie pointed out.

'Good for you. Very public spirited.'

'Seriously. A man is dead. You ought to—'

'I prefer to keep a low profile.'

Katie's mouth twisted. 'I hardly think they'll care about you crashing the wedding.'

'You noticed that, huh?' He pulled out a packet and stuck the unlit cigarette inside. 'And I thought I was so stealthy.'

'It wasn't that obvious. I was watching you, though —' Katie broke off. That was an embarrassing thing to say. He looked amused, which didn't help.

'That's good to know.'

'Because you seemed dodgy,' Katie said. 'Not for any other reason.'

He smirked. 'I'm Max, by the way.'

'Katie. So, big drama tonight.' She indicated the looming building behind them.

'Yep.' Max sat down again, his elbows on his knees.

'What were you doing in Mr Cole's room?'

'I was just passing, the door was open and I heard a noise.'

'Did you know him? The one who—'

'No.' Max shook his head quickly.

He was lying. Katie felt sick. It was unlikely that he had anything to do with the poor guy having a heart attack, but still. He was a liar. And he crashed the wedding which made him a thief, too. She felt a crushing sensation of guilt. She ought to have told the police about him. Ought to go back inside and tell them right now. He'd just lie to them, of course. And he seemed to be awfully good at it.

Like it or not, he was her responsibility. She sat down on the step next to him, probably a little too close for comfort but she'd always found this particular trick easier if she was physically near to the person she was trying to read.

She took a deep breath, concentrating hard, and trying to ignore the fact that she was close enough to catch the scent coming from his skin. 'Did you have something to do with his death?'

She watched him closely.

He frowned. 'Are you serious?'

'Just answer the question,' Katie said. Her voice was calm.

'No,' Max said. He looked disgusted. 'No, I didn't have anything to do with his death.'

He was telling the truth. Thank God. It wasn't his expression or the tone of his voice or the way his eyes met hers, it was something else. A certainty. Another of the Harper family intuitions but one that came in handy more often than most. 'Sorry.' She smiled, more at ease now. 'I'm just a bit shaken up, I guess.'

'Well, that's understandable—'

'It must have just happened when I found him. He'd called room service twenty minutes before. He was really cold, though.' Which was odd. Maybe. How long did it take for a body to get cold? Katie swallowed, feeling suddenly sick again.

'Oh, Christ. That can't have been fun.'

'Worse for him,' Katie said.

'No wonder you passed out. Are you sure you're okay? You still look really pale.'

'I'm always this colour,' Katie said. She started to

unwrap the cheesecake. Dessert would help. She needed some sugar to give herself the energy for the walk home. 'So, how'd you know the guy, Mr Cole. Were you two close?'

'I told you. I don't — I didn't — know him.'

Katie raised an eyebrow. 'If you keep lying to me I won't give you any cheesecake.'

'What makes you think I'm lying?'

'I know when people are telling the truth.' She smiled. 'It's a gift.'

Max tilted his head back and regarded her for a moment. Then he said, 'Remind me never to play poker with you.'

'So?' Katie used her fingers to break off a piece of cheesecake; it was messy. Messy and delicious. She closed her eyes to enjoy the creamy perfection and opened them to see Max looking at her with an odd expression. 'What?'

Max shook his head slightly, then said, 'He owed me money.'

'A lot?'

'Fair bit.' Max reached for the plate.

Katie moved it away. 'Why did he owe you money?'

'Do you play poker, as a matter of interest?'

'No,' Katie said. The sugar was helping, making her feel less weak and fuzzy. 'I used to play gin rummy with my dad all the time. I like whist but you need more than two and mum wasn't a card player.'

Max snagged the plate while Katie was talking and dug in.

'You know I'm not staying here, right?'

'Right.'

'Well, I'm just kind of passing through. When I'm

moving around I incur expenses. Petrol. Accommodation.'

'Food, when you're not crashing weddings, presumably.' Katie paused. 'Don't you get found out all the time?'

'Not really. I prefer corporate events, but big weddings are pretty easy. No one ever knows everyone at those things. If someone chats, you make sure to ask them first whether they know the bride or the groom and then you say the opposite. As long as you avoid the happy couple, you're golden.'

Katie shook her head. 'All for a free lunch?'

'I usually play poker in casinos or backroom games, but sometimes they're hard to come by, so I check out places like this that hold functions, turn up and make friends and play a few games of cards. For money.'

'You conned him?'

'No. Not really.' Max stared at the cheesecake. 'Maybe a little. Light hustling, perhaps.'

'And he croaked before you could collect your ill-gotten gains. Sucks to be you.' Katie stood up. 'Are you staying in town?'

'Uh-huh. At the delightful Cosy Inn.' He re-wrapped the cling film over the remaining cheesecake and got to his feet. 'I'll walk you home.'

Katie stifled the urge to laugh. 'I'm fine. Thank you.' She was Katie Harper. She was the latest in a long line of magical women. She was practically a witch, for goodness' sake, the dark was not a problem.

'Okay.' Max shrugged. 'You can walk me home.'

'Nice try,' Katie said, but, since they both had to walk down the driveway, there didn't seem to be much point in resisting too much. She'd have to break into a ridiculous trot to get ahead of him and that wouldn't be very dignified. Besides, the tall trees lining the driveway cut a lot of the moonlight and the driveway was incredibly dark. Katie didn't want to admit it, but she felt a bit shaky after seeing Mr Cole. A distraction was kind of welcome.

'So, you're a con man. I don't think I've met a real-life one of those before.'

'That's a bit harsh. I gamble a bit, sometimes I win, sometimes I lose.'

'But you hustled Oliver Cole?'

'You wouldn't be up in arms if you'd met him. I know it's not classy to speak ill of the dead, but the guy was a dick.'

'You said you hardly knew him.'

Max looked sideways at her. 'I'm a pretty good judge of character.'

The driveway curved down to the main road. Katie thought that she'd feel fine once she was out of the damn trees. The dark tunnel made her feel claustrophobic.

'So,' Max said after a moment. 'What do you think happened? I heard someone say heart attack.'

The unwanted image of Mr Cole's frozen face came back and Katie swallowed. He'd looked frightened. 'I don't know,' she said. *Nothing peaceful.*

Katie blinked away the image and said, 'So, why are you travelling around? Don't people usually go around, like, Venice and Paris and stuff? Not Wiltshire.'

He laughed. 'Not that kind of travelling. More of a road trip.'

They'd reached the end of the driveway and were on the steep hill into town. The lights of Pendleford shone in the dark like a constellation. The river was a velvet black ribbon. Soon they were on a street with lamps and Katie felt herself relax. 'A road trip on your own. Don't you have any friends?'

'Plenty.' Max gave her a twisted smile, but didn't say anything else.

They'd reached the brightly lit streets of Pendleford. All was well and Katie felt silly for her moment of weakness. So, she'd seen a dead body and fainted. It was unsettling and more than a little embarrassing but no reason to go to pieces.

'Well.' Katie stuck out her hand. 'It was nice to meet you.'

'I'll walk you home,' Max said.

'It's not far,' Katie said. 'I'll be fine. The Cosy Inn is down that way.' She pointed in the opposite direction to her flat.

'Are you sure? It doesn't feel right to leave you on your own.'

'Trust me, I'm perfectly safe in Pendleford.' Everyone in town knew that she was Gwen Harper's niece and half of them were terrified that she'd give them the evil eye. If she bumped into an idiot with a death wish or a clueless visitor, then she was covered with a home-made protection spell. Of course, she was bloody awful at spells, so she'd also armed herself with a practical option. Max was still hesitating, clearly torn over his misplaced ideas of chivalry. Katie pulled out her can of defence spray. 'I have this. See?'

Max took a step back and put his hands in the air. 'Is that legal? I thought—'

'It's not the good stuff,' Katie said. It was sticky spray, which had made her American friend, Alison, laugh for ten minutes after she'd explained that it shot goo, rather than pepper spray, but it said 'Mace' on the side in big letters. Plus UV-coloured goo had to be better than nothing. Especially if you aimed for the eyes.

Max looked into the spray nozzle and took another step back. 'I'm not going to win the "trustworthy" argument, am I?'

'Not tonight,' Katie said. She stuck out her hand again and he shook it. Katie tried not to notice how nice his hand was. Long fingers, knotty knuckles and the perfect size. It dwarfed her hand without seeming like a gorilla's paw. 'Nice to meet you, Max Thorne. Have a nice life.'

He tilted his head back, appraising her. 'You're kind of cold, you know that?'

The warm feelings she had been beginning to entertain fled. *Why were the good-looking ones always such wankers?* Katie sighed. 'Why do men think women are being cold if they don't fall at their feet?'

'Okay, okay.' Max turned away. 'I'm going.'

Katie watched him walk down the street. She told herself that she was making sure he was walking away, not going to follow her, but there was a part of her that just wanted to look at him one last time.

Inside her flat, Katie kicked off her shoes and stripped off her tights with relief. She'd been planning to get into the shower, but the headache was pulsing behind her eyes now. She took a couple of paracetamol and stumbled to the bedroom. When she lay down, the room seemed to be spinning, which reminded her uncomfortably of the one and only time she'd got drunk. It wasn't a good memory, but at least it pushed away the events of the evening. Katie closed her eyes and felt the adrenaline still running through her body, making her limbs tingle and her mind jump from one image to another. It was going to be a long night.

CHAPTER 3

Katie kept on seeing Oliver Cole's rigid face so, when she was finally dreaming and she found herself back in the upstairs corridor of The Grange, her hand reaching out to push open the door to The Yellow Room, she wasn't particularly surprised. *I can't be entirely asleep. I'm dreaming, but I know I'm dreaming. Weird.*

She moved into the room, knowing that she was going to see the body lying on the floor, half on the thick wool rug and half on the polished boards. But she didn't. He wasn't there. She turned, very slowly it felt, and looked around at the room. Everything looked normal. There was a suitcase open on the bed and she moved towards it. Men's stuff. Smart-looking trousers and neatly folded shirts. There was a book on the bedside table and a glasses case, a smudged water glass and a crumpled tissue. The toilet flushed and Katie looked towards the en-suite, suddenly feeling alarmed. Instinctively she wanted to hide; she felt guilty for being in this man's room. Even though it wasn't her fault. Even though it was a dream.

She stepped to the wall, next to the en-suite door so that when it opened it swung close to her face. Oliver Cole, alive and well, walked towards the bed. He was a bulky man and taller than she remembered. Of course, she'd only really seen him lying down. He started to undo his shirt and Katie panicked. She didn't want to watch this man get undressed. She willed the dream to change, but it didn't, so she stepped out from behind the door, heading for the exit as fast as her dream-slow legs could carry her.

Oliver turned in surprise, his expression trans-forming into horror as he caught sight of her. Then his hands were going to his throat, he was gasping, his eyes bulging and filling with blood as the vessels burst. She knew that expression; she remembered seeing it. He was terrified. His mouth was open as if he was screaming but Katie couldn't hear anything. Her own throat was hurting as if in sympathy and, suddenly, she was awake. In her flat. In her bed. Her hands clenched into fists and her breathing ragged as if she'd been running.

The sun was streaming through her curtains and it was already well past nine.

After several cups of coffee, Katie dragged herself up the hill to work. The Grange was Pendleford's nicest hotel. It was set on the outskirts, high above the town as if looking down on it. As it was a seventeenth-century manor house, it probably was. It looked just the same as always in the bright sunlight; there was no sign that anything untoward had happened the night before. Katie went around the back of the hotel and found

Anna propping open the kitchen door with a catering-sized tub of cooking oil.

'Oh, my God, I heard about last night.' Anna hugged Katie quickly. 'Are you okay?'

'Fine. I'm fine,' Katie said.

'Everyone's talking about it,' Anna said. 'Although watch out for Patrick. He doesn't want word getting out.'

Katie nodded and tried to step around Anna. She was staring into her eyes, as if waiting for something.

'You sure you're okay? I mean, finding Mr Cole like that—'

'Course,' Katie said, hating how stiff and formal she sounded.

Anna hesitated as if she was going to say something else, then she touched Katie's arm briefly and turned back inside.

The shift went quickly enough. Chatter from the staff was that Mr Cole had definitely died of a heart attack, although Katie wasn't sure if that was just gossip or whether it had been officially confirmed.

She marched through the downstairs rooms of the hotel, collecting stray glasses, straightening rugs and making sure all the flower arrangements had water. She loved how working at The Grange made her feel purposeful and efficient. She didn't want to do it for ever, but she liked being good at something.

At a momentary loss, Katie decided to check the library. MOPs were forever leaving the complimentary newspapers in an untidy pile or taking them away. She pushed the door to the small library open and found her boss sitting on the gold brocade sofa with his head in his hands.

He had a laptop open on the coffee table and was

obviously busy but Katie was too far into the room to back out again. He looked up, embarrassed, and straightened his spine. 'Hello there. What can I do you for?'

'Nothing, I was just—'

He stood up, running his hand over his head. 'Just checking the accounts. Beth is due on Thursday but... You know.'

Katie did know. Her father ran his own business and accounting was the bane of his life. That or invoicing for work. Or getting paid. The money side, anyway. And her aunt Gwen was self-employed, too. She'd run a market stall, Curious Notions, for years, but was successful enough now that she sold her work through galleries and took the occasional commission. It had taught Katie one thing: she wanted to be employed. Or be instantly so successful that she had a team of accounts and admin people to deal with all of that stuff. She gave Patrick a sympathetic smile and backed out of the room.

'Is the restaurant busy?' Patrick asked suddenly. 'I know occupancy rates are down but are we still getting drop-ins?'

'Not bad. Fairly full.' Katie didn't want to say that she and other waiting staff had noticed that it was nowhere near as busy at lunchtimes as this time last year.

'Good. Good.' Patrick looked distracted so Katie continued for the door. She was almost at safety when he said, 'Go and see Jo for me, will you? Check that the special offer menu is finalised for after the Greg Barton show.'

'Okay,' Katie said, not wanting to think about Greg Barton and his ridiculous stage act. She still couldn't believe Patrick Allen had booked something so tacky for his beloved hotel.

'I should've booked your aunt in.' Patrick was still talking. 'Would've been a damn sight cheaper, I bet.'

Katie didn't answer. The idea of Gwen doing a psychic stage show was too ridiculous to contemplate and didn't deserve a response.

Patrick closed the laptop and gathered the pile of papers next to it. 'Actually, I think I'll go and speak to Jo.' He gave Katie another look. 'Are you due a break?'

'Not sure,' Katie said. She was distracted by the feeling that an insect had just landed on her arm. She brushed it away.

Patrick was looking at her critically. 'You should take five minutes. I don't want people thinking I over-work my staff.'

Katie looked down. The hairs were standing up along her forearm but there wasn't anything there.

Patrick left the room, still muttering something about the lunch menu. The light slanting through the small panes of glass in the bottom of the window was cold and hard, which was peculiar when Katie thought of the searing heat outside. Her head was still sore from her fainting fit the day before and she felt stupid, too.

She wanted to be a wise and capable woman, like Gwen. A healer. A maker of spells. A fixer. Not a victim. And definitely not a delicate Victorian flower, requiring smelling salts and the loosening of her corsets at the sight of a dead body.

Katie gazed at the oak panelling and wondered how many fainting fits, corsets and the like they had seen. Maybe none, Katie thought, looking at the tall bookcases. Perhaps women hadn't been welcome in the library in those days. They used to think too much learning was bad for women, after all, and that novels rotted the mushy female brain. Katie wondered what the oak panelling would say about her shelves of giant books on herbalism and local history and then she caught herself wondering it and, instead, began to think that she had hit her head when she collapsed after all.

Maybe Patrick was right and she needed to take a small break. She leaned her head on the back of the armchair; the generous wings gave her something to rest her head against. It was gloriously comfortable and within seconds her eyes shut. She was having a hazy day dream, halfway between sleeping and waking, when a sudden rush of cool air woke her up. It was as if an external door had been opened and then closed on a cold day. The cold air dissipated quickly in the warmth of the room. Katie looked at the door and the window but they were both still shut. Besides, it was so muggy outside that you couldn't get a cold draught without an air-conditioning unit. The smell of pipe smoke made her sit up and look around again. There was nobody there, but she would've sworn that someone had just lit a pipe. Her grandpa had smoked a pipe and she remembered the rich, almost-sweet tobacco smell, utterly distinct from cigarettes. No matter, Zofia would still go mad. She had a hatred, not for smoking especially, but for guests that didn't obey the rules of the hotel. Was really funny about it, actually. Katie thought about going to find the perpetrator, but then sank back into the cushions. She was too tired.

Another blast of cold air forced her up and out of the chair. She was shivering, now, and every hair on her bare arms was standing up. The smell of smoke was stronger, the sweetness no longer comforting, but sickly.

Katie felt as if someone were actually blowing pipe smoke directly into her face. She held her breath and looked wildly from side to side, narrowing her eyes as if that would help her to see.

Nothing. There was nothing in the room. Nothing and nobody. She was just tired. The door opened suddenly and a teenage boy and his father walked in, arguing loudly. The father stopped speaking abruptly when he saw Katie.

She plastered on her work smile and swept past them into the warmth of the reception hall. Katie stamped on the feeling that she'd just been rescued and went outside into the sunshine. She took several deep breaths, banishing the pipe smoke with the scent of freshly cut grass.

KATIE HAD BEEN VISITING her aunt Gwen at End House on a Tuesday night since she was fourteen. They'd missed sessions, of course, for birthdays and holidays and when one of them was sick, but for seven years it had been a constant in her life. Pushing open the gate and hearing its familiar squeak and the thick scent of lavender as she walked up the path soothed her nerves. Things might not be perfect, but they weren't terrible, either. She'd decided that she wouldn't tell Gwen about passing out. It was probably because of the heat and the shock of finding Mr Cole and she was fine now. It would only worry Gwen and that was something she never wanted to do. Not again.

She could tell Gwen about her bad dream, though, and the weird feelings would go away; a problem shared and all that. And if not, Gwen might be able to give her a spell to make sure she didn't dream about Mr Cole again.

Cat jumped down from the garden wall and began winding around her feet. Katie bent to pet him and heard raised voices from inside the house. Gwen and Cam were in the kitchen and the back door was open, probably to let air through.

'It's not my fault,' Cam was saying.

'Are you saying it's me?'

Katie straightened up quickly. She shouldn't be listening; this was private. She wanted to announce her presence but couldn't make herself call out. She felt weirdly guilty even though she hadn't done anything wrong. Cat ran on ahead, squeezing through the gap in the door, making it swing open.

'I want this just as much—' Cam broke off as the door moved.

'Hello!' Katie called in a cheery voice. 'I've brought ice cream.'

Gwen was standing with her back to the sink, her face drawn and unhappy. Cam was at the opposite end of the kitchen. He smiled at Katie but it didn't quite reach his eyes. 'Mint?'

'Yep. And dulce de leche.' Katie unloaded her bag onto the table, not looking at Gwen or Cam. After he'd filled a bowl with mint choc chip, Cam kissed Katie on top of her head. 'I'll leave you two with your cauldron.'

'Funny,' Katie said.

After Cam had gone upstairs and Katie and Gwen had bowls of ice cream and spoons, the odd atmosphere dispersed enough for Katie to relax.

'What do you want to do this week?' Gwen already had a notebook open on the table. 'Have you been practising the heart's ease?'

Katie wrinkled her nose. No matter how hard she tried, she didn't seem able to make the remedies. She didn't seem to be cut out to be a healer like Gwen, which wouldn't be so bad if only she knew she was cut out for something.

'You've got to practise,' Gwen said. 'You can't do this stuff halfway. All or nothing.'

'I know,' Katie said. She sat down and tried to follow the preparation for Mr Byres's foot cream. The finished product was the right colour but it was runny where it should be gloopy. Gwen peered at it. 'I have literally no idea why that didn't work.'

'I'm useless,' Katie said, throwing herself backwards in her chair.

'No, you're not.' Gwen stretched. 'Maybe your heart isn't really in it. Do you want to try something else or call it a night?'

Katie sat forward. Incensed. 'But my heart is in it. I promise. I'm trying really hard.'

'I know you're trying, honeybunch,' Gwen said. She scooped the failed remedy into a plastic bag and tied the top. 'But sometimes trying isn't enough.'

'That's depressing.'

'Sorry,' Gwen said. She threw the plastic bag into the bin. 'It needn't be. If you want this badly enough then you won't give up, anyway, and if you don't want it badly enough then you'll stop trying and find the thing you really want to be doing and that can only be a good thing.'

'You don't think I should be doing this?' There it was, the thought she'd been avoiding. If she wasn't going to come into a power, a gift, and she was useless at the herbal stuff, then she had no place. No purpose.

Katie saw the future closing down like a thick forest growing over a path.

'I have no idea what you should be doing,' Gwen said, her face a perfect blank.

'I don't believe you,' Katie said. Being around a wise woman was hard work. You had the feeling that they knew more than they were saying, and it was hard not to resent that. Sometimes, just sometimes, Katie could see why people were wary of her family.

'Look,' Gwen put the kettle on, then turned to face Katie. 'I had the weight of expectation from my mother. She trained me, she told me every day that my destiny was to be just like her and I ran away from that. I'm not going to make the same mistake and tell you what you should be doing with your life. You can't fix things for other people. It doesn't work that way.'

'You fix things for people all the time,' Katie said. 'That's why they come to you.'

'That's different. You can't tell people what to do with their lives.'

'But Gran was right, wasn't she? You stopped running and came back and everything got better. You and Cam got together and you have a home and a life and you're happy. I don't want to run away.'

Gwen smiled but she looked sad. 'It's not a map. You can't follow my footsteps, you have to make your own path, make your own decisions. Maybe you should leave town, travel a bit, see the world.'

Katie felt as if she was going to cry. 'Why are you pushing me away?'

'I'm not. I swear I'm not. I just want you to be happy.'

'You don't think I can do it.' Katie knew that she sounded like a child and her voice wasn't helping any, cracking like that and making her sound pitiful and teary, but she couldn't help it.

'It's not that. I just think that you've been pushing on this particular door for a long time and that maybe it's time to try another one.'

'Fine, point taken,' Katie said. She stood up and grabbed her bag.

'Don't go,' Gwen said. 'We can watch a film or something.'

'No, I'm tired. I'll see you later.'

'Katie,' Gwen said, crossing the room and standing in front of the back door. 'Please don't be angry. I'm only trying to help.'

'I know.' And that made it so much worse. She wasn't a Harper woman; she was a client to be fixed.

'Stay,' Gwen said. 'I'll even let you choose the film.'

'I'm not in the mood,' Katie said. She gave Gwen a quick hug and stepped neatly around her to the door.

Gwen said her name again but Katie was halfway out of the door and she didn't stop.

Once outside, Katie let the hurt propel her forwards. She walked at double-speed, not caring that the warm evening air was making her hot and sweaty, that every breath felt like a gulp of soup. Soon, she'd turned off the main road into town and was inside the maze of cobbled streets that made up the tiny town centre. She saw familiar faces of people whose names she didn't know and several she did. Pendleford was that kind of place. Close-knit. Tiny.

She was a Harper. One day, she'd be living in a big house like Gwen's, dispensing wisdom and spells. A man with a dog on a lead nodded to her and she nodded back. Of course, she was going to have to get better at the spells and remedies, first. A lot better. The thing was, she knew she was going to do something brilliant. She knew she was going to rule the world or something equally amazing, but she'd always assumed the route to her something amazing lay in witchcraft. Suddenly, that didn't seem so likely.

At her front door, she paused to pet the cat that lived on the ground floor. It hissed and jumped onto a nearby wall. That wasn't usual. Katie might not have been a brilliant witch, but she knew animals. Katie knocked on the door of the cat's owner, Mr Davies, but there was no answer. She scribbled a note saying that she was worried the cat wasn't itself and had it been wormed, de-fleaed and checked by the vet recently, and shoved it under the door.

Upstairs, it took Katie several attempts to unlock the door as her hand was shaking. She was shivering, too, so violently that her teeth bashed together almost painfully. By the time she'd cooked a pizza from the freezer, Katie no longer felt hungry. Katie had always liked living alone, but now the flat seemed too quiet. She found herself wishing there were someone else around. If Anna were here, she'd make Katie a cup of Lemsip and crack bad jokes to check if she was delirious or not.

Katie bundled herself in a blanket and lay on the sofa to watch *The Lady Eve*. There was one plus side to probably having flu. It would explain why she'd screwed up Fred Byres's foot cream so badly. And why she'd fainted last night and was smelling pipe smoke that wasn't there. It had been an olfactory hallucination caused by a fever. She'd Google it in the morning. Relieved, Katie fell asleep.

～

Gwen put away the glass jars and re-hung the bundle of comfrey and meadowsweet from the wooden drying rack Cam had rigged up in the kitchen. She hesitated over the bowl of foot cream, still unsure how Katie had managed to mess it up so badly. The cream had separated completely, the oil emulsion sitting on top of the other ingredients, as if repulsed by each other. It had never done that for her.

Gwen emptied the whole mess into the bin and washed up the bowl, trying to think of something else to try with Katie. Herbal remedies certainly weren't her forte, but Gwen didn't know how to teach any of the other stuff. Most of it was experience, instinct; the right words at the right time. A kind of magic that was part psychology, part common sense. How Katie expected to have it, Gwen couldn't understand. At twenty-one, she'd hardly been able to find her own arse with both hands, let alone give sage advice. But there was no talking to Katie, no convincing her. She radiated need, thrummed with it. Gwen wanted Katie to relax, to enjoy her life, her youth, but she knew Katie didn't want to hear that.

Gwen heard Cam open the door from the hallway and a moment later she felt his hands on her waist; he pulled her gently backwards, against his chest, and put his face to her neck, inhaling deeply. 'What's that smell?'

'Foot cream,' Gwen said. She watched Cam kiss her neck in the reflection in the window and urged her nerve endings to respond. The glass was still cracked in one corner, something else she hadn't got around to fixing.

'I don't think so,' Cam said, into her ear.

It tickled and Gwen twisted away, fired with the

sudden need to move. She grabbed a tea towel and began drying up the bowl.

Cam stroked Cat, who was winding around his ankles. 'Katie gone already?'

Gwen slumped against the counter, hugged the bowl to her stomach. 'She was upset. She's not getting better — she's actually getting worse if anything.'

'Why doesn't she do something else? I wish she'd reconsider uni—'

Gwen interrupted him. 'I know. Me too. Ruby and David would be over the moon, too, but there's no budging her on it. She's convinced she needs to train with me. She takes being a Harper really seriously and that's good—'

'It shouldn't be everything, though,' Cam said.

Gwen turned away, put the bowl on the side. Cam tried, but he couldn't really understand what it felt like. Not really. He wasn't a Harper. He'd never woken up and found his life changed by a power that was at once external and completely part of him. He'd never felt the spark of power ignite inside his skin and watch it burn. He accepted her magic, her ability to find lost things and to make herbal remedies that were uncannily effective; he accepted that the people in their town came to the back door of End House at all hours of the day and night and that Gwen couldn't turn them away, had to help if she could with advice, a spell or some foot cream. He accepted, he supported, but it was never going to be a part of him. Gwen felt sick. No matter how close you were to another human being, you were never truly inside them. You were always alone.

Gwen realised that Cam had asked her something. 'Sorry?'

'Drink?' Cam was holding up a bottle of red wine,

already undoing the top. She heard the crack of the screw cap and did a calculation that had become a reflex. She'd only just had her period so there was no chance she was pregnant. She was safe to drink. Could drink herself into oblivion, if she wanted, in fact. 'Make it a large one,' she said and ignored Cam's raised eyebrows, his filthy smile. She felt the press of a thousand worries pushing down on top of her head. She couldn't even think about getting in the mood. She took the offered glass, thoroughly depressed. When had 'getting in the mood' become a chore?

KATIE WAS STILL SHIVERING the next morning, but she was certain it wasn't flu. She just felt cold. As if there were an air blower right next to her at all times. That wasn't right — it was more as if she were standing inside an air blower. If she could get used to the weird sensation, it might be quite nice. The man on the radio had already cheerfully assured her that today would be another 'scorcher' and she had an eight-hour shift at the hotel, starting with breakfast.

Katie avoided the main road out of Pendleford, which was choked with cars even at this God-awful hour of the morning. Commuters heading to Swindon or Bath or Bristol, sitting in their metal boxes and trying to pretend that the olde-world charm of Pendleford made their hellish drive every morning and night worth it. Katie took an old farm lane, instead, feeling more cheerful. Slinging cooked breakfasts at MOPs wasn't scintillating work but at least she wasn't stuck in an office cubicle.

The hedgerows were so lush and green that they

were hanging over the narrow road. The cow parsley had been thick and white, making the rows look covered in snow, but now it was dying back, overtaken by red poppies.

After half a mile or so, Katie realised something. It was too quiet. The birds weren't chattering. In fact, looking around, she noticed there didn't seem to be any birds around. No wrens or blue tits, no swallows swooping. She looked up, expecting to see a buzzard hanging motionless in the sky, frightening the little birds away. Nothing.

Feeling spooked, Katie looked carefully around. That horrible feeling of vulnerability was back. She hated her lack of knowledge, her powerlessness. Gwen would know why the birds were silent. Maybe there was a natural reason and maybe there was a magical reason but Katie was lost no matter what. She was cast adrift, floating between the two worlds. Aware that the magical one existed, but not powerful enough or clever enough to be truly part of it. She knew enough to be frightened and not enough to feel safe.

Then she saw it. A magpie, sitting on the wire fence a few metres ahead. It was looking straight at her.

'Good morning, Mr Magpie,' Katie said. She felt faintly ridiculous but that was the problem with superstition. It was hard to know which ones were based in fact.

The magpie didn't move. It continued to stare as she drew closer. Katie kept expecting it to get startled, to fly away, but it didn't. It shifted from foot to foot, twitched a wing, but continued to watch her approach. Katie was just thinking how weird it was when she was distracted by the warmth of the morning sun flooding through her. The cloud of cold air had disappeared and

Katie stopped walking from the shock of it. She'd got used to it and suddenly the heat of the day was there, on her skin. She could smell burning, too. Like a struck match. Then the magpie spoke to her. 'Watch. My watch. My watch.'

Katie looked at the bird. Magpies could imitate sounds, Katie knew, but those hadn't just been sounds. Those were words. Clear words.

Katie resisted the sudden urge to say 'pardon?' to the magpie. Perhaps she did have the flu after all. She put a hand on her forehead, tried to work out if she was running a temperature.

'My watch. My watch,' the bird said again. There was something urgent in its tone. Something pleading. It was staring at her as if willing her to understand something. And then she did.

'Mr Cole?'

The bird cocked its head. 'My watch.'

'What about your watch?' Katie said.

The magpie squawked and flew away.

CHAPTER 4

Katie slammed through the back door at End House. She'd phoned in sick to work and changed direction, heading to End House as fast as she could.

Her mobile buzzed as she half walked, half ran, and she slowed down to answer it.

'Please tell me you're not really sick,' Anna said. 'I wanted to go to the pub tonight.'

'I'm not really sick,' Katie said, out of breath. 'Sorry to leave you short-staffed for breakfast.'

'That's okay. There's hardly anyone here,' Anna said. 'Are you running?'

'Going to Gwen's.'

'Secret family stuff?'

'Kind of,' Katie said, feeling bad. Whatever Anna said, however accepting and chilled out she appeared to be, Katie still found it difficult to talk to her. Gwen had painted such colourful portraits of the dangers of telling people about their magic, but it was more than that: Katie was always waiting for Anna to realise that she wasn't such good friend material, after all. That the weirdness wasn't worth it. Katie wanted to be honest, didn't want to live a lie, so she ended up being cagey.

At End House she crashed through the back door and shouted, 'Gwen!'

'What's wrong?' Gwen was in a silk blue dressing gown, her hair up in a messy ponytail and a miniature rocking horse in one hand.

'Sorry, you're working.' Katie tried to push down on her panic, squeeze it into something manageable.

'Woke up with an idea,' Gwen said, pulling the door to the hall shut. 'Cam's still asleep.'

Katie winced. 'Sorry.'

'It's fine,' Gwen said. Then, 'What's wrong? You look pale.'

Katie laughed but the sound turned into a kind of hiccup. 'I had a really bad dream. About the man who died.'

'A man died?' Gwen said, her face draining of colour. 'Who?'

'At the hotel. Just a guest.' Katie shook her head, realising that she hadn't told Gwen. She'd planned to and then had heard her and Cam arguing and the weirdness of that had shoved it right out of her mind. 'I found him.'

'Oh, sweetheart.' Gwen put down the rocking horse, her face softened in sympathy. 'No wonder you had a nightmare.'

'And something weird just happened. A bird spoke to me. With a man's voice.'

Gwen put a hand on Katie's forehead. 'Do you feel sick?'

'I'm not ill. I think it was Mr Cole's voice. The guest. He had a heart attack.'

'Sit down,' Gwen said. 'I'll make some tea.'

Katie sat at the kitchen table, feeling comforted by the familiarity. Gwen's kitchen. A mug of tea. In a moment, Gwen would explain it all. Maybe the Harper powers always began with a chat with a magpie. 'Have you ever heard a magpie talk?' Katie said, over the sound of the kettle boiling.

Gwen was getting milk out of the fridge and the bottle slipped from her hand. Smashed on the floor.

Katie got up to help but Gwen stepped through the spreading milk and grabbed her hands. 'Are you sure it was a magpie?'

'Yes.' Katie would've felt insulted, they'd covered bird identification when she'd been fifteen, but Gwen sounded too freaked out. 'It said something about a watch. I think Mr Cole wants me to find his watch. Or do something with his watch. Or watch something, perhaps—'

Gwen's complexion had gone grey and her mouth was turned down. She suddenly looked much older than usual. 'A man who recently died spoke to you through a crow?'

'A magpie.'

Gwen shook her head as if she could erase Katie's words. 'No, no, no.'

Katie felt the hairs rise on the back of her neck. Gwen was usually so calm. This had to be bad.

'Gwen?'

She was staring to the left of Katie, her expression grim. 'I knew there would be consequences,' Gwen said, her voice bleak. 'This is my fault.'

'What are you talking about?'

'Blood magic.' Gwen seemed to be forcing the words out. 'I used blood magic. It's serious stuff. Dark. I knew there'd be a price.'

Katie frowned. Why did Gwen have to be so negative? And when was she going to be able to stop paying for that one little mistake? 'You don't think this is my Harper family thing? Maybe—'

Gwen shook her head. 'I don't know. I don't—' She broke off and reached for the nearest notebook, began leafing through it. 'I mean, I think there was something like this a long time ago, but—'

'That's it, then. I just inherited the crappest power. That's it.'

'None of them are simple,' Gwen said, still looking as if she was about to throw up. 'Lost things don't always want to be found.'

'I know that.'

'And giving people what they need isn't always fun.' Gwen looked angry now. 'Did you even read Iris's journals?'

'Of course,' Katie said.

'What about the stuff I wrote down for you? Did you read it? Did you take it in?'

'Yes! Of course I did. You know I did. I've been training with you every week for the last seven years. You know.'

'Well, it's a shame you didn't pay more attention.' Gwen snapped the notebook shut and frowned at Katie. 'Talking to a magpie? What were you thinking?'

'Charming,' Katie said, her anger matching Gwen's. 'What else was I supposed to do?'

'You need to be more careful.'

'I'm always careful,' Katie said.

'I'll look into it.' Gwen passed a hand over her eyes. 'There might be someone who'll know.'

'Not Gloria.'

Gwen shook her head. 'I won't tell her, yet. I need

to figure this out, first. Figure out what this means.' She grabbed Katie's hand. 'Don't tell anybody else.'

'So, do I look for his watch? I feel like he's asking for my help.'

'No. Don't do anything.'

'But—'

'It's probably not him. It's probably a curse or a hex or a rebalancing. This is not your power,' Gwen said. 'It can't be.'

Katie felt the disappointment. She was a victim again. Cursed. Or whatever. She was so careful, she trained hard, she'd read *Culpeper's Herbal* and *The Modern Herbalist* and everything else Gwen told her to read. She took notes in an A4 binder and never tried any magic unsupervised. She followed every rule Gwen gave her and now, when something had finally happened, Gwen was telling her to ignore it.

'Sit tight and don't do anything. I'll sort it out.' Gwen pulled her in for a quick hug. 'And if you see a magpie, put your fingers in your ears.'

'Are you being serious?' Katie's disappointment was rapidly growing into irritation. Gwen was dismissing her. It was like talking to her mother all over again.

'I'm completely serious. If this is a side effect of some kind, you've got to resist it.'

'Fine,' Katie said. 'I've got to go to work. I'm late.' She headed for the back door.

'I think you should stay away from that place. Just until things settle down.'

'It's where I work,' Katie said. She kissed Gwen's cheek and headed for the back door. 'Don't worry. I won't do anything stupid.'

∼

Katie crept along the upstairs passageway. She knew there weren't any guests in the rooms and she'd checked the time sheet for housekeeping and they should've completed the rooms on this floor. She flipped all the lights on and headed straight for The Yellow Room. The yellow police tape had been removed as per Patrick's instructions. Not letting herself hesitate, or think about what she was doing too much, she unlocked the door and slipped inside.

The room had been thoroughly cleaned since the incident. Housekeeping had done a bang-up job and the room looked just as it had on the day before Oliver Cole checked in, although someone had obviously knocked the thermostat as the room was freezing. She checked the en suite, not really sure of what she was doing, what she expected to find. The toiletries had been replaced, the loo roll was folded to a point, and the sink sparkled. Katie caught sight of herself in the over-sink mirror and grimaced. Pale skin, dark circles around her eyes and cracked lips. A frightening sight.

A sound from the bedroom made Katie's heart rate kick up. The door had been pushed open and there were footsteps, muffled on the carpet. Katie looked around wildly. She picked up the only portable item that wasn't a travel-size bottle of shampoo and edged to the doorway. A slice of the room was visible and she saw a male shape.

'Argh!' Katie sprang out of the bathroom, brandishing the toilet brush.

'Jesus, Mary and Joseph!' Max spun round.

'What are you doing in here?' Katie felt ridiculous, which made her furious.

'What were you going to do with that?' Max

pointed at the brush. He stepped forward, frowning. 'Is that a—?'

Katie turned around smartly and stashed the toilet brush back in its rightful place. She washed her hands to give herself a moment to regroup, then ventured out to find Max on the floor, peering underneath the bed.

'What are you doing?'

He shuffled backwards. 'They've cleared out this place, then.'

'Apparently,' Katie said. 'What's it got to do with you?' Then realisation dawned. 'You wanted to look through his stuff.'

'Don't you?' Max stood up, brushing down his jeans.

'No!' Katie said. The window was draped with heavy velvet curtains and they weren't fully shut. There was a section of sheer voile visible in the gap and it was rippling, distracting Katie. She crossed the room to shut the window but it was firmly closed. Up close the voile stopped moving and she wondered if it had been a trick of the light. She turned to find Max disturbingly close. 'You can't be in here. You're a MOP.'

'I just want to check a couple of things.' He shook the velvet curtains and then began searching the furniture — the bedside cabinet, the wardrobe, the chest of drawers.

'It's been cleared. His stuff is gone. It'll be with the police. Or his family.'

'Damn it.' Max had pulled the bottom drawer of the chest completely out and was up to his shoulder as he searched the space. 'Sometimes things slip down.' He glanced over his shoulder. 'Or, paranoid types tape their cash in unlikely places.'

'If you find anything, you'll have to hand it in. It's stealing.'

Max looked over his shoulder, affronted. 'I'm no thief. It's my money I'm after.'

'But he's dead. He can't pay you now.'

Max shook his head. 'It's my money. It's a point of honour to pay your debts in poker. It's the worst thing not to. I'm saving him from ignominy.'

Katie ignored the shiver that a good-looking guy using words like 'ignominy' gave her. She was going to keep her head. He was dodgy. And arrogant. And annoying. 'It's not right,' she said.

'Neither is not paying your gambling debt,' Max said. 'You play, you pay.'

'But the man has passed away.' Katie felt she was dangerously close to sounding like a Monty Python sketch, but she couldn't stop herself. 'He can't give you the money because he is no longer with us. He's dead.' She managed not to add that he was an 'ex-person'.

Max shrugged. 'Some things transcend death.'

'I can't believe you,' Katie said, revelling in the moral high ground. 'A man has died.'

He was on tiptoe, now, running his hands along the picture rail. His T-shirt rode up and there was a glimpse of bare skin.

Katie looked away.

I didn't say I didn't care. I hardly knew the guy but I'm sorry and all that. I just want to conclude my business with him and be on my way.'

'Well, you can't.' Katie was suddenly very glad of Patrick's efficiency. 'You'll have to speak to his family or something. Maybe they'll honour his debt. You never know.'

Max finished with the picture rail but was still

looking around in a distracted manner. Katie thought that he'd zoned out of their conversation and was about to say something when he looked at her in a disconcertingly direct way. 'I didn't get the impression that his wife was all that forgiving of his gambling habit. I'm not sure she even knew.'

'And you're squeamish about that? Rifle through a dead man's things, fine. Talk to his wife, no thanks.'

'Widow. And, no, I don't see the point in upsetting her. Upsetting her more, I mean. And it was his secret to keep or reveal, not mine.'

'I think your moral compass is a bit off.'

'I think you're money-obsessed.'

'What?'

'You're the one putting a man's money over his feelings.'

'How d'you know he didn't have very strong feelings about his money?' Katie shot back.

Max grinned. 'Fun as this is, I've got to go. Don't suppose you know of any poker games going on around here? Or blackjack?'

'In Pendleford? Not likely.'

'Oh, well. Something will turn up.'

'What will you do?'

Max shrugged. 'I have no idea. That's half the fun, though.'

'Funny kind of holiday.'

A strange expression crossed his face. At the door, he stopped and turned around. 'What are you doing in here, anyway? Don't tell me he owed you money too?'

Katie wasn't about to explain that she'd seen Mr Cole in her dreams last night and then a magpie had asked her to find his watch. 'Just checking that the room's ready,' Katie said, not able to meet his eyes.

She'd always had a policy of being as honest as possible, partly because she was completely useless at lying. She felt a blush begin on her neck, travelling up towards her cheeks.

'Right.' Max was looking at her intently, as if he knew full well that she wasn't telling the truth. Which he probably did.

He took a step towards her. 'Did you know Oliver? Mr Cole?'

'I didn't even know his name was Oliver,' Katie said, glad to be back on honest ground.

'You were at the wedding. Did you see him give anybody anything?'

'Like what?'

Max was still staring at her in an unnervingly calculating manner. Then his face cleared and he gave her a charming smile. 'Never mind. Don't worry about it.'

'I won't,' Katie said, irritated. The voile was moving again. Then the mustard velvet twitched. It billowed outwards as if there was something behind it, a figure hiding. Which was daft. Her eyes were playing tricks. Perhaps her blood sugar was low or something.

'Okay, then,' Max said. 'See you around.'

He left the room but Katie was distracted by the change in temperature. The room had been cool but now it was freezing cold, the skin on her arms goose-pimpling. She walked to the window but there was no breeze. The fabric of the curtain was moulding, funnelling into a solid column. There was definitely somebody hiding inside. Somebody moving.

'Hello?' Katie forced herself to speak, her voice coming out reedy and thin. Her insides went liquid with fear, but she stamped down on the urge to run. She certainly didn't mean to scream, but the curtains had billowed inwards, all towering thick cloth, which had suddenly seemed full of malicious intent.

Now, with Max back in the room and saying, 'What?' they were lying flat. Playing dead. She backed away from the window.

'I think there's someone in here, but I can't see them.'

Max didn't laugh, as she expected. He stepped up to the curtains and, before Katie could stop him, pulled them away from the window. Then he checked the bathroom, inside the wardrobe and under the bed. 'You're just a bit freaked out. After finding Cole like that.'

'No.' Katie shook her head. 'Look at the curtains.' The floor-length curtains had gone lumpy again, in the shape of a column or a person. She blinked and they fell slack.

'Did you see that?' Katie moved closer to Max. She looked around the room. 'Where'd they go?'

'Just some air or something,' Max said. 'I'll close the window.' He stepped forwards but Katie grabbed his arm.

'Don't!' Katie sounded properly panicked. 'Stop mucking about,' she said to the curtains. 'It's not funny.'

'It's okay,' Max said soothingly. 'There's nobody here.'

'I think there is. And it's really cold.' She was shivering and now her teeth clattered together. She felt Max's arm go around her shoulder and she wanted to lean into his warmth. But he was a stranger and a thief, so she stepped away.

'Let's go outside,' Max said. 'You'll feel better in the sunshine. Warm up a bit.'

'Something's wrong,' Katie said quietly. She turned her head, sniffed the air. 'Can you smell burning? And —' She broke off. Shook her head.

'There's nothing in here,' he began. Then a chair tipped over. 'Fuck!' He swore in surprise and moved to the door, Katie already a step ahead of him.

Max pushed Katie into the corridor and slammed the door shut behind them.

'Oh, my God,' Katie said. She took a ragged breath and leaned against the wall.

'That was odd,' Max said. His voice was level but he looked pale and his eyes were wide. 'Shall we go out for that sunshine now?'

Outside the air tasted good and the afternoon sunshine warmed the skin on Katie's face and arms, chasing away the chill. They walked around to the front of the hotel and down stone steps to the lower lawn.

Katie flopped down on the grass near to an enormous rectangular pond, the surface choked with lily pads.

Max sat carefully next to her. 'You okay?'

'Not really,' Katie said, but she smiled, to reassure him.

'Do you know anyone who would do this? To frighten you?'

Katie shook her head. 'I don't think so. I'm pretty popular.' She stopped, realising how arrogant that sounded. 'I mean. My aunt, Gwen, is something of a local celebrity. People either like her or they want something from her and I'm just kind of known by association. But people are nice to me.'

'You haven't fallen out with anyone? No big arguments?'

'Not my kind of thing.'

'Did you steal someone's boyfriend? Something like that?'

Katie snorted. 'No.'

Max looked as if he were trying to work out an algebraic equation. 'Anyone you know likely to play a joke like that? For fun?'

'That wasn't a joke.'

He shrugged. 'Maybe we've got heatstroke. Or we're drunk.'

'I haven't been drinking,' Katie said. 'Have you?'

'Not that I remember.'

Katie stood up, brushing grass off her skirt. 'I'm going to look for a watch.'

'What?' Max shaded his eyes and looked up at Katie.

She shrugged, looking embarrassed. 'Mr Cole's watch. I just need to find it. I'm going to check Lost Property.'

'Hang on,' he said, getting up. 'How do you know about the watch? Did he give it to you? I wouldn't put it past the old letch—'

Katie's eyes widened slightly. 'What do you know about his watch?'

Max put his hands on his hips and they stared at each other in silence for a moment or two. Max broke first. 'I need to find it.'

'Well, so do I,' Katie said. She turned and walked towards the hotel.

'It belongs to me. I won it,' Max said. He followed her across the grass.

'I don't know anything about that,' Katie said.

'What's your claim to it?' Max said.

Katie didn't answer.

'If you find it, you need to give it to me. It's mine.'

This wasn't good. Was Mr Cole's spirit asking her to get his watch off Max, because that seemed dangerous. Max seemed like the kind of person who wasn't going to give up in a hurry. Unless Mr Cole's spirit really did feel bad about not paying his gambling debt. Maybe he did want Katie to find the watch and hand it over to Max. If only the magpie had been a bit clearer. That was so often the problem with magic. It was so bloody cryptic.

Inside the hotel felt blessedly cool after the scorching garden. Anna was behind the reception desk, fanning herself with a brochure.

'Hello,' Max said, bypassing Katie and smiling at Anna. 'I've lost something and I was hoping you could help me?'

'Of course,' Anna said, putting the brochure down.

'I've lost a handkerchief,' Max said, leaning on the desk and gazing into Anna's eyes. He smiled a little. 'It's not worth anything, but it's of sentimental value.'

'You could look in Lost Property,' Anna said, dimpling back at him. 'I could show you—'

'A handkerchief,' Katie said. 'Really?'

'Katie was just on her way there. I'll tag along,' Max said. 'But thank you. Everyone has been so helpful.'

'We aim to please,' Anna said automatically, looking from Katie to Max.

'No chance,' Katie said, her hand on the door. 'Staff only. No MOPs.'

'What is this MOP business?' Max said.

Katie opened her mouth to tell him not to change the subject but Anna answered him: 'Member Of Public. MOP.'

'What about "lifer"?'

Anna frowned. 'Have you worked in a hotel?'

Max shook his head. 'I heard Katie say it.'

'Permanent resident,' Katie said. 'Like Hemingway or Fellini.'

'Yeah,' Anna said. 'Patrick would love a couple of those but I keep telling him this isn't London or New York. We don't get people with that kind of money.'

'Really? This place is pretty swanky.'

'Okay, say you were a millionaire with a yen to live in a hotel, with all the choices you'd have, would you choose this one? In Wiltshire?'

'Fair point but some people want the quiet life.'

'If you want it quiet, you don't live in a hotel. You live on an island or on your own private estate or something.'

'But there's quiet and then there's silent. If you live in a hotel you get to be around people, but not have to interact with them — at least, only on your own terms. You get to be alone but not lonely.'

'You sounded almost wistful then,' Katie said. She pushed open a door marked 'private', then turned to Anna. 'If I'm not back in five minutes, send out a search party.'

Anna gave her a thumbs up.

Katie stepped aside so that Max went in front of her down the short flight of stairs. If you walked in front of people on steps they could push you down them.

'You know, we don't keep any cash in Lost Property,' she said, wanting to distract herself from the fact that she was entering an enclosed space with a strange man.

Max shot a charming smile over his shoulder. 'Handkerchief, remember?'

'Of great sentimental value,' Katie said, her voice heavy with sarcasm.

He nodded. 'I'm distraught.'

'I can see that,' Katie said.

Downstairs, underneath the kitchen and next to the wine rack, was a short, wide corridor.

One side was completely filled with shelving and boxes.

Max pulled one out a little way and put his hand inside.

'I wouldn't do that.' Katie pointed to the hand-written label on the outside of the box, faded from time and barely legible.

'Teeth? You're serious?'

'You'd be amazed at the number of people who leave their dentures in their room.'

'Uh-huh.'

'And then there's the knickers.'

'Pardon?'

'Look.' Katie pulled out a bigger box from further along the row and produced a handful of silk and lace from inside. 'Women bring their best undies when they visit a hotel. Then they have a night of passion and leave them at the bottom of the bed. Totally forget about them and — bam — they end up in our knicker box.'

'Please tell me you've washed those?'

Katie dropped the crotchless pink thong back into the box. 'Of course. Well, Housekeeping did. Not me personally.'

'Why do you keep them?'

'In case their owners come to reclaim them. We're custodians of the lost pants, the dentures, the vibrators—'

'No. Really?'

Katie nodded.

'Any jewellery?'

'Sure.' Katie stepped closer and stretched her arm to reach for a shoe box on a high shelf. It was filled with watches. Leather straps, plastic straps, a red Swatch and a huge diver's watch. He scanned it quickly for his watch. It wasn't there. 'Why don't you send these on to the guests? You must have their details.'

'Anything really valuable — like a diamond ring — we do break the pact and contact the MOP, but for everything else...'

'What pact?'

'The pact of "see nothing, hear nothing". Very important in the hotel trade.'

'Okay,' Max said, looking confused.

'It breaks the illusion of invisible service if your knickers turn up in the post three days after your holiday. It's like slapping them in the face with them.'

'Right. Fair enough. But this is worth about three hundred quid.' He picked up the diver's watch.

'Really?' Katie peered at it. 'It's fugly.'

'It's waterproof to two hundred metres, measures depth up to one hundred metres and is made of titanium.'

'Woo-hoo,' Katie said.

'Ah, come on. It's shiny.'

'And being more evolved than a kitten that isn't enough to excite me. Sorry.'

There was a pause that lengthened past the point of comfort.

'Okay, then. Moving on,' Katie said, hating the fact that she knew she was blushing.

Max was standing close. He leaned towards her and, just for a moment, Katie leaned towards him.

Then she regained her senses and took a step back. 'You want to look for your handkerchief?'

'My what?' Max's voice had gone a bit husky. He cleared his throat.

'Your hankie,' Katie said. 'The deeply sentimental one.'

'Right. Is there a box for those?'

Katie pointed further down the corridor.

'Oh, bugger,' Katie said, sorting through the shoe box of watches. 'How am I supposed to know which one is his?'

'You didn't see him wearing it?'

'I wasn't looking closely at him, no.' Katie felt cross. She hadn't known she was going to be quizzed on Oliver Cole's accessories. *Culpeper's Herbal* had never warned her about that.

'May I?' Max held out his hand.

'I'm not letting you take Mr Cole's watch,' Katie said, gripping the box tightly. 'I don't care if you won it.'

He shook his head. 'I doubt we're after the same thing, that's all. The watch I won was a woman's one. Diamonds around the outside. Flashy in a mobster's moll kind of way.'

'So he was gambling with his wife's watch?' Maybe that explained why he wanted Katie to find it. Maybe his spirit felt bad about losing his wife's property.

'You didn't tell me why you need to find it. You don't even know what it looks like?'

'No.' She raked through the box, holding up the Swatch then dropping it back in. 'I'm an idiot. I'll just ask his wife. I'll say he mentioned it was missing — I don't need to tell her when he told me. Then I'm not lying. Perfect.'

'Perfect if you trust his wife not to pick the Breitling watch and sell it for a tidy profit.'

'Just because that's what you'd do.'

'In a past life, perhaps,' Max said. 'I'm turning over a new leaf.'

'Is that a fact?' Katie had the box held against her hip. 'You done, here?'

'Yeah,' Max said and they walked back upstairs, into the light.

CHAPTER 5

Cam was working late at the office and Gwen had taken the opportunity to go through all of Iris's journals. Back when she'd first inherited the house and had been reading the journals for the first time, it had often felt as if they fell open at exactly the place she needed. These days, she practically knew them by heart, but had to go through them in the normal way. Since there wasn't any kind of index system, that meant the slow way. After hours, in which the heat of the day made her want to put her head on the table and sleep, she wasn't at all sure the effort had been worth it.

When Katie arrived, Gwen delayed talking by making smoothies in the blender. As the fruit and ice whizzed noisily and Katie fetched tall glasses and straws, Gwen tried to think of a gentle way of explaining what she'd just read. Katie reached across and switched off the KitchenAid. 'What?'

'It's not good.'

'Tell me,' Katie said. 'I'd rather know.'

'Okay.' Gwen poured out the smoothies. She added a shot of vodka to her own and offered the bottle to

Katie who, as always, shook her head. Outside in the garden, Cat was stalking something in the undergrowth and the scent of lavender hung thickly in the air. The evening sun still had plenty of warmth, but it was gentler than earlier in the day. Gwen sat on her wooden bench, passing one of the cushions to Katie and rear-ranging another behind her own back.

Katie was gripping her glass and ignoring her smoothie. Gwen wanted to take away her tension, wanted to comfort her, but when she put her hand on Katie's arm, she shrugged it off. 'Please tell me you found something?'

'There was some information on haunting. Apparently, spirits do get trapped sometimes. They're either attached to a place, or an object, or a person.'

Katie sat back. 'Okay. So, Mr Cole is attached to me. I mean, he spoke to me through the magpie, so he's not stuck at the hotel.'

'That's what I thought,' Gwen said.

'So, how do I get rid of him? Not get rid, I mean, help him.'

'There isn't really anything about that. Iris is very cagey about speaking to the dead. She refers to it twice and both times she says it's a really bad idea.'

'What do you mean?'

'Apparently her grandmother could speak to the dead. Sort of.'

'What does "sort of" mean?'

'She touched corpses and knew how they'd died.'

'Like in *CSI*?'

Gwen nodded.

'Gruesome power,' Katie said, but she didn't look especially shocked. More intrigued. Gwen kept forgetting how strong she was, how motivated. She had to stop thinking of her as a frightened fourteen-year-old. 'So. What do I do about Mr Cole? Is there any way I can try to talk to him? Instigate contact, kind of thing. I mean, he's obviously trying to talk to me and if I want the nightmares to stop, maybe I should try harder to listen.'

That made perfect sense. Gwen felt uneasy about it, but she couldn't think of any way out of it. Katie was asking for her help. And since she was probably the one who had cursed her with this, she had to get rid of it. Cure Katie. 'There's a spell we can try. Like a sort of summoning.'

'Like a seance?'

'I suppose. Iris has put down the bare details but with so little description, it's clear she didn't approve.'

'Good thing she's not here, then,' Katie said. 'Can we get on with it?' She drained her smoothie, making sucking sounds with the straw.

'I thought you'd say that.' Gwen went back into the house and picked up the first candle to hand. It was a bergamot pillar candle she used in the kitchen to get rid of the smell after cooking curry. Back outside, she put it on the floor in front of the bench and sat cross-legged on the grass. Katie abandoned the bench and sat opposite.

Gwen lit the candle and reached for Katie's hands. They were cold and she squeezed them gently.

Katie looked excited, as if they were having an adventure. 'What should I be doing?'

'I think we just listen,' Gwen said. She stared at the candle flame and willed herself to relax.

'Focused or meditative?' Katie said, after a moment. That girl really had been reading her books.

'Meditative. We need to open a space for Oliver Cole to enter.'

'He's not entering me, thank you very much,' Katie said, but then she closed her eyes and went quiet.

Gwen did the same and, after a while, she felt herself slip into the dream space between waking and sleeping. Instead of a man who might be Katie's Mr Cole, she saw Katie lying in the hospital bed, aged fourteen and close to death. Gwen opened her eyes. Katie was in front of her. Twenty-one years old. Healthy. Alive.

Gwen was covered in goose bumps and she squeezed Katie's hands. 'Sorry. I can't.'

Katie opened her eyes. 'It's okay,' she said, evidently seeing something alarming in Gwen's expression. 'I'll find his watch. I don't need his help.' She smiled. 'I actually met someone else who is looking for it. He seems like the kind of person who gets what he wants. If I stick with him, I bet he'll lead me to it.'

'He?' Gwen said. She'd seen the kind of smile Katie was wearing before and knew exactly what it meant. 'Would this be an attractive kind of "he", by any chance?'

'Maybe,' Katie said. 'But don't worry, I'm being very sensible.'

'That's not what worries me.' Katie was always so cautious. She didn't trust people easily and was careful of every possible danger. While part of Gwen had welcomed that, knowing that Katie was never going to drink too much or take drugs or get into a car with a drunk driver, another part of her worried that she was never going to live either. That her safe world was going to get smaller and smaller until it comprised her own flat, End House, and that mausoleum of a hotel on the hill. Maybe not even the last one if Mr Cole continued to harass her from beyond the grave.

Katie drank some smoothie and laid her head on the back of the bench. She stretched into an enormous yawn, one that could rival Cat, and wiped her face. 'Sorry. Not sleeping well.'

'Take a nap, here,' Gwen said, taking Katie's glass and putting it on the ground. She might not be able to solve the restless spirit or possible black magic, but she could feed Katie blitzed fruit and give her a safe place to rest. Sometimes that was all you could do and, sometimes, that was enough.

GWEN WAS deep in thought as she walked along the canal path from Pendleford towards Bath. She'd set off early, before six, so that it would be quiet, but there were more dog walkers than she'd anticipated. A man was on top of his canal boat, smoking a cigarette in the dewy morning, and he said 'good morning' as she passed.

After a couple of miles, the rhythm of walking had quietened her mind and she felt as if she might be able to work when she got home. Gwen wasn't looking at the scenery, her mind was turned firmly inwards, so she didn't notice the woman until she was right in front of her. She jumped nimbly from the side of her boat onto the path. 'Gwen Harper, I presume?'

The woman had reddish black hair, the kind of colour you got with plenty of henna, and a yellow headscarf tied halfway back on her head, peasant-style. She was wearing dark blue jeans and a padded gilet over a checked shirt. She looked healthy and outdoorsy and looked oddly familiar. 'Have we met?' Gwen said, trying to keep her tone polite rather than worried.

The woman shook her head, holding out a hand. 'I'm Hannah.'

Gwen took the proffered hand. It was dry and the skin was a little bit rough, the nails cut square and short. Practical hands. 'Did you want something?' It was going to be slightly tiresome if people were going to start accosting her out in the open as well as coming to the back door at all hours of the day. No escape.

Hannah smiled. 'Not really. I just thought we should meet. Maybe we can help each other one day.' She shrugged. 'You know these things work. Tea?'

'Sorry?'

'Would you like to come in for tea?' Hannah gestured to the canal boat. It had the word 'Freedom' painted on the side in curling blue letters.

Gwen was torn between a desire to see inside the pretty canal boat and the feeling that getting into a confined space with a complete stranger was the kind of thing she'd warn Katie not to do.

Hannah narrowed her eyes. 'I knew Iris, if that helps at all.'

Gwen thought of Lily, her snake eyes and tiny teeth and the hard glint of insanity. She'd known Iris, too.

'I'm not surprised you don't trust people, after Lily Thomas.' Hannah appeared to be a mind reader.

'How do you—?'

'Oh, come on. Did you think the Harpers are the only gifted family in the world? I'm Hannah Ash.' She waited, as if expecting Gwen to do something. Gasp, maybe.

Gwen shook her head. 'I'm sorry, I don't—'

Hannah whistled. 'Wow, Iris wasn't joking when she

said she was the loner type. She really never told you about us?'

Gwen shook her head. 'I didn't actually know Iris. My mum and her had a falling out and we moved around a lot and—'

Hannah held up a hand. 'None of my business. I just wanted to meet you, to say "hello".'

'Hello,' Gwen said. She realised that she'd folded her arms across her body. Not very friendly. She forced them to unknot, put them by her sides.

'There are a few old families still around. My lot, the Ash family, are Avon way, the Irons are Somerset, I don't know the Willows very well but they're in Dorset. You know what it's like, can't live too close. That just causes problems.'

'Right,' Gwen said. She felt a little faint.

'I pass through this way at least once a month, usually around this time. Or you can ask one of the other river folk — they'll pass a message on. Just if you ever need anything.' Hannah gave Gwen a final look, raised a hand in a half-wave and jumped back onto the boat. She ducked through a low doorway and was gone.

Katie had arrived at The Grange for her afternoon shift. Anna was in the staff room, tying her hair into plaits and looking hot and bothered. 'Can you believe we've got to work in this weather? It's inhumane.'

'Agreed,' Katie said. Her back was damp with sweat just from walking through the grounds. She hung her bag on a peg and sat down to change her sandals for shoes. It was like forcing mini ovens onto her feet.

'I feel sorry for the bride,' Anna said. 'I mean, everyone wants sunshine on their big day, but this…' She waved one hand as if the heat had overcome her ability to finish sentences.

'Agreed,' Katie said again. She was trying not to think about Max, and failing. Raking through the lost property with him had been about the most exciting thing that had happened to her all year. 'What? Sorry.'

'Heatstroke,' Anna said, as if that finished the matter. Then she slugged back some water from a bottle and pushed through the door into the kitchen.

Katie was working the main function room, ferrying plate after plate of melon and prosciutto and dodging Frank's wrath. The sun was beating through the tall glass windows and everyone from the waiting staff to the groom was sweating.

As soon as she'd served the last of the starters, Katie went to find Anna. 'We need more fans.'

She set up three more electric fans around the edges of the room and a woman with silver-grey bobbed hair smiled and said, 'Bless you.' The air movement helped, but the temperature was still very high. Katie wondered how many guests would nod off during the speeches and she hoped the family would keep them snappy.

Katie had just finished serving sparkling wine to every table and making sure the kids had lemonade or orange juice when the best man rose and tapped his glass. The room fell quiet, apart from the drone of the oscillating fans.

Katie retreated behind the serving tables and carried on working as unobtrusively as possible. She knew from bitter experience that if you waited respectfully while the toasts were being made, you ended up in a mad rush afterwards. Fascinators bobbed gently in the breeze from the fans and the best man's voice, soporific in the best of circumstances, droned on.

'He's a bore, isn't he?'

Katie had been quietly boxing up slices of cake and hadn't noticed the woman approach. She had brown bobbed hair and a peach satin dress. Instead of the ubiquitous fascinator, she had a silver and black Alice band with a geometric design. She smiled widely at Katie's appraisal and lifted a hand to her head. 'Do you like it? It's the latest thing. Du mode.'

The woman was younger than Katie had first thought. Younger than her, in fact. Katie smiled politely. She didn't want to be rude, but carrying out a conversation, even quietly, was bad manners during the wedding speeches.

'What kind of cake is that?'

Of course, ignoring guests was probably worse. 'The bottom tier is chocolate cake, the middle tier is pineapple passion cake and the top tier is vanilla sponge. The boxes are labelled.' Katie indicated the pile she'd already filled. 'The bride wanted people to have a choice.'

The girl wrinkled her nose. 'Fruit cake is traditional. You're meant to keep the top tier and have it on your first wedding anniversary. Sponge will spoil.'

Katie looked around, anxiously, but no one seemed to have noticed their conversation. They were all watching the father of the bride and swigging table water, fanning themselves with wedding programmes.

'I don't understand the way people do things nowadays.'

Katie repressed the urge to laugh. The girl was seventeen or eighteen tops.

'And look at that.' The girl nodded towards the top table. 'The bride is making a speech.'

'And why not?' Katie shrugged.

The girl pursed her lips. 'It's not traditional.'

Katie wanted to tell her that wedding traditions like wearing white and taking your husband's name were throwbacks to a more sexist time but she didn't want to argue with a MOP. Plus, she had the sneaking suspicion that, given the opportunity, she'd be wearing one of those elegant ivory gowns, too.

'I'm Violet, by the way.' The girl trailed her hand lightly across the surface of the table. 'Is this real linen?'

'I don't know,' Katie said. She added 'sorry' to make it sound more subservient. Truth was, the girl was starting to make her a little bit uncomfortable. She had a very intense gaze.

'Would you like some cake?' Katie asked, holding out a slice.

'Oh, no.' The girl's hair didn't move as she shook her head; it made Katie's eyes feel funny. Maybe she really did have heatstroke. 'I don't eat cake,' Violet said. 'It's bad for the figure, you know.'

Fuck that, Katie thought. Out loud, she said, 'Oh, come on. You only live once.'

The best man pulled down a projector screen with a loud clatter and began showing photographs from the groom's life. Smiling pictures of the groom as a kid, groom as gawky teenager, and many, many pictures of him with groups of friends, red and grinning, drinks in hand. His life before meeting his beloved, of course. Back when he belonged to the best man and hadn't been bewitched by a female. Katie had only been half listening, but the best man's bitterness was seeping through.

Wrap it up, buddy, she thought. The emotions that came through during weddings were not always the ones you expected. Katie stopped staring at the carnage and turned to see if the MOP had any way of influencing the best man, but the girl had gone.

~

By the end of the shift, Katie was exhausted. The heat, combined with not sleeping well, made her feel like a zombie.

Outside, she found Max sitting on a low wall. He stood up as she approached and put his hands in his pockets.

'Hello, again.' Katie tried not to be pleased to see him. 'You're too late for the buffet.'

'I know.' Max flashed his boyish grin. The one that had probably been getting him out of trouble since he was a toddler. 'I was waiting for you.'

Katie stamped on the burst of excitement that flared in her stomach.

'I actually wanted to ask a favour.'

'Ah,' Katie said.

Anna came out of the staff door, pulling car keys out of her shoulder bag. 'Do you want a lift anywhere?' She caught sight of Max. 'Hello, again.'

'No, thanks,' Katie said. 'Anna, this is Max. He was at the Cole wedding.'

'Oh, I'm sorry,' Anna said.

'It's fine,' Max said.

'He crashed the wedding,' Katie said. 'So he's not bereaved.'

'Oh, good.' Anna looked confused. 'I suppose.'

'Nice to meet you,' Max said. 'Again.'

'Likewise.' Anna tilted her head slightly, appraising him. 'You don't live in Pendleford, do you?'

'Just passing through,' Max said.

'Lucky for you,' Anna said cheerfully. 'Are you sure I can't give you two a lift somewhere?'

'We're fine, thank you,' Katie said. Ignoring the significant way Anna was looking at her.

After Anna had walked away, towards the staff car parking area, Katie turned to Max. 'A favour?'

'I was hoping you'd let me into that room again. The door was open before but someone has locked it.'

'Probably because of the dodgy types hanging around,' Katie said. 'I'm not going to help you find money. I told you—'

'It's not that. I'm curious about what happened earlier. I wanted to take another look.'

'Why?'

'It might've been a ghost,' Max said. 'That'd be pretty cool.'

Katie crossed her arms. 'Are you going to tell me the real reason?' She waited for a moment and when Max didn't elaborate, she said, 'I don't think I should. I don't know you.'

'Fair enough.' Max shrugged. He began walking around the side of the hotel.

Katie followed. 'What are you doing?'

'Taking a look from the outside. Looking for wires or something rigged up that could've caused that effect with the curtains.'

Max stopped on the lawn and took several steps backwards, shading his eyes from the sun with one hand. 'Is that it?'

The window of The Plum Suite was on the second floor. It had one of the tiny balconies with thick stonework around the edge. Katie saw the window darken and she looked up at the sky, expecting a cloud to have crossed the sun. It hadn't.

'Nothing,' Max said. 'And I'm not climbing up there.'

He lay down on the grass and crossed his hands behind his head. 'It's too hot for one thing.'

Katie sat cross-legged next to him and then, feeling stupid for being so hesitant, lay down on the grass, a few inches of space between them. They were in a very public place, in broad daylight; there was nothing to worry about.

She put an arm across her face, shielding her from the sun.

'That room we were in?' Max said, his voice super-casual. 'Is it going to be Barton's when he arrives?'

'How do you know that?'

'Just a guess.'

'But you know he's coming here for a show?'

Max looked embarrassed. 'Yeah. I don't suppose you can get me a discount on a ticket?'

'Not my area,' Katie said. 'I thought you were just passing through.'

Max propped himself up on one elbow and looked down at her. 'Can I be honest with you?'

'I don't know,' Katie said, moving her arm so that she could look at him. 'Experience suggests not.'

He straightened up. 'Wow. You're really uptight, aren't you?'

'I'm big on honesty.' Katie shrugged. 'It's my thing.'

'Okay, then.' Max folded his arms. 'I wasn't just passing. I came to see Greg Barton.'

'The medium?' Katie tried to think of something

polite to add. 'I'm surprised,' she managed. 'You don't seem the type.'

'I'm not. Usually.' Max said. 'But I'm very interested in Mr Barton. I'd like to know more about him. You know, the man behind the show. His friends, his habits. If you could keep an eye on him for me when he checks in, let me know if—'

Katie moved back a little. 'I can't do that. I can't spy on a customer. That isn't right.'

'He's a public figure,' Max said. 'And a hotel is a public space.'

'That's not really true. Some parts of a hotel are public, some are extremely private. Plus, I can't trust you. You could be up to something illegal. I already know you're a liar.'

'Of course you can't — you just met me. Trust has to be earned.'

'That sounds almost noble.' Of course, he was a smooth-talking bastard. He would make it sound good.

'If you trust a person you've just met, that doesn't mean the person is trustworthy. It means that you're an idiot.' Max was clearly warming to his theme. 'There are two sorts of people in this world: mugs and marks.'

'Aren't they the same thing?' Katie leaned forward, interested despite her best intentions.

'No,' Max said seriously. He watched her intently as he spoke, as if it really mattered to him that she understood. 'Marks aren't necessarily stupid. The best marks aren't stupid at all. You need someone with the intelligence to see the possibilities. You can trick a mug, but for a con you need a mark. Marks are a little bit twisted. They have to be willing to do something they know is a bit dodgy because they want a part of the score being offered. That's why cons aren't often reported — the mark knows that telling the story will reveal his own part in it. That's what makes cons so beautiful.'

'There can't just be mugs or marks,' Katie said, forcing herself to look away. 'That's very bleak.'

'There are grifters, too,' Max said. 'Probably honest-to-God nun-types, too, but I've never met any.'

'You've never met a good person? You really are hanging out in the wrong places.'

'Nobody is pure as the driven snow. We're all living in the shades.' Max shrugged. 'I've never met someone who wasn't at least a little bit bent.'

Katie shook her head. 'My aunt Gwen isn't bent. Not even a little bit. She's always helping people. It's like, literally, her life's work.'

'I'm not going to comment on your family,' Max said. 'I'm not that stupid.'

'And what about nurses and those people who volunteer in Africa?'

'I didn't say people can't do good things. People do good things all the time, but that doesn't make them good.'

'But we are just actions — there isn't anything else. If you do good things you are good, if you do bad things, you are bad. That's how it works.'

'What about intention? What if you mean to do something good but it goes badly? Does that make you a bad person?'

'I don't—'

'And what about if you do bad things and good things? That's the usual thing.'

'You have to weigh them up,' Katie said. 'Some bad things are worse than others. If someone does loads of brilliant things and saves lives and stuff and then they nick a Mars bar from a shop, that doesn't cancel out all the good stuff.'

'Just makes a tiny dent in it?'

'Exactly.'

'And what if someone does something really bad? Can they cancel it out if they do enough good stuff afterwards?'

'Maybe,' Katie said.

Max smiled widely, genuinely amused. 'You believe in redemption?'

'Yes,' Katie said, irritated. 'Absolutely.'

Max shook his head. 'You're too nice.'

'I'm really not. Redemption isn't the same as forgiveness.'

'So, if I do lots of good stuff, you still won't forgive me for lying to you?'

'Oh.' Katie stayed very still while she thought about it. 'How good?'

Max smiled and she felt a low hum begin in her stomach.

'Like, maybe, kiss you,' Max said. At once, his face seemed very close. He wasn't leaning, though. Wasn't touching her at all. He was just sitting next to her and staring at her with such intensity, as if his whole life depended on touching her lips with his own, as if she were the centre of his universe. 'May I?'

Katie thought that nobody had ever looked at her that way. Then she realised that she wasn't breathing and took a gulp of air. When she managed to speak she had to clear her throat to stop it coming out all croaky. 'I don't know you. I don't kiss people I don't know.'

'But you want to kiss me?'

'I didn't say that.'

'Interesting.' Max tilted his head, as if considering

her. 'If you never kiss anyone you don't know, how do you get to know people?'

'Talking. Words. You know, the usual way,' Katie said. His confidence was making her feel more in control. If he carried on annoying her she wouldn't feel dangerously lustful.

'Kissing is quicker.' He smiled. 'You can tell a lot about a person from the way they kiss.'

Without meaning to, Katie thought about Stuart. Her first — and only — boyfriend. He had taken the advice to be gentle a little too much to heart and prefaced kissing sessions with a hundred or so tiny, feather-light touches to her lips, cheeks, chin. Every Single Time. It had been like foreplay performed by a butterfly. Katie felt her cheeks flush. To cover her embarrassment she said, 'You can tell a lot more from the total shite a person will say in order to cop a feel.'

He grinned. 'This is true.'

That smile punched her in the stomach. If she didn't move away, get distracted, right at this second she was going to take him up on his offer. What would kissing Max be like? She'd lay money it wasn't like a butterfly.

His smile widened, as if he knew what she was thinking. He leaned forwards, tilting his face to hers. 'Why don't you live a little?' He smelled of clean skin and sunshine and that indefinable bloke smell. He put a hand on her jaw, angling her face and then stopped, raising his eyebrows slightly in a way that asked for permission.

She tilted her head and leaned forward a fraction, closing her eyes so that she didn't have to look at his expression.

His lips on hers were firm and the pressure of them

made every nerve in her body crackle into life. Katie opened her mouth and tasted his. She felt as if she were melting into the ground, everything in her body liquefying. She put her hand on Max's cheek and felt that it was the perfect shape of a face, something that her hand had been waiting to touch for years.

Max was still leaning across, not touching her body in any way, and Katie was simultaneously glad and disappointed by his restraint.

He broke the kiss and smiled at her in a dizzy-making way. Katie resisted the urge to grab the front of his T-shirt and haul him on top of her. Barely. Instead she reached up and pulled him back down, capturing his mouth, testing to see if that first kiss had been a fluke. She was nothing if not scientific.

It was better. Max really was excellent at kissing. Not that she'd had that much experience, which, now she thought of it, was the perfect justification for necking with a complete stranger.

She felt his hand on her waist and then running up her side.

Panic washed over her.

Katie pulled away, her lust-drunk feelings draining away in a single moment of cold clarity. 'Sorry,' she said. 'I can't.'

'That's okay,' Max said. He moved away, lay back on his back and folded his arms behind his head.

'I mean, I don't know you.'

'No problem.'

It was annoying how cool he was.

Katie opened her mouth to say something else when there was a whistling sound and a massive crash. One of the large china urns from the balcony smashed into the ground inches from where they were lying.

'Fuck!' Max put a hand to his cheek and brought it away bright red. He looked at Katie. 'Are you okay?'

'Fine.' Katie got to her feet. She looked up to the balcony but there was no one there. The window was shut.

'How the——?'

'I don't know,' Katie said. She frowned at the sky, then got up to inspect the broken pieces of urn.

'You're shaking,' Max said. 'It's the shock.'

'I'm fine,' Katie said. Her mind was racing. Had she done it? Telekinesis wasn't a power she'd even considered coming into, but who was to say it wasn't possible? And she'd seen it with her own eyes. Although, if she'd done it, why had it been aimed at Max's head? She looked at him. Did she sub-consciously want to hurt him? Had she felt threatened or something?

'You should sit down. You're a bit pale.' His cheek was bleeding freely, giving a grisly cast to his unshaven chin, but his eyes were filled with honest concern. No. She was fairly sure she didn't want to stove anybody's skull in and definitely not Max's. It was too pretty.

'I'm pretty sure I didn't do it,' Katie began, 'but——'

'What?' Max looked at her as if she were crazy. 'Of course you didn't. Someone must be up there.' He looked up, hands on hips. 'There's no wind or anything. The window looks closed from here, though——'

'What if I did?' Katie was panicking, and the words were out before she could stop them.

Max stopped staring at the window and treated Katie to a long, sceptical look. 'You think you can move objects with your mind.'

'Telekinesis. It's a thing.'

'It's a made-up thing, yes.'

'If you knew my family, you wouldn't be so sure,' Katie said, under her breath.

'Okay.' Max shrugged. 'Let's say, for argument's sake, that it was you. Did you feel anything while it was happening? I mean, apart from being incredibly turned on by my amazing moves.'

'Funny guy.' Katie was determined not to blush. She didn't want to give him the satisfaction of ruffling her. He was insufferably confident. Maybe she had wanted to hit him over the head, after all.

Max was back to staring up at the window. 'It's weird that it came from the same room. Maybe it's a warning.'

Of course, someone else might want to hurt Max. It could be a curse. She sat up straight. 'Have you pissed anybody off?'

'Recently?' Max said. 'Probably.'

If he was hexed, he needed a cure. The next flying object might find its mark.

'Who has access to that room?' Max was still scanning the outside of the hotel. The stone balcony was tiny, just an ornamental feature, really. The window was an ordinary-sized one, not a door.

'If someone was out there, we'd be able to see them,' Katie said. 'They haven't had time to climb back through the window and shut it again.'

'Maybe someone rigged the room. With wires or something. Same thing that made the curtains go all weird.'

'Or one of us is hexed. 'Do I seem weird to you?'

Max glanced at her. 'Very. Why?'

'No, like glazed. Kind of drunk.'

He frowned. 'Why? Are you?'

'No.'

Max shook his head. 'We have to go and warn people. Someone could get hurt out here.' He picked up a couple of the pieces of broken urn. 'And I need another look in that room. See if it's been rigged. Although why—'

'You're right. We should tell Patrick.'

Katie headed to Reception to find him. He was behind the desk and, for a moment, Katie saw him as a stranger. A well-groomed man in his late fifties, with a patch of sunburned skin on his neck and a smile that didn't go anywhere near his eyes.

'I have a complaint,' Max said, before Katie had opened her mouth.

'I'm sorry to hear that, sir. My name is Patrick Allen and I'm the manager and owner of The Grange.'

'Someone is throwing stuff out of one of the upstairs windows. I was almost hit by this.' Max held out the broken pieces of china.

Patrick frowned. 'I don't understand.'

'From the balcony outside The Yellow Room,' Katie said.

Patrick shook his head. 'No one is staying there. That's the room—'

'Mr Cole's room, we know,' Max said.

Patrick looked at him. 'And you are?'

'I'm the guy who almost got his head split open at your hotel.'

'I'm very sorry for your shock,' Patrick said smoothly. 'I shall look into it and deal with the person responsible. Please dine free of charge during your stay. Which room are you in?'

'I'm not,' Max said. 'I was just visiting a friend.' He indicated Katie, who winced. 'On her break,' he added.

'Oh.' Patrick visibly relaxed. 'You were trespassing.'

'No. Visiting. As far as I'm aware this is a public building. It's a hotel. Visitors are kind of expected, yes?'

Patrick narrowed his eyes, which made him look like a lizard. A very well-fed lizard. 'But if you were thinking of taking legal action regarding the incident—'

'I'm not,' Max said, irritated. 'I just thought you should know that someone was upstairs taking potshots.' He handed the pieces of broken china to Patrick.

'I apologise,' Patrick said, with no sincerity. He tilted his head in Katie's direction. 'I assume you'll tell me the same story?'

'Jesus,' Max said, shaking his head. 'Your concern for your employee is touching.'

'I'm a very busy man,' Patrick said, his eyes snapping back to Max. 'What do you want?'

'Free tickets to see Greg Barton would go a long way to curing my shock.'

'I see.' Patrick's lips had gone very thin. 'I think I could manage that.'

'Thank you,' Max said. 'Incidentally, when does Mr Barton arrive?'

'I can't divulge personal information. Confidentiality is of utmost importance, I'm sure you understand—'

'I guess his people arrive before him, anyway. Sort things out. Make sure he only has blue M&M's, that kind of thing.'

Patrick looked nonplussed. 'What are you talking about?'

'Performers. They have riders, don't they? Like Van Halen demanding a bowl of M&M's with all the brown ones taken out.'

'Mr Barton has made no demands.'

'He's easy-going, then. Does he like to meet his fans before the show?'

Katie looked at Max. *Why the interest in Greg Barton?*

'I wouldn't know.'

Patrick's lip was curling. Not a fan, then. Or Max was just annoying him.

'They're probably a bit cagey about their methods,' Max continued, seemingly oblivious. 'These psychic types. Don't want to give away trade secrets.'

'I don't want to keep you,' Patrick said, and he waited until Max turned and left. Katie wanted to follow before he disappeared. The feeling that he'd been cursed had grown. Seeing him piss Patrick off so effortlessly made it more likely that someone disliked him enough to place a hex. 'Make sure he stays away from Greg Barton when he arrives. I don't want any complaints.'

Katie opened her mouth to explain that she didn't know Max, much less have any control over what he did or who he spoke to, but then she thought better of it. Patrick never listened to anybody and she needed to talk to Max before he disappeared.

'I think we should visit my aunt,' she said once she had caught up with Max, grabbing him by the hand and towing him around to the driveway. 'It's not far.'

'I'm not really one for family stuff,' Max said. 'Maybe another time.'

'Not like that,' Katie said. 'I think you might have heatstroke. And she's really good with things like that.'

'Is she a doctor?'

Katie towed Max along, and used the effort required as an excuse not to answer him. She had parked in the shade of some trees, but the car was still stiflingly hot. Katie felt the sweat run down the back of her neck and stick her vest top to her back. 'Lovely day for a run. Let me show you the sights of Pendleford.' She wound all the windows down and started the car to get air movement as soon as possible.

'Have you seen a medical professional about these mood swings?' Max said, but he belted up and stuck an elbow out of the window.

~

GWEN WAS in her back garden, a large hat shading her face and a book open on her lap.

'Code red,' Katie said, by way of greeting.

'So I see.' Gwen looked at Max and then back to Katie. 'Are you pregnant?'

'No! Christ, no.'

'Just checking.' She looked at Max again. 'Her mother fell at sixteen so you might want to be careful.'

'I'm always careful,' Max said.

Gwen smiled with absolutely no warmth. 'I bet you are.'

'There isn't time for this. Max, this is my aunt Gwen. She's not usually so hostile. Gwen, this is my friend Max. He just got hit by a falling vase.'

'Only a chip,' Max said. 'It's stopped bleeding. I don't know what the problem is.'

Gwen stood up. 'You'd better come inside.'

The house was pleasantly cool and Gwen went to the fridge. 'I can offer you apple juice or white wine. Or there's water, of course.'

'Water would be great, thank you.' Max looked even more out of place in Gwen's yellow kitchen than he had at the wedding.

'Where's Cat?' Katie accepted a cold glass from Gwen and drank half of it gratefully.

'Baking on the tarmac, I think. Hope you didn't run him over.'

'Don't joke about things like that,' Katie said severely.

'So, you're new in town,' Gwen said. She looked at Max appraisingly, her expression growing more thoughtful.

'I just thought we should have some lemon,' Katie said brightly.

Gwen glanced at her. 'Lemon?'

'Yes,' Katie said, raising her eyebrows at Gwen. 'In case we have heatstroke. We both feel a bit funny and you always said that lemon was good for heatstroke. Dried lemon, I think.'

Gwen gave a tight smile. 'Well, it's better to be safe than sorry.'

She turned away and began rummaging in an enormous canvas handbag that was hung over the back of one of the kitchen chairs. She produced an old tobacco tin. 'Come here. There's nothing to worry about.'

'I hate it when people say things like that,' Max said. 'They're usually lying. And I don't see why you think we have heatstroke. We've been indoors. I feel fine.'

'You just need to eat this. Ideally, let it dissolve under your tongue.'

'It's just dried, salted lemon. They use it as a salad ingredient in Greece, you know.'

'Salt's very bad for you,' Max said. His voice neutral.

'Drink plenty of water afterwards to counteract dehydration,' Gwen continued as if he hadn't spoken.

'I really don't think I've got—'

'Please,' Katie said. 'I know it's a lot to ask—'

'Fine,' Max said. He took the lemon from Gwen and put it in his mouth. 'This is fucking disgusting,' he said, pulling a terrible face. His jaw worked and his expression got worse.

'Try to let it dissolve. Leave it in your mouth as long as you can.'

'God,' Max said. 'It's horrible.'

'Think of it as one of your trials,' Gwen said, 'to win the hand of the fair maiden.'

'Hey,' Katie said. 'My hands aren't for sale, thank you very much.'

'Sorry.' Gwen nodded at Katie. 'My mistake.'

'Gah,' Max said. 'This is really grim.'

'At least it isn't pennywort. That makes you hurl. Gets the, um, heatstroke, out but purges everything else at the same time.'

'Mmm,' Max said, still chewing. He swallowed with a visible effort. 'Purging is still a distinct possibility.'

'Water,' Gwen said, thrusting a glass at him.

Half an hour later, they were back outside in the sunny garden. Max was lying on the grass, his hands behind his head watching the sky, and Katie was pretending that she wasn't watching him. Gwen wasn't pretending at all and had been staring at Katie with intensity for about ten minutes. Finally, Katie turned to her. 'What?'

Gwen didn't look away. 'Max. Would you do me a favour and go and refill my glass? Lemonade. Two ice cubes.'

Once he'd got to his feet and headed into the house, Gwen said, 'Tell me what happened again.'

Katie did.

Gwen leaned in. 'You know how Lily died?'

Lily Thomas, Gwen's ex-neighbour and genuine psychotic. 'The ceiling collapsed on her,' Katie said, reaching for the comforting shape of her revolver necklace. 'In the dining room.'

'It didn't just collapse. I think Iris did it.'

'Iris. As in dead Iris.'

'Yes,' Gwen said. 'I felt like she was still here. When I first arrived. The house had a specific feel and I know I was reading her journals all the time and there were notes from her to me, like she was talking to me from beyond the grave, but it was more than that. A feeling.'

'Fair enough. So Iris was haunting you and she dropped the ceiling on Lily. Go Iris. Hope you remembered to thank her.' A thought occurred to Katie. 'Is she still here? Have you seen her or anything?'

Gwen shook her head. 'I felt her leave. After Lily. Something changed in the house, suddenly, it was truly my house and Iris had gone.'

Katie nodded. It made sense. One witch in a house at any time. Any more than that and there was trouble. Just look at Gwen and Gloria.

'The man who died—' Gwen began.

'Mr Cole,' Katie said. 'You think this is something to do with him?'

'I don't know, but it's possible.'

'You mean the magpie thing might not be a curse? It might be a restless spirit, asking me for help?' Katie leant forward.

Gwen sat back. 'I have no idea.'

'So what should I do? Do I have to help him into the light or something? Is he throwing vases at me because he thinks I'm not paying him enough attention?'

'It's really not my area. Iris left of her own accord. I didn't make her go.'

'Is there anything else in the journals from ghost-whisperer granny? The *CSI* one?'

'No. Sorry. Iris doesn't write about it much. She's very damning about communicating with the dead,' Gwen said. 'She says that the dead ought to stay dead.'

'Ironic that she ended up haunting you, then.'

Gwen smiled. 'I hadn't thought of that.'

Katie wondered if there was a way to choose your power. She really didn't want to start hearing dead people. And she didn't want any more nightmares, either.

'Iris left once she'd protected me. Maybe it was unfinished business that kept her around. Maybe your spirit has something that's keeping them here.'

'Something that makes them want to knock Max unconscious?'

Gwen shrugged. 'Maybe. We don't know anything about him. Maybe he's bad news.'

'He does want Mr Cole's watch. Says he won it off him,' Katie said.

'He's too good-looking and he knows it,' Gwen said.

'He's not that good-looking,' Katie lied.

'Could be fun,' Gwen said, with a wicked smile.

Luckily, Katie was saved from answering by her uncle Cam. He opened the back door and said, 'There's a man in the house. Is he one of yours?'

'That's Max,' Gwen said. 'Be nice.'

'I'm always nice,' Cam said and disappeared inside.

'Uh-oh,' Gwen said, getting up.

'Why uh-oh?' Katie said, but she followed Gwen anyway.

In the kitchen, Max was leaning against the

counter, a glass of lemonade in one hand. Cam was leaning on the opposite counter, arms crossed, his expression unreadable.

'Why don't you go and change?' Gwen said, kissing Cam. 'You must be roasting.' Cam was still in his work suit. He put his arm around Gwen but didn't look away from Max.

'So, you're a friend of Katie's. That's nice.'

'I'm really sorry about this,' Katie said, crossing the room to stand with Max. 'They're not usually like this.'

'I got the lemonade.' Max hoisted the glass a little.

Standing closer, Katie could see Max was sweating although his face was quite pale. He had an unhealthy sheen. 'You have it,' Katie said. 'And sit down. You look a bit wobbly.'

'I'm fine,' Max said, but he sat down at the table.

Katie looked at Gwen. 'Could he have concussion? I thought just a chip of the vase hit him, but if it was going fast enough—'

'I don't think the lemon agrees with me.' He got up and stumbled out of the kitchen.

'Why are you being like this?'

Cam smiled. 'Your dad isn't here — I figured it was my duty. And I don't like him.'

'I got that,' Katie said. She filled a glass of cold water and drank it quickly, then rolled the glass against her hot forehead.

'Look at you, all protective,' Gwen said. She kissed Cam on the cheek.

'I'm serious,' Cam said. 'I don't think you should see him any more. He's bad news.'

'How can you possibly know that?' Katie didn't see any reason to inform her uncle that Max was almost certainly not going to be kissing her again any time soon.

'Honey, I was him,' Cam said. 'He's young and in heat and ready to sleep with anything that moves.'

Katie said, 'Ew, gross,' at the same time as Gwen said, 'Anything?'

'You just have to remember that he'll be doing all his thinking with his—'

Gwen stepped quickly away from Cam. She looked outraged. 'I didn't have you pegged as sexist.'

'What?' Cam said. 'I just don't want Katie to get hurt. Men like that—'

'Maybe she just wants to have fun, too. Did you ever think of that? Women like sex, too, you know.'

'Oh, God,' Katie said, practically running for the door. 'This conversation is not happening.'

'You don't need to be ashamed of your sexuality or your needs,' Gwen called after her.

'Bye,' Katie said. 'Thanks for the lemonade. Gotta go.'

Katie was relieved to find that Max had made it out to the main road. She didn't really want him to hear Gwen giving her advice on her love life. He was leaning against her car, looking queasy.

'Are you okay?'

'I will be when you tell me what all this is really about. I keep waiting for the other shoe.'

'What do you mean?' Katie put on her most innocent face. If he asked her outright about hexes, she wasn't sure she could lie convincingly.

'I don't know.' Max shook his head as if clearing his thoughts. 'I just expected some kind of con, I guess.'

'Isn't that your thing?'

'It's what I was brought up doing. My dad trained

me in this stuff. He had me running cons when I was still at primary school. It's not just what was expected, it was the only thing that was expected. You have no idea what that's like.'

'You're not a kid any more. You have a choice.'

'And I'm choosing to change. I'm turning over a new leaf. I'm not conning any more.'

'Turning over a new leaf? That sounds like something in progress. Something that you could just flip back whenever you decide it's all a bit too hard or too boring.'

'If I'd said "turned over a new leaf" you'd have accused me of arrogance.'

Katie fought the sudden urge to smile. 'Probably. But at least you'd have sounded more committed. Conning makes everything easy. I bet you've never done anything the hard way in your life.'

Max's face went blank and his voice matched. 'And you'd know about hardship. Pretty little rich girl living in the badlands of Pendleford.' He gestured to End House. 'You have no idea.'

'Well, at least you're being honest, now,' Katie managed.

'I'm sorry.' Max ran a hand over his face. 'I don't know why I said that. Maybe I do have concussion.' He tried a smile but it didn't sit. 'It's not been the easiest week.' He looked tired and worried and Katie felt a stab of sympathy.

Katie drove into town and dropped Max off at the Cosy Inn. 'Get some sleep,' she said as he got out of the car.

atie headed to the kitchen for an afternoon break. Jo often tried out the menu for the next day during the afternoon lull, and Katie was always happy to help her taste it. She found Anna sitting up on the counter in a shocking health-code violation. She was just about to warn her when Jo appeared from the walk-in fridge and gave Anna a look that could melt steel. Anna slid off the counter.

'Out,' Jo said. 'I'm working.'

'I'm just getting a Fab,' Katie said, changing plans. 'Do you want one?' Jo had bought Katie a catering-size pallet of her favourite ice lollies for her birthday and they had to stay in the hotel until she got the numbers down. She couldn't fit more than ten in her freezer compartment at home.

'Are you going to need help with that?' Anna said, nodding at the plate of cheese Jo was carrying.

Jo tilted her head slightly and narrowed her eyes.

'We were just going,' Katie said, hastily, pulling Anna by the arm. 'See you later.'

Outside, Katie shook her head. 'I thought she was going to throw that plate at you.'

'She's too uptight,' Anna said, squinting at the cloudless sky. 'And on such a beautiful day.'

'She's really nice when you get to know her,' Katie said. 'And you shouldn't annoy her when she's working.'

'I work without getting all arsey.'

Katie turned her face to the sun. 'The kitchen is her space. She doesn't deal well with others in there. It's fair enough, really.' The sun on her face was reminding her of the warmth of Max in the garden, his face in shade with the sun lighting up the tips of his dark curls, revealing hints of red. The scent of mown grass and musk.

'What?'

Katie opened her eyes to see Anna looking at her questioningly.

'Nothing.'

'Nothing, my arse. Spill it.'

'Okay, down there, though.' Katie moved away from the kitchen window and around to the side of the hotel. She handed Anna a Fab and unwrapped her own. 'Max kissed me.'

'Max? The poker player?'

'Mmm,' Katie said, and bit some of the white coating and sprinkles off her lolly.

'I thought you said he was dodgy.'

Katie couldn't stop herself from smiling. 'Oh, he is. He's a con man. He told me.'

'That doesn't sound very stealthy.' Anna looked confused. 'Is he staying?'

'I doubt it,' Katie said. 'I was just seizing the day, you know. Well, he was seizing the day and I was letting him.' She felt some of her good mood evaporate.

'Well, I'm glad. It's nice that you finally fancy someone. I was starting to think you needed hormone treatment or something.'

'Hey. I fancy people,' Katie said, stung. 'I want Jon Snow to put down his massive sword and do borderline illegal things to me.'

Anna laughed. '*Game of Thrones* doesn't count.'

'I've loved James Stewart since I was six.'

'Ew. Neither do dead film stars. I mean real people. You don't fancy real people. I was beginning to worry about you.'

'I fancy people,' Katie said. 'I've had boyfriends.' Kind of.

'Not in the time I've known you,' Anna said. 'It's not natural.'

'There's more to life than sex, you know,' Katie said.

Anna gave her a long look. 'Who said anything about sex? No wonder it's on your mind, though. You must be frustrated. Have you got a rabbit?'

Katie stuck her fingers in her ears. 'La, la, la.'

'When was your last relationship?'

Katie pretended to think, as if there'd been more than one. 'Stuart. We were together for nearly a year. He was really nice. Steady. Reliable.'

'Sounds like you're describing a car. What happened?'

Katie shrugged. 'Just fizzled out, really.' Not that it had ever been on fire, Katie thought. When she'd tried to talk to Stuart about their problems in bed, he'd said that everything was fine, that some people just weren't very sexual.

'Mmm. You're so due a grand passion.' Anna took

a big bite of her lolly and winced. 'Too cold,' she said around the ice.

'I definitely shouldn't be kissing men I only just met, though. That's a bad idea. Passion doesn't mean putting myself at risk.'

'Strangers are just friends we don't know yet.'

Katie raised an eyebrow. 'Are you trying to make me vomit?'

'It's a fridge magnet.'

'Oh, well,' Katie said, trying to lighten the mood again. 'You can't argue with a fridge magnet.'

Anna pointed her lolly at Katie. 'Exactly.'

BACK DOWNSTAIRS, Katie was trying not to look at Max, but every time she walked into the bar area to get a drinks order for the restaurant her gaze seemed to rest, immediately, on him. She told herself that she was keeping a professional eye on him, just in case he was under some kind of hex, but she knew that wasn't true. He was talking to one of the temp staff, a girl with a smooth honey-blonde bob. He was relaxed and smiling, and she was laughing at something he'd said, looking up at him as if he were a god.

Katie poured a glass of white wine, wishing she could slug one back herself, and opened a bottle of Coke. She carried the tray back through, hoping that Max was watching her, too. Would he glance up and watch her walk out of the room? Gwen had always said that intuition was something you could train, like a muscle in the body. Katie had thought hers was pretty good, but now it seemed to have deserted her.

She was at the exit when a communal gasp made

her stop and turn round. An unoccupied table in the middle of the bar was floating. Levitating. People were shoving their own chairs back and standing, gasps and shouts and nervous laughter. Then it crashed down, tipping onto its side and teetering for a moment before falling onto the floor.

Katie hurried over to put the table back up and bumped into Max, who was doing the same. Patrick was waving his arms around and telling everyone not to worry, it had been a trick of the light. One of the temp staff from the agency, a guy Katie didn't recognise, picked up the table and carried it out of the room, as if it were a naughty toddler.

'Trick of the light, my arse,' Katie said under her breath.

'Pardon?' Max said.

'Nothing.'

'Who was nearest the table?' Max said.

'I don't know. Maybe her?' Katie looked around, but the punters had mostly stood up and moved places. Katie hadn't been paying all that much attention to them before and it was impossible to remember who had been where.

She spotted Violet, standing next to an older man and woman who must be her parents. They were dressed in neatly pressed shirts and beige chinos and looked utterly ordinary next to Violet in her flapper dress. Katie looked harder. The same vintage-style dress she'd been wearing at the wedding.

'Excuse me,' Katie said to Max and crossed the room. 'Pretty exciting, huh?' she said to Violet. 'Listen, I don't know if you saw who was near the table just now. Was anybody touching it?'

Violet's mother gave her a quizzical look. 'I'm sorry, are you speaking to me?'

'Um, maybe. Did you see anything?'

'I just saw a table fall over,' Violet's mother said at the same time as Violet said, 'No one was touching it.'

Katie looked from Violet to her mother. They really looked nothing alike. And Violet was still wearing that beaded headband thing.

'Excuse us.' Patrick had hold of her elbow and was steering her away. 'What are you doing?' he whispered. 'You'll alarm the clientele.'

'It's okay, I've talked to her before. She won't mind.'

'I mind,' Patrick said.

'Fine.' Katie pulled her arm away from Patrick. 'I'm going outside for some fresh air.'

On the patio outside the French doors, the wisteria flowers were tumbling in profusion from the vines that climbed the side of the building. The sun was low in the sky, casting a warm honey glow over the view. Katie took a deep breath and told herself that arguing with her boss was not the smartest move.

There was a gust of cold air and Violet appeared next to her. Katie blinked. Violet had actually appeared next to her. She hadn't walked out from the dining room or from the side of the hotel. 'Violet?'

'I think it might've been done with wires. Like puppetry.'

'I don't see how that would work. And who would do that anyway?'

'Parlour trick. I once saw a medium make a table fly. We were all sitting in a circle, channelling our energy, but still. Larks.'

'But why?'

'The medium wanted us to believe she had magical powers, of course.'

'No, I mean, in there. Why would anyone set up wires to make a table tip over?'

'Talking to yourself is the first sign of madness, you know.' Max wandered through the French doors, a bottle of beer in one hand.

'I'm talking to—' Katie said as she turned to indicate Violet, but she'd gone. Disappeared.

'So, what do you reckon that's all about?' Max jerked his head backwards.

'Huh?' Katie looked left and right and then turned to look out across the lawn. No Violet. She couldn't have walked back through the French doors because Max had been coming that way and Katie had been watching him do it.

It was simple. Either Violet was a powerful wizard who was capable of vanishing into thin air or she was a master of disguise and had thrown on a cunning costume in the seconds Katie had been turned away and was now camouflaged as a planter or a deckchair. Or, the third option. Violet was a ghost.

'Excuse me?' Violet was standing next to them, as if she'd just appeared there.

Max rubbed his arms and peered up into the cloudless sky. 'That's weird. It just got really cold.'

'You're a ghost,' Katie said to Violet.

'Rather blunt, don't you think?' Violet said. 'What if I didn't already know? That would be quite a shock.'

'What?' Max said. 'Hang on, who are you talking to?'

'I'm sorry,' Katie said.

'That's all right.' Violet sniffed. Then she disappeared again.

Max was peering at her. 'Katie?'

'I've got to go,' Katie said. She didn't feel faint. She didn't even feel frightened. She just had to get away so that she could think. She headed away from the terrace and through the gardens.

That was no hallucination. She had just met a ghost. She could talk to ghosts.

She found herself at the vast ornamental pond and sat on its low stone border. She stared at the lily pads and the encroaching algae and pond skaters and let the elation run through her. It was like electricity, starting at her toes and buzzing through to the top of her head. She could talk to ghosts. She was a Harper.

CHAPTER 7

Max followed her into the garden. 'What was that? Are you trying to make me believe that there is something ghostly going on here?' He looked tense. The dangerous, predatory look was back and Katie fought the urge to get up and run.

'I'm not trying to make you believe anything,' Katie said. 'You followed me.'

'Katie?' She looked towards the hotel and saw Patrick Allen barrelling towards them, looking like a man on a mission.

'Oh, come on,' Max said. 'This is practically "haunting for dummies". A flying table, broken china, billowing curtains, you pretending to talk to thin air. All you need now are creepy twin girls saying "redrum" and you're sorted.'

'I'm not doing anything,' Katie said. 'Those things are happening. I just happen to be nearby when they do. Don't get all over-excited with that cause and effect business.'

Patrick reached them and scowled at Max. 'What are you doing here?'

Max held his hands up. 'Not a thing.'

'What's wrong?' Katie asked Patrick. He was redder than usual and breathing heavily.

'Not in front of——' Patrick gestured to Max.

'Don't worry. I don't think he's your target audience.'

Patrick nodded. 'True. I think The Grange is out of his price range.'

'I'm standing right here,' Max said, but he looked more relaxed. Katie wasn't fooled.

'I was hoping you could help,' Patrick said. He turned to Max. 'Could you give us a moment, please? This is a private matter?'

Max shrugged and walked away a couple of steps.

'Okay,' Katie said. 'What's up?'

Patrick glanced at Max, who had turned his back and was studying the lily pond. 'I don't know. It seems as if something a little out of the ordinary is going on. Maybe something...' Patrick lowered his voice to a whisper '...supernatural.'

'I don't see what I can do,' Katie said, truthfully enough.

'Oh, come, I know your family. If you can't help me, perhaps you can ask your aunt on my behalf.'

'Ask her yourself,' Katie said. She wished she could take the words back. If Patrick Allen asked for Gwen's help, Gwen would feel duty-bound to say yes even though she hated the man. Gwen was big on duty.

Patrick had the grace to look slightly ashamed. 'I don't think she'd help me. I've not always been, um...' He paused, then tried again. 'We've not always seen eye to eye.'

Katie nodded, acknowledging the truth of his state-ment. After a pause, she added, 'So?'

'Please.' Patrick seemed to force the word out. 'Everyone says that you're like Gwen. Please help me. I can't afford to lose any more guests. The restaurant is due to be assessed for an AA Rosette, which would put us on the map, and I'm trying different events to bring in more customers, but it'll all be for nothing if I can't stop this nonsense. We're a boutique hotel — we offer spa treatments and afternoon tea. I can't have this—'

'Do you have any enemies?' Max said, turning around.

'I beg your pardon?'

'Have you made any enemies in the hotel trade?' Max said, speaking more slowly.

'You can't make an omelette without breaking eggs,' Patrick said. He puffed his chest out, a sure sign he was about to make a proclamation of some kind. 'Show me a businessman without any enemies and I'll show you a destitute one.'

'I'm not criticising you,' Max said. 'Just making a point. Mind you, it's a bit of an odd way to go. I would've thought a touch of food poisoning in the kitchens would be more effective. That'd shut you down —' Max clicked his fingers '—like that.'

'What do you know?' Patrick said, looking wary and not a little angry.

'Lots of things,' Max said. 'I know about cons, scams and hoaxes. I bet you'll find you've got a disgruntled ex-employee or a business rival.'

'It's possible, I suppose,' Patrick said.

'That does seem most likely,' Katie said. 'I mean—' she forced a short laugh '—it's hardly going to be haunted, is it?'

Patrick tilted his head back a little and regarded her. 'I grew up in this town and I've owned businesses here for over thirty years. Besides, you don't get to be mayor of a town like Pendleford without keeping an open mind.'

'Right,' Katie said. She couldn't wait to tell Gwen that Patrick Allen was asking her for help. On the other hand, it would be brilliant for Jo's career as a chef if the restaurant got upgraded. And Patrick looked truly wretched. 'I'm not saying that I know anything about these kinds of things,' Katie said, 'but I'll look into it.'

'You're getting scammed.' Max was scowling.

'Not by me,' Katie said. 'I'm not asking for anything.'

'I appreciate it,' Patrick said, ignoring Max completely. He clasped Katie's hand, then turned back to the hotel.

Max waited until he had reached the stone steps leading back up to the main building, then turned to Katie. 'So, is everybody around here crazy, or what?'

'He's just keeping an open mind.'

'He thinks the hotel is haunted,' Max said. 'That's beyond an open mind. That's—'

'Don't say "crazy" again,' Katie said. 'I'll think less of you. Plenty of people believe in ghosts.'

'So, you think a poltergeist threw that vase?'

'I'm not jumping to any conclusions,' Katie said.

Max put his hands on his hips. 'Isn't it more likely that a real live person is behind this? On account of ghosts not being real?'

'That's your opinion,' Katie said.

'Isn't it more likely to be a real live person who is invested in the myth of the afterlife like, say, Greg Barton?'

Katie thought about Violet. She was real. Not the

kind of haunting you could fake. 'I don't think so,' she said.

'What if he set these things up? To drum up some publicity for his shows?'

'You really don't like him, do you?'

'Did I hear that this place is short-staffed at the moment?'

'Yes, why—?' Katie began, but Max had already moved away. Katie watched him take long strides towards the hotel and thought: that can't be good.

BACK AT THE FLAT, Katie had only just kicked off her work shoes when her mobile beeped. Her head hurt and for a split second she thought about ignoring it.

It was Gwen. 'Can I borrow a scarf?'

'I knew you'd succumb,' Katie said, rubbing her aching feet with one hand.

'What?'

'Accessorising. I knew you'd follow the wisdom of my ways eventually. What's the occasion?' Katie was smiling, imagining her and Cam having some lovely anniversary celebration. Something couply and normal and safe.

Gwen's voice had gone cold and a little bit panicked. 'You forgot.'

'What? No.' Oh, God, was it an important anniversary? Like a silver or a gold or something? No, that couldn't be right...

'My opening. You said you'd be there.'

Gwen's exhibition. At the Rotunda Gallery in Bath. 'Of course I will.' Katie walked rapidly to her wardrobe and began hauling clothes off hangers.

'Starts at six, right? I'll be there. You wanted a scarf? What colour?'

'Doesn't matter, really,' Gwen said. 'I'm wearing black.'

'Like a true artist,' Katie said approvingly.

'Yes, but I thought something, maybe a little floaty thing around my neck.'

Katie paused, picturing Gwen. Then she said, 'I'll bring a couple and you can choose, but you might not need it.'

'Okay,' Gwen said. 'Thanks.'

She sounded tense. 'It's going to be brilliant,' Katie said, desperate to get off the phone and get ready.

Katie pulled the cover off her sewing machine and sat down. She had a black and white prom dress from Gwen's Curious Notions days and she'd been meaning to alter it for ages. This was the perfect opportunity and a deadline always sharpened her skills. She'd flipped the dress inside out and pinned new darts under the arm holes and at the waistline, where the newly tucked waistband had an excess of material bunched above it. It wasn't going to be a perfect job, but she had a wide belt that she was going to wear, which would cover any small bumps in the new seam.

Katie worked the pedal and ran the material through the machine. As always, she got a buzz from the sound of the motor and the needle shooting in and out of the fabric at high speed. Sometimes she thought about becoming a curtain maker, just so that she could spend hours sewing straight lines, full speed ahead.

She should have raised the hem of the dress a little higher — it was sitting too low beneath her knee — but some strappy red sandals with a two-inch heel saved it. She added the wide belt and a wrap to cover her shoulders. Wearing the same necklace all the time made accessorising nice and simple; she adjusted the tiny charms to make sure they were sitting straight and she was ready to go.

Katie arrived at the gallery only half an hour late. She had never been inside the Rotunda Gallery before and it was like the Tardis — bigger on the inside than she expected. Most of Gwen's shadow boxes were mounted on the white walls, but a few of her more recent creations were on square plinths in the middle of the gallery space, so that you could walk all around them. Katie walked around the nearest one, which was reminiscent of a revolving stage set. One side showed a cosy cottage kitchen, not unlike the one at End House, while the other was a strange night sky over a bleak flat landscape.

'You're here.' Gwen swooped over and kissed Katie, hugging her. 'Oh, God, I feel ridiculous. What if nobody comes?'

'People will come,' Katie said.

'Hey, kiddo.' Cam was standing behind Gwen looking simultaneously proud and tense. But then, Cam often looked tense. He put an arm around Gwen and kissed the top of her head. 'They'll come.' He nodded at the tables set up at the side of the vast room. 'Free wine.'

Katie shot him a look. 'And beautiful art.' She flung her arms wide, encompassing the room, the shadow boxes, and the gallery staff dressed in chic black. 'Look at this. It's amazing.'

'Thank you,' Gwen said. 'I can't believe this is happening. My little boxes.'

Elaine Laing, Cam's terrifying mother, clacked across the polished wooden flooring in staggeringly high heels. 'Gwen, darling,' she said, ignoring Katie and Cam. 'You must come and meet the man from *Art Now* magazine.' She paused. 'Are you wearing make-up? You look a bit washed out.'

Katie remembered the scarf, dug in her bag for it. 'I brought your scarf.' She held out the scrap of silk and Elaine plucked it from her hand and tied it around Gwen's neck, knotting it at one side with a practised ease that Katie felt a grudging admiration for.

'There,' Elaine said. Then she turned to Katie. 'Excellent choice.' And to Gwen. 'Come along.'

After Elaine had towed Gwen away, Cam smiled at Katie and asked her about her day. They chatted while the room filled up. Slowly at first and then in a great rush, as if an art-loving coach party had just arrived.

Cam was staring over her head at where Gwen was standing with Elaine and a man with a goatee. 'I think I'll just—' he said, and left Katie for Gwen.

Katie watched him slip an arm around Gwen's waist, saying something that made everyone laugh. Gwen looked up at him as if he was both the question and the answer, and the expression of trust and affection in her eyes made Katie's throat go suddenly thick. Sometimes Katie thought that Cam and Gwen had set an unrealistic expectation for adult relationships and that was why she was dissatisfied, so picky all the time. Perhaps she should've stayed with Stuart. He was a good man, at least. A good person. Perhaps she was searching for something that didn't exist.

Katie picked up a glass of orange juice and sipped it while watching the crowd. She wanted to support Gwen, but the temptation to slip away was suddenly very strong. Anna and a few of the others from The Grange were going to the pub to play pool and she could meet them there. Anna had asked about the art opening but Katie hadn't wanted her to feel obliged to come. Now she wished she had; it would be nice to be standing with Anna, rather than on her own.

Gwen walked up behind Katie and linked arms with her. 'Have I told you that you look amazing, tonight?' She squeezed her arm gently. 'You do dressing up so much better than me.'

'You look really good,' Katie said. 'And thank you.'

'People are always saying that youth is wasted on the young. They obviously haven't met you.'

'Ha. I don't know about that.' Katie tried not to think about all the ways she wasn't enjoying her life. She should be out in the world, taking risks, having adventures. Ever since she could remember, she'd had the horrible feeling that she was doing it wrong. Her life. That everybody else knew exactly what they were doing and she was the only one who hadn't received the handbook.

'Are you seeing that boy again? Max?'

Katie forced a smile. 'Subtly done.'

'Well?'

'He's got a job at The Grange, so probably.' The question wasn't so much 'would she see him again?' as 'could she make herself stop wanting him now that she knew he was a crook?'. A real-life crook. A thief.

'Oh.' Gwen took a swig of her wine. 'That's good.'

'Really?' Katie said. 'Aren't you going to say something serious and parent-like?'

'Oh, I leave that side of things to Cam. He does intimidating so well. Besides, I quite liked Max. There's something about him.'

'He thinks he's charming,' Katie said.

'He's not wrong,' Gwen said. 'You deserve charming. That Stuart was a bit—'

Katie was desperate not to hear Gwen's opinion on Stuart. He might not have set the world on fire but he was the only romance she'd ever had. 'I've got to tell you something.'

'Wonderful show,' a man with a glass of wine in each hand said as he walked past.

'Thank you,' Gwen said. She steered Katie out of the room, into a corridor. 'What is it? Are you still having bad dreams?'

'Yes,' Katie said, 'but—'

'No more flying vases,' Gwen said. Her voice was light, but her eyes deadly serious. 'No more crows—'

'I've actually got good news,' Katie interrupted.

'Oh?'

Katie took a deep breath, savoured the moment. 'I can see ghosts.'

Gwen looked stricken. 'What do you mean?'

'You know how you were saying you sensed Iris in the house when you moved in? Well, I've met a ghost. A real live one. Her name's Violet and she lives at The Grange.'

Gwen didn't say anything and Katie rushed on to fill the silence. 'Isn't it brilliant? The Cole thing isn't a hex or anything bad, it's just his spirit talking to me. He must be, like, a weaker ghost or something. Violet looks like you or me. You could mistake her for living — which I actually did — but, I guess, you wouldn't because you wouldn't be able to see her. Max can't. Other people can't. Just me.'

'It could still be a curse. An effect of the magic I did when you were younger,' Gwen said. 'This is bad. Your power should be something full of life, not death. You're just a kid.'

'I'm really not,' Katie said, frustrated. 'I'm twenty-one. And this power could be positive. It's about helping people, right? Just because they happen to have passed on, doesn't mean they don't deserve help.'

'That's one way of looking at it,' Gwen said. She didn't look convinced.

'Can't you be happy for me? I was so worried I was going to turn out like Ruby.'

'There are worse things,' Gwen said, still looking worried.

'I know that. She's my mum, I love her, but I don't want her life. We're very different.'

'Maybe this is temporary,' Gwen said. 'Maybe you're just developing your intuition and this ghost-business will fade away as you learn to control it. I'll look through the journals, again. I must've missed something. There must be a spell or something that can make this go away.'

'I don't want it to go away,' Katie said, trying to hide her irritation.

'It's not natural,' Gwen said, her lips in a thin line.

Katie wanted to point out that death was about as natural as it got, but Gwen looked too upset. 'Come on,' she said instead. 'We should get back to your party. You need more champagne.'

'It's just sparkling wine,' Gwen said, but she followed Katie back into the gallery.

THE NEXT DAY Katie was sitting behind the front desk, enjoying a jaw-cracking yawn, when Patrick walked into Reception. She hastily covered her mouth. 'Katie, I've had a report from The Plum Suite. Could you take a look?'

'What kind of report?' Katie said. She still felt foggy, as if she hadn't woken up properly. She guessed it had to be the heat since she hadn't exactly been partying until dawn. In bed by half eleven after half a glass of sparkling wine and three orange juices. Wild.

Patrick looked significantly in the direction of the brocade two-seater sofa that sat in the bay window. A female MOP was reading the paper, a bulky handbag at her feet.

They moved into the hallway and Patrick spoke quietly. 'Mr and Mrs Moore just checked out but Housekeeping won't go into the room. She says it doesn't feel right. She keeps making this sign at me and speaking in Dutch.'

'Polish,' Katie said. 'Zofia's probably speaking Polish, not Dutch. On account of that being her first language.'

'What?' Patrick was already distracted by something on his phone.

'Because she's Polish. Never mind. I'll talk to her,' Katie said.

He looked up. 'And check the room?'

'Okay. Sure.'

Katie found Zofia in the first-floor corridor, restocking a housekeeping cart from the supply closet.

'Are you okay?' Zofia had a round, pretty face that was usually smiling. It wasn't now.

Zofia piled handfuls of miniature shampoo bottles onto the trolley and disappeared into the closet.

'Patrick asked me to talk to you.' Katie stood awkwardly by the closet door, unsure whether to follow

Zofia inside. 'About The Plum Suite. He said you had some kind of fright.'

A clattering noise indicated that Zofia was getting the industrial vacuum cleaner out.

'Zofia?'

She appeared, dragging the machine. Katie put a hand onto her arm and Zofia froze. 'Please. I need to talk to you.'

Zofia stared at the vacuum but she stopped moving away.

'It's about the room. The Plum Suite.'

'I'm not cleaning that room.' Zofia shook her head, still not looking at Katie. 'I'm sorry. Tell Mr Patrick I'm sorry but I'm not cleaning. He must—'

'It's okay. You don't have to. I'm here to help.'

Zofia looked at her then and Katie flinched from the naked panic in her eyes. 'You mustn't!' Zofia said. 'Stay out. Lock the door. It's no good now. No one can stay in there. No point cleaning, no point.'

'Zofia,' Katie said gently, 'I can help with what you saw in the room. Can you tell me about it?'

'No. Not good to talk about it. Very bad.'

'But if you could just tell me what you saw? It would be helpful.'

Zofia closed her lips into a tight line and made the sign of the devil. Then she moved down the hall to plug in the vacuum.

Marvellous.

Katie went upstairs to The Plum Suite. She opened the door using her universal keycard and had a quick look around. The room was reasonably clean and tidy; Zofia had obviously started on her housekeeping before whatever scared her did its thing. Either that, or Mr and Mrs Moore were the cleanest guests in the history of hostelry.

The suite consisted of an enormous bedroom, the walls painted a muted mustard that should've looked horrible against the dark purple soft furnishings but somehow didn't. The furniture was dark wood, antique and very heavy. Katie's eye was taken by the gigantic triple wardrobe. It had two full-length mirrors either side of a central unit that was filled with drawers of differing depths. She could see herself in the edge of one of the mirrors, the burgundy flash of her uniform. She moved over and regarded herself, wondering why it always felt different to look in a mirror that wasn't your own. She had a full-length mirror bolted to the wall of her bedroom, but the room was about a third of the size of this one and she supposed she was always a lot closer to the mirror when she was checking out her outfit.

Katie turned to the side and smoothed down the tabard. She quite liked the way it looked, almost like a sixties mini-dress. Maybe in a different colour... Katie caught sight of movement in the other mirror. She glanced across and just managed to stop herself from screaming. It was the girl from the wedding. Violet. She'd just appeared in the room. Instantly materialised from nowhere. If there had been any doubt in Katie's mind, it evaporated. Violet was a ghost.

'What are you doing?' Violet said. Her voice sounded normal. Real.

Katie forced herself to look away from the image in the mirror and at the person standing a couple of feet to her left. 'Hello again,' she said, marvelling at how steady her voice was.

'I don't like your clothes,' Violet said. 'You could borrow something of mine, if you like.'

'Um,' Katie said. Violet was still wearing exactly the same as before, down to the beaded headband. Katie supposed if you ended up as a ghost, you stayed in the same clothes. Were they the clothes you died in or the clothes you imagined yourself wearing? Katie had so many questions, but she settled for, 'What are you doing here?'

Violet's forehead creased lightly. 'It's my house.'

Katie wanted to say 'not any more' but that seemed unfeeling.

'This is my bedroom,' Violet said, looking around. 'Was my bedroom. I don't need one any more. I don't sleep. And I'm too old for my doll's house.'

Katie blinked. Where the desk with telephone and hotel stationery had been a second ago, there was a massive doll's house. It had tiny leaded glass windows, a couple of which were half open.

'What did you do to Zofia?'

'The maid?'

'Housekeeping assistant,' Katie corrected automatically. 'We don't say "maid" any more.'

Violet sniffed. 'Same job.'

'What did you do to her?'

Violet walked to the doll's house and crouched down in front of it. 'I used to spend hours with this. Hours.'

'Zofia?' Katie said.

'I can't open the doors now, though. It's very frustrating.' Violet reached out. Her fingers looked solid enough to Katie, but Violet was having difficulty in getting them to hook around the edge of the house. 'Can you help me?'

Despite the weirdness of the situation, Katie was suddenly curious to look inside the doll's house. She hunkered down next to Violet and attempted to open the front. It was the kind that the entire front should swing out, forwards, but it became more nebulous as soon as she tried to touch it. Her fingers hit something solid and she was excited for exactly one second before she realised she'd just hit the chair that was tucked underneath the desk. She could see them through the image of the doll's house, now.

'I don't think it's really here. That's why neither of us can touch it.'

'But why am I here?' Violet said. 'Why aren't I in the same place as my doll's house?'

Exactly the question Katie had been planning to ask. But if Violet didn't know, who would?

'I'm bored to sobs,' Violet was saying. 'You have no idea.'

'Is that why you frightened Zofia? Because you were bored?'

'Who's Zofia?'

'The maid. Housekeeping assistant.'

'Oh, her. I was just experimenting. I blew into her ear.' Violet pursed her lips to demonstrate. 'I didn't know if it would work.'

'Well, you really scared her,' Katie said. 'It wasn't very kind.'

Violet turned and gave her a disgusted look. 'You shouldn't be so concerned about her. Maids see everything, you know. When you think you're alone and your face falls because you've just been gutted like a fish, your maid sees it. And don't ever think they're your friends. They're not on your side, not even for a second. They'll sell you out in a heartbeat.' Violet walked to the bed. The floaty movement gave Katie a headache.

'Can't you just, I don't know, move on?'

'How? I can't leave the house. I've tried. I can walk as far as the pond and then I wake up back in the house. In the cellar, actually, which is rather embarrassing. Not to mention grubby.'

Violet had a very refined accent, the word 'rather' coming out 'raaathar'.

'Not move out of the house, move on. You know, into the light or something.'

Violet gave her a sudden, piercing look. 'Die, you mean? Properly?'

'Um—'

'No, thank you. A shred of life is better than none at all. Just you wait, you'd be the same in my position.'

Katie swallowed. She hoped, fervently, not to find out.

'But if you're so bored,' Katie began.

'What do we have here?' Violet had floated over to the bed and was peering at the padded headboard. 'A hair. A long brown hair.' She tried to pluck something from the fabric surface but couldn't.

'Left by Mrs Moore, I imagine. You frightened Zofia away before she could turn the room around.'

Violet flapped a hand. 'She's fine. I didn't really frighten her.' Her face turned petulant. 'Why are you so worried about her? What about me? In case you hadn't noticed, I'm dead. It's not fair.'

The shimmering was worse and Katie felt as if she was going to be sick. 'What can I do?'

Violet didn't answer; she was still trying to pick up the hair from the pillow, watching her own ghostly fingers intently.

Katie wanted to ask Violet the obvious question, but she wasn't sure how. She plumped for the direct approach. 'How did you die?'

'Rude girl,' Violet said, but she smiled. She really was extraordinarily pretty.

'Did somebody hurt you?'

'Oh, yes.' Violet turned away, the movement strange and fluid, as if Violet were becoming a little more insubstantial and ghost-like. 'I imagine that's why I'm still here. I'm probably supposed to be absolutely furious about it, but I can't seem to summon the feeling any more. It's funny how these things just fade away.'

'Violet,' Katie tried again. 'What happened to you?'

'Why don't you look it up?' Violet said. 'Violet Leticia Anne Beaufort.' And then she disappeared.

Across town at End House, Gwen Harper closed her eyes and wished that, just once, she could swap her power from 'finding lost things' to 'shutting people up'. Amanda had been going non-stop since she arrived and Gwen's head was still pounding from the white wine at the opening the night before. She closed her eyes and lightly massaged her temples.

Amanda had covered the shockingly narrow aisles at their local small supermarket, her mother's weird obsession with linen napkins, and something about a C-list celebrity who'd been photographed with, as far as Gwen could gather, a B-list celebrity. Which made it news, apparently. She tried to tune Amanda out, just for a moment, just to let the pain in her head abate a little. She'd had some tea and about three pints of water, surely—

'What about the chalk man in Dorset? You could visit him.'

Gwen opened her eyes. 'Chalk man?'

'Like the white horse. Only a man. With a massive willy.'

'Ah.' Gwen closed her eyes again. She had a horrible feeling she knew what Amanda was going to say next.

'You shag on it. You and Cam, I mean. It's supposed to cure infertility.'

'Who told you that?'

'Oh, everyone knows that. It was in the paper and everything.'

'A chalk man. On a hillside.' Gwen tried not to show her distress. Amanda was only trying to help. And it was her own fault for confiding in Amanda in a moment of weakness. She should've been more like Iris and kept her thoughts firmly confined to her journals.

'The fertility rates around the hill are above national average — all the women around there have, like, three kids each. At least. It's been proven.'

'I really don't want to talk about this,' Gwen said. 'I'm sorry, but I just can't.'

Amanda put her hand on Gwen's arm. 'I know it's painful, but talking can help. And surely anything is worth a try. I'd have thought you'd be open—'

'How are your kids?' Gwen interrupted Amanda with the topic of conversation guaranteed to distract her.

Amanda pulled a face. 'Monsters. Milo has decided five is the best time to start the day and Lucy refuses to poo in the toilet.'

'That sounds—'

'She's trained, I mean, she's able to hold it, but she won't do it unless I put a nappy on her.' Amanda shook her head. 'You don't know how lucky you are.'

'Indeed,' Gwen said.

'Oh, crap.' Amanda clapped a hand over her mouth. 'I'm so sorry. I didn't mean—'

'It's fine,' Gwen said. She busied herself by topping up their cups from the teapot. Chamomile with essence of burdock.

'Can't you cure yourself?' Amanda didn't seem to be able to leave the subject alone. She'd always been the kind of woman to wedge her foot so firmly into her own mouth that the only conceivable option was to keep on pushing, perhaps in the hope that it would eventually appear out the other end.

'Apparently not.' Gwen thought of the spells she'd tried, the herbal remedies she'd downed. She'd had enough evening primrose and dandelion root to last her a lifetime.

'It'll happen,' Amanda said, cosy certainty in her voice. 'Maybe if you stop trying. Lots of people find that. They give up, and they adopt or just decided it's not happening or whatever, and then they get pregnant —' she clicked her fingers '—like that.'

Gwen dug her fingers into her palm to stop herself from screaming 'shut up, shut up, shut up' into Amanda's face.

Amanda drained her mug and stood up. 'Well, I'll let you get on. You must be so busy. I saw that piece in *The Guardian*. We're going to try and make it to your launch-party thing. If we can get a sitter. If not, me and Kev are going to go into Bath this weekend. We'll take a look, then.' She laughed a little nervously. 'Won't be able to buy one, though. Out of our price range.'

Gwen smiled. 'Don't worry about that.'

'I won't keep you,' Amanda said again and, miracle of miracles, she actually headed towards the door. Amanda never stayed for just one mug of tea. It was unheard of. At the door she hesitated. 'Is it true you're doing one of your box things for the Bath City of Culture thing?'

Gwen nodded.

'Fancy,' Amanda said, approvingly. 'You'll be too famous to talk to us little folk soon!'

Gwen waved and closed the door. Amanda had never asked her about her work before. Not in detail. She felt a creeping pride and realised that one of the best things about the magazine coverage and the exhibition was that her friends and neighbours actually believed that she was working now. She'd just been dabbling before. Being eccentric. Making funny little boxes. Now, it was a proper job. Nothing had changed except people's perception, which meant, of course, that everything had changed.

CHAPTER 8

The Grange was filled with MOPs determined to have a good time, many of them ignoring their children while they did so. Katie dodged several toddlers and even a crawling baby on her way to and from the kitchen.

She'd just dumped a tray of empty glasses on top of the bar and told Anna that she was taking her break, when Max took hold her elbow. 'Let me buy you a drink.'

'Don't you mean steal a drink?' Katie said, trying not to be pleased.

'I'm working now. I pay when I can.' Max gave her a look. 'I'm willing to talk about what you believe is going on here. With an open mind. Can't you lay off just for a bit?'

'Sorry,' Katie said. 'I don't know you. I don't know your life. I've got no right to judge.'

'That's okay.' Max looked surprised.

'You're staff now, right?' Katie said.

'I guess.'

'That means you can enjoy the Costa del Sol.'

Katie led the way round to the back of the hotel. A screened-off area hid the bins from MOP view and there were a few straggly deck chairs arranged around an old picnic table. 'It's the summer staff room. Fag-break area. It's grim.' She gestured to a faded pink plastic chair. 'Sit.'

Katie fetched a couple of Fabs from the kitchen. Something had tried to knock him out with a ceramic, he'd been de-hexed by Gwen and menaced by Cam and he was still speaking to her. He deserved an ice lolly.

His eyes lit up when she returned. 'God, I haven't had a Fab in years.'

'When you said you were a con man,' Katie began, after a few minutes of companionable lolly-induced silence, and then stopped. She realised that there was no good way to finish that sentence.

Max didn't help, just lowered his eyes and concentrated on finishing the rapidly melting lolly.

'Have you been travelling around for long?' She wanted to ask where home was. What he really did for a living. Just how black his heart truly was. But how did you do that? How did you say 'are you dangerous?' without sounding unhinged? Without inviting the truth she didn't want to hear or the lie she expected?

'Couple of months,' Max said. 'I've been feeling sort of dissatisfied for a while and then something happened. It made me want to take some time off.'

'From conning?'

'Sort of. From that life, yeah. But it's not that simple.'

'It is. You just stop stealing from people.'

'Send me a postcard from where you live some time.'

'What?'

'Where everything is so black and white.'

Katie nibbled the sprinkles and chocolate that covered the top part of her lolly. It was black and white. Stealing and lying equalled bad. Max was a bad person. She should walk inside and talk to Jo, instead. She shouldn't speak to him ever, ever again. 'So, what happened? What made you reassess your life of crime?'

'I was already taking it easy, having some time away. I was moving around, playing lots of poker tournaments. Nothing dodgy for once, not really gambling.'

Katie made to interrupt but he pointed at her with his empty lolly stick. 'Playing poker isn't gambling. Well, it is. But if you have skills then you have a good chance of winning. You can influence the outcome to some extent.'

Katie licked some strawberry that was threatening to run down her wrist. 'Right, so—'

'One place, I had a bit too much to drink and got knocked out of the game early. You know what it's like when you're already drunk and you just keep drinking?'

No, Katie thought. Not really.

'I don't know how much I'd had, but I ended up seeing Greg Barton's act.'

'You must have been really slaughtered.'

Max nodded. 'It wasn't exactly my intention. I wasn't thinking clearly.'

'To say the least.'

'Exactly. I had found a comfortable seat and fallen asleep for a while. When I woke up the show had started and my head was pounding so I just stayed put. I got sucked in, though. The man is a real pro,' Max said, his voice full of admiration. 'I mean, you should see his cold reading.'

Katie felt sick. 'So, what, he's like some kind of hero to you?'

Max's eyebrows drew sharply down. 'Hardly. I think he's scum. He preys on people when they're vulnerable, grieving. He breaks all the rules. No scruples whatsoever. But, you know, sometimes you gotta admire technique.'

Katie wasn't sure about that, but she didn't want to stop Max talking.

'But then he spoke to me. Called me out in the audience. I mean, I didn't even have a ticket. I definitely hadn't been at the meet and greet before the show, when the runners pump people for info, which they can feed back to Barton for the show. I'd stumbled in there, dead drunk, passed out in an empty seat.'

'What did he say to you?'

Max's smile vanished. 'It's personal.'

'Fair enough,' Katie said. 'But it shook you up?'

'It got to me,' Max said. 'I know all the tricks and I know it's a kind of con, but the things he said... Put it this way. I'd really like to prove he's a grifter.' He smiled a little. 'I'm going to prove it.'

'You should be careful. I read about a medium. Got accused of faking in a newspaper and he sued them for a load of money.'

'I know,' Max said, his smile fading. 'But I'm hoping I can catch him out, anyway. I would love to ruin his sordid little career.'

'Sordid career? Pots and kettles spring to mind.'

Max shook his head, deadly serious now. 'He's violating the code.'

'There's a code?'

'Of course.' Max counted off on his fingers. 'Only

steal from the crooked, only scam the dishonest, family's off limits.'

'I'm sorry.'

'Thank you,' Max said, standing up. He held out his hand for Katie's lolly stick, which, she now realised, she'd been mangling while they talked. She passed the twisted bit of wood to him and stood up. 'Back to work, I suppose.'

'Are you really working here?'

'Just temporarily.' Max smiled. Not his usual small one, but a wide, loopy grin. 'I quite like bar work. An honest day's work and all that. I could get used to it.'

'You'd better not.'

'Don't worry, I won't outstay my welcome.'

'Bit late,' Katie said, automatically, and was rewarded by Max's smile growing even wider.

'I know you don't mean that,' he said, pointing at her with the remains of his Fab. 'But don't worry. I think Patrick only hired me because he's desperate. As soon as he finds a permanent replacement, he'll chuck me out.'

Katie felt an alarming mix of feelings. Terror, because he wasn't joking about being a con man and that was bad. That was really bad. And sympathy because he seemed genuinely sad about something, and Barton had upset him and she could see it had shaken him in some fundamental way. And arousal because, well, because Max just seemed to have that effect on her. Which brought her neatly back to terror.

～

THAT NIGHT, Katie sat cross-legged on her sofa and fired up Google on her laptop. Gwen might be convinced that seeing Violet was some terrible curse, but Katie felt properly awake for the first time in months. The magical world that she'd always known was there, hiding in the shadows of the mundane world of toast and television, had finally come into sharp focus. She was linked to it and she wasn't about to hide under her duvet until it went away. If Gwen wasn't going to help her, she was going to do it herself and she was going to start by helping Violet.

Katie typed Violet's name into the search engine. She paid for a subscription to *The Times* so that she could search the past issues and was rewarded by a scanned-in story from the beginning of August, 1937.

THE CASE of missing heiress Violet Beaufort took a sinister turn today with the news that some personal effects of the young lady have been recovered from the Beaufort estate in Avon. Lord Beaufort maintains that his daughter was away at the time of her disappearance, visiting friends in Norwich, and until now the search has been centred upon the route. The alarm was first raised on 7th July when Violet Beaufort did not arrive as expected and there have been no clues to her whereabouts and no statements released by the police regarding the investigation since the initial appeal for information.

KATIE BLINKED. Why would it be odd to find 'personal effects' of Violet's in her home? Maybe they were items that no young lady would leave behind when planning an extended trip away. Or, perhaps, they'd been hidden. Another thought popped into Katie's mind: perhaps they had blood on them.

It would've been so much easier if Violet had just

told her what had happened. Katie felt bad for her frustration. Violet was bored and had, most likely, suffered some horrible fate all those years ago. She probably deserved some excitement and happiness in her afterlife. Even if it had to be at the expense of Katie's sleep. She rubbed her grainy eyes and drained the rest of her coffee. Perhaps if she read about the Beauforts as a family she'd stumble across something.

An hour later, Katie was none the wiser. The Beauforts were an ancient and moneyed family, connected closely to the royals — although not as close as they'd like. Apparently someone tried to tell Queen Victoria that a Beaufort marriage back in the day had been legitimate, making the Beauforts' claim to the throne stronger than the current royal family, and the queen had simply taken the papers and thrown them on the fire. Katie liked that. Amoral, but decisive.

She researched The Grange, too. It'd been a family home of the Beauforts for many years before, although the family moved out en masse in 1987. The house was left empty for a number of years before the family sold it to Patrick. He turned it into a hotel six years ago.

Katie rang Patrick and got the name of the person he dealt with when buying the hotel. 'You're not going to ask them any strange questions, are you?'

'No,' Katie lied. 'Just investigating. You know.'

Patrick had bought the house through Strakers solicitors and the seller was a Mr Roberts who, it turned out, had only set foot in the place once. He had bought it on behalf of his client, a Texan oil magnate called Boon who wanted an unusual anniversary present for his fourth wife. Katie couldn't find a contact for Boon, although she did find him listed on the board of several companies.

Katie searched for news stories about the house or surrounding area during 1987 but didn't find anything. Of course, Violet would know. It would be simplest to just ask her. She didn't know why Gwen was so against her talking to ghosts. It was fun.

～

THE NEXT DAY, Katie went into The Plum Suite and called Violet. There was nobody there, no cold spots and no sign of Violet's doll's house. Katie tried not to feel disappointed. She tried to tell herself that it would be a good thing if she turned out to have had a dose of heatstroke after all.

As she locked the door the hairs on the back of her neck suddenly stood up.

'Oh,' Violet's voice said. 'It's you.'

'I wish you wouldn't jump out like that,' Katie said, forcing herself to look at Violet. When she wasn't with Violet, she couldn't stop thinking about her, hoping to see her again, but the first few moments were still alarming. She was looking at a dead person. A ghost.

The alarm wasn't helped by the fact that Violet was looking particularly spook-like today. She was floating a foot or so above the hall floor and looked cross. 'I would say "boo" but you're no fun,' Violet said.

Katie swallowed her panic; the fear made her snappy. 'I've been reading about your family. What made them all leave in eighty-seven?'

Violet shrugged elegantly. 'I haven't the faintest idea.'

'Okay. What were they like, the people who lived here? After you, I mean.'

Violet looked at her oddly. 'I don't know. I died, you know.'

'But you're here now.'

'I died and the next thing I know I'm waking up to the sound of the world caving in. A loud, grumbling, roaring.'

Katie frowned. 'What—?'

'It was machinery, of course. Not a dragon or an earthquake, but everything felt very odd and fuzzy for those first few months. It might've been a digger. That man. Mr Allen. He'd hired one to tear up the vegetable garden. If my father had been alive, he would have had him shot.'

'You don't remember the years in between?'

'I didn't know there had been years, not at first.'

Katie tried to digest this. 'Were you frightened?'

'A little bit, perhaps.'

'I'm sorry.'

'It's hardly your fault,' Violet said, suddenly sounding a lot more grown up. 'Besides, the fear was small and didn't last. It was almost as if I felt fear because I thought I should. As soon as I stopped forcing it, it went away.' Violet looked sad at this memory.

Another question had been bothering Katie. If Violet couldn't touch things, who had tipped the urn off the balcony? 'Are there other people like you here?'

'Ghosts?' Violet said. 'I don't know. Maybe.'

'Are they here now?'

Violet gave her a funny look. 'Why? Can you see some?'

'No. But something threw a vase at my friend's head and I couldn't see that. I wondered if they were invisible, or something.'

'I'm invisible,' Violet said. 'Usually, anyway. Sometimes little children can see me and animals, I think, but you're the first grown up.'

Katie took a deep breath. 'These other ghosts. Is it possible one of them tried to kill Max?'

Violet tapped a lip. 'I couldn't really say. I'm pretty sure there are other spirits in this house — I hear them sometimes. Banging. Strange music. And there's a very cold wind in the servants' old hallway.'

Katie couldn't believe her ears. The ghost was being haunted. 'But you haven't met any?'

'Nobody like me. There might be some weaker spirits.' Violet looked thoughtful. 'They're more like echoes. Barely here.'

Katie's skin prickled. She looked around, wondering how many echoes were in the room with them. She didn't like the thought that there were things she couldn't see.

'I wish I could touch things,' Violet said. There was longing in her face and Katie tried to imagine what it must be like, drifting through this world, unable to touch anything, affect anything.

'Do you—?' Katie began but Violet disappeared.

'Thanks, Caspar,' Katie muttered. She sat on the bed and stared around the room, trying to feel if there were any other spirits hanging around. Gwen would say that she needed to relax, but Katie didn't know how that was possible. In this world, a hundred and one things could hurt you, and that was before she knew about the ghosts.

Katie took the back stairs to the kitchens and bumped into Max coming the other way. He was wearing black shirt and trousers and had a name badge that said 'Lee Smith'.

'Where are you going?'

'Just looking around,' Max said. 'Investigating.'

'Barton hasn't checked in, yet, you know.'

'I know that.' Max smiled at her. 'But I'm still looking for my watch, too. I'm a man of mystery with many missions.'

'Not very mysterious,' Katie said. 'You seem a bit forthcoming for a con man.'

'But you said you could tell if I was lying and I'm hoping you'll decide I'm a good guy and give me my watch out of the goodness of your heart.'

'I don't have it.'

'But maybe you'll tell me if you find it. You know, now that we're friends and colleagues.'

Max's brazen confidence was difficult to deal with. And he was standing too close, which made thinking especially difficult. Katie settled on, 'Does this kind of approach usually work?'

'No idea,' Max said. 'I usually lie my socks off but I told you. New leaf.'

Katie was a couple of steps above Max so their faces were level but if she continued she'd have to squeeze past him on the narrow stairs.

As if reading her mind, Max turned to the side, flattening himself against the wall to make room. Just when she'd decided he was an untrustworthy lech, he did something like that.

Not allowing herself to think about it too much, Katie angled her body to face his and kissed him.

The reaction was immediate. Max grasped her shoulders and kissed her back. She opened her mouth and the kiss deepened. Her body's reaction went from zero to sixty in the half a second. Katie had never had such a visceral reaction to being touched before. It made her feel wildly awake. Alive. She clasped her hands behind his head, pulling him closer, making the kiss harder and deeper.

Max swung her around so that she was against the wall and pressed up against her. Her body sprang to life, a thousand tiny points of sensation, every single one of them wanting to be touched.

Max had one hand on her neck, the other roamed across her body, trailing fire wherever it went. Katie arched her back, pressing herself against him, and a tiny sound escaped from her mouth. It was a small moan and she instantly felt self-conscious. What was she doing necking like this on the stairs? She was embarrassing herself. She felt cold. Max's hands on her body felt suddenly heavy. He was still touching her, but the sensation was gone. His tongue in her mouth was suddenly just a lumpen thing. Stuart had been right: she wasn't very sexual.

Katie concentrated on getting the feelings back. She kissed Max, trying to remember how to move her lips. She thought about Gwen and Cam, barely able to keep their hands off each other. The passion and affection fizzing between them at practically every moment. Katie wanted that. Maybe that was what she should've been training in all these years — forget magic. Although it would be beyond weird to talk to Gwen about sex. She was too much of a mother figure. It took Katie a moment to realise that Max wasn't kissing her any more. His face was a couple of inches from hers and when she met his gaze, he tilted his head and smiled tentatively. 'Are you okay?'

'I'm fine,' Katie said. Katie's honesty policy allowed for white lies and she didn't want to hurt Max's feelings. It wasn't his fault she was dead from the neck down.

'I kind of lost you there, didn't I?'

'I was thinking about my aunt,' Katie said.

Max let go of her. 'That's not as sexy as you might think.'

'Sorry,' Katie said. 'It's not you. It's me. That was very nice. Thank you.' And then wanted to slap herself in the head. 'Very nice'? 'Thank you'? She tried a quick smile. 'I'd better get on.'

'Fine.' Max stepped back. 'No problem.' He turned and took the stairs, two at a time. No doubt desperate to get away from her.

KATIE HAD BEEN so busy with Violet and Max at The Grange, and then with reading over the notes she'd made on the Beaufort family and Googling 'ghosts' and 'helping ghosts', that she made herself late for her training session with Gwen. She walked towards End House, her head swimming with the overload of information. She'd decided she wasn't going to talk to Gwen, though. She wanted to solve the mystery on her own and then say, 'Ta-da, look what I did.' She was going to prove to Gwen that this was her power, that she could cope on her own.

Gwen was out on the road and walking away from the house when Katie arrived.

'Sorry, honeybunch. Rain check on tonight?' Gwen hoisted the rucksack higher on her shoulder and started down the road. 'I need to visit Fred. His garden is getting out of control.'

'I'll come, too,' Katie said. Some fresh air and a bit of exercise would do her good after being hunched over her laptop for hours. 'It's not like I've got anything better to do.'

Gwen shot her a sideways look. 'Aren't you seeing anyone? It's been ages since Stuart. You should be out there, having fun.'

Katie did not want to talk about her love life. 'How is Fred, anyway?'

Gwen looked away. 'Not so good. He's pretty much housebound, now. His eyesight has pretty much gone and his legs are too painful to walk far.'

'Can he even see his roses?' Katie said once they'd got to Fred's terraced cottage. She was looking at the massive flower bed that covered most of the front garden, and remembering, abruptly, how much she hated weeding.

'In his mind, he can,' Gwen said.

Katie thought about asking why Gwen was spending her evening tending roses that Fred Byres was probably never going to see. That was her aunt, though. Caring. Giving. She was a natural earth mother, really, which was why it was odd she didn't have kids of her own.

'We need to add this to the mulch.' Gwen pulled a plastic bag with the words bone meal on the side out of her rucksack. 'And pull up any weeds, check for greenfly, signs of distress, the usual.'

Katie put one hand on her hip. 'Distress?'

'Brown leaves, sickly petals.'

Katie shook her head. 'They're just flowers.'

Gwen gave her a long, thoughtful look, until Katie started to feel uncomfortable. Instead she grabbed the bag of fertiliser and began opening it.

'You'll need scissors,' Gwen said, but Katie had already gouged a hole in the bag with one of her nails and was now ripping it open. 'What is this stuff, anyway? It stinks.'

'Bone meal.'

'For real. I thought that was just the name. So, roses eat bones. I knew there was a good reason I didn't like them.'

'You mean, besides the thorns and their old lady image problem.'

'I'd forgotten about the thorns,' Katie said, picking up one of the thick pairs of gardening gloves off the floor. 'Nasty sneaky bastards, luring you in with their pretty flowers and then, wham, spiking you.'

'Worse than spiking you,' Gwen said. 'They hook you. Ever tried pulling a rose thorn out of your skin? It's not just painful, it's bloody difficult.'

'Why the hell are they so popular?'

'Beats me.' Gwen shrugged. 'I don't care why Fred likes them, just that he does. While he's under my care I'll do whatever I can to ease his pain. Believe me—' Gwen stopped weeding and stretched for a moment '— this is the easiest of it.'

'I'm sorry about Fred,' Katie said, lifting up the head of a yellow rose to check underneath the leaves for aphids.

'Thank you, honeybunch,' Gwen said. 'And thank you for helping me with this. I know it's not your idea of a good time and I know things aren't progressing exactly the way you want them to, but I'm sure things will work out in the end. Sometimes the only way forward is through.'

Katie thought about telling Gwen that she'd made progress, that she was going to solve the mystery of Violet's death and give her eternal peace, but she hugged the information to herself. She shook her head. 'You're such a wise woman, these days. Do you ever say anything that isn't, like, totally profound?'

'Cheeky sod,' Gwen said, smiling. 'Heed my warning, grasshopper.'

After they'd finished in the garden, Gwen rummaged in the front pocket of her rucksack. 'I almost forgot. I've got something for you.'

Katie was arching her back, trying to stretch out the ache. Weeding was hard work.

'I made you this.' Gwen held out a tiny silk pouch. 'Thread it on a chain and wear it. It should keep spirits away. Stop you being bothered by any more ghosts.'

'Violet doesn't bother me,' Katie said. 'She's actually quite nice—'

'She's a spirit. She shouldn't be here.' Gwen held out the pouch. 'Just take it. Please.'

'Okay.' Katie tucked the pouch in her pocket.

'You don't know what she wants,' Gwen said. 'She might seem nice, but her essence is kept here for a reason. That reason might not be good.'

'I hear you,' Katie said. She had absolutely no intention of warding off Violet. She was going to help her. It was her purpose. Her power.

Gwen was looking at her as if she knew exactly what she was thinking. 'Just be careful.'

'It's fine,' Katie said. After all, even if Violet did turn out to be a bad spirit or whatever Gwen was worried about, it wasn't as if she could do anything. She couldn't touch things. She was completely harmless.

Gwen looked at her watch. 'It's time for Fred's dinner. Do you want to join us?'

Katie shook her head. 'I can't. I'm going out with Anna.' It wasn't true but she couldn't face seeing Fred when he was so ill. Another sign she wasn't cut out for the life she'd chosen. She pushed the thought away.

Gwen was looking at her as if she knew she was lying. Which she probably did. 'Fair enough,' Gwen said, but she didn't look happy. 'I can't make you.'

'I know it's part of the deal, but he's got you. I don't need—'

Gwen held up her hand. 'You don't have to explain to me. Nobody likes this stuff. Nobody finds it easy.'

As Katie made her way back to her flat, she couldn't shake Gwen's unspoken words. Nobody found this stuff easy, but if she wanted to be a Harper, she had to deal with it anyway. That was part of the package. For the first time, Katie felt a pang of uncertainty. What if she didn't want to follow in Gwen's footsteps, after all?

THAT NIGHT, Katie wrapped a teaspoon each of lemon thyme and dried valerian in a square of cotton muslin and put it underneath her pillow. She'd been too afraid to try any of the remedies for nightmares in the journal Gwen had given her, but, now that her power had appeared, maybe she was going to get better at spells again. Maybe everything would just magically unlock.

The journal was red leather and Gwen had presented it to her with great ceremony when she 'came of age' on her seventeenth birthday. Gwen had always said that seventeen was more significant than eighteen because at seventeen you could pledge your life to another or drive a potentially lethal machine, both of which were far more significant than being able to buy a pint of lager.

Maybe, four years later, she was finally going to be able to use it properly.

Katie felt calmer than she had in weeks. Everything was going to be all right now. She was on the right path. She had come into her power and all she had to do was to embrace it. She fell asleep easily, one hand tucked underneath her pillow to feel the comforting softness of the cotton muslin and the herbs inside.

❧

SHE WAS BACK in The Yellow Room at The Grange. She could see Mr Cole, whole and healthy, moving around his room. Part of Katie knew she was dreaming, that this was the same dream she'd had before, but it wasn't strong enough to change the story. She watched helplessly as Oliver Cole undid the buttons on his shirt. He turned and caught sight of her, his mouth falling open in an expression of terror.

Dream slow, he fell to the ground, gasping and red. A beached fish, his mouth working for air, eyes bulging. His mouth kept moving, as if trying to form words. His face filled Katie's vision so she could see every wrinkle, every pore, in close-up. She could smell his breath as he gasped out two words. 'You. Watch.'

Katie woke up sweating and sick. The red numbers on her alarm clock said four minutes past three. She swallowed hard, the taste of vomit burning the back of her throat.

CHAPTER 9

*P*agans came from far and wide; those that didn't go to Stonehenge came to Avebury to watch the sun rise behind the stone circle on midsummer's day. Gwen had never expected to join them. Perhaps this was what rock bottom looked like for a Harper woman. Joining the tourists for a clichéd bit of sun celebration. As always, her thoughts immediately jumped from 'rock bottom' to 'perhaps I'll get pregnant'. Every single thought led back to that. Gwen could no longer really remember a time when it hadn't.

The line of cars snaked down and through the village, moving slowly as people found parking spaces in the field that had been commandeered for the purpose after the National Trust car park had filled up. The campsite was packed, too, had been fully booked since the previous solstice, in fact.

Gwen hooked the straps of her rucksack onto her back, locked the car, and began the two-mile walk to the village. The sounds of revelry carried through the night air, albeit at a more subdued tempo. It was three in the morning and even the drum enthusiasts were beginning to get a little tired. They lit fires, partied and drummed and sang through the night, and then greeted the sun on the longest day. Gwen walked through the first camping field, picking her way as quietly as possible past closed tents. The occasional group, sitting around a glowing fire, raised hands in greeting or salute.

Gwen didn't feel warmth towards her fellow man. On one level, it was nice that people were keeping the old traditions, but Gwen felt empty inside. A blank coldness where happiness and fellow feeling should sit.

After organising so carefully for Cam to stay in London, she wished he were with her. He'd be uncomfortable, of course, and was practically allergic to the sound of tribal drumming, but he'd hold her hand and everything would seem lighter.

It didn't help that this felt like a last chance. A final-ditch attempt. It had the air of finality to it, which, if she were counselling a friend, she would say was never going to work. You couldn't put that kind of pressure on a situation, on yourself, and expect a miracle. But that was what she wanted. She wanted a damn miracle and she wanted it now.

Gwen had planned to sit alone in her misery, not wanting company or to infect anybody else with the waves of negativity that she felt were uncurling from her body like black tentacles, but hadn't banked on the popularity of the event. She found a space between a couple with Boden clothes and cute blond twin boys, and a group of dreadlocked teens with a home-made bong. She put down a folded blanket and sat on it and tried not to stare at the toddler twins with hungry eyes. Even though she had a fleece and a thick waterproof, she still felt cold. There was dew on the grass and the dampness felt as if it was coming up from the earth itself. Gwen had never felt so aware of the thin skin of life, of the miles of cold rock beneath her. She looked up at the sky and felt the perspective that she always did. The vast sky and the dead spaces between the stars.

'Would you like some hot chocolate?' The father of the twins was holding out a flask. Gwen shook her head. Forced her voice out. 'No, thank you.' I'm having an existential crisis. Catering is not required. 'Thank you, though,' she remembered to add, feeling proud of herself for managing civility when her soul was screaming to the sky.

There was a faint glow on the horizon. The drumming increased in tempo and Gwen thought, uncharitably, that the musicians' arms were going to get very tired indeed if they started that nonsense now. Sunrise was going to take a while. At once, Gwen felt ridiculous. What was she doing sitting in a field in the middle of the night? If all her so-called powers hadn't helped her, all the knowledge from her great aunt Iris's journals — and she'd been through every single one, tried every possible remedy and spell — then why on earth did she think that watching the sun rise with a load of tourists was going to help?

After an hour, Gwen's backside was numb and she was thinking about going home. She pictured the waves of negativity that she was projecting, probably souring the experience for all those around her. She felt toxic.

Then she saw a familiar figure picking her way through the mosaic of seated bodies. She was wearing a tiny flared skirt over leggings and a giant hoodie that Gwen remembered her having when she was still just a kid. Her dark hair was back in a ponytail and, despite the early hour, her trademark eyeliner was perfectly in place. Gwen felt her insides squeeze. She stood up and waved so that Katie would find her.

'Hey, honeybunch,' Gwen said, hugging Katie. 'How did you know I was here?'

Katie shrugged. 'I don't know. I just had a feeling.' They sat down, squeezing onto the blanket together. 'And I couldn't sleep.'

Gwen looked at her niece's profile, pale and sharp in the gathering light. 'Are you still having nightmares?'

Katie nodded quickly. 'It's getting boring, now.'

Gwen felt the Harper intuition tickling at the back of her mind. Katie was holding back. She ignored the feeling. People were entitled to their secrets, after all.

'So, what's this all about?' Katie gestured, taking in the field and the crowd and the standing stones of Avebury.

'Solstice. Longest day, turn of the year. You know—'

'Yeah,' Katie said quickly. 'It's just you always said it didn't matter whether you paid attention to the solstice or not, because it happened anyway. You said that was the point.'

Gwen was surprised, as she always was, to hear her own words parroted back. She'd slipped into Iris's old role in Pendleford, dispensing advice and remedies and mediating disputes, but she still found it weird how much Katie listened to her. It was a huge responsibility.

'I'm not doing brilliantly well at the moment,' Gwen said, picking her words carefully.

'Are you ill?' Katie said quickly, her voice panicky.

'No, nothing like that. It's complicated.'

'Are you and Cam all right?'

Gwen nodded, suddenly unable to speak. Her

throat had closed up.

Katie looked at her. 'Something's missing? Something you can't find.'

Gwen blinked back tears. 'Bloody intuition.'

'Sorry. Christ. Sorry. I'm being like Gran, aren't I? Insensitive.'

That broke the spell. 'You are nothing like your gran, honeybunch. I promise you that.'

'Do you want to talk about it?'

Gwen shook her head. 'Some time. Not now.'

'Okay.' Katie turned her face to the rising sun. 'I'm here when you're ready.'

Gwen patted her knee. 'So, what's up with the bad dreams? Do you want me to try and get rid of them for you?'

'They're the least of my problems.'

'What's going on? You haven't spoken to that ghost again?'

Katie's mouth twitched. 'A couple of times.'

'No.' Gwen didn't mean the word to come out like that. So harsh. So stark.

Katie looked at her as if she'd lost her mind. 'Why are you so against my gift? You, of all people—'

'It's no gift. And it's my fault.' Gwen felt the tears build again, behind her eyes as if they'd never left. She couldn't start crying. She didn't think she'd be able to stop. She didn't know what she was upset about any more. Everything just seemed so bleak and so frightening.

'I don't want to argue with you,' Katie said. 'Please. Let's just watch the sunrise.'

Gwen took a deep shuddering breath, forced the wave of darkness back down inside herself. She'd felt so sure, ever since saving Katie's life, and making End

House her home. Things had been so sure and so good and so right. Now she couldn't even remember how that felt. It was like imagining another person, another life.

As the sun rose Gwen tilted her face towards it. She felt Katie's hand take hers and squeeze it. The feel of Katie's hand anchored her, pulled her back from the darkness, and she squeezed it back. Together they watched the light from the sun spill over the horizon.

Katie watched the sun rise, its warmth flowing over the landscape and into the people sitting on the ground, welcoming it. She looked at Gwen's profile and hoped it would help with whatever was upsetting her so much.

When Katie had woken up, the bad taste from her Oliver Cole nightmare stale in her mouth, she'd felt the compulsion to drive here. It was the kind of intuition that Gwen had said was her birthright and, thank goodness, it seemed to be coming back. 'I wish you could be happy for me,' Katie said. 'All I've ever wanted is to be like you.'

Gwen blinked. 'I'm just worried.'

'I know. But it isn't helping,' Katie said. 'I need information. I need help. And I don't know why you keep denying what is happening to me. I thought you'd be proud of me—' Katie hadn't realised she was going to say those words until they were out of her mouth but she felt a peculiar ripping feeling, as if something had torn in half. She wrapped her arms around her body.

Gwen was looking at her with something close to horror. 'But I am proud of you. I'm always proud of you. How can you—?'

'But you keep saying this isn't a good thing, that it's a curse or something. It's like you think I've done something wrong. Like you're ashamed of me.'

'No,' Gwen said. 'I'm worried that I've done something wrong. I feel like I've messed everything up.'

'What have you messed up? What's wrong?' Gwen did everything right and lived the perfect life. Gwen was Katie's blueprint for adulthood, her roadmap to the future.

Gwen squeezed her hand. 'Nothing. I'm being daft.' She glanced at the sky and seemed to gather herself. 'And I'm not ashamed of you. That's crazy talk.'

'You can talk to me, you know. I'm not a kid any more.'

'Protecting you is a hard habit to break,' Gwen said. 'But, I'll try. Deal?'

'Deal,' Katie said, suddenly not sure she liked the turn of the conversation. She wanted Gwen to respect her, see her as an adult and an equal, but could use all the protection she could get. She turned her face to the morning sun and tried to feel strong.

THURSDAY NIGHT MEANT film night and Katie was expecting Anna, popcorn and a DVD or three. She wasn't expecting Anna to be looking shifty and to be accompanied by a tall, brown-haired con man. Anna started speaking the moment Katie opened the door, as if anticipating an objection. 'Max was at a loose end tonight and I said I couldn't let him hang about Pendleford on his own, so I invited him to film night. Hope that's okay?'

'These are for you.' Max stepped forward and

thrust a bunch of flowers that had clearly been collected from gardens on the way over and a bottle of red that was, suspiciously, the same type as the house wine they served in The Grange.

'I'm sure Max only agreed to be polite,' Katie said. 'I'm sure there's all kinds of trouble he'd rather be getting into.'

'Not at all,' Max said. 'I'm thrilled to be here.' He flashed a wide grin at her and moved through the door so she was forced to step aside or risk him brushing against her.

'You won't like the film,' Katie called after him. Then she turned back, ready to question Anna, but she'd kicked off her shoes and was making a beeline for the living room. 'You can run,' she muttered under her breath.

In the living room, she grabbed Anna by the arm. 'Excuse us,' she said to Max and towed Anna into the kitchenette. 'What are you doing?'

'Giving you a little push,' Anna said, lifting her chin. 'I know you like him, so don't try to deny it.'

'That's not the point.' Katie dumped the flowers on the draining board. 'I don't need to be set up.'

'Really?' Anna said. 'Remind me, how long is it since you went out with anyone?'

'By choice,' Katie said. 'My choice.'

'Uh-huh.' Anna picked up the flowers and began snipping the ends of their stems. 'And how much of this choice is based on fear?'

'You can talk. You're having an imaginary relationship with that cricket player.'

'I didn't say I had it sorted. Which is all the more reason for you to grab this opportunity. I'm living proof that they don't come along every day.' She took a pint glass down from the shelf over the counter and half filled it with water. She put the flowers in and put it on the window sill.

'It'll be fun,' Anna said. 'Remember fun?' And she picked up the bottle of red wine and walked back into the living room.

Katie put popcorn into bowls and poured herself a Diet Coke. She liked to keep a clear head at the best of times and it seemed particularly important at that moment. She was delaying walking into the living room, could hear the rumble of Max's voice, punctuated by Anna's laugh, and every sound made her anxiety go up a notch. She wasn't cut out for this. She was cut out for safe. For dates at the cinema with a boy who was as predictable as he was sweet. Not for Max sprawled on her sofa with his long legs and his sarcasm. The timer on the oven went off and she hauled the chocolate orange muffins she'd put in earlier.

'Those smell amazing,' Anna said when she carried them through. She snagged a muffin from the plate. 'You should move in with me.'

'They're just muffins. Anyone can make muffins. They're like fairy cakes or flapjack. Impossible to get wrong. My aunt Gwen is the real cook,' Katie said. 'I bet you can bake muffins.'

'Nope,' Anna said cheerfully. 'I have other talents.'

Max unscrewed the top from the wine. 'Glasses?'

Katie pointed to the kitchen doorway. 'Help yourself.'

Anna had taken the armchair, which left the sofa for Max and Katie. 'Move,' Katie whispered. Anna shook her head, smiling.

Max came back through a moment later with a

Winnie the Pooh plastic tumbler, a shot glass and a mug.

'I'm fine,' Katie said quickly, holding up her Diet Coke.

Max sloshed wine into the plastic tumbler and took a healthy swallow. 'Okay, I'm ready to be bored senseless.'

'That's the spirit,' Anna said and pressed play on the DVD.

'I'm kidding,' Max said, leaning back and stretching one arm along the back of the sofa.

'I'm very cultured,' he said, over the sound of the opening titles. A moment later, he said, 'Subtitles?'in a disgusted tone of voice.

Katie kept her eyes fixed on the screen and tried not to think about Max sitting a few inches to her left. She didn't want to lean back in case she touched his arm. It might look as if she wanted him to put his arm around her, as if this were a date.

When Max leaned forward to get a handful of popcorn and offer her the bowl, he moved his arm and didn't put it back again. Katie sank back against the sofa cushions and tried to concentrate on the film. She loved *Amélie* with a passion and had been looking forward to showing Anna. Now, she wished it were something a little less romantic. Why couldn't this have been the night they watched *Platoon*?

After *Amélie* had finished, Katie clicked off the television and turned to Anna. 'See? Greatest film ever. Well, in the last twenty years, anyway.'

'I prefer *Hitch*,' Anna said. 'But I did like it.'

'I'm going to ignore that,' Katie said, hoping that Anna was teasing her.

'What shall we do now?' Max said, stretching his

arms above his head. Katie tried not to stare at the way his muscles flexed. It was ridiculous. She'd seen men before. Seen muscles, seen arms, seen flat chests and nice jaw lines and all that. Why was this particular mix of them making her feel so off balance? He smiled at her in a way that suggested he'd noticed her looking.

She got up quickly and went to refill her glass.

In the kitchen she took a moment to regain her equilibrium. Max joked around as if he were Mr Easy-Going, but he had a focused intensity she found alarmingly attractive. He had a way of looking at things as if he was calculating the odds of every single possibility. Katie felt as if she'd met hundreds of guys who were good at having a laugh. Guys like Stuart who were friendly and fun and would move furniture for you if you asked them nicely. At first, Katie had loved Stuart's relaxed attitude to life, but she'd felt as if she had to keep cracking jokes to remind him of her existence. Max never gave the impression that he'd forgotten about her. It was flattering. And probably an act. She wasn't going to be naive and get sucked in by the first charming guy she met.

She smoothed down her skirt. She was going to keep her head and keep her distance. Not let things get too personal. And he was here to see Greg Barton's show. After that, he'd be on his way. She was perfectly safe, as long as she kept her head.

'So,' Max said, when she finally picked up the courage to walk back in. 'Anna tells me you're a witch. Is that for real?'

Katie almost dropped her glass. 'What?'

'I didn't,' Anna said, waving her wine glass, her face flushed. 'Jo told him and I just confirmed it.'

'Jo told you I was a, what?' Katie had practised her

look of innocent confusion, adding increments of outrage until she had just the right blend of 'what the fuck?'. It was hard, trying to work out how a normal person would react to that kind of statement. She suspected most people would just laugh, but she'd never been able to pull that off. Fake laughter was really hard.

Anna was sitting forward. 'Oh, come on. It's not like it's a big secret. Everyone in town knows. It's nothing to be ashamed of.'

Katie took a sip of her drink to buy time.

'I've been wanting to ask you about this stuff for so long. I mean, you're a Harper. Your aunt—'

'I don't want to talk about my family.'

'But it's so cool,' Anna said. 'And Max was saying that he met Gwen the other day. I mean, you took him to End House, so I assumed—'

'No,' Katie said.

Anna looked devastated and defiant in equal parts. 'I thought we were friends. I thought you'd open up eventually but I guess I was wrong on both counts.' Anna got up.

Katie wasn't sure if she was mock-offended or really offended, but she knew she didn't want to lose her. She took a deep breath. 'There are certain abilities in my family, yes.'

Anna let out an excited little squeak and sat back down. 'See!' She turned to Max. 'They can do this stuff for real. I heard that Gwen can find lost things and then there's all that stuff that grows in her garden—'

Max was looking at her with an amused but faintly disgusted expression.

'Can you read my cards?' Anna was practically bouncing on the chair. 'I've wanted to ask ever since we met but then we became friends and I didn't want you to think I was using you or anything—'

'But you're fine with it, now?'

'Please,' Anna said. 'Everything's a bit rubbish at the moment.' She tried to calm down, look serious, but she was too hyper to pull it off. 'I think it would really help.'

'Fine,' Katie said. She didn't dare look at Max.

She fetched her tarot cards from the bookshelves and opened the box. 'I'm not really good at this, but I can do a little bit. My gran has the fortune-telling gift. She's scary good.' Katie fixed Max with what she hoped was a compelling gaze. 'And I do mean scary.'

'Me first, me first,' Anna said, even though Max hadn't shown the slightest inclination to want to join in.

'Okay. Can you sit opposite me?'

Katie moved the cups and mugs to the side of the coffee table and put a bowl of popcorn on the floor. She opened the wooden box and unwrapped the black silk from around the cards.

Max's expression was stony, but she ignored him and put the stack face down in the middle of the table. 'Okay,' she said. 'I'll do the tree of life but I warn you now, if I don't think you'll benefit from knowing something, I won't tell you it.' Katie had had enough lectures from Gwen on the importance of responsibility. Apparently her gran had a different policy — you asked, you got answers. Even if it meant you left her house in tiny little bits.

'Fine,' Anna said, sitting forward.

Katie put a hand over the pack and held it there, waiting for the tingling sensation that had always come before. Nothing. She picked the pack up and shuffled it. Put it back on the table and held her hand over it again.

Anna said, 'Do I ask a question or something?'

'No.' Katie shook her head. 'I can't do it. Sorry.'

'Why not?' Anna looked disappointed.

The familiar sense of failure settled across Katie, making her feel tired and a little bit weepy. 'There's nothing there.' She gestured to the pack of cards. 'I don't know why. Maybe I'm tired.'

'Some other time,' Max said. He looked at his watch. 'Don't we have more filmage? Unless you want to go to the pub, instead?'

'No.' Anna stretched and stood up. 'I'm knackered. I'm going to head home.' She picked up the empty muffin plate and took it to the kitchen.

Katie followed. 'Don't you dare.'

'I'm tired.' Anna didn't meet her eye. 'Early shift tomorrow.'

Katie's stomach swooped. 'Are you angry with me? I'm sorry about the cards—'

'It's okay,' Anna said, but she still didn't look up. She eased past Katie and back into the living room. Katie heard her saying goodbye to Max and then she was gone. Katie willed her heart to stop hammering. She was okay. He was a stranger but he wasn't dangerous. He was just a guy. And Anna was right: she was never going to meet anybody new if she didn't take little risks now and then.

Max was standing in the middle of the room, looking at the art prints and postcards on the walls.

'Do you want more wine?' Katie said.

'Aren't you having any?'

'No.' Katie shook her head. 'I'm not a big drinker. Especially with people who think I'm insane.'

'Sensible,' Max said. His calculating expression was back again.

'What?'

'Why didn't you read the cards for Anna?'

'You know why,' Katie said. 'I couldn't do it. I don't know what's wrong with me, but—'

'But you know her — you'd hardly have to cold read her. You could've just made some stuff up, made a few vague statements.'

Katie put a hand on one hip and regarded him coolly. 'I don't do that. I'm not pretending. The women in my family have unusual abilities. For real.'

'I think you really believe that,' Max said slowly. Then he smiled. 'Luckily, I have a high tolerance for weirdness.'

'Thanks a lot,' Katie said. His expression made her bold, made her want to shock him. 'I can talk to ghosts. There's one at the hotel and her name is Violet. I was talking to her the other day. And I've been dreaming about Mr Cole. He keeps asking me to look for his watch. That's why I want to find it.'

Max waited a beat, as if expecting her to smile and say she was joking.

'You were brought up with conning. I was brought up with this,' Katie said. 'I don't expect you to believe me, but I think it was a ghost that dropped the vase the other day.'

'It's a theory,' Max said.

'I'm only telling you for your own safety. If you get cold all of a sudden, look out for flying ceramics.'

'Okay, this is just your thing,' Max said. 'Like a hobby. And it's not that weird. To be fair, lots of people believe in ghosts. Not so many claim to chat to them, but—'

'Just because you can't see the giant rabbit, doesn't mean it isn't real.'

'You're seeing rabbits, now?'

'No,' Katie said. 'Like in *Harvey*. Jimmy Stewart could see this rabbit but no one else in the film can.'

'Like in *Donnie Darko*? There's a rabbit in that, isn't there?'

'No,' Katie said severely. 'Like in *Harvey*. It's not a scary rabbit. It's life-affirming.'

Max shrugged. 'Sorry. I haven't seen it.'

'I'm going to have to educate you.'

'You and I have very different ideas about education.'

'We have very different ideas about a lot of things. It's one of the many reasons I'm not going to drink with you.'

'You will eventually.'

'Now you sound dodgy and arrogant again.'

'Sorry,' Max said. 'Occupational hazard.'

'How's that new leaf going, anyway? Are you liking an honest day's work?'

'The bar?' Max said. 'It's fun. For now.' He moved closer to her. 'Not as much fun as this, though. I just wish you weren't frightened of me.'

'I'm not frightened,' Katie said. 'I'm being sensible. You're only here because you think I've got your watch.'

'Not any more. You're not stupid so if you were trying to con me, you'd be making a better job of it than this.'

'Thanks,' Katie said. 'I think.'

'Besides, I don't think I've ever met anybody less suited to grifting. I mean, you were embarrassed tonight. When you couldn't do that card trick, but you didn't gloss over it or pretend.'

'Tarot isn't a card trick.'

'Not always, apparently,' Max said. 'I still think Barton is faking, though.'

Katie frowned. 'Don't put me in the same category as him. A true psychic would never get up on stage and dish out information. It's morally corrupt, unethical, wrong. And it's not even the way it works.'

'You're not a fan, then,' Max said, looking a little bemused. 'I'd have thought—'

'Well, you thought wrong.'

'Do you want to come and see the show? See if we can catch him out together? I've got a plus one on my ticket.'

Katie felt a rush that started from her toes and went straight to the top of her head. He wanted to see her again. She was crap at kissing and had told him she could see ghosts and he still wanted to see her again.

He dipped his head. 'Katie?'

Katie realised she was clutching her necklace and she made herself let go of it. Safety-wise, it was one of the best dates she could accept. She would be in the hotel, surrounded by people. On the other hand, it would involve sitting next to Max for an hour or two. A prospect that made her heart rate kick up and her palms go all sweaty.

He gave her a quick smile. 'No problem if you've got other plans or would rather jump off a bridge. I can take a hint.'

'No,' Katie said.

'It's cool.' Max held up his hands.

'No. I mean, I don't have plans. Yes. I'll watch the show with you.'

'I'll say goodnight, then.' Max kissed her quickly on the cheek, then got up from the sofa and made for the door. 'Until tomorrow.'

Katie sank back onto the sofa and stared at the glasses on the coffee table. She was going on a date with a con man. Ex-con-man, whatever. She couldn't stop picturing Max and every time she conjured his face, her own split into a wide grin. This wasn't good. The last time she'd felt this excited she'd been fourteen and madly in love with Luke Taylor. That hadn't ended well, but, no matter how much she tried to frighten herself with bad memories, she couldn't ignore the fizzing in her veins. It was as if her blood had been replaced with lemonade and her vital organs filled with helium. Katie pictured Max's face as he'd asked her out, replayed the sound of his voice when he'd said 'until tomorrow' and then had to cover her mouth to stop an excited squeaking sound escaping. *Tragic.* She was glad that Shari wasn't around to witness her giggling and gurning like a fool. One thing was clear, though: she had a crush on the con man.

'Not, sensible, honeybunch,' she said out loud, trying to channel Gwen and regain some semblance of sanity.

Unfortunately, Gwen's voice echoed back saying, 'Women like sex, too,' which wasn't at all helpful. She got up and cleared away the glasses and took them into the kitchen, before heading to bed.

For once, she was glad when the Oliver Cole dream began its nightly rerun. At least I'm not dreaming about jumping Max, she thought, before the dream took over and she was back in The Yellow Room watching Oliver Cole die.

THE NEXT DAY, Katie went to find Mrs Cole. She'd been

distracted from Mr Cole's watch but it seemed pretty clear that the bad dreams weren't going to stop until she found it. She used the hotel database to find the address and drove to the Cole residence in a cul-de-sac in Chippenham.

The houses in the street were all detached new-builds with conservatories and at least two cars to fill their double garages. The woman who answered the door was wearing stretchy workout clothes and a purple sweat top. She must've been in her late fifties but had incredibly shapely legs. Katie dragged her gaze upwards. 'Mrs Cole?'

'Yes?'

'I'm very sorry to bother you,' Katie said. 'This is a bit awkward, but it concerns your late husband. May I come in?'

Mrs Cole narrowed her eyes. 'Are you one of his?'

'I'm sorry?'

'You're a bit young, even for him.' Mrs Cole gave her an exaggerated look up and down.

'No,' Katie said. *Ew.* 'I work at The Grange.'

'Oh.' Mrs Cole looked confused. 'Is there a problem with the bill?'

'No, nothing like that. I'm really sorry to bring this up, but had your husband lost a watch? Before he passed away?'

'I knew it, you're of them—'

Mrs Cole went to shut the door and Katie stepped forward to stop her. 'I didn't know your husband. I'm just trying to recover some property. Did he give you a watch? It belongs to a friend of mine.'

'That ugly thing? Pass on my condolences to your friend.'

'So, you did see a watch?'

'It was in his wash bag. In a gift box all ready to give to one of his whores.'

'I'm sorry?'

'You think I didn't know?' Mrs Cole said. 'I knew. I knew all about his extra-curricular activities.'

'The thing is, the watch belongs to my friend.' Katie didn't think gambling would seem worse than infidelity, but it still didn't feel right to out Mr Cole. 'I don't want to speak ill of the dead—'

'Oh, go ahead. It's what the bastard deserves.'

'Right. Well. He was supposed to give the watch to my friend and he didn't. I'm sure he was going to, but, well—'

'He popped his clogs.' Mrs Cole was looking at Katie in an appraising way. 'You're not one of his girls, are you? You don't seem the type.'

'No,' Katie said. 'I swear.'

'Then I'm sorry. I gave your friend's watch to the Red Cross shop, along with all his clothes and CDs and the fucking ugly coffee table he made me live with for the past ten years.'

'Oh,' Katie said, taking a step back. Mrs Cole took advantage of the moment and swung the door closed.

'Which Red Cross shop?' Katie said, but the door banged shut. *Fabulous.* Katie looked at the door for a few moments before returning to her car. On one hand it was good that Mrs Cole wasn't sentimentally attached to the watch, but Katie was still none the wiser as to what Mr Cole wanted her to do about it. And the more Katie found out about Mr Cole, the less inclined she was to help him. When she'd thought about helping others, she'd always pictured nice people like Fred Byres. She hadn't planned on being an errand girl for a lying, cheating scumbag like Oliver Cole.

The hotel car park was full long before Barton's show was due to start. There were vehicles parked along the driveway and in front of the main house. Patrick watched the audience enjoying pre-show drinks in the bar with evident delight. Katie was surprised he wasn't actually rubbing his hands together. 'Have you seen this crowd?' he said to Katie. 'Unbelievable. I had no idea the show would be this popular.'

'There's no accounting for taste,' Katie said.

'Are you working?' Patrick said, his eyes still on the crowd.

'Excuse me.' One of the temp staff appeared. 'Mr Allen? There's a couple here who want to sleep in the haunted room. I wasn't sure—'

'What?' Katie whipped around, but Patrick was already hurrying towards Reception. Then she got distracted by the sight of Max walking in through the French doors, which were open to the terrace.

'Hey, Nancy Drew,' he said, kissing her on the cheek. 'Ready for our hot date?'

'We're going to watch a man we both abhor. Really sexy.'

'And you dressed for the occasion.' He looked at her work uniform.

'I've just finished my shift.'

'I love a woman in uniform.' Max gave her an appreciative look that she felt down to the tips of her toes.

'Bloody hell, does this approach actually work for you?'

'Usually,' Max said. He offered her his arm. 'M'lady.'

'Idiot,' Katie said, but she reached out anyway and let him tuck her hand around his upper arm.

The tables in the function room had been stacked in the breakfast room, and every available chair in the building pressed into service. The rows of seats faced a makeshift stage at the front of the room with a spotlight trained onto two modern armchairs with a low table between them. It looked like the set for a business seminar. A young woman dressed in black trousers and T-shirt placed a bottle of mineral water and a glass onto the table and then fiddled with a microphone stand, angling it towards one of the chairs.

The people filling the room were chatting quietly and there was an air of intense anticipation. 'We should've got here earlier,' Max said, suddenly sounding tense. 'We're too far back.'

Katie looked around at the crowded space. She knew that Gwen had a steady stream of people coming to the back door at End House, asking for remedies and advice, but that was different. That actually helped. She shook her head. 'There must be a hundred MOPs in here. Patrick will be delighted.'

Max didn't reply. He was leaning forward, his hands gripping his knees in claws.

'Are you okay?'

Max shrugged quickly. 'Not exactly. I really don't like this man.'

'You mentioned that once or twice.' Katie nudged him, trying to lighten the mood.

'But I kind of want him to be the real thing, too. I want him to, I don't know, give me a message—'

'I'm sorry,' Katie said, hit by his sudden vulnerability, the spark of hope in his voice. 'I don't think that's likely.'

Katie took his hand and squeezed it. The final stragglers were coming into the room; some had bottles of water and some were clutching personal items like talismans. One man had a gold carriage clock. He hesitated, scanning the rows for a spare seat and then took the final one. Katie tried not to think about all the sad, grieving, frightened people, in the room. It was too awful.

Someone put the lights off in the room and the chatter stopped almost instantly. The spotlit chairs seemed to grow in size with the weight of expectation in the room. A door opened and the female assistant appeared. She was carrying a couple of wireless microphones and she passed one to a Grange staff member and they crossed to the other side of the room, waiting. Then, a short man in a sharp suit came through the open doorway and stepped quickly up onto the stage. Greg Barton smiled with dazzling teeth and welcomed them all to his 'house of spirits'. He had odd, puffy hair that rose in a stiff bouffant above his rather jowly face. His skin had an unreal orange tinge and Katie wondered whether he was addicted to sun beds or had overdone the stage make-up.

'Thank y'all for inviting me here,' he said in a strange transatlantic accent that seemed to span Yorkshire and America by way of the deep south. 'Before we begin, I need you to switch off mobile phones and to remind you that strictly no filming or recording of this event is allowed. It annoys the spirits.' He smiled, cocking an eyebrow at someone in the front row.

'So that no one plays it back and realises he was cold reading the whole time,' Max said quietly.

'Can I please ask for silence while I summon my spirit guide?' Barton pressed his hands together and closed his eyes. Max rolled his at Katie, but he still looked oddly tense.

Part of Barton's skit was that he was in touch with a spirit called Magda. She was apparently the ghost of an American heiress and she helped Barton connect with the other side. Out of the goodness of her dead heart, apparently.

Barton opened his eyes. 'Magda says there is somebody with her now. A man. Does the name John mean anything to anyone here?'

'John is only one of the most common male names in the Western hemisphere,' Katie leaned in close to whisper into Max's ear and she caught the scent of his skin. She leaned away again quickly.

A woman in the third row had her hand up. 'My husband was Jonathan.'

Barton walked to the edge of the stage. The runner had already passed along a hand-held microphone to the woman and she spoke into it. 'My husband—' she began.

He held up a hand, silencing her. 'Magda says this

man is very sad. I'm getting the letter "P" — does that mean anything to you? And the letter "S".'

The woman gasped.

'The letter "S" is very strong. I'm sensing that's important.'

Nice fishing. Katie wondered how many letters Barton usually had to throw out before he got a hit. Two? Three? In a crowd this size, he could always switch to someone else, claim the spirits were talking to them now. It made her sick. All of these poor people, looking for answers. They wanted the comfort that knowledge could bring and Barton was feeding off them.

'Our son is Simon.'

'He says he doesn't like to see you upset. Does that sound like him?'

Yeah, that sounded like everybody, ever.

The woman had a tissue pressed up against her face. She nodded mutely.

Katie shifted in her chair. It was painful to watch the act, when she knew that the man was alone up there. No spooks. Or ghosties or ghouls.

She turned to Max and found him sitting forward, looking as if he wanted to hit something. She didn't blame him.

A young woman in the front row burst into tears and Barton looked down at her, his face a picture of sympathetic benevolence. 'Your granddad says "hi".'

'No, he doesn't.' Violet's unmistakable cut-glass tones sounded in Katie's right ear. Katie whipped around but she couldn't see her. The large man sitting next to Katie gave her a funny look, though.

'Where are you?' she said, very quietly. Almost under her breath. The man next to her glanced anyway, then looked away very quickly. *He thinks I'm mad.* She resisted the urge to say, 'You're the one paying to watch a man pretend to be psychic.'

Barton threw his head back and the audience gasped. His eyes rolled back in his head. Katie had read up on him and apparently he was famous for being 'taken over' by a spirit. He spoke as them, in a strange high voice and it was, according to *The Birmingham Gazette*, 'not to be missed'.

'Mummy?' Barton spoke in a high squeaky voice and Katie had to stuff her hand into her mouth to stop herself from laughing out loud. She didn't dare look at Max's face or she knew she wouldn't be able to keep quiet.

'It's dark,' Barton squeaked. 'I want my mummy.' He dropped his head, his arms going limp and then, after a few seconds of stillness, he raised his head and stared, seemingly sightlessly, out across the assembled people.

'Peek a boo.' He wasn't doing the squeaky voice any more but something in his tone made all the hairs stand up on the back of Katie's neck.

'What a funny fat man. Shall I make him dance?'

Barton's eyes were wide, now. Terrified.

'Stop it,' Katie said, standing up. 'Violet. Just stop.'

'You're no fun.' Barton's lips were moving and it was his vocal cords that were making the sounds, but the inflection and accent was pure Violet. It was her, speaking through Barton as if he were a puppet.

Katie watched in horror as Violet detached herself from Barton. It was hard to focus on, gave Katie a headache to try, but she saw Violet appear from within Barton. As soon as she was separate, he sagged forwards and one of the assistants ran up on stage to catch him before he hit the floor. Violet, meanwhile, was sort of filling up again, becoming more solid as Katie watched. Once she was corporeal-looking again, she gave Katie a beatific smile and sauntered off stage left.

'Ladies and gentlemen.' Barton had almost straightened up. Katie had to hand it to the man: he was a trooper. 'What you just witnessed was interference from an evil spirit.' He held up his hands. 'Don't be alarmed. Magda has seen off the evil but I must remind you all that this is why you must only ever attempt to communicate with the dead through an experienced professional such as myself.'

Violet had disappeared. Katie scanned the room, looking for her, her mind racing. Violet could step inside a human being and make them move. Which meant she could touch things after all. She could've thrown the vase after all. *So much for harmless.*

The audience was still fussing, but Greg Barton was getting them back. His voice carried through the room, blanketing with phrases like 'part of the process' and 'it's okay to feel emotions' and 'intense spiritual experience'.

MAX WAS DISTRACTED after Barton's show. He kissed Katie on the cheek and thanked her for accompanying him. She'd expected him to make some kind of move, and was almost disappointed when he didn't. Maybe he'd decided that he didn't fancy her after all. Or that she was too uptight to be worth bothering with. That wasn't unlikely.

'I'm just…' Max trailed off. He was looking into the middle distance, his eyes unfocused.

'Are you okay?' Katie wanted to talk about the show. She found she even wanted to tell Max about what Violet had done. He wouldn't believe her, of course, but the urge was there. Which was a bit weird.

'Yeah. Just tired.' He didn't meet her eye. 'I'm going out for some fresh air.'

Katie watched as Max walked away from her and tried not to feel hurt that he hadn't wanted her company. A walk outside sounded nice.

Instead, she headed upstairs to talk to either Barton or Violet. Whichever one she found first. She knocked on the door to Barton's suite and pushed it open. He was sitting on the burgundy sofa, a tumbler of amber liquid in one hand and a newspaper open on his lap.

'I'm sorry to bother you, Mr Barton—'

He didn't look up. 'Just put it on the table.'

'Um... I'm not—'

He glanced up then, with an expression that probably would've been a frown on a more mobile face. His eyebrows raised ever so slightly.

'I just wanted to speak to you for a moment, if that's okay.'

'Signed photos are in the case. Help yourself.'

'Thanks,' Katie said. She walked into the room but left the door wide open. One of the first rules of working in a hotel was never to enter a room with a MOP by yourself and definitely never to close the door. Personal safety 101. 'But I actually wanted to ask your advice.'

Barton heaved a theatrical sigh and flipped his newspaper shut. He looked at her and then gave her a long look up and down that made Katie's skin crawl. 'I knew there'd be a catch.'

'Sorry?'

'The free room. I knew there'd be a catch. This is why I usually avoid staying in the venue. Did you see the show, sweetie? Want a private session? You should know that I'm very expensive.'

Katie narrowed her eyes. 'Fine. I just thought you'd want to know more about what happened to you up there. I thought we could help each other out. Friendly, like.' She turned to leave. 'Sorry to have bothered you.'

'What do you mean?'

Katie turned back. 'I'm guessing that doesn't usually happen? Possession?'

'I'm a direct voice medium — the spirits talk through me all the time. That's what I do.' Barton's tone was pompous but his forehead was beaded with sweat. Off-stage, he didn't look all that well.

'Is it usually out of your control like that?' Katie said.

Barton's face twisted slightly. 'My spirit guide is on my side. She looks after me.'

Katie had Barton down as a cold-hearted fraud, but she was starting to wonder if he believed in his own hype. Intense self-deception? Or maybe real ability? She felt a spark of excitement. Maybe he could help her. Maybe she wasn't alone in this.

'Did you see Violet come out of your body?'

'Violet?'

'The spirit that possessed you. She's called Violet,' Katie said. 'Don't be angry with her — she's usually very nice.'

'I felt a loss of control of my own body. It was a

violation. Nothing nice would do that,' Barton said, his expression one of disbelief and anger.

'Maybe she did it by accident,' Katie said. Then something occurred to her: if Violet could move into a person's body and move it according to her own will, she'd be able to write on walls, throw vases. Anything an alive person could do. Crap.

'There's a spirit in this hotel that I'm worried about. An angry one and I was hoping you might have some advice.'

'We could hold a seance,' Barton said. 'I usually charge two hundred but as a personal favour I'd do it for one fifty.'

'I can see ghosts. I don't need to pay you to pretend to talk to them,' Katie said, anger running through her body. 'I just hoped you'd have some advice. For me.'

Barton leaned forward, an expression of interest on his face. 'You can see ghosts? Communicate with them?'

'Yes. Well, I've only talked to Violet so far but I saw a boy commit suicide in the cricket pavilion, too.'

'And you want my advice?' He smiled like a lizard.

'Yes, please.'

'Start charging.' Barton sat back. 'Get some flyers printed up. Start small. You can't expect to play places like this—' he waved a hand '—until you're more established.'

'I don't want to charge people,' Katie said. 'I want to know how to get rid of the angry ghost. And how to help the sad ones.' She tried not to see the blood dripping down the boy's arms, his terrible expression.

'Then you're a fool.' Barton picked up his newspaper again.

'Thanks for nothing,' Katie said, backing out of the

room. The disappointment was a bitter taste in the back of her throat.

Barton looked up. 'I did meet a ghost-hunter type, once. When I was on *This Morning* with Phil and Fern. They had the most darling little canapés in the green room and the best make-up girl I've worked with.'

Katie paused, waiting for Greg to stop blowing hot air.

'Anyway. He said that he exorcised ghosts by digging up their bones and burning them.' Barton gave an elaborate shudder. 'Ghoulish.'

Katie turned to leave and walked straight into Max. He caught her arms and stopped her from stumbling over, then did a double take at the room number on the door. His face hardened. 'You know Barton. Of course you do.'

'I don't,' Katie said. 'I was hoping he could help me with something, but—'

'I'll bet,' Max said. He looked disgusted. He stepped to the side, leaving an exaggerated amount of space for her to walk past. 'See you around.'

CHAPTER 11

Katie watched Max walk into Barton's room and shut the door. She wanted to tell him that he shouldn't do that, that you should always leave a door open when visiting a MOP or cleaning a room, but she was still in shock from the anger in his voice. The look of betrayal on his face. Maybe she'd let him calm down first.

She was halfway downstairs when the smell of Chanel No. 5 and a blast of cold air alerted her to Violet's presence. She ran the last few steps and went into the Ladies, hoping to outrun the ghost. She'd stepped inside Barton. She'd made him move like a puppet. For the first time, Katie felt frightened of Violet.

She looked at herself in the mirror. Her eyeliner had smudged so she wet her finger and swept it underneath her eyes, leaning close to the mirror to scoop the gunk from the corners. A slight movement in the edge of the mirror made her whip round. Violet was leaning against one of the stall doors. 'You should take better care of your skin, you know,' she said.

'Hello, Violet,' Katie said, keeping her voice even. 'How are you?'

Violet shook her head, using that fluid motion that gave Katie a headache. 'Why did you run away?'

'How long have you been able to do that? Possession?'

Violet looked confused for a moment, then she giggled. 'That was my first. Wasn't it fun?'

'It wasn't very nice,' Katie said.

Violet was peering at her own reflection, didn't seem to be listening.

'You shouldn't do it — you shouldn't take a person's free will like that,' Katie said, trying to catch Violet's eye in the mirror.

'I thought I was helping. Your young man doesn't like him. I thought it would make him happy.' She cast a disparaging look at Katie. '*You* don't seem to be trying.'

'I don't have a young man,' Katie said.

'You'll lose him if you're not careful.' Violet turned away from the mirror. 'You talk to him too sharply. And he looked really angry just now.'

'Were you watching us?'

'You mustn't make him angry,' Violet said, her body vibrating. The air around her began to shimmer like a heat haze and her voice rose. 'Men don't like that.'

'It's okay,' Katie said, putting her hands up. 'Max is fine. We're fine.' In her desire to calm Violet down, Katie forgot for a moment that she wasn't with Max, that this entire thing was a bored ghost's fantasy. 'And you've got the wrong idea — we're not together.'

Violet shook her head again. 'Well, that's even worse. You should be.'

'I don't think so,' Katie said, glad that Violet had

stopped vibrating. She leaned close to the mirror and re-applied her liner.

'He's handsome,' Violet said.

'He's a con man.'

Violet pressed her lips together. 'You don't know how lucky you are.'

'That a man is interested in me? Oh, please—'

'Not that.' Violet waved a hand. 'Someone interesting is interested in you. That's far more rare.'

Katie had to concede that Violet had a point.

'And he has a motor car.' She wrinkled her nose. 'It isn't very clean, but you can't afford to be so choosy.'

'What do you mean?'

'Well…' Violet tilted her head '…you're getting on a bit.'

'I'm twenty-one.'

'Exactly,' Violet said. She smoothed down her dress. 'I'm so bored of this frock, you have no idea. I can't even change my make-up or spritz on a little perfume. It's hellish.'

'You don't need to spritz,' Katie said. 'You smell like Chanel No.5. It's how I know you're there even when you're trying to be subtle.'

'Oh.' Violet's mouth turned down. 'That's rather galling. One hates to be predictable.'

'And I think you're right and there's another spirit around here, because I keep smelling pipe smoke and this whole place is non-smoking.'

Violet looked disgusted. 'Poor you. I hate pipes.'

~

KATIE WENT TO FIND MAX. He was in the ornamental

garden, pacing up and down the gravel path, and muttering to himself.

'Someone once told me that was the first sign of madness,' Katie said.

He shot her a look. 'What do you want?'

'To clear the air. I'm not working with Barton or visiting him for his autograph or whatever it is you're upset about. I think he's scum.'

Max stopped pacing. 'So, what were you going to see him about?'

'You know I've been talking to a ghost called Violet? Well, she sort of stepped into Barton at the end of his act.'

'The "fat man dance" bit?' Max said. 'I thought that was different. I didn't think Barton was that good an actor and something funny happened with my eyes, too. I thought it was the lights.'

'It wasn't the lights.'

'You are absolutely serious, aren't you?' Max said. He was watching her in an alarmingly intense way. After a moment, he said, 'I watched that film. *Harvey*.'

'Don't tell me if you didn't like it. It'll only make me think less of you.'

'I liked it. It also gave me an insight.'

'Careful. Those can be dangerous.'

'It's his thing. Dowd. It's the thing that lets him face the world, his comfort blanket. But rather than growing out of it, he's kept it as a kind of personality trait.'

'I'm not sure that's—'

'I just wanted to tell you that you don't need to see ghosts to be interesting. You're already interesting. To me.'

'Thank you,' Katie said. 'But you'd have difficulty being further from the mark.'

'I mean it.' Max took a step forward. 'You're funny and clever and beautiful and different.'

'Thank you,' Katie said, a little off balance. She reached for her necklace and traced the shape of the charms with her thumb.

Max took her hand, folding his fingers around her own. 'You always fiddle with this when you're nervous.'

Her face went warm. 'I'm not nervous.' She was embarrassed that she had such an obvious tell and excited that Max was watching her closely enough to notice it. Plus, his fingertips were brushing her collar-bone and it was making it difficult to think straight.

He smiled, ignoring the obvious lie. 'I like it, by the way.' He opened his hand and looked at her necklace. 'I saw it the first day I met you. I thought perhaps you were a gambler.'

Katie frowned. She'd made the necklace years ago, using Gwen's supplies. She didn't know why she'd chosen the bone die, the silver feather or the tiny revolver, only that she always felt good wearing it.

'You know,' Max was saying. 'Guns and dice, very Vegas.'

'Death and chance and hope,' Katie said, offended. *Bloody Vegas, indeed.*

Max's smile got wider. 'You see. You're always saying things I don't expect. You're sarcastic and a bit mean but you have a good heart.' He stepped closer. 'A really good heart.'

'You hardly know me.' Katie was working hard not to be flattered. He was a con man. A professional liar. He knew how to charm people and she was a fool if she fell for his act. He was probably only talking to her because he wanted to get his watch back.

'I know enough. And you don't have to make your-self any more mysterious.'

Katie crossed her arms. 'You think I'm pretending to see ghosts in order to make myself alluring to you?'

'Not just me. Everyone. But you don't need to hide behind that.'

'I'm not hiding behind anything.' Katie spread her hands. 'I'm right here. Plain sight.'

'I think you're using it as a defence mechanism. To keep people away from you. To stop anybody from getting too close.'

'That's not true,' Katie said. 'I live in a different reality, though. That's fact. You can't understand. No one can understand. Not really.'

'That's very convenient, isn't it?' Max put his hands on her waist. 'Why don't you admit you're scared of letting people get close to you.'

'I've had a boyfriend. I've got friends.' Katie forced herself to step away. 'Has it occurred to you that I might not want to get close to you? That maybe I've got more sense than to get involved with a—'

'I believe you kissed me the other day,' Max said. 'Or are you going to claim you have an identical twin running around? Which would be quite interesting, by the way.'

'That was just lust,' Katie said, then mentally slapped herself in the head.

'Lust?' Max quirked an eyebrow. 'I can work with that.'

'I don't think so,' Katie said. 'You're a con man. A thief. A liar.'

'But I've been honest about my dishonesty. Do I get points for that?'

'One point,' Katie said. 'Which doesn't help you much. You're still in minus figures.'

'But you believe in redemption, remember?'

'So, redeem yourself. You should.'

'And then you'll go out for dinner with me?'

'No.' *Maybe. Yes.*

Max leaned closer, his lips brushing her cheek. 'I think we'd be good together.'

Katie felt the breath leave her body. Max was too close. She could see the hairs of his stubble poking through his skin, smell the sweat on his T-shirt. His head was tilted, his lips close to hers. All she had to do was move a fraction of an inch and she'd be kissing him. They'd be kissing.

'Katie?' Max said.

She stepped back. Just because he had no morals didn't mean she couldn't do the right thing. She wasn't looking forward to seeing him walk away, but there was no point prolonging it. She'd tell him about his watch and he'd disappear from Pendleford and she could get her mind back where it belonged.

'I know where your watch is.'

'Great,' Max said, and he pulled his car keys out of his pocket. 'Let's go.'

Katie hesitated. Maybe she should give him a chance. 'If I tell you, you can't steal it.'

Max frowned. 'I can't steal it because it belongs to me. At most I can regain my rightful property.'

'You said you wanted to redeem yourself. You keep talking about turning over a new leaf. Prove it.'

'Fine,' Max said. 'I promise I won't steal it. Where is it?'

'Mrs Cole donated it to charity. It's in a Red Cross shop in Bath and you can't steal it because that would be stealing from a charity. It doesn't matter how it got there. It was donated by Mrs Cole.'

'I promised,' Max said. 'I'll buy it back. Happy?'

Katie nodded, relieved. 'It must be really important to you. Is it sentimental value?'

'It's not of sentimental value. It's of real value,' Max said. 'I was playing poker and the pot was up to ten grand. I'd run out of cash, so I put it down.'

'A watch worth ten grand? That's obscene. You could buy a car for that.'

'The stakes can go up quickly in poker. That's part of the attraction.'

'Jesus Christ.' Katie shook her head. 'I had no idea Mr Cole was that rich.'

'Yeah, well, he wasn't an entirely honest business-man, put it that way.'

'But you won the game, right? So, you won this watch which is worth loads of money, but you didn't actually see it? And he didn't give it to you? That seems a bit—' Katie was going to say 'stupid' but that seemed harsh, so she finished with 'trusting'.

'I knew he had it because he'd won it off me the night before. I met Oliver Cole in a back-room poker game the night before the wedding. I shouldn't really have been playing with it, but, like I said, I ran out of cash and I wanted to stay in the game. It was a slight error of judgement.'

'Oh, my God, you think?' Katie felt wobbly at the idea of losing that much money. 'How on earth do you have a watch that valuable? Oh, no. Did you steal it?'

Max gave her a serious look. 'It was my dad's watch. My inheritance.'

'I feel ill just thinking about it. Ten thousand pounds.'

Max shrugged. 'Other families have ISAs, we have watches.'

'Watches, plural?'

'Okay,' Max said. 'Here's the deal. One of Dad's favourite short cons was the pigeon drop and he always carried a spare watch for it. Cheap as dirt, but fancy-looking or antique-looking. Like this.' Max pulled a fob watch out of his coat pocket.

'Nice,' Katie said, reaching for it.

'Not nice.' Max shook his head. 'Junk.'

'What's the con?'

Max rolled his shoulders then, speaking in a softer, lighter voice than his own he held the watch out. 'Excuse me, miss, did you drop this?'

'No,' Katie said, playing along.

'I just found it.' Max gestured over his shoulder. 'It looks pretty old. Is there, like, a lost property box or something here?'

Katie opened her mouth to say 'yes' when Max made the sound of a ringing telephone with his mouth. It was uncanny.

'Wow, you're like a mynah bird. Or that impressions guy, what's his name?'

Max continued to ring like a telephone until Katie got sick of the noise and mimed answering one.

'Hello? Is that The Grange hotel?' Max had changed his voice again. He sounded deeper, older, and far more commanding.

'You're through to Reception. How may I help you?' Katie said.

'I was in your restaurant for lunch earlier and I think I left my grandfather's watch. Maybe on the table — I was showing it to some folks — or maybe it fell out of my pocket. Thing is, it's really important to me. I want to offer a reward for its safe return. Two hundred quid.'

'Actually, sir,' Katie said into her hand, 'it's just been found.'

'Great. Keep it safe, will you? I'll be there in half an hour.'

'Then,' Max said in his normal voice, 'the first guy tells the receptionist or shop assistant or whoever, that they're running late for a job interview and they can't wait around to collect their reward, but that they'll happily split it halfway. The mark hands over a hundred quid and takes possession of the watch, knowing full well that they're going to be up a hundred quid. They don't think there's any danger because, if nothing else, they're in possession of a valuable watch.'

'And the caller never turns up?'

'Correct.'

'And the watch is worthless?'

'A tenner at most,' Max said.

'I'm confused,' Katie said. 'Is the watch you won off Mr Cole worthless, then?'

'No. Dad didn't trust banks or lock-boxes or his own kids, apparently. He hid a diamond-studded watch amongst the cheap crap that he used for pigeon drops.'

'And he didn't tell you?'

Max shook his head. 'I only found out last month. Most of the watches had fake authentication certificates. For insurance, you know?'

'Right—'

'I wanted to get them all checked properly. I've been wanting to make a fresh start, to clean everything up and it seemed like a good idea.'

'And you found out that the watch that you pretended was worth ten grand in a poker game, really was worth ten grand. Bloody hell. Talk about poetic justice.'

'Sixty.'

'What?'

'The watch that I lost to Mr Cole and then won back but can't find is worth sixty grand.'

'Why didn't your dad tell you? You weren't kidding about your family having issues.'

Max gave her a long look. 'Would you trust me with sixty grand?'

He had a point.

Three days late. Gwen flipped back through her journal and double-, then triple-checked. Yes. Today was day four, really. She'd been so worried about Katie, she'd lost track of the days. She couldn't remember the last time that had happened.

She felt her breasts. Tender, but then they were when she was due on; it didn't mean she was pregnant. Still, she couldn't entirely burst the little bubble of hope that had appeared in her stomach. She felt her chest again, pressing the sides underneath the armpits. Definitely sore. And, was it her imagination, or had her breasts got a bit bigger during the night?

She took a sip of her tea, trying to decide if it tasted a bit odd. Your tastes changing was another early pregnancy symptom, as was a metallic flavour in the mouth. Gwen took a piece of honey cake from a tin and took it into the garden. She took a bite and then buried the rest underneath the oak tree that spread its branches over the back corner. It was a superstition, but she wasn't ruling anything out. Not any more. She and

Cam had been trying for a baby for three years, now, and had had every test known to medical science. The verdict was unexplained infertility, which, as Cam had pointed out, was just a fancy way of saying 'we don't know'.

Gwen couldn't help worrying that there was an explanation. That she was being punished for the blood magic. Or that, somehow, Lily was still exerting her evil influence from beyond the grave. Which was silly.

More likely was that it just wasn't meant to be. She had her quota of good fortune; Cam, her artwork and a beautiful home. Katie was healthy and, she hoped, happy. She was lucky. So very lucky. Perhaps trying for motherhood as well was just greedy.

Gwen patted the earth down on top of the cake and said an incantation. She couldn't help it. Greedy or not, unwise or not, she wanted a baby. She wanted to be a mother. The depth of this need had come as a complete shock and it consumed her. Only working on her shadow boxes let her forget it for minutes at a time, but as soon as she wasn't focused on creating, it flooded back in with a strength that was physical.

She'd tried to explain to Cam. The desire squeezed her insides; she actually felt her centre contract around the empty space. The empty space that should hold a baby.

She was contracting now, in fact. A clenching pain low down in her stomach. Below her stomach. A dragging sensation that a moment too late Gwen identified as her period. *No, no, no.* She hurried inside to the bathroom and sat on the toilet. There, the bright red evidence of another failed month. Gwen leaned back against the cool cistern and let the hot tears flow over her face unchecked.

It was good to get out of the hotel for the day and even better to spend it with Anna. Katie had been worried that she'd blown things with Anna and had been overjoyed when she'd invited her to spend the day together, even if it did involve watching cricket.

Katie silently thanked the world for her day off and stretched out on the grass at the edge of Pendleford's town green. It crackled underneath her, all the moisture evaporated by the thirsty sun. 'Can you believe this weather?' She adjusted her tortoiseshell cat's-eye sunglasses and folded her hands behind her head. The sky was an almost unbroken blue, just a couple of wispy white trails to highlight the colour of the rest.

Anna was propped up on her elbows, her hand shading her eyes as she watched the distant figures in white. 'Watch Nicolas bowl. See his arms. They're so powerful. And long. Honestly, I feel like they could wrap round me three times.'

'That's a bit of a weird image.'

'Yeah,' Anna said. 'Hot, though.' She lay back next to Katie.

'I can't believe people still play cricket,' Katie said. 'It seems really old-fashioned. It doesn't belong in the same world as Wi-Fi and 3D television.'

'And it takes for-bloody-ever.'

'Yeah. You'd think, in this modern age when we're all supposed to be so busy all the time, they'd at least have shortened it. Quickie cricket.'

'No chance,' Anna said. 'That's why they like it.' She gestured to the players. 'It's like golf. Half the appeal is being away from their real lives for an entire day.'

'But it's so boring,' Katie said. 'Why not just lie on the sofa and watch films all day?'

'I'm so hot,' Anna said. She pulled at the edges of her shorts. 'I wish I could lie here naked.'

'Go ahead,' Katie said, lazily. She closed her eyes and felt as if she could fall asleep. 'It would give the fielders something to look at.'

'The grass would tickle,' Anna said. 'It's so dry it feels like little bits of paper.'

'Coward,' Katie said, smiling.

'Uh-oh. Someone's hot and bothered.'

Anna's tone made Katie open her eyes. She lifted her head and saw Nicolas walking to the edge of the pitch. Even from this distance, she could see his scowl.

'That'll be Ed,' Anna was saying. 'Nicolas says he cheats.'

'Oh.' Katie knew that wasn't much of a response but the heat had made her so drowsy.

'Look.' Anna nodded at a skinny man with black hair. 'He's gloating.'

'You're really getting into this, aren't you?'

'It's important to take an interest in each other's hobbies. It's the secret for a happy relationship.'

'The secret?' Katie teased.

'Well, one of them. I read a book about it once.'

'Let me guess, you should listen to each other, spend quality time together and give him a blow job every night.'

Anna laughed. 'You're disgusting.'

'So, does he show an interest in your hobbies?' Katie wasn't sure if Anna had any hobbies, but she was all for equality.

'Oh, he doesn't know I exist. My relationship with Nicolas is purely theoretical, but I'm working on it.'

'Naked sunbathing would probably help with that,' Katie said.

The skinny dark-haired guy was bowling. She watched as he took a run, his arm windmilling. Just before he released the ball, though, moving so quickly that Katie thought she'd have missed it if she'd blinked, another player grabbed him around the middle and pulled him to the ground.

'Jesus!' She sat up.

Anna laughed. 'Oh, my God, what an idiot.' She looked over at Nicolas, smiling. 'That'll cheer him up.'

'Won't their team lose, now, though? For cheating or something?'

'Why?' Anna frowned at her. 'Ed tripped. It's hardly their fault.'

'What are you talking about? He was tackled by that guy.' Katie looked for the blond player.

Anna was looking at her as if she'd lost the plot. 'He just fell over. Tripped over his feet or lost his balance doing that over-arm throwing thing.'

'That guy.' Katie spotted the blond man who was

walking swiftly away from the game. She pointed. 'Him.'

Anna looked in the direction Katie pointed but didn't lose her frown. 'What's he look like?'

'Blond hair. Pink face. Cricket whites.'

Anna looked back at the game. 'I think you've had too much sun.'

'No,' Katie said. 'Over there.'

She turned to point as the blond guy walked towards the pavilion.

'I don't see a blond.' Anna squinted. 'Do you mean Mark? His hair is kind of strawberry blond.'

Katie felt cold. Anna couldn't see the man.

She got to her feet. The blond guy was walking purposefully towards the pavilion. He looked solid. He looked real.

Katie looked down at Anna. 'Back in a minute.'

Katie walked towards the pavilion. The door was propped open to let air through and the man had just gone inside.

She followed him. To the right was the entrance to the locker rooms and to the left, a door marked private. Straight ahead, after a short corridor, was the bar area. It had seen better days. Cracked lino on the floor, a seventies wooden bar with three optics behind.

'Hello?' The place was deserted. He must've gone into the locker room or the public toilet. Katie waited, unsure what to do. Did she really want to follow a strange man into the changing rooms to accuse him of... What? Tripping up a player? Being a hallucination? No.

Her body didn't seem to be listening to her brain, though, and she shoved open the door. 'Hello?'

The changing room was empty. A row of lockers against one wall and a long bench on the other. The pegs above the bench were filled with clothes and there were shoes tucked underneath. No blond guy. There was a blue shower curtain pulled across the entrance to the communal shower area and it was spotted with mould along the top, probably the source of the smell of decay that was lying underneath the scents of sweaty feet and deodorant. Katie couldn't hear a shower running but she expected to hear it start any moment. She waited. After a couple more minutes, there was still no running water so she called again. 'Hello? Excuse me? Can I talk to you?'

Nothing. He obviously hadn't come in here, after all. Well, Katie wasn't going to look in the toilets and, suddenly, she wasn't at all sure why she was looking for him anyway. To verify that she wasn't seeing things, she supposed. To prove that she wasn't going nuts. Well, creeping around the men's changing rooms probably wasn't the best way to demonstrate that.

Still. Just to be thorough, Katie walked to the silent shower area and pulled the blue curtain to one side. She almost screamed. The blond boy was standing in the corner of the shower area, facing the wall. He was fully dressed, still in his cricket whites.

Katie opened her mouth to say 'hello' again but she couldn't manage it. Her throat was too dry. Then the boy turned. He moved smoothly, in a way that didn't seem quite human. Katie wanted to take a step back, but she was filled with a numb buzzing, pins and needles in her spine. His face was the same pink-cheeked one she'd seen outside but the eyes were wrong. All black as if the pupils had swallowed the rest. Those terrible eyes were facing her, but didn't give any sign that they could see her. Then he lifted one hand, a hand that now held a razor blade and sliced down his forearm.

'Don't,' Katie said, her voice echoing off the tile. Panicky and thin.

He took the blade with the sliced arm and, as Katie took an involuntary step forward, neatly did the other side. The blood flowed instantly and thickly, running off the tips of his fingers and onto his white trousers. Then he disappeared.

Katie blinked at the suddenly empty space where the boy had just been standing. She looked instinctively down, expecting to see blood all over the tiles. It had been so real.

Katie pushed her way out of the changing room, choking on the smell of bleach, which seemed to have developed an undertone of iron.

That's your imagination, she told herself. She'd seen blood so she expected to smell it. Stupid brain. A wave of sickness washed over her and she swallowed to keep it down, bolting for the ladies' toilet, just in case.

Katie ran cold water over her wrists and took several deep breaths, willing herself not to be sick. After a while, the nausea passed and she turned off the cold tap. She stared at her face in the mirror while her mind ran over the last ten minutes in a kind of holding pattern. *We're sorry, but Katie is not available to take your call at the moment. Because she is freaking the fuck out.*

Katie blinked, trying to focus. She'd seen a ghost. Another ghost. It was nothing like Violet, though. It was terrifying. And sad. Overwhelmingly sad. Her face in the mirror was streaked with tears so she splashed water over her face, too.

Katie dried her hands and headed outside. Anna was back in their spot, lying on the grass and watching the match.

'You okay?' she said.

'No. Definitely not.' Katie took a deep breath. She was too upset to think about lying or evading. She had to tell someone, had to say it out loud. 'I just saw a ghost.'

'Really?' Anna sat up. 'Here?'

Katie nodded. 'In the pavilion. The blond boy. I met one at The Grange. Violet. I've been talking to her, but this one was different. He couldn't hear me. Just killed himself.'

'Killed himself?'

'With a razor blade. I guess he must've committed suicide and now is reliving it or something.'

'You're serious, aren't you?' Anna said. She poured her a tumbler of water and passed it across. 'Drink this.'

'Thank you.' Katie took a sip and felt a little better.

'Are you sure they're ghosts?' Anna said. 'In *Doctor Who* they always turn out to be aliens or something. There was one where the ghosts were Cybermen.'

Katie couldn't believe how well Anna was taking the news. 'Violet's not a Cyberman. Trust me.'

'I do,' Anna said.

'Thank you,' Katie said. 'I know it's a lot to take in.'

Anna pulled a face. 'After my gran died, she used to visit me. She stood at the end of my bed.'

'Really? That sounds—'

'Horrifying,' Anna said. 'I know. But it really wasn't. There was just a lovely comforting feeling. I knew she was watching over me.'

Katie drank the rest of her water. There was

nothing comforting about the boy in the shower. She didn't want to see ghosts everywhere. Violet was one thing. At the hotel. Contained. This was different.

CHAPTER 13

*K*atie had never wished she drank hard alcohol more. She'd called and Gwen was on her way, but as she sat on the bench outside The Red Lion she wished she could down a whiskey or two. Anything to numb the panic a little, to calm the twisting thoughts. She kept seeing the boy from the cricket pavilion, the blood running down his arms.

'Honeybunch.' Gwen swooped down and hugged Katie. 'Tell me.'

Katie went through it again, adding more detail than she had on the phone. The way she'd smelled the blood, the blackness of the boy's eyes. She felt a little lighter as she did so and she wondered if Gwen was using a spell or whether it was just comforting to talk to her. Katie still didn't know if she was going to be angry, tell her to be more careful, so when Gwen patted her and said, 'It's going to be okay,' she almost cried with relief.

'I don't know how much research you've managed to do,' Gwen said, 'but I went to see a woman whose family has a history of this kind of thing.'

'A family like ours?' Katie said. 'How did you find her?'

'She found me,' Gwen said. 'Her name's Hannah Ash. She lives on a canal boat and passes through this way quite often.'

Katie didn't know what to say; she'd never considered the possibility that there were other magical families. 'Do you trust her?'

Gwen shrugged. 'I think so. I'm not about to rush out and start swapping secrets, but I did talk to her about you—' Gwen broke off and held up a hand. 'Don't worry, nothing too personal, but I did ask her about this ghost thing.'

'We need all the help we can get,' Katie said, touched that Gwen had spoken to someone about her. Gwen tended to deal with everything on her own and Katie knew speaking to an outsider wouldn't have been easy.

'That's what I thought,' Gwen said, not looking happy about it. 'For what it's worth, she said there were different types of ghosts. Some are hardly here, more like echoes of a life. Others are fully formed spirits or souls. They have will and personality and feelings, just like any human being.'

'Aren't they human, still?'

Gwen shrugged. 'I don't know. Hannah said they might look like us and sound like us and sometimes even act like us, but they're something else. Something other.'

Katie was finding it hard to concentrate on Gwen's voice. There was a woman on the town green. She had her back to the town and seemed to be staring out over the river. There was something odd about her. Katie focused on the woman's feet, but they were firmly planted on the grass. Her body looked solid and wasn't doing the weird shimmery, vibration thing that Violet was so fond of.

'What?' Gwen said and turned to follow Katie's gaze. 'What's wrong?'

'Ghost,' Katie said. She'd finally worked out why the woman seemed odd: she was wearing strange clothes. Old things that belonged in another time. A brown dress in a rough material and a woollen shawl. Her hair was long and matted and there were stains down her back. There was the smell of burning, too. Not like the struck match that she'd detected at the hotel, but a proper bonfire. Wood smoke and something else. Something meaty that turned Katie's stomach. She stood up. 'Can we walk?' Without waiting for Gwen, Katie headed towards the main road, away from the green.

Gwen was looking around. 'They're here?'

Katie blinked back sudden tears. 'I'm starting to think they're everywhere.'

'It's amplifying,' Gwen said. 'Makes sense.'

'Does it?' Katie was walking fast, but it didn't feel like enough. She wanted to run.

'When my power came in, I managed to control it quite well.'

Of course, Katie thought.

'But when I moved back to Pendleford, I couldn't any more. I couldn't stop it from happening, even though I really didn't want to use it.'

'Really?' Katie slowed down a little and looked at Gwen. 'You had trouble?'

'Oh, yes,' Gwen said with feeling. 'Lots. But it got better. I stopped resisting it and it just got easier to handle. It was like it stopped fighting me when I relaxed.'

'I'll try,' Katie said. She didn't know how she was going to relax around the scary spirits, but she'd do her best. 'Maybe I'll get used to it.'

'I wish you didn't have to,' Gwen said. 'I know I've been preoccupied, but I'm going to look into it more. There might be a spell that can help.'

'Thank you,' Katie said.

'Of course,' Gwen said, pulling Katie in for a hug. 'You don't have to do this alone.'

This ghost was unmistakable as anything else. He was clearly one of the echo-type ghosts Gwen had talked about, the ones that were barely here at all. He was faded and semi-transparent; if Katie concentrated she could make out the art nouveau pattern on the tiles in the fireplace he was standing in front of. Leaning, really. He was leaning against the mantel in a pose that suggested he ought to have a pipe in one hand. His hand was in his pocket. He was wearing a suit with loose-cut trousers, a waistcoat and a pale shirt with honest-to-God cufflinks. They shone as if lit by the glow from a fire, even though the hearth was empty. He wouldn't have looked out of place in a golden era black and white and Katie wished that she'd be able to speak to him.

'Is it too much to ask?'

His voice, deep and full-bodied, made Katie jump, her knees instantly turning to water.

'One minute of solitude.' The ghost raised his eyes to heaven with great drama.

'I'm sorry,' Katie found herself saying. 'I'll leave you

in peace.' She turned to get out of the room, but the man was turning around, his face a pure expression of surprise that probably echoed her own.

'You can hear me?'

Katie nodded. 'And you can talk. I didn't realise—'

'You can see me?' The man's face was moving as he spoke, but the transparency of his features was disconcerting; it was giving Katie a headache so she focused on his chest instead.

'Yes. You're a bit...thin...but I can see you perfectly well.'

He hesitated, then stepped back to the fireplace, pulled a pipe from his pocket. 'I don't suppose you have a light? I'm dying for a smoke.'

'No,' Katie said. 'I could go and get one, though.'

'Don't bother.' He looked sadly at the pipe and then slipped it back into his pocket. 'It won't work.'

'Why?'

He shrugged. 'Beats me. Maybe it's part of my punishment.' He gave her a crooked smile that made other parts of her body go a little bit liquid. 'I have tobacco but no light. I can see food but I can't eat it.'

That didn't sound nice. 'I thought ghosts didn't feel hunger.'

He gave another elegant shrug. 'Force of habit.'

'I'm Katie,' Katie said, deciding to take control of the conversation. 'Have you been here long?'

'In this house or this room?'

'The house.'

'A while. I'm Henry.' He tilted his head back and seemed to be appraising her; it was hard to tell with the little glimpses Katie was taking of his face. She took a longer look, then had to swallow down a sudden burst of sickness.

'What's wrong?'

'You're all, wavy. It's making me feel queasy.' Katie added, 'Sorry,' as she didn't want to seem rude. It wasn't his fault, after all.

'How's this?' Henry shimmered for a moment and then, somehow, did seem to be a little more solid, but perhaps she was just getting used to the sensation.

'So, how long have you been here?' Henry's voice really was nice. Deep but soft.

'Just a couple of hours.'

'You're taking it well,' he said. 'How'd you die?'

'What?'

'I apologise if I sound blunt. I haven't conversed with anyone for a long while.'

'I'm not dead,' Katie said.

Henry frowned. 'So, how are you able to see me?'

'I have no idea,' Katie said, ignoring the itch behind her ear.

'You're alive,' Henry said musingly. 'Now, that is peculiar. I was beginning to think this was purgatory.'

'Haven't you seen people before?'

'Seen, yes. But not spoken with. I had assumed they were echoes of life or perhaps hallucinations sent to torture me. So close to life but not part of it,' he said in a dramatic voice. Then, in a more ordinary tone, 'That kind of thing.'

'No. This is reality. The real world. Earth.'

He nodded. 'Okey-doke. That is interesting. And how long have you been able to see people like me? Lost souls.'

'Ghosts? About a week. I'm still getting used to it.'

'I'll bet.' Henry sounded sympathetic and Katie had to tamp down the sudden urge to tell him all of her fears.

'How long is it since you—?'

'Died? I'm not sure. I don't know what year this is, but I passed in 1948.'

'Over sixty years. Have you been here all that time?'

'I don't believe so. I was in a dark box for a long time.'

Katie shuddered. 'You were conscious inside your coffin?'

Henry held up a hand. 'Please don't use that word. I prefer "storage".'

'Fair enough,' Katie said. She could feel a headache coming on; her temples pulsed in time with Henry's shimmering form. She was going to have to leave and lie down in a dark room. Just for a week or so. She closed her eyes against the pain. 'Are you usually here? In this room?'

'Why?' Henry said. 'Would you like to call on me again?'

'If I may,' Katie said, keeping her voice as polite as possible. She opened her eyes a crack.

'I would like that very much,' Henry said. He began to fade, the flickering getting worse.

'Wait.' Katie had a sudden thought. 'Why do you think you're being punished?'

Henry smiled his disconcertingly attractive smile and said, 'Because, Katie, I'm a very bad man.' And then he disappeared.

CHAPTER 15

When Katie got home she realised that she had several missed calls from Gwen's number. She cursed the rubbish mobile reception at The Grange and called her back, excited to think that Gwen had found something useful about controlling her power already.

'It's Fred,' Gwen said, sounding shaky. 'He's worse. I don't know how much longer—'

'Five minutes,' Katie said. She didn't want to waste time changing out of her work clothes, but she swapped her skirt and black tights for a long cotton one and sandals and headed back out into the heat.

Gwen was waiting outside Fred's cottage, her enormous canvas bag slung over one shoulder. Katie hugged her, her heart hurting for Gwen. Fred was a fixture of Pendleford; it was unthinkable that he might not be there for ever.

'Are you coming in?' Gwen put a hand on Katie's arm. 'You don't have to.'

'No.' Katie squared her shoulders. 'I want to see him.' That wasn't strictly true. She'd prefer to remember Fred the way he was before he got sick. Ancient and grumpy, but always ready with a cup of disgustingly strong tea.

'He'll like that. He might not be able to show it—'

Katie didn't want to talk any more, could feel her anxiety growing. If they didn't walk into Fred's terraced cottage soon, she was going to lose her nerve completely.

Inside, the house smelled of disinfectant and the foot cream Gwen made for him. Fred had become so devoted to it, the smell was linked to him, like another man's aftershave or the smell that came from Max's skin. Katie blinked. She didn't want to think about Max.

The district nurse had made up a bed in the living room, as the bathroom was on the ground floor and Fred hadn't been able to manage stairs for some weeks. Last time Katie was here, Fred had served them mugs of tea and plates of custard creams and he'd sat in his favourite chair and they'd watched the snooker together. His chair was tucked into the corner, now, facing away from the rest of the room like a naughty child, and Fred was lying flat on his back. He was very still and very straight, his nose pointed to the ceiling. Katie swallowed.

Gwen crossed to the opposite side of the bed. She was limping very slightly and Katie knew that was the knock-on effect. She'd been siphoning off Fred's pain for weeks, now. One of the tricks she'd learned from Iris. Gwen said she was nowhere near as good at it as Iris had been, but she was clearly skilled enough.

Gwen had shown Katie Iris's journals. Iris had been really good at taking other people's pain, something that went hand in hand with her gift of giving people what they needed. The pain had to go somewhere; that was the problem. You didn't just wave your hands and make things disappear; they always went somewhere. Iris had talked of losing toenails and Katie's toes pulsed in sympathy just thinking of it. She wondered how badly Gwen's feet hurt. How much longer she was going to keep taking it for Fred. As usual, Katie felt completely inadequate next to her aunt. Her selflessness, her bravery. Her power. 'Did you want me to try and help?'

Gwen shook her head. 'That's not why I asked you to come. I just wanted you to see him.'

Katie kept her expression neutral with an act of will as she approached the bed. Not just for Fred, whose eyes were closed but might open at any moment, but for Gwen. She knew Gwen was watching her. Wondering how she would cope. No doubt worrying, as usual. She wanted to prove to Gwen that she was strong.

Gwen reached for Fred's hand, and Katie watched her visibly prepare herself for the wave of pain. After a moment, her shoulders went down a notch and she looked at Katie with tears in her eyes. 'He's close,' she said, quietly. 'Do you want to say goodbye?'

Katie stepped closer to the bed, took Fred's free hand. Fred's hand was cool and dry. His fingernails were yellow and ridged and Katie quickly stopped focusing on them. She tried to look at his face, but it already didn't look like Fred. His expression, in sleep, was slack, and his colour wasn't right. His skin looked like wax, like a bad copy of a human being. Katie didn't want to think it, but he already looked dead.

Gwen passed a hand over his forehead, leaned in and spoke close to his cheek, so quietly that Katie couldn't hear what she said. When she sat back, Katie leaned in, ready to say goodbye. As she did Fred's fingers tightened on her own. She leaned closer, thinking perhaps he might open his eyes, maybe even say goodbye himself. Katie felt her eyes prickling with tears and a lump formed in her throat. Fred was the closest thing she'd had to a grandfather and now he was slipping away in front of her. Katie felt a strange tingling in her hand, and an itch in her shoulder that travelled down her arm, making her muscles tense.

Colour was flooding into Fred's face. His cheeks went from pallid to pink and seemed to plump up. The itching in her arm was turning into discomfort, which was quickly turning into painful pins and needles. Katie tried to pull her hand away from Fred's, she wanted to move her arm, to rub life into it, but his grip was tight now. 'My arm,' Katie said, fear rushing through her. 'My hand.'

Gwen's voice sounded very far away and there was a roaring sound in her ears. The edges of Katie's sight went black. She felt Fred moving, sitting up, his hand still grasping hers, and then she felt nothing at all.

GWEN LOOKED from Katie's slumped form to Fred, who was struggling to sit up, for a single, paralysed second, her brain trying to work out what her eyes had seen, and then she darted around the bed. 'Lie down,' she said to Fred, not caring that her voice was harsh, only wanting to simplify things for a moment. Fred was holding Katie's hand, his knuckles white, and Gwen tried to peel his fingers away. 'Let go of her,' she said. 'Fred. Let go.' Fred looked down as if surprised to see himself gripping Katie and his hand sprang open.

Katie's eyes fluttered open. 'Gwen?'

'You're okay,' Gwen said, relief making her giddy. She put her arms around Katie and helped her to sit up. 'You're okay. You just fainted.'

'Crap,' Katie said, her eyes already clear, her colour back to normal. 'Not again.'

'What do you mean?' Gwen said, her heart squeezing. 'Again?'

'When I found Mr Cole. Didn't I tell you?' Katie shook her head, as if trying to clear it. 'I've been feeling faint a lot at work, too.'

'Are you pregnant?' Gwen spoke without thinking. She tried to ignore the stab of pain that the words gave her.

'Christ, no!' Katie looked outraged. It would've been funny if Gwen had any room in her mind for humour.

'Flu?' She put her hand on Katie's forehead. It was cool and dry.

'I'm fine.' Katie leaned back in the chair. 'Just a bit tired.'

'May I sit up, now?' Fred said in a meek voice.

'Sorry, Fred,' Gwen said, on automatic pilot. 'Hang on.' She peered into Katie's eyes, checking her pupils, and watched colour returning to her face. *What had happened?*

Katie closed her eyes, waved a hand. 'I'm fine, really.'

Gwen helped Fred to sit up. She'd wanted to protect Katie from pain and loss and, of course, she didn't want Fred to die, but this was beyond anything she could've imagined. Fred leaned forwards and Gwen arranged pillows behind him. The man who had been on the brink of death for the last week and who, Gwen would've sworn, had taken his last breath three minutes previously leaned back with a contented sigh. It wasn't right. He was supposed to be dead. Goddess help her for thinking it, but it was the truth. Gwen couldn't stop looking from Katie to Fred. Katie had done something, but what kind of magic could cure a person that sick? A person whose time had clearly come?

Fred smiled at her, his top dentures slipping a little. 'I could murder a boiled egg. Do you know how long it's been since I've felt hungry?'

As the woman who had been trying to coax him to eat for the last six months, Gwen had an idea, but she shook her head.

'But first, I must pay a visit.' Fred pushed the covers back and began to swing his legs over the side of the bed.

'Fred—' Gwen moved to stop him. 'You can't.'

'Nonsense, girl.' He pushed on the bed with his hands and rose unsteadily to his feet.

Gwen followed him as he walked to the bathroom, seeming to get stronger and more steady with every step. She went into Fred's kitchen and put a small pan of water onto the electric hob. There were eggs on the counter; she'd brought them earlier in the week. She remembered choosing the small box, thinking that he'd never finish a dozen. That he wouldn't live long enough.

Katie walked into the kitchen, her arms wrapped around her body as if she was trying to hold herself together.

'Are you sure you should be up?' Gwen didn't know how to act around Katie, wasn't even sure if the young woman standing in Fred's kitchen was truly her niece at all. She wasn't sure if she should be gentle or motherly or whether she should take her by the shoulders and scream, 'How did you do that?'

'I'm fine,' Katie said, sounding as uncertain as Gwen felt.

Gwen put the lid on the saucepan and turned to face Katie. 'What happened in there?'

Katie looked miserable. 'I was hoping you could tell me.'

Gwen shook her head. 'I'm sorry, honeybunch. I'm useless.' She felt tears in her eyes and blinked them back.

'You're not useless,' Katie said, 'but that was strange. Wasn't that strange?'

'Strange is definitely the word,' Gwen said carefully.

'Unless he wasn't as sick as we thought,' Katie said. 'Or, maybe he's just having a little rally. Maybe he'll go back to bed in a minute.' She stopped speaking as the sounds of Fred whistling in the bathroom reached them. 'Or maybe we should visit Hannah Ash. See if she knows anything about this kind of thing.'

'I don't know.' Gwen was sick of feeling uncertain but maybe going public would be a bad idea. Who else might want to use Katie's power, use Katie? 'You brought him back to life,' she said, needing to hear the words out loud. 'You made him better. I saw it.'

'I don't think—' Katie began, then stopped. 'Is that even possible?'

'I've never heard of it. Unless you're talking about blood magic. The bad stuff.'

'The stuff you used. To save me.'

Gwen nodded. 'Exactly. But you didn't do anything like that.'

'No,' Katie said. 'I swear—'

'I know you didn't. You just touched him and he got

better. Magic that powerful is... It's huge. I can't even—'

'What's huge?' Fred Byres appeared in the doorway. Still old, a little hunched, and very skinny, but unquestionably alive. His eyes went from Gwen to Katie and back again. 'I hope you're talking about my egg because I'm starving.'

CHAPTER 16

Gwen kept calling, wanting to talk about what had happened with Fred, but Katie didn't have room in her mind to process it. She'd touched Fred and felt something shift and then she'd passed out. When she'd woken up, he was better. Alive. Healthier than he'd been for month, maybe years. Katie had filed it under 'good news' and was concentrating on Violet Beaufort. If she could solve the mystery of Violet's disappearance, help her to move on or whatever it was she needed, then she'd know her power was positive. And it would give her a way of dealing with the voices and spirits that seemed to be surrounding her every waking moment. Her only other thought was that she wanted to see Max. Which wasn't good. He probably wasn't even in Pendleford, any more, much less in a mood to help her. Still, he seemed like a man with certain skills and Katie didn't feel she had many other options.

When she saw him in the staff room, downing a can of Coke, she felt as if the air in the room had been sucked out. She went to hold her necklace, remembered that Max would notice, and forced her hands back to her sides.

'I thought you'd be long gone,' Katie said. She lowered her voice, even though there was nobody else in the room. 'Your watch—'

Max offered his can. 'Thought I'd stick around a while longer.'

'Oh,' Katie said. 'That's—'

'I told you. I have a high tolerance for weirdness.'

'Pendleford's not that weird.'

He grinned. 'Uh-huh. Besides. You owe me dinner.'

'I don't think I ever agreed to that,' Katie said, pleased. 'Besides, you invited me out, which means if anybody owes anybody anything it would be you owing me. Dinner.'

Max finished his can and Katie took the opportunity to mentally slap herself in the head. She had to stop babbling. 'I actually need a favour. Can you help me find someone?'

'Ghost?' Max stood up and began tucking in his black shirt.

'No. Alive people. At least, I hope so.'

'No problem,' Max said.

'The Beaufort family moved out of this place in 1987 and I want to know why.'

'People move, you know — it doesn't mean it's significant.'

'This house belonged to the Beauforts since it was built in 1698. Imagine, your family lives in a place for almost four hundred years, and then you all just leave. Just like that. Why?'

'Money troubles most likely.'

'But they didn't sell it straight away. It was left empty.'

Max looked up. 'That is odd. Give me a moment.'

He took his phone out of his pocket and stabbed buttons for a moment before putting it on the table.

'Aren't you going to Google?'

'I know someone,' he said, and gestured to his phone. After a moment it rang. 'Yeah,' Max said. 'I need a favour.'

He was looking out across the room while he spoke and Katie watched the slope of his shoulders, the lines of muscle that ran down his arms. He seemed to change when he spoke to the mystery man on the phone, become tense and different. Not her Max. Of course, Katie realised, she didn't know him at all. This man. This man she had been hot and heavy with. She felt a shiver of fear. What was she doing?

He finished the call and turned to her. 'Juliet's going to find us a Beaufort.' He stretched, putting his head to one side and then the other. 'Do you want to get out of here for a bit?'

'Who's Juliet?'

'Private detective. She finds people on a professional basis.'

'I can't afford—'

'Favour,' Max said. 'I'm calling it in.'

'Oh.' Katie hesitated. 'Thank you.'

～

KATIE HAD FINISHED her shift and was thinking about having a Fab when Max came into the staff room.

'Juliet came through.' Max waved a slip of paper. 'I've got a live Beaufort. Name, address, phone number, email, Facebook, the lot.'

Katie took the paper. Michelle Beaufort. 'Michelle. That's not a very aristocratic name.'

'She married into the family. Kept the name Beaufort after she divorced out of it again.'

'Right.' Katie looked at Max's handwriting and contemplated ways to start the conversation with Michelle Beaufort. 'Hi, you don't know me, but I'm being haunted by your ex-husband's ancestor. Any chance of a chat?'

'Do you want me to phone her?' Max said. 'Or are you going to email first?'

Email was tempting. Easier. And Michelle wouldn't be able to slam the phone down.

'That's okay,' Katie said. 'May as well get it over with.'

The phone rang a few times and Katie was beginning to think Michelle wasn't home when there was a click and silence. It was the dead air quiet you got when the phone was connected, though, so Katie waited. There was a muffled thump and then some heavy breathing.

'Hello?' Katie said.

Another thump. Then a child's voice, far away, calling, 'Mummy.'

Katie waited again, watching Max reading through the notes she'd made while she did so. His hair was curling in the humidity and she couldn't take her eyes off one lock that curled under his ear. The skin on his jaw line was bumpy from shaving and the nails on the hand that held the sheaf of paper were bitten, the skin around the cuticles ragged.

'Yes?'

'Michelle Beaufort?' Katie said. 'My name is Katie Harper and I work at The Grange hotel—'

'I'm not buying anything,' Michelle said.

'I'm not selling anything,' Katie said quickly. 'I'm working at The Grange.'

'Where?'

'It's a hotel in Pendleford. But it's the old Beaufort manor house.'

'Oh, Christ. That place.'

'I've become fascinated by the history. I was hoping you could talk to me about it.'

Max had stopped reading and was listening. He pulled a face at her and she turned her back. 'Ms Beaufort?'

'I'm going to be in Malmesbury tomorrow for Toddlers. I could meet you after that. Eleven-thirty. Do you know the Little Teacup?'

'I can find it,' Katie said. 'Thank you very much.'

MAX INSISTED on coming with her, but she point-blank refused to let him drive her. It was a forty-five-minute drive and Katie took as many minor roads as possible. She miscalculated one and had to inch along a narrow lane, the hedgerows overgrown and brushing the sides of the car. The hedgerows were thick with cow parsley and the hawthorn trees were covered in creamy white flowers. It was as if the green hedges were covered in snowfall.

Max was browsing through her iPod. 'Why don't you have any music?'

'I have music,' Katie said.

'You have twenty audio books, lots of comedy — which I applaud—'

'Thank you,' Katie said with as much sarcasm as

she could muster. Max didn't seem to notice.

'But hardly any music.'

'I've got plenty.'

'Best-of compilations don't count. Where are your albums?'

'Albums? How old are you?'

'Twenty-five. How old are you? Seventy-five?'

'Rude,' Katie said, suppressing a smile. Bickering with Max was more fun than she'd ever had in bed.

Malmesbury was another pretty Wiltshire town. Nice architecture, honey-coloured stone, traffic-choked streets. Katie found parking behind the ancient abbey, and she and Max walked up through the town until they found the Little Teacup. It had bunting in the window and the tea was served in mismatched vintage china. There was also a generously sized children's corner with beanbags, a play kitchen, garage, and low bookcase.

Max sat at a corner table, his back to the wall, and leaned his head against the lilac-painted wall. He looked completely out of place. Like the devil at a teddy bear's picnic.

A waitress came over and took their order. As she turned away the door opened and a petite blonde woman came in. She was holding the hand of a little girl, who tugged free as soon as she saw the toys. The woman was looking around so Katie stood up and did a half-wave.

The woman came over to their table. 'I'm Michelle Beaufort.'

'Katie,' Katie said, 'and this is Max.'

Michelle gave Max an appreciative look and sat down. She was wearing an elegant slash-neck top that had to be silk and skinny jeans. She had lightly tanned skin and perfectly highlighted and styled hair. As far as Katie could tell, she could've been aged anything from thirty to fifty. But then, she'd been married back in eighty-seven. Katie's insides clenched. What if Max's information was wrong? What if this was the wrong woman?

Michelle was gazing at Max. 'Where's your camera?' she said. 'No photos of Rosie, mind. She's not part of the deal.'

Katie thought: What deal? But Max just nodded as if he'd expected as much.

Michelle turned to Katie. 'What do you want to know?'

'You lived in the Beaufort house?'

'For a short while. I married Thomas when I was nineteen—'

The waitress brought drinks for Max and Katie, and Michelle paused to order hot water with a slice of lemon and a gluten-free muffin.

'It must've been amazing,' Katie said. 'The house is—'

'That's one word for it,' Michelle said. 'I used to get lost getting from one end of that pile to the other. I hope they've modernised it.'

'Yes, they've—' Katie began.

'That's a lie,' Michelle interrupted. 'I wish they'd bulldozed the whole place.' She gave Katie an apologetic smile. 'Not the happiest time of my life.'

'Ah. I'm sorry—'

'Not your fault. I shouldn't have married Thomas and I shouldn't have stayed in that mausoleum after the first night.'

'What happened on the first night?'

'I'd been in the house lots beforehand, of course,

but I'd never stayed the night. Old-fashioned values and all that. First night was after we'd come back from honeymoon. We were in the east wing, for privacy, you know, and old man Beaufort was being less of a drunken—' Michelle glanced at Rosie, who was cooking with a plastic saucepan; she lowered her voice. 'Thomas's father was not a nice man. Neither was Thomas as it turned out, but I didn't realise at the time.'

'At least you married rich,' Max said cheerfully and Katie kicked him under the table.

Michelle smiled thinly. 'That's what everyone says but I had to sign a pre-nuptial agreement. I didn't come away loaded, whatever anyone says. In fact, it would be helpful if you could put that in the piece. I mean, half my family are after money I don't even have.'

'You weren't left penniless, surely.'

'Not entirely,' Michelle said. 'But that's why I kept the name. I was damn well going to have something of value. Not that it's done me much good.'

'So, the first night,' Katie prompted.

'Right.' Michelle looked suddenly nervous. 'I don't want to make me sound like a loony. I was really young and the house was creepy and old and I think I just got spooked.'

'Fair enough,' Katie said, containing her impatience as best she could. 'What did you see?'

'I didn't see anything. I heard voices, though, and music playing.'

'Could it have been other people in the house?' Max said.

'Thomas's father was passed out in his study in the other wing of the house. Everybody else was away. The staff had gone home.'

'They didn't live in?'

'He couldn't keep live in staff. Nobody stayed very long so he gave up trying and just hired day staff.'

Katie shot a look at Max.

Rosie toddled over, clutching a plastic bowl with a wooden tomato and a yellow plastic blob that could have been scrambled eggs. She plonked it in front of Michelle and said, triumphantly, 'Eat!'

'Ooh, thank you,' Michelle said in the exaggerated sing-song voice people used with small children. 'Yummy, tomato and eggs.'

Rosie's face clouded over. 'No. It's soup.'

'Silly me,' Michelle said, taking the plastic spoon and pretending to eat some. 'Mmm. Lovely soup.'

'Silly, Mummy,' Rosie said and marched off to her corner.

Michelle watched her go with a soppy expression. 'She's my little angel. My miracle.' Michelle leaned in and lowered her voice. 'I was forty-three when I had her. Can you believe it? I'd almost given up hope.'

'Wow,' Katie said. She couldn't imagine wanting a mini dictator in her life any more than she could imagine being forty-three.

'IVF. Four rounds. It was hell.'

Katie nodded politely and then took a sip of her tea so that she wouldn't have to say anything.

Max was looking intently at the menu.

'But so, so worth it. You don't really know love until you become a mother.'

'So you heard voices.'

'And music. It was creepy but I kind of got used to it. I avoided the back stairs — they were always cold — and I used earplugs at night.'

'You were brave,' Katie said.

Michelle gave her a tight smile. 'I was distracted. Being married to Thomas was scarier than anything else. I didn't really have time to worry about it. I told myself it was an old house, settling sounds. Radiators. I really wasn't scared. Not after the first night. That's why it was such a surprise.'

'What was?' Max was looking at Michelle.

'Thomas going that way. I mean, he'd been acting strangely for ages, but I put it down to eccentricity. He also was a bit odd.'

'Why did you marry him?' Katie couldn't stop herself from asking.

Michelle gave her a pitying look. 'When Thomas Beaufort asks you to marry him you say yes.' She hesitated. 'Don't write that down. Write that I was young and in love.'

'What?' Katie said just as Max said, 'No problem.'

Katie could see Rosie approaching, her tongue stuck out in concentration as she carried two plastic bowls, piled high with plastic fruit. 'Why did the family move out of the house?'

Michelle closed her eyes. 'Thomas was convinced it was haunted.'

'Was it?'

Michelle opened her eyes. 'Of course not. Ghosts don't exist.'

'But Thomas believed in them?'

'He was very spiritual anyway, believed in all kinds of crackpot theories. His great-grandfather or someone had been interested in all that stuff, too. He had a really freaky collection of books and weird objects. Like, there was this horrible shrunken head from Peru and Neolithic axe heads. I told him that stuff should've been in a museum, but between you and me I think it should've been sent to landfill. I didn't like it being in the house but by then I'd realised that my opinion meant exactly nothing.'

Rosie placed a bowl of fruit in front of Max. 'Banana surprise!'

'Thank you, madam,' Max said, his voice completely serious, and Rosie giggled delightedly.

She put the other bowl down a little shakily and a plastic orange skittered across the table. 'Is that for me, darling?' Michelle said, reaching for it.

'No!' Rosie pushed the bowl to Katie. 'Eat.'

'So Thomas was predisposed to believing odd things, but what made him desert the estate? I mean, it had to be something big——'

'Pinocchio died.'

'Dog?' Max said, before Katie could ask.

Michelle nodded. 'Thomas thought it was an evil spirit. Said he wasn't waiting around for the same thing to happen to him.'

'Did he say who the spirit was?'

Michelle looked thoughtful. 'He thought it was his great-grandfather at first, but later he decided it was an archaeologist. A friend of the family back in the thirties. Kept going on about digging up the corpse and burning it, if you can believe that. I used it in the divorce. Unreasonable behaviour.'

Katie tried to look sympathetic, even while her mind was jumping with excitement. Violet had died in 1937. It couldn't be a coincidence. 'Did he actually do it? Burn the body?'

'Ew. Don't be disgusting.'

'Are you sure?'

Michelle gave her a look that was borderline frightened. She glanced over to where Rosie was playing, then began to get up.

'Please,' Katie said. 'I know it's a weird question—'

'His great-grandfather had been cremated,' Michelle said. 'It was in his will. He was very specific about it. Why do you want to know? What kind of article are you writing, anyway?'

'I'm not—' Katie began, but Max cut across her.

'Thank you so much for your time. We really appreciate it.' He held out his hand and Michelle shook it quickly. She picked up her handbag and, with one last alarmed look, grabbed her daughter's hand and left.

'Well, that was interesting,' Max said after the café door closed behind Michelle. 'I'm starting to think you're onto something with this ghost business.'

'Thank you,' Katie said, surprised. 'Have you decided I'm not a weirdo, after all?'

'I wouldn't say that,' Max said. Outside he took Katie's hand and held it as they walked back to the car. 'But I've got a high tolerance for weirdos.'

'Is that supposed to be nice?'

'I'm being romantic,' Max said. 'Shush. Let me tell you about my dad. He thinks the number four is evil. Like, properly, evil. He thinks it's out to get him.'

Katie laughed. 'You can't out-weird me with family stories. Trust me, I'll win.'

'Is that a challenge?' Max said, and all the way back to Pendleford they swapped stories. He matched every Harper-family fact with one of his own. Like the fact that his father's best friend had an imaginary dog, who he insisted on giving a bowl of water to at poker games. Katie dropped Max back at The Grange and watched him walk away.

CHAPTER 17

*K*atie looked around the hotel for Henry. She checked the living room where she'd first seen him and all of the unoccupied bedrooms. He wasn't in the kitchen, although Jo was experimenting with a new sweet fruit tart for the next day's menu and Katie snagged a freebie for her elevenses.

Katie had given up her search and decided to find a sunny spot on the lawn and rest until her shift started when she saw a figure by the ornamental pond. As she got nearer she saw it was Henry. He was standing motionless and staring out over the water.

'Hello,' Katie said. 'Am I disturbing you?'

Henry turned and although Katie had prepared herself for his image to do that shimmery-shuddery thing, it didn't seem as bad. Maybe it was the sunlight, but Henry definitely seemed more solid than last time she'd seen him. 'Not at all,' Henry said. 'I'm delighted to meet you again.'

Katie tamped down on the lift that gave her. The man was just being polite. Plus, he was dead.

'I didn't realise you could come out here.' Katie indicated the gardens.

'I've tested my boundaries and I can get halfway down the driveway to the front and just beyond the ha-ha at the back.'

'Why do they call them ha-has?' Katie said. 'It's always seemed rude. As if the landscaper is laughing at you for being fooled.'

Henry frowned at her. After a moment, he said, 'You have a singular mind.'

'Thank you.'

Henry looked briefly annoyed. Then he smiled thinly. 'I've been thinking about you since we last spoke and I have questions. May I ask them?'

'Fire away.' Katie sat down on the stone bench overlooking the pond.

'Have you met many like me?'

'A few. Lots can't talk, though. They're very thin. They just seem to repeat something. It's like they're not really here but I'm looking through a special glass and seeing into somewhere else.'

Henry nodded. 'And the ones who can talk. What are they like?'

Katie thought about Violet. 'Variable.'

Henry turned away from the pond and moved a little closer to Katie. She felt a wave of cold air, as if an enormous cloud had gone across the blazing sun.

'Have you met any others? Ghosts?'

'No.' Henry looked irritated. 'I told you, I can't leave this place.'

'But, there are others here. Lots, probably. I mean, this place is old.'

Henry was very still. 'There are other lost souls here?'

'You've never seen another ghost?' Katie realised how little she knew about her new reality. 'Aren't you guys all connected on, like, a spiritual plane or something?'

'I can't speak for anyone else, but I'm not.' Henry looked miserable. 'I told you, I haven't conversed with anyone for a very long time.'

'Perhaps you're all on different planes.'

'In soap bubbles, floating around you.' Henry smiled. 'You're at our centre, aren't you?'

'I don't think I'm important. I'm just the lucky girl who can see ghosts.'

'There must be a reason. I can feel the power coming from you.' Henry took a deep breath. 'Can't you see how I get stronger when you're near?'

It was true: he did seem more solid again. 'You think I'm doing that?'

'I think you've no idea what you can do.'

'My aunt, Gwen, she finds lost things and she's really good at making remedies, giving advice, that kind of thing. The women in my family often have special skills. I think there was even someone who could talk to the dead, kind of, but nothing like this, nothing like...'

'Nothing like you.' Henry smiled. 'Why does that not surprise me?'

'I just wish I knew why. I mean, the gifts in our family are usually useful in some way. I tried to speak to a ghost, to help him, and I couldn't. He looks miserable and I can't help. What's the point of that?'

'I wonder why you can talk to some spirits and not others.' Henry tilted his head back as if to appraise Katie more fully. 'Perhaps you're not really trying.'

'I did try,' Katie said. 'He just didn't hear me.'

'Perhaps you need a physical connection. This ghost you say you tried to help, did you touch him?'

Katie shook her head. 'Something told me not to.'

'Your selfishness, perhaps.'

'Hey.'

Henry lowered his eyes. 'You felt frightened, yes? The little voice that lives in the back of our minds and tells us when to run, when to hide, it spoke to you, yes? And you listened because that was easier than helping this poor unfortunate.'

'That's not true,' Katie said and wished she couldn't feel the tugging in her left ear lobe. She had been frightened. She was frightened, now. She didn't want to touch the ghost, didn't want to be anywhere near him when he produced that horrible sharp blade and began cutting.

CHAPTER 18

Katie needed to get away. She needed a break from the hotel, from Violet and from Max. He wasn't entirely wrong when he said she didn't want to get too close. She didn't like feeling attracted to him. It made her feel weak and vulnerable. As if she could do something stupid at any moment. It was all very well for Anna to say she should 'live a little', but she didn't know how seriously wrong that could go. Trust the wrong person and you could wind up dead. That was Katie's reality and all the fridge-magnet homilies in the world couldn't change it.

The streets were busy and Katie dodged window shoppers and dawdling couples. The bridge was choked with tourists. Some were leaning over the parapet and gawping at the water as if they'd never seen a river before. Katie blamed the weather. The sun was low in the sky, casting a yellow-toned glow onto the scenery, and the air was warm and still. It made the place feel Mediterranean and holiday-ish.

As she stepped around a couple of girls who had stopped in the middle of the pavement to snap pictures with their mobiles Katie felt a rush of cold air. Before she had time to process the familiar feeling, a man who was too translucent to be alive reared up in front of her. 'Have you seen it?' His voice was a quiet rasp and Katie took an instinctive step backwards.

Katie opened her mouth to reply and, remembering that she was surrounded by people, closed it again. She shook her head as discreetly as possible, lowered her eyes and moved on.

Katie's flat was on the middle floor of a town house. One of the Victorian ones on Elm Road, and something the people of Pendleford had an irritating habit of referring to as the 'new houses'. Just because Pendleford had houses and streets from medieval times and had originally been a Roman settlement, didn't mean they had to shout about it. And it certainly didn't mean they should get away with referring to Victorian as 'new'.

The streets were quieter once she was off the main road, but the whispering voices she'd started to hear seemed to get louder in response. It was like having a receiver in her mind, constantly flicking between radio stations with varying receptions. Maddening.

When Shari had lived in the flat, Katie had developed a habit of walking into the living room with her eyes aimed on the carpet. That way, if Shari and her boyfriend were engaged in naked sofa gymnastics, they had time to disentangle or, at least, pull a throw over themselves.

At first, Katie had loved being able to walk anywhere in the flat, her gaze held high and without fear of seeing a stray boob or random penis, but today it didn't seem like such a terrible price to pay for company. She unlocked the front door and walked into the quiet hallway, ignoring the wisp of a ghost that she could sense around knee height. She didn't look down. The child ghosts were the worst. They looked so forlorn, so empty. Yesterday, she'd seen a boy of about eighteen months crawling along the aisle of the local supermarket. He'd been dressed in layers of woollen clothes, which made him look like a bulky sort of cater-pillar, and he'd been crying so hard that there were trails of snot and tears hanging from his face to the floor. She'd had to leave her basket of shopping on the floor and still couldn't think about his unhappy face without crying, herself.

In the bathroom, she clicked on the light, illumi-nating the cracked white tiles above the sink and the black mould that was advancing across the ceiling. The room was freezing, as always, and the creaky extractor fan wheezed into life. Katie contemplated the black mould that had colonised the sealant about the sink and had turned the tile grouting a speckled grey. It was comforting to think about normal things like bleaching the walls and how she needed to phone her landlord about the dodgy noises coming from the boiler.

Katie squeezed toothpaste onto her brush and ran the cold tap, turning it all the way on just to get a measly trickle of water. That was the only thing with the characterful old properties in Pendleford: they were high maintenance and she wasn't exactly the house-keeping type.

The overhead light flickered and the extractor fan stopped working. She began brushing her teeth, closing her eyes against the light in case it started a migraine.

When she opened them, leaning forward to spit, she caught sight of a figure. An old man with a heavily lined face and big pouched bags under his eyes. She yelled, a fountain of toothpaste foam and saliva pouring down her chin. The light flashed off and then on again in a split second and there was nobody there.

Katie looked around the bathroom, shaking so badly her teeth were cracking together. The room was colder still, the hairs on her arms standing upright. This was another problem with the old houses in Pendleford. Lots of ghosts.

KATIE WALKED to Pendleford green on her own. Gwen had told her to trust her instincts and she had to do something about controlling her power. She couldn't shake the feeling that she was supposed to help the spirits and she was determined to work out how to do that on her own. Besides, she didn't want to bother Gwen with this ghost business unless she had to. Katie couldn't shake the feeling that something was very wrong with Gwen. She was draped in a sadness and Katie didn't know where it had come from or why it had descended now. Maybe Gwen was working too hard? Maybe the attention for her shadow boxes was more stressful than everyone realised.

Katie had a plan, though. She was taking control and going to work things out on her own. She had brought a blanket to sit on and a book to read, but she couldn't concentrate. She kept watching the players, waiting for the boy to show up. She was half in hope and half in dread and her eyes danced over the page, turning the text to gibberish. After a while, she gave up on her book and just watched the match. There was something hypnotic about the thwack of the ball on the willow bat and she found herself being drawn into the game. So much so that when the boy appeared it took her a second to recognise him. Katie had wondered if her new knowledge would make him appear differently, but he was just as solid-looking as before.

She'd seated herself conveniently close to the pavilion and was able to slip inside ahead of him. She went into the changing room, crossing fingers that it was unoccupied. It was.

Katie didn't have long to wait; the boy appeared in the middle of the room, between the benches. He was looking straight ahead, unseeing, and his walk had that odd flowing quality she'd got used to seeing.

'Hello,' she said as loudly as she could. The boy didn't show any sign of having heard and Katie proceeded with the next part of her plan. She followed the boy into the shower but before he could reach the corner, turn around and do away with himself, she darted into the corner ahead of him and plunged her hands straight into his chest. She willed herself to believe that her hands would sink inside him and, just as Henry had claimed, they sank into the boy as if he were vapour. Which he was. Unbelievably solid-looking vapour. Katie could feel more than vapour. Nothing solid and certainly not what she would be feeling had she put her hands inside an actual corpse, but something with substance. A squishy sensation, pressure around her hands and fingers. Something. Katie tamped down on the urge to throw up and said, 'I'm here to help you.'

The boy's eyes grew wide in surprise. He opened and closed his mouth like a guppy.

'I can help,' Katie said. 'You need to let go. There's nothing here for you now. If you let go of this place, you can move on.'

The boy looked anguished but Katie had no idea if he was overcome with emotion at being spoken to for the first time in thirty years or whether having her hands inside his ghostly body was as unpleasant for him as it was for her.

'You need to move on,' she said. Then, feeling rather self-conscious, she said, 'I release you from this mortal plane.'

The boy seemed to be getting more solid than before. The sensation around Katie's hands was getting more pronounced; she could imagine tissue and muscle and blood pressing around and between her fingers. The boy's expression was getting more frightened, his face splitting into a scream.

Katie pulled her hands away and the boy disappeared.

Katie washed her hands and then ran cold water over her wrists until she felt less sick. She walked into the sunshine and tried to feel triumphant. Katie tried to convince herself that something good had happened, that she'd released him from torment, but her gut told her otherwise. She ran back inside and just made it to the sink before throwing up.

CHAPTER 19

On her way home, Anna called, sounding excited. 'I'm going to look at a flat. Can you meet me?'

Katie stopped walking and sat on a bench to wait for Anna. She was delighted to have a distraction, a reason not to think about the boy in the cricket pavilion or Violet or her nightmares or any of it. At least for a little while.

'I'm sick of travelling from Bath every day,' Anna said, when she arrived. 'I want to walk into work. There's a new development down from the old mill.'

'By the river? I bet that's expensive.'

'Too much on my own, but it's two bedrooms.' Anna shrugged. 'I was hoping you'd come and look at it with me. You know, if you want.'

'I want,' Katie said. She took the particulars from Anna and checked the rent. It was practically the same as her current place. 'Why is it so cheap?'

Anna looked at her. 'You think that's cheap?'

'Well, nothing around here is cheap, but you know—'

Anna shook her head. 'I forget you're rich.'

'I'm not rich,' Katie said.

'Your family is, though. It makes a difference. You know you've got a safety cushion, whatever happens.' Anna spoke without rancour, but it still stung.

'I pay my own way.'

'I'm not having a go,' Anna said. 'I'm jealous.'

'But I don't take money from my dad.'

'I'm not saying that you do. Just that if it all goes tits up, you know he'll bail you out. It's security.'

'That's not—'

'When your car needed a new clutch last month, who paid for it?'

'That's different. I need a car and there's a service-agreement thingy with the garage—'

'Which your dad bought. When he bought the car.'

Katie forced a smile. 'You might have a point.'

'Now, take me.' Anna pointed to her chest. 'I can't afford a car not because I can't buy one, but because I know I don't have the income to fix it when it goes wrong or needs a service or whatever. I want to start a business but I don't have the capital and no bank will lend me the money so I'm stuck working for Patrick Allen. For now, at least.'

There was an awkward pause. Then Katie said, 'We could always rob a bank.' She offered Anna the bottle of water.

'It's good to keep our options open,' Anna said. 'It's a shame you can't magic up some cash. That would be handy.'

Katie did not want to talk about magic. 'When shall we visit the flat?'

Anna's smile could've been seen from space. 'Now?'

The flat was in a new development by the river,

imaginatively called the Riverside Development on a hoarding that Katie had been walking past and not really seeing for the past year or so.

'I thought this would be luxury. You know, the million-pound stuff.'

'Patrick told me that the contract was dependent on them building affordable housing. Something to do with government quotas.'

'Oh, God, Patrick doesn't own these, too, does he?'

'Not sure. He might've just been involved because of the mayor thing.'

'I keep forgetting about that. It's so archaic.'

'It's nice, though,' Anna said, looking up at the building.

Some of the windows had tiny balconies and it had that clean, Lego-look of a brand-new modern build. They'd added decorative touches, moulded to look reminiscent of the Victorian mill that stood further up the river, but not gone overboard.

'Besides,' Anna said, pressing the entry phone, 'I think the million-pound set require original fireplaces for their cash. They wouldn't touch a box like this.'

Inside, the letting agent showed them around. The second bedroom was, predictably, smaller than the master, but it wasn't too bad. Not bad enough to cause seething resentment, which, in Katie's experience of shared accommodation, was very important. The kitchen was actually a little bigger than the one in her current flat, with more cupboard space and a tiny breakfast nook for dining. Everything was painted tasteful cream, the floors were newly laid laminate and rubber tile, and the switch plates and plug sockets were shiny chrome. It smelled of paint and MDF and was utterly quiet.

Katie stood in the middle of the living room while Anna was checking out the water pressure in the bathroom and listened. Nothing. No voices, no echoes, no weird feelings, no coldness. She looked around, studying the blank white walls and the air around her. No ghosts, no after images, no floating lights. Just some dust motes in a shaft of sunlight falling on a pristine, wood-grain-effect floor.

Katie heard the agent and Anna talking and then they came in from the hall. 'It's a really good use of space,' the agent was saying.

'Do you know what this was built on?' Katie said.

'Sorry?'

'This building. Was there something here before? Or was it just open space?'

'Um…' The agent hesitated. She looked at her clipboard as if it might contain the answer. 'I don't think there was anything here. It was just, like, ground.'

'What do you think of it?' Anna asked. Her eyes were shining and her expression was hopeful.

'It's perfect,' Katie said. 'I think we should take it.'

'Yay!' Anna grabbed her in a hug.

Katie hugged her back, thinking of how perfectly peaceful the flat was. No history. No ghosts.

CHAPTER 20

The feeling of triumph didn't last for long. Anna had suggested a celebratory drink in The Red Lion and Katie had called Max. She had just finished telling them about her success at the cricket pavilion when she felt the atmosphere change.

'So, where did he go?' Anna said, her eyes wide.

'I don't know,' Katie said, trying to maintain a breezy tone. 'Heaven, if you believe that stuff. Or nowhere, I suppose, if you don't.'

Max shook his head. 'I can't believe you went to a ghost for advice. And then killed another one. And you called me immoral.'

'I didn't kill anybody. He was already dead.' Katie put her hand to her necklace and touched the revolver.

'Semantics. And you're being too trusting of this Henry guy,' Max said. 'I don't like it.'

'He told me he was bad. I'm sure he'd have lied if he was really bad, if you see what I mean.'

'Or maybe he could sense that you'd know if he was lying, or maybe he was feeding you the "bad guy trying to go straight" line. Girls love that.'

'You'd know, of course,' Katie said.

'I told you, I was brought up to con. It might not be nice, but it can be useful. Like now. It's useful and it's telling me that this ghost is not to be trusted—' He broke off. 'I can't believe I just said that.'

'I don't trust him, but I know he wants something and he thinks I can deliver it. He wants something, I want something. I don't have to trust him completely — I'm not marrying him or anything.'

'But he can't hurt you, can he?' Anna said, her eyebrows pulled down in concern. 'He's a ghost.'

'What about when Violet took control of Barton? You're telling me you're willing to let Henry do that to you?'

'I don't think I have a choice. I can't live like this. Have you got any idea how many dead people there are? I mean, seriously, there are ghosts everywhere. They're noisy. They're scary. They're angry. They're really, really sad. I've got to be able to control this or I'm not going to cope. I'm going to go mental.'

'I know.' Anna put her hand on Katie's arm. 'It's okay. It's going to be okay.'

'But it isn't,' Katie said. 'I'm sorry to be dramatic and everything, but I really, really, can't do this any more. I can't have all these voices and feelings. I need to have some control over it.'

Anna shot a worried look at Max and Katie took a deep breath to try and calm herself. She didn't want to frighten Anna. She didn't want to burden her but at the same time she wanted to lay her head on Anna's shoulder and cry.

'There must be another way,' Max said. 'There must be other people who can do what you can do. If we can find them, they'll be able to tell you how to control it.'

'What about your aunt?' Anna said. 'She's cool.'

'No.' Katie shook her head. 'I don't think she can help.'

'Back to you, then,' Max said. 'What about Violet? What if she's like your spirit guide? The kind of thing Barton claims to have. What if you're supposed to work with her, relay messages or whatever?'

'I'm nothing like Barton,' Katie said, insulted.

'I know that,' Max said gently.

It would be nice if it were that neat. 'I don't think so. Apart from anything else, Violet isn't in contact with any other spirits. They all seem to be separate, unaware of each other. It's like they're occupying different dimensions or something.'

'Like in *Doctor Who*,' Anna said triumphantly. 'I told you.'

KATIE WENT TO END HOUSE. The back door was open and she called, 'It's me,' as she stepped inside. Gwen and a woman with a red headscarf over short grey hair were sitting at the kitchen table. 'Sorry,' Katie said, making to walk through into the hallway. 'Don't mind me.' Gwen's consultations didn't usually take that long.

'This is Hannah Ash,' Gwen said, standing up. 'We're glad you're here.'

Great. Two wise women. Katie turned around and sized up Hannah Ash.

'I've got something to tell you,' Hannah said. 'It's my thing. I get these messages, things I have to pass on. I don't always understand them, sometimes they're in a language I don't even speak, but I have to pass them on. There was one in Russian once, it sounded amazing but I had no idea what I was saying and this bloke, well, he...' She trailed off.

Katie folded her arms. 'Go on, then.'

'Rude,' Gwen said. 'Sorry,' she said to Hannah.

'No skin off my nose,' Hannah said. 'Keep the light.'

Katie waited a beat then, when Hannah took a sip of her water, she said, 'That's it? Helpful.'

'The light as in "go into the light"? Like with ghosts?' Gwen said.

'I don't think so,' Hannah said. 'It's a message for her, not the spirits.'

'Does it mean anything to you?' Gwen said. She looked so anxious that some of Katie's irritation drained away. It wasn't Gwen's fault. She shook her head.

Hannah was getting to her feet. 'Thank you for the water.'

'That's it?' Katie said. 'You drop some unhelpful, cryptic rubbish and then leave? What kind of power is that?'

Hannah gave her a steady look. 'You tell me.'

'I'm sorry,' Gwen said again. 'Katie—'

'I've had worse,' Hannah said. 'Besides. She'll feel really guilty when she works out what it means. I don't get messages about the small stuff.'

'I won't,' Katie said. She was being childish but she didn't care. Hannah Ash could take her special sodding message and shove it where the sun didn't shine.

'I met a girl from the Iron family once, she gave messages, too, but they were trivial ones. Like about which brand of washing machine to buy, or to wear blue more often because it suited them. Imagine that, travelling across the country to find someone you don't know just to give them advice on whether to make chocolate or vanilla cupcakes for the school bake stall.'

Katie crossed her arms and stared at Hannah Ash, not saying anything, until Hannah gave a slight nod and turned to leave.

Gwen followed Hannah out, still apologising, and Katie helped herself to a glass of water.

'There was no need for that,' Gwen said when she came back.

'Things are a bit difficult right now,' she said. 'I don't need wannabe witches giving me cryptic tips. I need proper information. Real knowledge.' Katie was annoyed to feel her throat closing up. 'And I don't trust her,' she finished.

'There's a surprise,' Gwen said. She got up and filled the kettle. 'Tea? Or are you angry with me, too?'

Katie hadn't intended to tell Gwen about the ghost in the cricket pavilion, but she found that she couldn't stop herself. She was glad she'd waited until Gwen had put down the kettle, though, as she looked as if Katie had punched her. 'You did what?'

It wasn't the reaction Katie had been hoping for. The bad feeling she'd had after the boy had solidified got worse. 'I was trying to help him to pass over or whatever ghosts are supposed to do.'

'How?' When she was angry, Gwen looked a bit like Ruby. Katie stifled the urge to tell her. That wouldn't improve Gwen's mood.

'I don't know. I put my hands inside him. Here.' Katie pointed to her own chest. 'And I told him it was okay to move on but he didn't. Then I took my hands away and he disappeared.'

'How many times have I told you not to mess with something if you don't understand it? You could've been hurt.'

'But I wasn't. Besides, I don't have any way of understanding this. Unless Iris left some instructions you're not telling me about—'

'No.'

'And she doesn't appear to be here.' Katie waved around the kitchen, angry now. 'I can't exactly ask her. I can't ask anyone. I'm doing my best.'

'I know,' Gwen said. 'I'm sorry. I told you it wouldn't be easy.'

'I've got to believe that I'm supposed to help them,' Katie said. She reached for Gwen's hand and squeezed it. 'I thought the boy would want to move on because why would he want to stay? Reliving his last moments over and over again.'

Gwen sat forward, her face suddenly pale. 'Do people get trapped like that?'

'I think so.'

Gwen bit her lip. 'What if something is trapped here? Things haven't been exactly working for me recently and I wondered—'

Katie got up and left the kitchen. She walked around the house slowly, pausing in each room and listening. There were echoes. A feeling of happiness in Gwen and Cam's bedroom, a slight sense of alarm in the living room, and a coldness in the dining room. Katie looked up at the ceiling. It was smoothly plastered now. There was no evidence of where the ceiling had come down, killing Lily Thomas. Lily Thomas had given Katie a spell that had almost killed her and then she'd attacked Gwen with a knife, but the ceiling had caved in and killed her instead. As if the house itself had been protecting Gwen. 'Iris?' she said, feeling a little bit foolish when there was no reply.

'Nothing,' she said to Gwen, back in the kitchen. 'Clean as a whistle.'

Gwen's expression was a mixture of relief and misery.

'What's wrong?' Katie said. 'Do you miss Iris?'

'I've got as much of Iris as I ever had — I've still got her journals.'

'But you felt like she was here, didn't you?'

Gwen nodded. 'After Lily died I thought I felt her leave. Like she was done.'

'That makes sense. Everything I've read suggests spirits stay on because of unfinished business, something they feel they need to do.'

Gwen took a breath and then didn't say anything.

'What is it?' Katie said. 'I promise you Lily isn't here.' It felt strange to be the one comforting Gwen, the one with the information for once.

'Do you think the house has bad karma?' Gwen said finally. 'Because of Lily?'

'Definitely not.'

Gwen smiled and there were tears in her eyes. 'Okay.'

Katie had the feeling she was missing something important, but she figured Gwen would tell her when she was ready.

'I'm so sorry,' Gwen said. She put her head in her hands. 'This is all my fault.'

Katie knew what she meant. Gwen had been carrying around a weight ever since Katie was fourteen; it was almost visible above her head. Katie said the same thing she always said, the same thing she'd heard

Ruby say and Cam say a million times over: 'You've got nothing to be sorry about. You saved my life.'

'At what cost?'

Katie took a deep breath in through her nose. It didn't help. 'Have you considered pulling your head out of your backside for a second?'

'Pardon?' Gwen looked as if she was trying not to smile.

'This. Is. My. Power.' Katie put a hand onto Gwen's arm, to soften her words. 'I need your help and you can't help me while you keep denying that. I can't just ignore it. I can't just avoid the hotel. They are everywhere.'

'Okay,' Gwen said, looking Katie in the eye. 'But I don't know what to do.'

'But you always—' Katie began, looking frustrated.

Gwen held her hand up. 'Head is firmly extracted from backside, I promise. I just don't know, I really don't—'

'Tell me what to do,' Katie said, desperation leaking into her voice. 'Everyone says they can help. Max says it's a psychological tic, Barton says I should go on the stage, Henry says he will help me if I help him, Hannah Ash is dropping in to witter on about light bulbs.'

'Just light, I think,' Gwen said, mildly. 'You have to trust someone.'

'I trust you. That's enough.'

'But I can't help you. I want to, but I'm drawing a blank, you know that. Is Barton any use?'

'I doubt it. My instinct says he's a fraud, but I might be wrong,' Katie said. 'What if he isn't? And we don't know Hannah Ash. She seems genuine, but I've not always been the best judge of these things.'

'Lily Thomas was a long time ago,' Gwen said.

'Seven years,' Katie said. 'Not long enough.'

'What do your instincts tell you?'

Katie closed her eyes. 'It's too noisy in my head. I don't know.'

Gwen poured the tea. 'I know that feeling.'

They sipped tea for a few moments and Katie enjoyed the feeling of peace Gwen's kitchen always gave her. Cat wound around her ankles purring loudly and she reached down and scratched behind his ear. She felt a spark, like static electricity, and it reminded her of holding Fred's hand. Fred Byres's recovery was the elephant in the room. She wanted to ask Gwen how he was getting on, but she didn't want Gwen to look at her with that awful expression again. The one that was part shocked, part frightened.

She stroked Cat and he arched up, rubbing his head against her hand. She felt the spark again and moved her hand away. 'Why did the ghost in the pavilion get all solid like that? When I touched him?'

'I've been through the journals twice, I swear,' Gwen said, 'but there's nothing.'

'Is it linked to what happened with Fred?' Katie forced the words out. 'I thought I would help the ghost, like I helped Fred, but it doesn't seem to work that way.'

'I don't know. No one in our family has ever been able to heal someone with a touch.'

Katie tried not to hear the accusatory tone in Gwen's voice. It had almost been better when she'd been powerless and a disappointment. 'That's because it's impossible,' she said. 'There's always balance. You told me that.'

Gwen sipped her tea and then said, 'That's exactly what worries me.'

CHAPTER 21

*K*atie was wandering through the hotel, looking for Violet, when Patrick opened the door to the library and gestured to her.

'I need you.'

Katie's first thought was that Henry had discovered a way to move things and was floating books or something equally unhelpful, so she wasn't ready for a real-live person to be in the room, rising from her chair and holding out a hand.

'Come in, come in.' Patrick ushered Katie forwards. 'This is Gillian Lewis from the *Chronicle*.'

'Good to meet you.' Gillian held out a hand. Katie ignored it and spoke to Patrick. 'I'm not speaking to a journalist.'

Violet popped up in front of her. 'I don't like this,' she said. 'Make him stop.'

Katie gritted her teeth to stop herself from answering Violet. The last thing she wanted was to encourage Patrick.

'This building has a fascinating history,' Patrick said. 'And a tragic one.'

Katie and Violet both looked at him.

'The Beaufort family built this house in 1698. You can imagine the births and deaths, love and laughter, that these walls have seen.' Patrick paused to look around at the walls. 'Guests have reported hearing music playing quietly in the back corridor, a table was seen to move without anybody touching it, and House-keeping reports seeing indentations in the bed in The Plum Suite where nobody has slept.'

The journalist was scribbling furiously in a note-book. She looked up. 'Anything else?'

'Well, there was a ghostly woman in a white dress seen in the library. She is sitting with a book on her lap and some people have reported seeing a kitten playing by her feet.'

'And you think that is Violet Beaufort?'

Katie couldn't stop herself from looking at Violet. A mixture of disgust and interest was fighting it out on her face.

'Well, having looked into the history of the house, Violet Beaufort fits the description and she did mysteri-ously disappear in 1937.'

'Disappear?' Gillian cocked her head. 'Not die?'

'Presumed dead, after a few years, I believe,' Patrick said. 'As I said. Mysterious.'

The journalist nodded. 'Okay. That's good.' She tapped her notebook. 'Perhaps we could get the police to reopen the case. That would make it current affairs, too.'

'There was a suggestion of scandal at the time. A love triangle gone wrong—'

'No,' Violet said. 'I don't like this.' She turned to Katie. 'Make them stop. I don't want to know.' Then she did her disappearing trick.

The journalist was looking at Katie expectantly. She had a neat brown bob and a kind face. Katie wasn't fooled. 'This is the first I'm hearing about this,' she said. She forced a little laugh. 'It all sounds rather far-fetched.'

'Katie saw the table flying and has been looking into the occurrences. She belongs to a family known for its sensitivity to—'

'Mr Allen,' Katie broke in loudly. 'The Pink Room has a blocked sink in the en suite. Can I have the plumber's number?'

'In a moment,' Patrick said.

'Fine.' Katie turned on her heel and left the room. She wasn't playing a part in Patrick's little charade.

He caught up with her in the hall, and put his hand on her shoulder. 'Go back inside.'

'No,' Katie said, shrugging away. 'I'm not talking to a journalist. I want no part in this. Whatever you're doing.'

'You think I like this?' Patrick said, his face red. 'My wife is furious and the town council is going to have a fit. But this hotel is a disaster. It wasn't profitable enough before and now I've got too many loans. My hands are tied.'

'This is not the right way to go,' Katie said.

'It's too late,' Patrick said. 'Word is spreading that The Grange is haunted. Either I jump on board and make it a feature, or it'll bury me. Barton's doing another show and he's happy to talk about the spiritual presences he's sensed at the hotel.'

'I'll bet he is,' Katie said.

'He says that ghost tours are big business. If we can get listed as a haunted hotel, we might even get picked up by the television people.'

'You don't want The Grange to be known for this,' Katie said, appealing to his vanity. 'It's not very upmarket, is it?'

'There's a programme called *The Real Ghostbusters*. With enough publicity, Barton says he can convince them to film an episode here and that'll really put The Grange on the map.'

'What kind of map?' Katie said. 'Surely ghosts are bad for business. They're throwing stuff around — people could get hurt.'

'Ah.' Patrick wagged a finger and Katie stamped on the urge to smack him. 'Haven't you heard of the phrase "if you can't beat them, join them"?'

'Haven't you heard the phrase "don't poke a sleeping lion"?'

Patrick tried an avuncular chuckle. 'I hardly think a spirit is as dangerous as a lion. Besides, maybe Barton will be able to get him to move on. I mean, it's not like you've had any luck in that department.'

'No.'

'Not that I don't appreciate your effort.' He all but patted her on the head.

Greg Barton walked down the main staircase, shooting the cuffs on his suit jacket. 'It's Katie, isn't it? Be a dear and run up to my room—'

'What the hell do you think you're doing?'

'I'm milking it, darling, and if you had an ounce of sense you'd do the same.' He looked at her critically. 'You're quite attractive, really. You've got a good face for television.'

'I'm not talking to any journalists and I'm definitely not going on television,' Katie said automatically.

'Suit yourself.' Greg shrugged theatrically. 'I was just trying to be kind.'

'I doubt that,' Katie said, and Greg smiled with no humour, then opened the door to the library.

Katie moved away so that she wouldn't have to listen to Barton smarming at Gillian Lewis.

Patrick's face had gone bright red. 'Are you really not going to help me?'

Katie crossed her arms, tried to gather some inner strength. 'It's not part of my duties, so I've no obligation to speak to a journalist. And I am trying to help you, you're just not listening.'

She fixed her gaze over Patrick's shoulder, so that she wouldn't have to watch his expression. She saw a familiar figure in a burgundy housekeeping tabard come through the staff door and cross the hall.

'Ah, finally,' Patrick said, and moved to usher Zofia into the library.

Katie reached out for her first. 'What are you doing?'

Zofia looked at the ground. 'Mr Allen says that I need to speak with the lady from the news.'

'You don't have to do anything you don't want to.'

'Please,' Zofia said, pulling her arm away. 'I need this job.'

'Patrick,' Katie said. 'Tell Zofia she doesn't have to speak to the press. Or anyone she doesn't want to speak to. Ever.'

Patrick gaped at her. 'I beg your pardon.'

Katie looked him in the eye. 'Don't make me tell you again. Unless you want me to call Gwen up here.'

After a moment, Patrick said tightly, 'You don't have to go in there.'

Zofia looked fearfully at Katie and hurried away.

'If you keep bullying your staff, it'll come back to haunt you.'

'What?' Patrick started, looking genuinely alarmed.

'Sorry,' Katie said, not meaning it. 'Poor choice of words.'

Katie went up to The Plum Suite to find Violet. She looked angry.

'The newspaper people are going to start researching it, now. You may as well tell me.'

'I don't know. I already told you.'

'You disappeared, Violet. Your body was never found.'

Violet took another swipe at the ghostly doll's house. 'So?'

'What if it's the reason you're here? What if we're supposed to find out? Supposed to make it public or something? Bring the person responsible to justice?'

Violet pinched her fingers together, her face a picture of concentration. She was trying to pick up a tiny dog that was just in front of the main entrance. Her fingers slipped through it and she growled under her breath.

'Violet?'

'I told you, I don't like to think about it.'

'Please. What if it's connected to the stuff that's happening, now? What if it's the key to your being here?'

'You want to get rid of me?' Violet stopped trying to pick up the dog and turned large wet eyes onto Katie. 'You want me to go?' Fat tears began coursing down her face and her mouth opened in an ugly shape. 'Why do you want me to go? This is my house. You should be the one to leave. Not me. It's not fair.'

'Violet, I'm not trying to get rid of you. I promise.'

Violet turned back to the house, swiping her hand wildly at the figure of the dog. It connected, the dog spinning away across the polished hardwood floor. 'I thought you were my friend,' she said, her voice rising into a wail.

'You touched the dog. Did you see?'

Violet wrenched open the front of the doll's house and began picking things up and throwing them. It wasn't exactly as if she was throwing them at Katie, but many were certainly in her direction. Katie felt the strangest sensation, like a whole body shiver when a small chest of drawers flew at her chest, rebounded and fell to the floor. The doll's house was getting more solid with every second.

'Vi—' Katie began, fear gripping her.

'No!' Violet snapped. 'You don't talk now.' She turned back to grab another missile and Katie fled.

ON THEIR NEXT DAY OFF, Katie and Anna moved into their new flat. Katie took the smaller room. She was still smarting from Anna's casual insistence that she was rich and privileged. She was, but really. Of course, she thought, as she unpacked her sewing machine onto its little side table and tucked a basket underneath, if Anna had wanted her to take the smaller bedroom without any fuss then giving her a sense of guilt first would've been a very smart move. Max would no doubt have a field day; he'd probably make a little Post-it note with the word 'mug' on it and stick it on her forehead.

Katie made the bed with her new bedding, her moving-in present to herself, and piled cushions at the headboard. The room was the perfect blank canvas and Katie decided not to put up her old prints and knick-knacks, shoving them underneath the bed. She was going to live with the blank walls for a while and then decide what she really wanted to look at every day.

She put her books onto the bookshelf, along with the red journal Gwen had given her years before. She hadn't read it for a long time. Losing any ability to cast spells or read cards had been so soul-destroying, she realised now that she'd been going through the motions during Tuesday night training. She'd been saying she was trying her hardest, but she hadn't really. Now she felt different. She was frightened a lot of the time, but there was a kind of fizzing energy that hadn't been there before.

Katie sat on her bed and flicked through the journal. Spells and cures and advice from Gwen and Iris were jumbled alongside snippets of family history, anecdotes and quotes. She began reading in earnest, turning back to the beginning and settling back against her pillows, the shadows lengthening down the blank wall opposite.

A few hours later, Katie emerged from her bedroom, a plan forming in her mind. It was full moon, which was perfect timing, something Katie decided to take as a sign.

The living room was already looking more lived in, with fairy lights around the minimalist fireplace with its non-functional fake-fire, and a big glass bowl filled with coloured glass pebbles and more fairy lights.

'Do you think we might have too many fairy lights?' Katie said, squinting at the room.

'You can never have too many fairy lights,' Anna said. She opened a bottle of Diet Coke and handed Katie a glassful. 'Cheers.'

'Here's to us.' Katie clinked her glass against Anna's.

'Are we going to have rules?'

'Housemate agreement?' Katie said. 'Is this where you reveal I'm moving in with Sheldon Cooper?'

'No. I just don't want to be another Shari. I want us to stay friends.'

'I'm still friends with Shari,' Katie said, shocked. 'Shari's brilliant.'

Anna shook her head. 'But you complained about her all the time. I don't want you to be at work, bitching about how I don't clean out the grill pan.'

Katie sat on the sofa next to Anna. 'I'm sorry. I didn't realise I'd been such a moany cow.'

'You weren't,' Anna said. 'I just don't want us to fall out.'

'All you have to do is agree not to have sex on this sofa.' Katie held out her hand and they shook.

'Never on the sofa,' Anna intoned. 'I swear.'

Katie tilted her head back. 'You're thinking about doing it on the chair, aren't you?'

Anna opened her eyes wide. 'I have literally no idea what you're talking about. Besides, the chair looks uncomfortable.'

Katie laughed. 'Actually, you can have sex wherever you like, just don't use my toothbrush.'

'Shari used your toothbrush?' Anna wrinkled her nose. 'Yuck.'

'You have no idea,' Katie said.

AFTER A PLEASANT EVENING sorting out the kitchen with Anna, making flapjack and singing along to the radio, Katie changed into a dark hoodie and jeans. She wasn't going to be exactly incognito when she lit the candle, plus the light from the massive full moon, but there wasn't much she could do about that. All she could do was hope Violet and Henry and the other ghosts were busy and that none of the staff or guests of the hotel were out for a late-night stroll.

'Where are you going?' Anna caught her on her way out of the door. Katie thought about lying, then decided it would be better if someone knew where she was. Just in case.

'I'll come,' Anna said, after she'd explained. 'Give me a sec.'

Katie waited while Anna put on trainers and a grey bobbly cardigan over her pyjamas.

The gardens at The Grange were quiet. The pond looked even bigger and deeper in the moonlight than it did during the day. Katie sat on the wide stone edge furthest from the house and set up her candle. There was a gentle 'plop' sound as a fish came to the surface to investigate.

'What're you hoping to do, again?' Anna sat cross-legged on the other side of the candle. 'Can I help?'

Katie thought. Anger was dangerous, but it would also give a boost of power. 'Could I hold your hand?'

Anna smiled. 'Are you kidding? I've been wanting to try this stuff since we met.'

Katie considered launching into her 'be careful' spiel, memorised from the countless times Gwen had delivered it, but then decided she couldn't be bothered. The way she'd been recently, nothing was going to happen anyway.

'Okay. When I light the candle, I want you to hold my hands either side of it, like this.' Katie held her arms up to demonstrate. 'Look into the candle flame and try to relax.'

'Do we chant?'

'Nope,' Katie said. 'If it's going to work it'll be pretty quick. I might zone out for a bit. Don't worry about it and don't wake me up.'

'Right, let's go.'

Katie glanced up at the moon, then lit the candle. She held Anna's hands and tried to relax her mind. She wanted to reach out to the memories that might be held in the hotel. In the grounds. She wanted to know what Violet wasn't telling her.

'Am I doing it right?' Anna whispered. Her voice seemed to be coming from far away and Katie found she couldn't open her mouth to speak. The light of the candle flared until her vision was filled with hot white light. The white light turned to sunlight and Katie felt a release; she couldn't feel Anna's hands any more. She was sitting in the same place, but the sun was bouncing off the water, the glare hurting her eyes.

A man with tremendous mutton-chop whiskers and a waistcoat was standing to her left. Just as she became aware of the sunshine, the birdsong and the thwack of a croquet mallet she realised that the man was talking. Hectoring, really. His voice resolved into words as Katie's mind adjusted to his speech. 'You can't see this man again. I forbid it.'

Katie looked down at herself. A white sundress with more ruffles than was strictly necessary. Dainty feet in soft silk slippers. Not her feet. She felt a lurch of sickness.

'Daddy, please.' Katie felt her lips moving, the breath leave her body, but the voice wasn't hers. It was familiar, though.

'This conversation is at an end. You will not see that

man, you will not speak to that man, and, come June twenty-sixth, you will marry Lord Somerset.'

Her father's face softened. 'This is for your own good. You'll see in time.' Mutton chops had become her father, suddenly familiar and beloved and infuriating. Then his face darkened as if covered by shadow and the garden scene disappeared to blackness.

Katie felt the familiar panic take her but a moment later Anna was shaking her. 'Wake up. Oh, God, wake up.'

'I'm okay.' She sat up.

'Thank Christ.' Anna looked white in the moonlight. 'I thought you'd died or something.'

'I'm fine,' Katie said. She couldn't stop smiling. 'I did it.'

Gwen took the canal path, not really holding out any hope that she'd meet Hannah Ash again. Perhaps there'd be a likely looking person who could pass on a message, though. It was early and the sun was welcome, cutting through the cloud and damp of the night. It was clear it would be too hot again soon enough. As always, Gwen's first thought was how that might affect her chances of baby-making. If Cam was too hot to fancy sex, they could go into the garden. At least End House was secluded.

Gwen reached the first of a series of locks and paused to watch a boat come through. The person who was opening the lock, winding the mechanism with rapid turns, had green canvas trousers tucked into black wellington boots and a voluminous overcoat. The only sign that this was a woman was the bright red head-scarf knotted over short silver-grey hair.

She said 'good morning' in a perfunctory sort of way, then did a double take, looking at Gwen with one hand shielding her eyes from the sun. 'Oh, it's you.' Her voice was pleasant but she turned away without smiling and disappeared into the body of the boat.

A moment later her head reappeared. 'Are you coming?'

Gwen hesitated, then clambered after her.

Inside, Hannah was at the far end of the boat, putting tea bags into blue enamel mugs. A kettle on the small burner began to whistle.

The inside of the boat was neat and ingenious. A small cushioned bench ran along a narrow table and a curtain hung at one end, screening off the rest of the living area. The walls were filled with tiny compartments and drawers, which made her feel as if they were standing inside a giant bureau. Gwen felt a stab of nostalgia for Nanette, her beloved van.

'Sit.' Hannah gestured to the bench. 'Do you take sugar?'

'No, thank you.' Gwen looked around the interior, part of her mind planning a canal-boat-themed shadow box.

'You need advice about your niece, I take it?' Hannah opened a tiny window above the cooker and let the steam in the kitchen escape.

'Did you sense a disturbance in the force or something?' Gwen said.

Hannah shrugged. 'You know what it's like.'

'She's communicating with the dead. Spirits.'

'And the problem is?'

'I don't think it's a path she should be on.' Gwen accepted the mug of tea and blew lightly on its surface while she tried to marshal her words.

'You're worried that you brought death into her life?'

The tea slopped dangerously close to the rim of the

mug. 'Yes.' *And no.* Katie had brought Fred back to life. That wasn't death but it wasn't necessarily good, either.

Hannah shook her head. 'I don't know about that. Except that it doesn't matter. What matters is what she does with it now. Is she all right? Coping?'

'She wants to help them.' Gwen felt herself go warm, thinking about Katie.

Hannah sat on the bench underneath a porthole-shaped window. 'There was someone in our family who could talk to ghosts. My mother's cousin.'

'Could she talk to Katie? Help her?'

Hannah shook her head. 'She stepped off this mortal coil. Well…' Hannah pulled a face. 'Stepped off a kitchen chair with a rope around her neck, actually.'

'Oh, Christ,' Gwen said. 'I'm sorry.'

'I'm telling you this so that you can warn your niece.' Hannah looked suddenly very fierce. 'Tell her that she can't help them. She mustn't let them get too close.'

'What do you mean?'

'It's not like spells or cures or any of that. The dead aren't in our world, not really. If you can see ghosts it's like you're looking through a window into another reality that's just really close to ours.' Hannah gestured to the porthole. 'You mustn't let her open that window.'

'What will happen if she does?' Gwen didn't know if Katie would even listen to her any more.

Hannah shrugged. 'She better be damn sure she can shut it again, that's all.'

Katie found Violet in The Plum Suite, staring out of

the window with a moody expression. 'Peace?' Katie said.

'Only because I haven't any better options,' Violet said. She pouted for a moment longer and then gave way, her lips turning up at the corners. As a ghost, Violet was utterly irrepressible. A force of nature. God only knew what she had been like in life. 'I do have something to show you, though,' Violet said. 'Come.'

Katie followed Violet as she ran along the floor, pausing for a skip or a twirl here and there. She stopped in front of the mahogany wardrobe with its full-length mirror and sighed. 'I do wish I could see myself.' Then carried on out of the room and onto, Katie assumed, the balcony. Katie opened the door wider and stepped out onto the tiny area, half expecting Violet to have disappeared. She wondered if Violet could just float into the air if she wanted to, fly around the building like something out of *Peter Pan*.

Violet was leaning on the stone balustrade, gazing out into the distance with a thoughtful expression that looked manufactured.

'Can you fly?' Katie said.

'Why?' Violet said. 'Are you going to push me over the edge?'

'No!' Katie took a step back, keen not to appear threatening. She'd only just got Violet speaking to her again. And she had a favour to ask. 'I was just wondering. I thought it might be fun. Like a perk.'

'A perk of being dead,' Violet said. 'Goodness knows there are precious few of those.' She shook her head. 'It's not such an awfully big adventure, after all.'

Katie smiled. 'I was just thinking about Peter Pan.'

'Most things aren't how you expect them to be, though, are they?' Violet turned and gazed at Katie with a forlorn expression. It was heartbreaking on her pretty, young face. A fact of which Violet was no doubt well aware, but, still, Katie felt her heart squeeze in sympathy.

'What did you want to show me?' Katie spoke gently. She wanted to put a hand on Violet's arm, something comforting but didn't know whether her hand would pass straight through thin air or whether there would be something, some kind of electrical energy, to touch. She didn't know which would be worse, either.

'Down there.' Violet indicated the gardens.

Katie looked at the grounds, the lawn, the hedges and flower beds, the ornamental pond and the red brick wall with the iron gate in the centre that led to the old orchard. The cultivated land stopped after the ha-ha, and beyond there were fields and, in the distance, a copse. It must've been the view, more or less, from when Violet lived here with her family, her brothers and sisters, mum and dad. She had just been a girl, not very different from Katie, dreaming of her life to come. Maybe falling in love. 'What am I looking at?' Katie said, trying to keep her voice light, trying to fight off the blanket of melancholy that had draped over her shoulders.

'I saw you kissing that man,' Violet said. 'There, on the grass. It was quite revolting.'

'Oh, come on,' Katie said. 'Revolting is a bit harsh. Like you never snogged anyone in the garden.'

'What is snogged?'

'Kissed.'

'You shouldn't do that sort of thing if you're not married. It gives entirely the wrong impression.'

'Look, I know you come from a different time.

More refined. Strict rules. I get that. But if you want me to believe that you never snogged — kissed — a boy, then I'm afraid I reserve my right to disbelieve you. Strongly. Disbelieve. You.' She waggled her eyebrows suggestively, trying to make Violet laugh and was pleased when she did. She had such a nice laugh. For a ghost.

Violet slapped a hand over her mouth, which was sweet, too. 'Very well. I might've kissed a boy once. Just once.'

'Once can be enough if the kiss is good enough.'

'Ain't that the truth, honey.' Violet put on an American accent, stuck a hand on one hip.

Katie laughed. 'I'm glad it was good. Everyone should be kissed really well at least once in their lives.' She thought of Max. That man had moves.

Violet's face had fallen. She was staring out at the garden again. 'I was in love, once,' she said.

'I know,' Katie said, feeling guilty. 'You told me to look it up, so I did.'

'That wasn't in a book,' Violet said, turning to her. 'I don't understand.'

'I used a spell,' Katie said. 'I peeked into your past and I saw your dad, really angry about a boy. I'm sorry. It was rude of me.'

Violet hesitated. It looked as if she was trying to decide whether to get angry or not. Then her shoulders went down a notch and she sighed. 'I wish I could do spells. How exciting.'

Katie smothered a smile. The ghost was jealous of magic. Of course. 'I'm not very good, to be honest. Not like my aunt. This—' she gestured to Violet '—is my special talent. And I don't know what I'm supposed to do with that.'

'You'll work it out,' Violet said. 'You're awfully clever.'

'Thank you,' Katie said, surprised.

'Not like me,' Violet said cheerfully. 'I'm a complete clot. Daddy always said it was a good thing I was pretty.'

'Did he?' Katie wished she'd slapped Daddy when she'd had the chance. Perhaps she'd head back into Violet's past and aim a kick at his shins.

'Who did you love, Violet?'

'There was an archaeologist. He was excavating Silbury Hill, you know, near Avebury? And Mummy and Daddy met him at an event of some kind, I don't know where, but they made friends. He wasn't titled, but he had a lot of dough. His father had made a lot up north somewhere, something to do with manufacturing. I didn't really pay attention. So, he was iffy, you know?'

'Iffy?'

'New money. It wasn't the sort of thing that was supposed to matter, not after the war and with the depression and all, but it still mattered to a lot of people. Including my dear old parents.'

'And you fell in love with him?'

'Worse.' Violet pulled a face. 'His apprentice. I may as well have gone googly-eyed over a footman.'

'Oh,' Katie said. 'I keep on forgetting how weird everyone used to be about class.'

'Used to be?' Violet laughed. 'How many lower-class people are welcomed into this hotel?'

'That's not about class, it's money.'

'My darling girl,' Violet said, suddenly sounding a lot older than twenty, 'it's always been about money.'

'But everyone has the same opportunities, now,' Katie said, realising as she spoke that this was utter nonsense. She felt embarrassed, suddenly, by the twenty-first century. She ought to have something better to tell Violet. Something superior to compare with the dark ages of the nineteen thirties.

'I was the daughter of a lord, and there were certain expectations. I was expected to play the piano or sing, I was expected to show compassion to animals and the lower orders but to remain above reproach as regards my behaviour, and I was expected to make a good match. Lord Somerset had spoken to Daddy and was going to propose on my birthday. I was going to say "yes" and then I would be parcelled up and moved from this estate to my husband's in Cornwall.'

'Cornwall's nice,' Katie said weakly. The thought of being that powerless made her feel faint.

Violet gave her a withering look. 'I was a fool. I thought Daddy would change his mind. I thought he would meet Henry and see how much in love we were and relent. I thought it would be like *Top Hat*.'

'You loved Henry?' Katie went very still.

'Yes.' Violet stared out at the garden. 'I died loving Henry so I still love Henry. I will always love Henry.'

Katie tried to contain her smile. This was it. Her purpose. To reunite the lost lovers. It was romantic; it was beautiful; it was perfect. She was going to give Violet her happy ever after. Well, as close to that as she could get, considering the circumstances.

CHAPTER 23

*K*atie went to find Max. She wanted to tell him about her success and to have a closer look at the stored junk in the basement. She'd been wondering why Henry was haunting the building when he hadn't died here, and Gwen had said something about spirits being attached to objects. Perhaps if she found the thing that was keeping Henry here it would help her to connect him to Violet.

'I was looking for you,' he said, before she could say anything.

'Want to help me play detective?' Katie said.

'I thought you'd never ask.'

Katie pushed him lightly. 'Behave yourself,' she said, ignoring the urge to push him again, just to touch him.

Henry appeared as they walked past Lost Property. He looked more translucent again, the shelves of boxes clearly visible through his torso.

'Is it me or is it cold in here?' Max said.

Katie rubbed her arms and glared at Henry. 'Very.'

'This place is a tip,' Max said. 'Has Patrick ever really looked down here?'

There were a couple of new mattresses, still in plastic wrapping, on the floor with several lampshades perched on top. A vacuum cleaner with a broken handle sat next to a pile of cardboard boxes, and there were mysterious lumps underneath white and dusty sheets and a wall filled with broken chairs, side tables, and a chest of drawers, with half its drawers missing.

Henry pulled a face and walked close to Max, as if inspecting him. Max shivered. 'Is that Violet?'

Katie pushed aside a lampshade and sat on the stack of mattresses. 'I wanted to talk to you about my periods.'

Max raised his eyebrows. 'Okay.'

'Come and sit down.' Katie patted the mattress next to her and smiled, trying to look inviting but slightly unhinged. She'd bet anything she'd nailed it.

Max closed the door and sat, the mattress sagging a little. 'What's wrong?'

Katie raised her voice, just in case Henry was putting his fingers in his ears. 'I want to talk about my women's periods. My monthlies. My flow.'

Max winced. 'I said all right — you don't need to shout.'

'I've got problems with my uterus. My ovaries are aching.'

'What?' Max looked confused. She didn't blame him.

'My Fallopian tubes are twisted,' Katie said, 'and my vagina—'

Henry disappeared.

'—is weird,' Katie continued, looking around to check Henry wasn't hiding in a corner or behind them.

'I'm sorry to hear that,' Max said. He was leaning away from her, probably unconsciously, but Katie couldn't help laughing.

'It's okay,' she whispered. 'My tubes are fine.'

'Is this some kind of test?'

'I just wanted to get rid of Henry and I noticed he was squeamish. Got that old-school reserve thing going on, too. My clothes disgust him, let alone talking about my secret lady parts.'

Max swallowed. 'Right. He was here, then.'

'Yep,' Katie said, cheerfully. She stood up and pulled at one of the sheets, raising a massive cloud of dust. Once she'd finished coughing she said, 'That's why it was cold. Can't you feel the difference now he's gone?'

'Yes,' Max said thoughtfully. 'He really exists. Ghosts really exist.'

'Welcome to my world,' Katie said.

'But your vagina isn't weird,' Max said. 'Just to clarify.'

Katie gave him what she hoped was a withering look and didn't reply. She began investigating the boxes.

'What are we looking for?'

'That collection of odd stuff that Michelle mentioned. I thought it might still be in the hotel. It's not in the library or any of the public rooms, so I thought I'd try here. Next stop is the attic.'

'Why did you want rid of Henry?'

'Because I don't know how he'll react to our looking through his stuff and...' Katie hesitated '...partly because you're right. I know I shouldn't trust him.'

Max looked pleased. 'While you're listening to me, I've got news.' He took his phone out of his pocket and began scrolling through photographs. He held up the screen and there was a fuzzy picture of a paper. 'Love letters. To Violet Beaufort.'

'Are you serious?' Katie leaned in to look. The handwriting was slanted and dark, cramped together as if written by a very energetic but controlled hand. She didn't think she'd be able to read it even if she were looking at the real thing rather than a grainy photo on a screen. 'How——?'

'I went to the folk museum in town.'

'I didn't know Pendleford had a museum.'

'It's tiny. A few black and white pictures of the high street and the names of the town mayors, that kind of thing. It's practically run out of the owner's front room.'

Katie felt mortified that she hadn't known about it. She was really going to have to work on the wise-woman act.

'Anyway, the woman there was about three hundred years old and she was happy to talk about The Grange. She had a problem with some of the renovation work that Patrick has done, but, once I got her off the conservatory, she told me that there was a big scandal here. When Violet Beaufort went missing.'

Katie went still. 'Did she know anything else?'

'Apparently our Violet was very popular. She was being pursued by two men.'

'I know,' Katie said. 'That's what I was going to tell you. Lord Somerset and Henry.'

Max shook his head. 'Alexander James and Henry Keele. They were excavating Windmill Hill, apparently, and they got to know the Beauforts. These letters are from Alexander. He was in love with her.'

'Maybe he's just being polite. It was a different time, different ways of speaking——'

'He talks of her beauty, of what a good mother she

will make for his children and he signs them "for eternity".'

'Thank you,' Katie said. He had taken time to go and research ghosts. Ghosts he probably didn't really believe in. For her. She went on tiptoe and kissed Max on the cheek.

Max caught her around the waist, his hands on the bare skin between her skirt and vest top. 'You're welcome.' And he bent to kiss her full on the mouth.

Katie reached up to meet him, giving herself up to the kiss. Everyone deserved a second chance. Even a con man.

After a moment, she broke away. 'Not that I don't appreciate this, but I really think we should look for that collection. While we have the chance.'

Max released her. 'You should be more irresponsible, you know. Live a little.' But he turned and began moving the broken chairs to get at a pile of boxes behind.

'I tried irresponsible once,' Katie said. 'It did not end well. I'm now all about education.'

'Didn't you drop out of uni?'

'I didn't go in the first place,' Katie said. 'University wasn't going to teach me what I need to know. Knowledge is power, but it's got to be the right kind.'

'You sound like my dad. I wanted to study maths but he thought I was crazy. He said I already knew its practical applications so what was the point.'

Katie tried to imagine a younger Max, thinking about studying rather than grifting. It was hard. 'What do you mean?'

'Card counting, mainly.' Max took a penknife out of his pocket and ripped open the tape on the first box. 'Old flyers,' he said, putting the box on the floor.

'However, autodidactism is all well and good but what about having fun? That doesn't have to be dangerous. That can just be fun. I mean, we're young, we're healthy, why shouldn't we have fun together?'

'You make it sound like playing tennis.' Katie tried not to get turned on by him saying 'didacticism'. Honestly, the man looked like a wise guy, spoke like a professor. It was confusing. And very hot.

'It's not far off. Gets your heart rate up, very good cardio—' Max broke off as he reached into the box. 'Hello. I think we have a winner.' He held up a bit of twisted brown metal. It had a faded cardboard luggage tag tied to it. Max tilted it to the light. 'Bronze brooch, c.1000 BC. Avebury, 1935.'

'Well, that should definitely be in a museum.'

'I wonder what it's worth,' Max said. Then, 'What? I'm just curious.'

Katie plucked the brooch from Max and put it on the seat of the upmost stacked chair. 'What else?'

Max began unwrapping newspaper from something the size of a tennis ball. Katie reached in and pulled out a box with a faded picture of a toothy smile on the lid. There were random bits of sticking plaster with some sketchy blue marks that might have, once upon a time, been writing. She opened the box and found the tiny, perfect skull of a bird. The image of a magpie flashed through her mind. She closed the box and put it with the brooch.

After three bits of pointy rock that might have been flint arrow heads, a box full of geodes and agates packed in cotton wool, and many free-floating paper labels that had become unattached from their objects, Katie found a burgundy leather photo album with half the pages empty. Some had yellowed squares and empty photo corners where pictures had once been, and some had clearly never been filled. Katie flipped through until she found a picture of a man in funny tweed trousers standing by a mound of earth and holding a pipe in one hand and an object in the other. Maybe a rock? Katie held the album closer but it didn't help.

She turned a page and there was a photo of two men standing in a formal garden. The man from the previous page and a familiar face. Henry. There was nothing written underneath so Katie slipped the picture from its crumbling corners and checked the back. Alexander James and Henry Keele June, 1936. She held it out to Max who whistled between his teeth. 'There's lover boy.'

'Lover boys. Henry and Violet were an item. But her father didn't approve.'

'How do you know?' Max said. 'Research?'

Katie nodded. She'd explain some other time. Maybe.

'Look at this.' Max was unwinding cloth from a spherical object that Katie assumed was a glass fishing float. Once the cloth was removed it looked more like an oversized Christmas bauble. Max read the label. 'Witch's ball, circa 1890. You could give this to your aunt.'

Katie held out her hands and took the ball. It was a burnished coppery gold and felt warm in her hands. She didn't want to give it away. She wanted it. It was hers in a way that seemed completely natural and inevitable. She put it on top of a packing case, nesting it carefully in the material so that it wouldn't roll. A reflection of the room was held in the curved side of the ball, a perfect tiny reproduction of their world, complete with a tiny Katie and tiny Max. 'This is the best thing I've ever had,' Katie said. 'Seriously. It's beautiful.'

Max gave her a funny look. 'Don't you consider it stealing?'

'I don't think Patrick Allen is going to miss it,' Katie said, hugging it closer.

Max held his hands up. 'You don't need to convince me. I don't care.'

'Good,' Katie said. She couldn't explain why, but she felt that it was hers. *Finders keepers. Hers.* She felt an alarming violence rising up inside her at the thought of anybody trying to take it away from her.

CHAPTER 24

Gwen looked at the doctor, willing her to say something more useful.

'I'm very sorry,' she said. 'There's nothing else we can do. Unless you want to discuss treatments for infertility such as IVF or—'

'No, thank you,' Cam said. They'd discussed all of the options at great length. For months. Gwen thought she had resigned herself to this diagnosis; they'd been warned often enough that sometimes that was the outcome. Unexplained infertility. A fancy way of saying 'we don't know' or 'life can be cruel'. It didn't tell you why your body was betraying you in this awful, unforgivable way and it didn't tell you why it was happening to you. Why she couldn't get pregnant when they'd passed three teenage girls on the way through town, pushing babies, dragging toddlers, practically tapping fag ash onto their unwanted, accidental newborns.

Gwen felt the bile in the back of her throat. This wasn't her. She wasn't this mean, this judgemental. But she was just so fucking angry. Why couldn't they have a baby when so many people seemed to manage it with such painful ease? Why?

'Ms Harper? Would you like a glass of water?' The doctor was looking at her with professional concern. Suddenly, Gwen had to get out of that office. That building. She needed fresh air and somewhere private to scream.

She leaned on Cam as they walked out of the building, feeling as if her legs might give way at any moment.

'Shall we go for a walk?'

Gwen couldn't answer him. She didn't know what she wanted to do. She wanted to be with Cam, but alone. She wanted to be outside but also underneath her duvet, curled into a foetal position. She wanted to put loud music on and scream until her throat was sore and to sit quietly with no sound whatsoever. Most of all, she didn't want this. She didn't want these feelings; she didn't want this need; she didn't want this emptiness and desolation that seemed both inside her and bigger than her.

'There's still a chance,' Cam said. 'There's nothing actually wrong with either of us—'

'Don't,' Gwen said. 'Please.'

'Sorry.'

They got into the car in silence. Gwen waited for Cam to start the engine but he sat, his hands resting on the steering wheel, and stared out of the windscreen. He wasn't crying, but the expression on his face was so bleak it was worse. Gwen felt it like a stab of reproach. She was depriving him of children. She was defective. No matter what the specialist said, she knew, with the awful Harper certainty, that it was her fault. Cam would've fertilised any other woman within seconds.

'It's my fault,' Cam said, surprising her out of her shame spiral.

'What?'

'I work too hard. Long hours. Stress.'

Gwen was too shocked to speak for a moment. Then she said, 'That's nonsense. Everything is fine, physically. You know that. You've got the slip of paper to prove it.'

Cam turned to her, looking wretched. 'Not on paper. It's like I'm not making room for a baby in our lives so one isn't going to come along. I know that sounds crazy, but what if I haven't wanted it as much as you have and that has somehow stopped it?'

Gwen went cold. 'You don't want a baby?'

'I want to be a dad. I want to have children. Definitely. But what if the universe can sense that I work too hard or something? Or...' Cam glanced away, embarrassed '...what if I've pissed off Mother Earth or something? I mean. If you tell me I have to paint myself green and dance around a tree, I'll do it. I'll do anything.'

'It doesn't work like that. This isn't either of our fault. And it isn't destiny or fate or the universe. It just happens.' In comforting Cam, Gwen felt the load lighten a little. She was right, she knew. This wasn't because of blood magic or hexing or any of it. This was just life. She reached for Cam and pulled him to her; his head fitted onto her chest. She wrapped her arms around him and stroked his hair chemically while he cried.

ACROSS TOWN, Katie was taking a tea break and staring

at her new most favourite thing in the world when Zofia walked into the staff room. 'What is that?'

Katie quickly put the cloth back over the sphere. 'Nothing. Just an ornament.'

Zofia reached out and flipped the material back. 'Oh.' She sat back on her heels. 'That is good news.'

'What is?'

'You have a trap. That is very lucky. You should put that in your home. Although—' Zofia glanced around the room '—maybe keeping it here might be best. Here is very bad.'

'What do you mean "trap"?'

Zofia put her head on one side. 'You know that's a witch's ball?'

'Yes, that's what the label said.' Katie showed Zofia. 'It's an antique.'

'They trap evil spirits. I've seen glass ones before. You hang them in a window or a doorway, somewhere like that.'

'Like a dream catcher?'

Zofia shrugged. 'I don't know why you'd want to catch dreams. But bad spirits, yes, please.'

Katie nodded. 'I couldn't agree with you more. Do you know how it works? It's a bit big to carry around with me, but—'

'I don't know,' Zofia said. 'I think it just does. If you just have it near, it can draw them. Like a magnet.'

'Thank you,' Katie said. 'I know you probably think I'm mad, but—'

'Not mad,' Zofia said. 'I'm glad to see you have this. I'm glad you're taking this seriously. He doesn't.'

Katie knew she meant Patrick Allen.

'There are evil spirits here,' Zofia said. 'We all need to be careful.'

'They're not all evil,' Katie said, thinking of Violet.

Zofia blew air over her lips, making a disgusted face. 'They're not supposed to be here.'

'Do you know how we could get rid of them?'

Zofia pulled a face. 'My grandmother would know. She's very wise. Knows about Wila. Spirits.'

She gave Katie a shrewd look. 'She'd be able to help you. I think you have more to fear than most of us — am I right?'

Katie swallowed. 'Maybe. Or maybe I'm luckier than everyone else. I can talk to them. I can see them. I'm hoping I can help them.'

Zofia shook her head. 'You can't help evil spirits. Only banish. That's what my grandmother would say.'

'Does she know how to do it?'

'Oh, yes. She'd have this tidied up—' Zofia snapped her fingers '—like that.'

Katie felt her hope rising, but she kept it in check long enough to ask, 'Is she in Poland?'

Zofia nodded.

Katie's heart sank.

'But I can email her.'

'Would you?'

Zofia patted her arm. 'Of course.'

KATIE LOOKED for Violet in every public room of the hotel. The place had filled up with MOPs and The Plum Suite had a 'Do Not Disturb' sign hung on the door handle. Katie hoped, for their sake, that Violet wasn't in residence. She went outside to check by the pond and then wandered around the gardens.

She found Violet in the walled garden. The borders

were a little overgrown, but in a very attractive manner with blowsy summer blooms tumbling over one another and butterflies dotting the shrubbery. Katie looked at the different colours of roses, visible through Violet's body, and breathed in the mix of floral scents.

'I can't smell them,' Violet said, turning slowly. 'I've been standing here for hours and I can't smell a thing. Not the grass, not the flowers, not even my perfume. Why is that?'

'I'm sorry. I don't know,' Katie said. 'But I have got something to tell you.'

She took a deep breath, hoping her news wasn't going to be like a rose. She wanted to give Violet soft petals and happiness, no nasty hidden thorns.

'Are you getting married?' Violet clapped her hands together.

'What? No.'

'Oh, you were staring at the flowers. I thought you were planning your bouquet.'

Katie shook her head. 'Henry's here,' she said, and then mentally kicked herself. *Nice gentle way to break the news. Really smooth.*

Violet had gone very still but Katie could tell she was upset by the way she had floated upwards and was now suspended at least a foot above the lawn. 'He's dead?'

'Um, yes. I'm afraid so.'

'But he's like me? And he's here?' Hope and pain were fighting it out across Violet's face. 'Why can't I see him? Is he with us now?'

Katie shook her head. 'No. He's usually in the library. I don't know why you can't see each other. I think it's something to do with how and when you died, but I'm not sure.'

'It's not fair,' Violet said. 'What did I do? What did I do that was so terrible?' She sank down to the grass and sat cross-legged, looking even younger than usual. She passed a hand across her face and looked up at Katie with an expression of frustration. 'I should be crying but I can't—'

'I think I can bring you together,' Katie said. 'If that's what you want.'

Violet unfolded from her position and twirled in the air by way of an answer. Violet was moving so fast, she was just a blur and it made Katie feel sick. She closed her eyes and felt a brush of cold lips on her cheek.

'I take it that's a "yes, please",' Katie said to the empty garden.

Inside the hotel, Max was polishing the bar with a cloth with more force than was strictly necessary. 'Why is he still here?'

'Who?' Katie turned around and spotted Barton sitting at a table in the corner, reading a newspaper. 'Oh. Patrick has offered him another show. Popular demand, apparently. He's doing it on Friday night and Patrick is putting him up for free until afterwards.'

'Can't you stop him?'

'Patrick? Unlikely,' Katie said.

Max was still glaring at Barton, anger and something else across his face.

Katie reached out and put her hand on top of his. 'I know he bothers you, but it might not be all bad. Maybe he comforts some people.'

'With lies,' Max said.

'I'm not defending him.' Katie squeezed his hand. 'Just trying to lower your blood pressure.'

Max made a visible attempt to relax. He passed a hand over his face. 'I'm fine.'

'Do you want to talk about it?' Katie said. 'I'll buy you a beer?'

'I'm working,' Max said, but he got a bottle from the fridge and popped the cap.

Katie hoisted herself onto one of the bar stools. 'What did Barton tell you that was so awful?'

Max took a long pull on his beer and for a moment Katie thought he wasn't going to answer her. Then he closed his eyes and said, 'I tried to get him to take it back. I went to his room after the show and I asked him straight.'

'And did he?'

Max gave her a bitter smile. 'He said I needed a private session. Only two hundred quid for an hour.'

'What a bastard.' Katie glanced at Barton, who was still reading, oblivious. 'I hope you spat in his drink.'

He tilted the beer towards Katie and she shook her head. 'You know he's a fraud, though.' Katie put a hand on Max's arm. 'Why do you need him to take it back? Or prove he's lying or whatever?'

'I didn't say it was logical. I know he's lying, that he just got a lucky hit, but there's that little bit of doubt.' He lowered his voice. 'And now I know that ghosts exist, it makes it all so much more possible. Afterlife. Messages from beyond the grave, all that.'

Katie wanted to ask him what Barton had told him, but she was afraid he'd say, 'It's personal,' again.

He read her mind. 'I know you must be curious—'

'It's okay, you don't have to talk about it.'

Max looked relieved. 'Thank you.'

Damn it. Maybe Anna was right: maybe it was time she took a leap of faith. If she opened up to him, maybe he'd do the same back. Gwen had told her once that when a client was being hesitant about explaining a problem, she shared something personal or embarrassing first. Like swapping vulnerabilities. Like making a deal. 'I know what it's like to be lied to. There was a woman who talked me into trusting her. She said she was going to show me how to harness my power, make me strong like Gwen.' Katie swallowed. 'She showed me just enough magic so that I believed her, showed me how to do things.'

Max was leaning on the bar, nodding. 'She gave you what you wanted. Perfect con.'

'And then she tried to kill me. Nearly succeeded, too.'

'Jesus,' Max said, straightening up. 'You mean that metaphorically, right?'

Katie swallowed and shook her head.

Patrick sailed up to the bar and Max swiped his beer off the top.

'Where's Housekeeping?' Patrick said, not even bothering to look up from the tablet he was carrying.

'Zofia?' Max said. 'Behind you.'

'Ah, good.' Patrick tapped at his gadget a couple more times, then frowned at Zofia. 'I've just had another complaint. Mrs Thomas in The Blue Room says her bed wasn't made today.'

Zofia shook her head. 'I did that room. I made all the rooms.'

'What's wrong?' Katie stepped in front of Zofia.

'This is unacceptable,' Patrick continued hectoring Zofia over Katie's head. 'People expect a certain level of service and if you're unable or unwilling to provide that service—'

'She did the room,' Katie said. 'She just told you.'

'This isn't like the good old days. There's the

Internet now. People go on their computers and write bad reviews that the world and his wife can read.'

'So, give Mrs Thomas a free meal or a spa treatment or something.'

Patrick finally seemed to notice Katie. 'I thought you were looking into this?'

'I am,' Katie said. 'Did you check the room?'

'Look for yourself,' Patrick said and marched away.

'Sorry,' Katie said to Zofia. 'Just ignore him.'

Upstairs, Katie knocked on the door of The Blue Room to make sure it wasn't occupied and then used the master key to go inside. There was a suitcase on the luggage rack, a few personal items on the bedside tables and desk and the curtains were open. Sunlight streamed onto the unmade bed. Sheets were tangled on the floor, the blanket scrunched up at the foot of the bed and what looked like a toaster-full of crumbs on the bottom sheet.

Katie crossed her arms. 'Violet! Come out here right now!'

A waft of Chanel No.5 and a dramatic drop in temperature gave her away.

'Where I can see you,' Katie said, using her strictest tone.

Violet glided out from the en-suite bathroom with a studied look of innocence on her face.

'What have you got against poor Zofia?' Katie indicated the bed. 'She's the one who catches trouble for this stuff, you know.'

'Nothing,' Violet said. 'Although I don't know why you care so much. Maids are all the same. Sneaky.'

Katie closed her eyes. *Of course.* 'Did a maid tell your father about Henry?'

Violet tossed her hair. 'She spied on us then went

running to him. She got Henry sent away. Father wouldn't even let me write to him. It was awful.'

'I'm sure it was,' Katie said.

'I trusted her,' Violet said. 'I confided in her and she betrayed me.' Violet looked anguished and Katie felt the stab of betrayal in her own heart.

'But you mustn't punish Zofia. It's not her fault.'

'You won't let me have any fun.' Violet pouted. 'And I'm dead. It's not fair.'

'Vi—'

'Fine.' Violet curtseyed, holding out the skirt of her dress. 'Your wish is my command.'

'Are you talking to a ghost right now?' Patrick emerged from behind the door, which Katie had left open out of habit. He'd followed her upstairs, had been listening in the hallway.

Katie looked at Violet. 'No.'

'You were,' Patrick said. 'You said "Violet". Is that Violet Beaufort? The girl who was murdered?'

'I don't know what you mean.'

'Barton said he could sense a lot of energy here, but I didn't really believe him. This is brilliant, though.'

'I told you before. I'm not talking to any journalists.'

'What about ghost leading a ghost tour?'

Patrick wasn't listening to her, so Katie tried a different tack. 'Didn't you say the town council objected? What about Pendleford's traditional family values?'

'What could be more traditional than history?'

'Well, count me out,' Katie said. It was difficult not to glance in Violet's direction; she was plucking at Patrick's sleeve.

Patrick shivered. 'You know your future employment relies on this place staying open.'

Katie stepped up and looked Patrick straight in the eye. 'Don't threaten me. You have no idea what I can do.'

Violet put her arms around Patrick and Katie felt the coldness she knew would be enveloping him. She watched Patrick turn pale with great satisfaction. He turned and half ran down the hall, the fire door at the end slamming shut behind him.

'Fun!' Violet clapped her hands. 'Who else can we do?'

~

PATRICK AVOIDED Katie for the rest of her shift, which was just perfect. The bar was so busy that Max didn't have time to scowl at Barton any more and Anna finished early in the restaurant to go on a date with Nicolas, the cricket player.

'I'm so pleased for you,' Katie said, giving her a quick hug goodbye.

'You inspired me,' Anna said. 'You took a chance and now look at you. All loved up.'

'I wouldn't say that,' Katie said, trying not to smile.

'Oh, please,' Anna said. 'You dribble whenever you see Max and he can't take his eyes off you.'

'I don't dribble,' Katie said. 'That's slander. Does he really watch me?'

Anna pulled on her denim jacket and adjusted the collar. 'He doesn't just stare at you, he gets this really dopey expression. Like this.' Anna pulled a moony-eyed face.

'He does not,' Katie said, glowing all over.

At the end of her shift, Katie went to the freezer to liberate a couple of Fabs. Max joined her outside and

294

she filled him in on Violet's latest antics. She couldn't stop smiling, but Max was quiet.

'What?' Katie said.

'I don't understand. You and Violet are so friendly, why do you have to investigate her death? Why not just ask her what happened?'

'She says she doesn't remember,' Katie said. 'I don't know if she just doesn't want to talk about it or if she really doesn't—'

'So she's lying to you? And you wonder why I don't want you to trust them—'

'She's frightened, I think. Or maybe she really can't remember. It was a long time ago.'

'I think she'd remember her death. It's pretty important.'

'The dead seem to have a different concept of what's important. You'd be surprised.'

He didn't know Violet the way she did; he didn't understand. Violet was trapped and bored as a ghost and she'd been trapped and bored when she was alive, too. She deserved to live.

Max put his hands on the tops of Katie's arms near her shoulders. They were hot but dry and she felt the shock of his touch right down to her toes. Max put his face close to hers. 'Don't you think that's an even better reason not to trust them?'

Katie tried to focus on his words, tried not to get distracted by his nearness, by the feel of his hands on her skin. He was holding her firmly, not gripping, but she could see the tension in his arms. The muscles were standing out and the sleeves of his T-shirt had ridden up, exposing a line of lighter skin.

'I know you like Violet,' he was saying, 'but she's dead. At the very least she's got this whole other perspective, something we can't imagine. I mean, maybe life doesn't seem all that important to her any more, or maybe it does. I don't know. You don't know. That's what I'm saying. We. Don't. Know.'

'If I can help her, then I should.'

'I know you believe that, but you have to stay safe, too.'

'Believe me, that's always been my view. My priority. But I'm sick of being scared.'

'I get that,' Max said, gently. 'I really do. And I know you like Violet.'

'It's more than that.'

'You don't have to prove anything. Not to me. Not to anyone. You can just walk away.'

'It's not that simple.' There were whispers in every shadow; the suggestion of a face was looking through the window — it had been getting clearer and clearer the whole time Max had been speaking. Spirits seemed to be everywhere she turned, getting stronger and louder by the moment.

'We could go away,' Max was saying. 'Together. Just for a while.'

'Maybe,' Katie said. She tried to focus on his face, but she felt very cold. The hairs were standing up along her arms.

'I think a break would—' Max broke off. 'Are you okay? You've gone really white—'

'Headache,' Katie managed. A shape rose out of the concrete floor and the flickering image of a woman ran through Katie, filling her with a paralysing ice.

'Do you want a tablet?'

'Please,' Katie said, trying to sound normal, trying not to alarm Max. 'And a glass of water.'

'I'll be right back,' Max said and disappeared into the hotel.

'Find my baby,' a deep voice, like a woman who had been smoking cigars for the last hundred years, and then another 'help' and another and another.

Katie curled into a ball on the floor. She wasn't sure how long she'd been there, hours or minutes. She wrapped her arms around her head and tried to block out the voices that were coming from all around. She couldn't make out the words any more; it was just a babble of different tones. There were screams, too, one getting louder and higher pitched. Somewhere, at the edge of the noise but still, somehow, achingly clear was a newborn's thin and heart-wrenching cry.

Katie was crying, now; she couldn't stop the tears falling and she couldn't stop the voices. She had her fingers wedged so tightly into her ears that they hurt but it didn't help. The boundary between her and the voices seemed blurred. It was as if they were screaming inside her head.

She didn't realise that she was rocking, or that she was making sounds of her own, but she felt a shaking of her shoulder. She jerked up and saw Henry reaching down for her. He put his hands on her head and she jerked away. He came forwards, his hands out and Katie scrabbled backwards, pure instinct driving her from beneath the pain and terror.

'I can help,' Henry said. At least she thought that was what he said. She watched his lips move and heard him, just barely. Darkness was edging in around her vision and she felt her old terror of passing out. She was not going to be helpless. She was not going to let the darkness take her. She couldn't think coherently enough to know why, but she just felt that inner steel, the same thing that stopped her from having more than one beer, the voice in her head that told her she had to stay alert, in control.

The pain was a band around her temples and it was squeezing tighter and tighter, the voices just an incoherent roar. *In a moment my head is going to pop like a ripe mango.* The thought was horribly clear. She let Henry put his hands on her. He took her hands from her ears and replaced them with his own. His palms softly cupped her ears, his fingers ran underneath her hair at the back of her neck and, for once, the icy touch of a lost soul felt like a balm. The voices faded almost instantly. Katie caught a couple more separate voices again and then, blissfully, they went quiet.

She gazed into Henry's pale eyes, willing the miracle to stick. It did. The quiet was so absolute that she became aware of the sound of her own ragged breath.

'Better?' Henry spoke quietly.

Katie swallowed. 'Yes. Thank you.'

He moved away, then, and Katie closed her eyes, expecting another onslaught. Nothing.

Katie sat back on her heels and pressed her palms over her eyes. She could see flashing lights. Perhaps she was getting a migraine. Anna had described hers once and they'd begun with fuzzy vision and ended with intense pain.

'What was that?'

'At a guess,' Henry said, 'you're not in control of your own power.'

That was wearingly familiar. 'It's not my fault.'

'I didn't say it was your fault. It'll be your funeral, though.'

Katie took her hands away and looked at Henry.

He looked completely calm. 'Are you trying to frighten me?'

'I don't think I need to do anything. Surely you can see that, long term, hearing the voices of every echo and fragment of every person who has felt strongly enough to leave some kind of trace on this world is not a tenable position.'

'Not tenable. I think my head is about to split open.' I thought I was going to die.

'Precisely.'

'You stopped it, though.' Katie tried to sound appropriately grateful, rather than terrified and angry. 'How did you do that?'

'I've had a lot of time to practise and it seems that my unfortunate position is not without its own abilities.'

'Can you help me?'

Henry smiled. 'Absolutely. But there is something I want you to do for me in return.'

'You won't do it out of the goodness of your heart?'

'Not really my style, I'm afraid,' Henry said. 'But I can show you how to control your power. You'll never need to be scared again.'

'What do you want?'

'I want a friend.'

Katie opened her mouth to say that she was already Henry's friend, but he pre-empted her.

'Not you, dear girl. A friend like me.'

'A ghost.'

'Precisely. I don't want to be alone any more.' Henry looked embarrassed and a little forlorn and Katie felt her heart clench in sympathy. But still. 'I don't know how to give you what you want. You all seem to exist in different, like, dimensions or something.

Were you with anyone when you died? Maybe I could find them and if they're linked somehow—'

'I think you're the key.'

'What?'

'To linking. I think I'd be able to cross over to another dimension if you, shall we say, invite me.'

'And how would I do that?'

'As I say, I think you're a key. I think you open the doors between the different planes of existence. In fact, you're like a skeleton key — you fit everyone's lock and that's why you can hear us all.'

'I still don't see how—'

'If I step inside you, then I think I'll be able to talk to the other ghosts who can talk to you. You'll be a conduit.'

'But you can't stay inside me for ever,' Katie said, horrified. 'You'll be back to square one afterwards.'

'I don't think so. I think you can hold me and another soul inside at the same time. We'll become linked because we'll occupy the same dimensional space. You.' He smiled. 'Temporarily, of course.'

'And then you'll, what, step out of me again?'

'Naturally. If we do it at the same time, then I'm hoping we'll still be linked.'

'Will that work?'

'I have no idea, but I think it's well worth a try.'

'And you swear you'll leave me again?' Katie couldn't believe she was considering it. The idea was abhorrent. Awful.

'It would just be for a moment,' Henry said. 'Then I'll never trouble you again.'

Katie felt a stab of guilt. 'You're not troubling me,' she said. 'I really do think of you as a friend, you know.'

'That's kind,' Henry said. 'But I must face facts.

You'll leave this place, your life will take you onwards, and then I'll be alone again.'

'I could take you with me. If I could work out what you're anchored to, I could maybe move it, give you more freedom.'

'But you'll grow old and die and I'll still be me. Same age. Same Henry. Still alone. Besides…' He hesitated. 'Now I know that Violet's here I won't rest until I see her again.'

Katie swallowed. 'You know about Violet?'

'I heard you talking to your friend.' Henry wagged a finger. 'You should've told me. Naughty girl.'

'I was going to,' Katie said, wondering what the hell Violet saw in Henry. He was unbelievably arrogant. 'I was waiting for the right moment.'

Henry spread his hands. 'I believe we've found it. You give me what I want and I'll help you control your awkward little psychic gift. I'll make sure you're never troubled again.' He was moving towards her and Katie took a step back. 'Imagine the peace and quiet.'

'Let me think about it.'

'Of course.' Henry gave a small smile. 'I've got all the time in the world.'

Max came back with a box of paracetamol and a pint glass of cold water. Katie swallowed two tablets and half the water.

'Do you believe me, now?' Max said. 'You need a break from this place. I'm going to take you home and you're going to have a good night's sleep and then tomorrow we're going somewhere. Anywhere. How about the Lake District? Or Cornwall? Ireland?'

'You're taking me on a mini break.'

Max managed a tense little smile. 'It's for your own good.'

'You said you'd help,' Violet said. She floated towards Katie, her eyes wide, arms outstretched, looking more ghoul-like than she ever had before.

'I know,' Katie said. 'And I will. I just need a bit of time.'

'Is she here now?' Max was squinting in Violet's direction. 'You see. They don't leave you alone for a moment.'

'I'm not bothering Katie,' Violet said, indignant.

'Hang on,' Max said. He squinted in Violet's direction. 'I think I can see something. It's like heat haze. The air is kind of shimmering.'

Katie looked at Violet. She could smell burned matches and an undertone of Chanel No.5. The light was catching off the stones in Violet's headband and her dress moved as if blown by a draught. She reached out and touched Violet's fingertips. There was a crackle of energy, like an electrical current jumping from Katie to Violet, and she snatched her hand away.

'Christ.' Max stumbled backwards. 'I saw her.'

'That's interesting,' Katie said. She was rubbing her fingers. They felt hot, almost singed.

'I just saw a ghost,' Max said. 'A real ghost. Fucking fuck.'

'Is he talking about me?' Violet said. 'His language is appalling.'

The scent of cigar smoke gave Henry away a few seconds before he appeared. 'What are you doing?'

'Chatting to Violet. I think I'm making her stronger.' Katie felt as if something very important had happened but it was hard to concentrate with Henry and Violet and Max all near her.

'She's here?' The sudden need in his face was heartbreaking. 'Tell her I love her.'

'Henry's here,' Katie said to Violet. 'He says he loves you.'

Violet clasped her hands to her chest and smiled, tears shining in her eyes. 'Tell him I love him for ever.'

'Right-oh,' Katie said, but Max had hold of her arm, pulling her close. He put both hands on her cheeks and made her look at him. He was pale, his lips thin. 'I just saw a ghost.'

'Violet. Yes.'

'Did you tell him, yet?' Violet said, her voice close.

'Just a sec,' Katie said. Looking into Max's eyes, she said, 'Are you okay?'

'I will be.' He let his hands drop as if suddenly realising that he'd been touching Katie. 'Sorry.'

'It's okay. It's a shock.' She couldn't help adding. 'I did tell you.'

'I know. And I believed you. I thought I believed you. I just—' He stopped. 'It's a shock.'

'What's more interesting is why did me touching Violet make her solid enough for you to see?'

'I think we should go to the pub,' Max said. 'Right now.'

'Okay,' Katie said. 'If that's what you feel like doing...' Honestly, show a man evidence of the afterlife and all he wanted to do was go and play pool and drink beer. She really didn't know anything about the opposite sex.

Max practically carried her out of the hotel, he was so desperate to get out. Once they were in Katie's car and almost at the centre of Pendleford, he said, 'Shall I show you the museum?'

'I thought you wanted to go to the pub?'

'That was just the first thing that came into my head. There were ghosts around. I wasn't thinking straight.' He looked at her. 'Why are you so calm?'

'I've had time to get used to it.' *And I'm not that calm.*

'That's not it,' Max said, staring at her with eyebrows raised. 'Back in the beginning, when that table was flying around the bar—' He stopped. 'Was that real, then? Christ.'

Katie concentrated on parking the car. It was strange to be described as calm. She always felt such an insecure mess inside.

'How are you not freaking out?'

Katie applied the handbrake and turned to face Max. 'You know I told you that my family has certain abilities? It's more than that, really. It's like having a totally different way of seeing the world. Once you know that magic exists, that people can be cursed or cured with words, it colours everything. You can't help seeing magic in everything around you.'

'That's just like conning,' Max said. He held up a hand to stop Katie interrupting. 'Not that I'm saying your stuff is dishonest — it's just that when you've been brought up to grift, you see it everywhere. It changes the way you see things. Situations. People. Everything.'

Katie nodded. 'You can't switch it off. If there's a plane crash on the news, I wonder if the pilot was hexed—'

'And if I see a total bastard waving wads of cash around, I get an itch to relieve him of it.' He looked at her carefully. 'Did you just say "magic"?'

'What else do you call the ability to find lost things, to know what a person needs, to tell fortunes, to stop an argument with some herbs, to—?'

He reached out and cupped her cheek. 'Magic and ghosts. Okay.'

'Okay?' Katie said. 'Just like that?'

He leaned across and kissed her quickly. 'Just like that.'

Katie grabbed the front of his T-shirt and hauled him back for a proper kiss. She was definitely getting better at it. She was able to shut her mind off for whole seconds at a time. She opened her eyes and watched his eyelids and eyelashes close up, the pores of his skin, felt the slight scrape of his stubble on her cheek.

Max pulled away. 'I lost you again, didn't I?'

'No,' Katie lied.

'You think too much,' he said and got out of the car.

'That's impossible,' Katie said, following him.

The museum was just as tiny as Max described. It occupied the bottom floor of a small Tudor house, up a narrow cobbled street. The house was packed in by cottages on either side, which almost seemed to be holding up its sagging walls. The half-timbered façade was bowing outwards, and the roof looked as if it was going to come down at any moment. There was a small printed card in the bottom pane of one of the small windows. It had faded in the sun, but up close Katie could read the words 'Pendleford Folk Museum. Open Daily. Ring Bell'.

The woman who answered the door wasn't as old as Max had described. Maybe only in her eighties or nineties. She had white hair and was dressed in moss-green tweed. She led them to a surprisingly bright and modern-looking exhibition and then shuffled off in what appeared to be tweed slippers.

Katie scanned the printed boards, skimming over the history of Pendleford as a Roman settlement, through Saxon times, to its prosperous seventeenth-century years as part of the textile industry. She was caught by an image of a weaver's cottage, realising that it was familiar to her as the crystal shop on Silver Street.

'Over here.' Max pointed to a board dedicated to the Beaufort family. It described the history of the Beaufort estate, rehashing the information Katie had already cribbed from the Internet. Next to it was a glass-fronted cabinet with the letters Max had photographed. The display read, 'The mysterious disappearance of an heiress'.

Violet Beaufort was an enigma even before her mysterious disappearance in 1937. A socialite heiress with a penchant for archaeology, she is known to have taken a great personal interest in the Neolithic excavations at nearby Avebury and Windmill Hill.

When she first went missing, it was widely assumed that she had eloped with Alexander James, a wealthy Yorkshire businessman who was conducting the archaeological digs, some of the first of their kind in Britain. Love letters (fig. 1-5) from Alexander seem to bear this out, although the couple must have left Britain as there are no recorded sightings of either one after July, 1937.

Some locals still believe that something more sinister occurred and that a police investigation was hushed up and, perhaps, even cut short, by Lord Beaufort, who was mindful of the family's reputation and wished to avoid further scandal.

'Have you asked yourself why there aren't any letters from Violet?'

Katie looked at Max. 'She didn't love Alexander, she loved Henry. She told me—'

'Okay,' Max said, 'but why aren't there letters between her and Henry? Why isn't Henry mentioned in any of the news stories?'

Katie shrugged. 'Violet's affair with Henry was secret. They just did a good job of keeping it that way.'

'But she must've been murdered. Don't you think it would've come out during the investigation?'

'Don't say that. Maybe she eloped with Henry. Maybe she can't tell me how she died because she really can't remember. Maybe she lived a long and happy life in America and died in her sleep aged eighty and the Violet I know is just an echo of her younger self or something. Why does it have to be murder?'

'Hey, I'm not the bad guy. I'm just pointing out the most likely scenario.'

'Well, don't.' Katie knew she was being ridiculous but she liked Violet. She knew she had to work out what happened to her, but at the same time she simply didn't want to know.

'I just don't see why you're so quick to trust them.'

Katie's hand flew to her necklace. 'I'm not.'

Max was clearly frustrated, but Katie couldn't come up with an answer that would make him happy. Unless she lied.

'I'm out of options,' she said.

'What makes you think you can trust Henry?'

'We've been over this,' Katie said. Her head was pounding again and she wanted to lie on the sofa in the quiet of the library, not argue with Max.

'And you're still not listening. These things are dead. They are echoes or spirits or whatever, but they're not even people any more.'

'They're inside my head,' Katie said. 'It's like the top layers of my skin have been peeled back and I'm feeling everything all the time. I can't go on. I'm tired. I'm so bloody tired.'

'I know.' Max reached for her. 'I know. I'm sorry. I wish I could do something. Can I do something?' He looked so sweet and earnest and Katie leaned against him, feeling a rush of gratitude that he was there. She couldn't believe she used to think he looked predatory. He was always watching, always calculating, but he had been trained that way. It wasn't his fault.

'Please, hold off,' he said, speaking into the top of her head. 'Just give us a bit more time to research this stuff. Talk to that woman, Hannah, again. Talk it through with Gwen.'

'Okay,' Katie said. 'Another few days won't do any harm. Violet's waited this long.'

Katie had been hoping to sit somewhere quiet with Max for five minutes before her shift started and do some serious kissing. She felt in need of a boost and kissing Max was like being plugged into a car battery. In a good way. The scent of pipe smoke told her that wasn't going to happen. *Shouldn't have arranged to meet in the library. Stupid.*

'You are making me stronger,' Henry said. 'I can feel it. I'm more connected. I can see more.'

'That's nice,' Katie said, still thinking about how much she wanted to kiss Max. She wanted Henry to go. She wanted to be alone with Max and have just a couple of minutes to herself, then his words sank in. 'Wait a minute. What do you mean "connected"? To this world or the spirit world?'

'Both,' Henry said, looking smug. 'I'm hearing all kinds of things. For example, has your young man told you why he wanted to connect to the other side?'

'Max? A medium told him there was a message for him. He didn't really believe it, but these things can get stuck in your mind, you know—'

'Was the message from a young lady of his acquaintance?'

'I don't know,' Katie said, her stomach suddenly cold. 'What do you know?'

Henry waved a hand. 'I would say lover.' He rolled the word around his mouth, as if he was enjoying himself. 'These days, I believe the term is "girlfriend".'

'Max wanted a message from his girlfriend?' Katie said.

'What girlfriend?' Max walked in, wearing his black work shirt and a name badge.

'Henry's here.' Katie moved closer to the ghost. She felt the coldness of Henry, but pictured light filling her, warming her up, and she felt a little less chilled. Maybe Hannah was right. If she held onto the light, she could get close to the ghosts, help them, without passing out. That would be nice.

Max stared to the left of Katie, then shook his head. 'Can't see him. Maybe if I—' He screwed up his eyes into a squint and tilted his head to one side.

'He killed her.' Henry's voice was flat with none of his usual teasing tone.

Katie felt the energy rush out of her. Henry seemed taller suddenly. 'What?'

'Ask him,' Henry said.

'No.' Katie shook her head. 'No.'

'What's wrong?' Max stopped squinting.

'You're lying,' Katie said.

'Are you talking to me or him?' Max took a step towards her and Katie took a step back. 'He says you killed your girlfriend.'

The colour went out of Max's face. After a long, horrible moment, he said, 'Did Laura tell him that? Is she—?'

'You're not denying it.' Katie took another step, edging towards the doorway. Fear was thumping through her now. She was such an idiot. No intuition. No clue on who to trust. He'd told her he was dodgy but she hadn't believed him. Hadn't wanted to believe him. Had been seduced by his nice voice and lopsided smile and warm eyes. She'd listened to Lily Thomas, trusted her, and now she'd made the same mistake all over again. Another step.

'It was an accident,' Max said, very quietly. So quietly that Katie almost didn't hear him. There was a roaring in her ears but her mind felt frozen solid. As if it had shut down.

'I have to go.' Katie stumbled out of the room. She ran through the hallway and out of the front door. Outside, the air was like soup. The mugginess of the last day had intensified. Katie dragged in warm breaths, trying to calm her heart, trying to think clearly. She wasn't a kid, any more. She wasn't helpless. Max wasn't going to hurt her. Apart from anything else, they were in a hotel. A very public place. She would get Anna or Jo or even Patrick to tell him to leave and she wouldn't even have to see him again. Not ever.

The light had gone strange. Filmic. Katie half expected to see floodlights and cameras. The colours of the garden were saturated, the edges of everything clearly defined, making it look hyper real or like a painted backdrop. There was a roll of thunder some- where far off and fat rain drops began to fall. The weather was finally breaking. And then the rain got heavier and she realised she was getting drenched.

'Katie. Can I talk to you?' Max was there. Of course he was.

'No,' Katie said. She walked past him and ducked

into the large porch. Through the glass panels of the front door, she could see Anna step behind Reception. She could open the door and ask her to phone the police. Max was a thief and a liar and, maybe, a killer.

'Please.' He reached out as she walked past and she turned, feeling fury thump through her body.

'This is not a rom com. This is not the bit when we stand in the rain and you make a speech and make everything all right.'

'Laura.' Max swallowed. 'It was an accident. I was driving. It was dark and the road was really wet and we were arguing. It was three years ago and I've felt terrible ever since. When Barton said he had a message for me, from Laura, it hit me hard. I didn't believe him but I wanted to believe him — you know that feeling when—'

'You lied to me.' Katie held onto her pendant, feeling the reassuring shape of the bone die, the sharp point of the silver feather.

'I didn't.' Max shook his head. 'I have never lied to you.'

Katie opened her mouth in amazement. The man had nerve; she had to hand it to him.

'Never,' Max said. 'I told you I crashed that wedding when we first met. I told you I hustled poker. I told you I was brought up to con. That I was a grifter. You just didn't believe me.'

'I believe you now.'

'I have never lied. I might not have given you every single detail, but—'

'Laura is a pretty big detail.'

'I know,' Max said. 'But I told you I wanted to prove Barton was a fraud and that was the truth. I told you I didn't agree with what he did and that was also true. I told you there was a personal reason I was turning over a new leaf. All true.'

Katie felt wet on her face. She wiped the tears away with the heels of her hands. Part of her knew that this was true, that what he was saying made sense, but she felt as if an empty cavern had opened up inside her. She was hollowed out. 'I told you,' Katie said. 'I told you what happened to me. I trusted you.'

'I know.' Max looked stricken. 'But you can trust me. I swear, you can trust me.'

Katie wrapped her arms around herself. 'Stay away from me.'

Max's face crumpled and Katie couldn't stand that, either. 'Just for a bit. I just need——'

'Whatever you want.' Max's voice was dull.

Katie pushed through the front door, letting it swing shut behind her.

CHAPTER 28

Across town in End House, Gwen lay in Cam's arms and waited for her breathing to return to normal. Cam stretched against her, curling one arm to bring her closer. Ever since the solstice she'd felt lighter. She hadn't cursed Katie, so maybe she hadn't cursed herself either. She wasn't at peace with the idea of not having children, never would be, but the dark lens that had clouded her vision over the last few months had finally lifted. And there was Cam. Sweet, loving, steady, funny, Cam. He'd just been patiently loving her, the way he always had, waiting for her to come back to him.

'I'm so lucky,' she said. She felt she could see clearly again. Maybe even start to see the joy in life again.

'Yes,' Cam said, kissing her.

'I don't think we should ever leave this bed,' Gwen said, kissing him back.

'I agree.' His stomach gurgled. 'Although we should've packed a picnic.'

'Okay, we'll raid the kitchen and then we'll never get out of bed again. Ever.'

'Does that mean you'll never get dressed? Because I'm in favour of that.'

'Never ever.'

'And I don't have to go to the office?'

'Nope.'

He smiled into her mouth. 'And we'll just make love?'

'All the time,' Gwen said, snuggling closer.

'And cuddle.'

She smiled back. 'And sleep.'

'And do the crossword on Sundays.'

'Do you think the paper boy can be persuaded to deliver to the bedroom—?' Gwen stopped. 'What's that?' The wind had been howling with the storm that had finally broken, but the noise that she'd thought was branches being knocked against the windows sounded more like someone thumping on the back door. She sat up and retrieved her bra from the foot of the bed, then went searching for her discarded sundress.

Cam sat up. 'What happened to not getting out of bed?'

Gwen hurried downstairs as thunder rolled around the house.

Hannah Ash was standing on the back step, drenched. Her blue shirt was sodden and stuck to her body and her headscarf had slipped. 'Is Katie here?'

'What's wrong?'

Gwen stood back to let Hannah into the kitchen.

'I was doing some research. In the family archive.'

Gwen bit down the urge to hurry Hannah, didn't want to interrupt and have her start at the beginning again. She was one of those people who had a certain number of words in their head and they had to get every single one out, no matter what.

'When I have a message like I had for Katie I don't usually think about it again. You know what it's like. But there's something about your niece—'

Gwen dug her fingernails into her palm. She could hear the door upstairs, Cam's footsteps on the landing.

'Well, I think I was wrong. I don't think she's a doorway.'

'What is she, then?'

'I think she's doing it. Bringing them to life.'

'Ghosts?'

'The light is Katie's life force and she's like a running tap. They're all drinking the water, so to speak, getting nice and strong.' Hannah shook her head. 'No. Tap isn't right. They don't run out.'

'Katie will run out? Her energy will run out?'

'I think it's possible. If she doesn't stop dishing it out, I'm worried what will happen.'

Gwen was already at the phone in the hallway, but the electricity was out and it didn't work. She used her mobile but the landline at The Grange was dead and Katie's phone went straight to voicemail. She hesitated, wondering which was quicker, walking or driving to The Grange, then sat down and pulled on her trainers.

'What is it?' Cam was in the doorway, fully dressed.

'Katie,' Gwen said. 'We need to tell her not to let the ghosts touch her.' She looked to Hannah for confirmation.

Hannah nodded. 'If they touch her, they can drain her that much quicker.'

Cam nodded and began lacing his walking boots. 'The paths are going to be rivers by now.' He grabbed waterproofs and they headed out into the pounding rain.

KATIE WALKED, zombie like, into the library. She wanted to be alone, but she didn't know where to go to avoid Henry and Violet; they could follow her anywhere. Barton and Patrick were sitting in the wing-back armchairs and Henry was in his favourite position by the fire. 'I'm sorry, dear girl,' he began and Katie held up a hand.

'Don't.'

The rain was sheeting down outside, now, and the windows were a blur of cascading water. There was a crack of lightning, followed closely by a deep rumble of thunder and the lights went out. 'Well, this is atmospheric,' Barton said.

'I'll find some candles,' Patrick said, getting up. 'How many guests do we have in at the moment?' Katie knew that Anna had stashed wind-up lanterns around the hotel last winter, that there was one behind the desk in Reception, so she went to fetch it.

Patrick followed her. 'Have you reconsidered my proposal? I would be very grateful—'

'No,' Katie said. 'The answer will always be no.'

Zofia was taking the main staircase. She had a carrier bag with a round object in it, which she tried to hide behind her back.

'That's mine,' Katie said.

'This is very bad,' Zofia said. 'These people—' she gestured around '—they will annoy the spirits. Who knows what will happen?'

'Oh, that's perfect,' Patrick said. 'The frightened maid. How do you feel about your photo going on the hotel website, Sophia?'

'Her name is Zofia. She's Polish,' Katie said, irritation with Patrick breaking through her sadness and confusion. Irritation felt good, so she went with it. 'And I told you to leave her alone.'

Patrick shook his head. 'You're so short-sighted.'

There was a bang from upstairs and a voice called, 'Hello? My television's stopped working.'

'Better check on the MOPs,' Katie said, sweetly. 'And cross your fingers the freezer doesn't defrost.'

'Oh, Christ,' Patrick said, and hurried away.

'It's okay,' Katie said to Zofia. 'I'm going to help them. You'll see there's nothing to be afraid of. They're just like us. Only—'

'No.' Zofia was backing away. 'You're a fool if you think that.'

'Please, Zofia. I promise it'll be fine. Trust me.'

'You need to use this,' Zofia said, flashing the carrier bag. 'My grandmother emailed me. All you have to do is hold it close and, as long as the spirit isn't anchored to anything else, they'll be drawn into the trap.'

Katie hesitated. What if reuniting Violet with her true love meant that she was no longer anchored here by the mystery of her death, or whatever was holding her? What if she got accidentally trapped in the witch's ball? 'Keep that away from me,' she told Zofia. 'Violet's my friend—'

'It is time?' Violet appeared in the doorway, just next to Zofia, who shivered and moved away.

Henry floated in the doorway to the library. 'Is she here? Is it time?'

The naked need on his face made up Katie's mind. Why not now? Why make them wait? The afterlife was like this life — you never knew what was going to happen, how much time you really had. Why should

Henry and Violet wait another moment for their happiness? *Someone* should get to be happy.

'Yes,' she said. Katie led the way into the library, letting Henry go ahead of her. It seemed rude to just walk through him. And a bit creepy.

Barton was still wedged in his armchair and Katie ignored him to focus on Violet.

She was so close to Henry it was odd to think they couldn't see each other. But then, most people couldn't see either of them.

'Did it just get cold in here?' Barton said, sitting forward.

'That'll be the ghosts,' Katie said. The irritation that she'd felt with Patrick ignited into full-blown fury in front of Barton's ignorance. 'You know. The sort you're supposed to be so attuned to.'

'Katie?' Violet said. 'Why are you shouting?'

'I'm not.' Katie made a supreme effort to focus. This wasn't about Barton lying to Max. Or even about her and Max.

'Are you sure about this?' Katie said to Violet. 'Anything could happen. You might pass over—'

'I'm ready,' Violet said. 'Besides, it'll be a change.' She smiled bravely at Katie. 'And I want to see him again, my dear Henry. If there's a possibility I could see him again, it's worth any risk.'

'Okay,' Katie said. There had been a part of her that hadn't been sure she was doing the right thing. She didn't trust Henry, her instincts told her that, but if Violet loved him, and that was her business, then she was doing a good thing. Reuniting the lost lovers. She was like the apothecary in *Romeo and Juliet*. Okay, that was a bad example.

'Are you ready?' Henry said. He looked hungry.

'Yes,' Katie said. She fixed Henry with her very best witchy look. 'I will hold you both for a couple of seconds, then you have to get out again. I'm trusting you.'

Henry nodded, impatient now. 'As you said before. I remember.'

Violet was bouncing up and down, so excited that she was forgetting to balance properly on the floor and her feet were floating a couple of inches above it. She looked so young.

Zofia grabbed Katie's hand. 'I don't like this.'

'It's fine,' Katie said, with more confidence than she felt.

'May we begin?' Henry floated closer to Katie, looking more ghost-like than he had for a while. Which was good, Katie told herself; it would be really weird for a completely solid-looking person to step inside her.

She was just wondering how it was going to work and whether she needed to reach out and pull him in or whether she should take hold of each of their hands at the same time, when Henry darted forward. In one moment he was directly in front of her, his chest uncomfortably close to her face, and the next moment, she was filled with ice.

'Are we starting, yet?' Violet said. Her voice seemed to be coming from very far away.

Katie opened her mouth to answer but found she couldn't. She tried to move, to raise a hand, to nod, even blink. Nothing. Panic rushed through her. She felt her heart trying to race, trying to beat faster, but it couldn't. It was beating slowly. She could hear it in her head, as if she were underwater.

Max opened the door to the library and, seeing

Barton, made to walk out again. She wanted to call out to him, but couldn't.

'It's okay,' he said. 'I know you don't want to speak to me.'

Katie wanted to shake her head, to ask him to stay, but she was too cold.

Max was standing next to Violet and she saw what a handsome couple they made. With that random thought, a flare of white-hot jealousy ignited in the front of her mind. Violet looked beautiful. Beautiful and as virginal as the day he'd seen her last. It was perfect. Joy was there now; a wild joy and a need to touch her, to speak to her, to be with her. To be with her the way he couldn't before. There had been people standing in their way before. People clouding Violet's mind, stopping her from seeing him. Well, she'd seen him now.

Katie realised that Henry was in the front of her mind. She was tucked somewhere at the back. As if she'd been pushed out of the service entrance in a restaurant and was hanging out by the bins. She wanted to giggle. That was a silly thought. Bins. Restaurants. Food. By God, she was hungry. Or was that Henry? She had to concentrate. If only it weren't so bloody *cold*.

'Hold my hand,' Katie said. She could feel her mouth and tongue moving to form the words, but it wasn't by her own volition. Then her arm was lifting, with great effort, like moving a branch of a tree.

'Are you okay?' Max was frowning at her. 'Katie?'

Her arm was stretching out to Violet, but at once she wanted to snatch it back. She wanted to warn Violet. This didn't seem like such a good idea after all. Although, it had been her idea. She needed to stay calm; it would be over soon. It was just the cold and the horrible pushed-out-of-her-own-head feeling. No need to panic.

Violet's hand was in hers. Henry clasped it tightly, gazed into her gentle brown eyes, and, finally, finally, pulled her to him.

Katie saw Violet's eyes widen. First in surprise and then fear and then they disappeared. Katie's corner, round the back of the restaurant, by the bins, shrank. She knew Violet was there, too. Somewhere tucked away but she couldn't see her.

'—thou art in heaven, hallowed be thy name, thy kingdom come, thy will be done—'

Violet's voice. Terrified. Crying. Reciting the Lord's Prayer.

Something was wrong.

'Katie? Speak to me? Are you sick? Has something happened?' Max's voice was there, but Katie had her eyes closed. She couldn't see. Henry had the eyes. Her eyes.

Katie stamped hard on her own panic, tried to think clearly. She remembered something: she and Max had worked out a system. A sign she could give him if things went wrong. The problem was, Katie wasn't in control of her body in order to give it. They hadn't thought of that.

Henry was thinking; she could hear him. He thought, I regret this, truly.

They walked out of the hallway and into the sheeting rain. Katie knew that they were heading for the pond, before Henry turned that way. She could hear Violet praying; she knew that Henry was walking to the pond to drown her.

'Why?' she asked him, silently.

'You're the door but in order for me to be with Violet, I need you to die.'

'You knew that all along.'

'Since we're sharing one mind, there's little point in my denying it.'

Katie struggled, but she couldn't stop her legs from moving. She watched the pond get closer and hoped that Max would do something. Surely, he'd know something was wrong.

Her body spun around, a flash of pain on her arm. Max had it in a grip, was facing them. 'What the hell are you doing?'

'Just needed some fresh air,' Henry said in Katie's voice. 'I feel a bit light-headed.'

'In the rain?' Max looked concerned. Not concerned enough, though.

'Help!' Katie shouted with her mind. She tried to force her eyes to convey anguish, to telegraph 'help me, I'm possessed' with her facial expression.

Henry sat on the low wall bordering the pond. He leaned down and Katie, fired with pure terror, put everything she could into stopping her body. It continued smoothly down, her face an inch above the surface.

'Oh, fuck,' Max said, his hair plastered against his head.

'—forgive us our trespasses—' said Violet.

'Don't struggle,' Henry said. He plunged them into the water. Shocking and cold. Katie felt it shoot up her nose and down her throat. 'Violent death. You'll probably hang around. Be an unquiet spirit. You'll live for ever.'

'I'll be dead for ever,' Katie said. 'Violet, stop praying. Help me. Stop Henry.'

'He's not Henry. He's a bad man,' Violet said, her voice little-girl and frightened. Katie felt despair. Violet was too far gone, too frightened. She couldn't stop Henry; she couldn't move her body. He was too strong.

Her body was jerked backwards. Air on her face. She tried to cough out the water, felt her body's natural instincts override Henry's determination and a waterfall spewed out of her mouth.

Max was pulling her backwards, she fell on top of him on the grass, but Henry was fighting back control. Then he went limp. He lifted his head and said, 'Max?' In a wavery tone. 'Oh, Max.'

Katie felt Max's arms around her. Saw him looking into her face. A flash of lightning illuminated his face into a circle of white. 'What happened? What the fuck was that?'

'He tried to kill me.' Henry was using a stuttering, frightened voice. It was Katie's frightened voice, echoed in her own mind, but they weren't her words.

Don't believe him, she urged Max. Don't listen. *It's Henry.*

'Jesus, you scared me. How could he do that?'

'Henry took over my body but he's gone now. I overpowered him.'

'Where's he gone?' Max was holding her tightly, looking around wildly as if a ghost were about to shout 'boo'. 'Where's Violet?'

Katie reached out to Violet, one trapped soul to another. She pictured herself patting Violet, telling her that everything was all right and that if she could just stop reciting the Lord's Prayer, then perhaps they could join forces and eject Henry from Katie's body. Regain control.

Katie felt Violet's thoughts. In an instant she knew it all. The man calling himself Henry was not Henry. He was the other man in that photograph, the archaeologist Alexander James. And Katie knew why Violet was so frightened. Alexander James had killed Violet. He'd drowned her in that pond in a jealous rage when she'd chosen Henry. He'd been so angry. That she'd chosen a mere lackey over him, a great historian, a man of money.

Her bones were lying in the bottom, amongst the silt and the stones and the slimy weeds. Katie felt Violet remembering that as if it were her own memory, big hands around her neck, the terror as she realised she couldn't take a breath and that Alexander wasn't going to stop, wasn't going to let go. Katie felt it all as if it had happened to her, not Violet, and she felt the pull of her bones down in the deep cold water. They were calling.

Violet was folding in on herself, getting smaller and weaker. 'He's going to kill me again,' she whispered. Her voice was quiet, just an itch at the back of her consciousness. But Katie's thoughts were cloudy. Had she dreamed that she was a girl called Katie, working as a waitress and living in a tiny flat? Or was she Violet Beaufort?

Katie felt herself being squeezed smaller; she wasn't sure any more whether she was Katie or Violet. It hardly mattered. Alexander was getting stronger and stronger and she was getting weaker. Katie blinked, tried to see out of her own eyes, see past the fear and the ice. The black water of the ornamental pond was being pelted with rain so that the surface was dancing. The black clouds shifted and the evening sun lit the water for a moment and Katie thought of the warm light. There was something important about the light. Something strong and comforting. She remembered her name. Katie Harper.

'Not murder, Violet.' Alexander was speaking out loud, with Katie's voice. 'I don't want to kill you, my love. I never meant to hurt you.'

The warm light of the sun was on her face, reminding Katie that she had light of her own. She reached inside and found the light, gathering and stretching it around her. Then, as she felt a little stronger, she pictured breaking a tiny piece off and giving it to the form she knew was Violet's soul, feeding it like a baby bird.

'We can be together, for ever.' Alexander was still talking with Katie's voice. 'I was angry before but that's all in the past now. This is all we have dreamed of.'

Something turned over inside and Katie felt Violet disappear. She stepped out of Katie's body as if she were shedding a skin. 'I don't think so,' Violet said, looking whole and solid and very un-ghost-like.

'Behave yourself,' Alexander said, sounding scared.

Violet winked at Katie and then stepped into Max.

Katie wanted to scream but she couldn't. She saw the surprise on Max's face and felt horror, but only in a very faint way. She was being squeezed tighter and tighter; her essence was being crushed. Alexander was getting stronger with every second. Katie had gathered the light around herself, but Alexander was digging in as if it were an all-you-can-eat buffet.

Max reached into his pocket and pulled out a small copper-coloured object. It was the bronze brooch they'd found in the archaeologist's things. In Alexander's things.

Max winked, in an exaggerated way that looked nothing like Max and entirely like Violet. Then he threw the brooch into the pond and said out loud, 'You want me, come with me.'

Katie felt a rush as Alexander left her body. She staggered back as the ghost dived after it, the water not even rippling as he hit the surface and disappeared.

Violet stepped from Max. One moment, Katie could see her in his face and posture and the next moment she was next to him and Max was doubled over making retching noises.

'Where did Violet go?' Max said, once he'd caught his breath. 'I felt her. I saw her thoughts, everything. That was—' He sat down heavily. Shook his head as if he needed to clear it. 'That was fucking horrible.'

'She's gone.' Katie looked around. Zofia picked up the witch's ball and wrapped it in its black cloth. She passed it to Katie. 'You should break this. Then he can't come back.'

'She's really gone.' Katie couldn't concentrate on anything else. She'd seen Violet step out of Max and then seen her disappear. Nothing dramatic, no flames or dust or bright light, just a flicker of a bulb, here one moment and gone the next. 'I felt it,' Katie said.

Zofia put her hand on Katie's arm. 'It's for the best.'

'I feel terrible. She saved my life. And now she's gone God knows where.'

'She saved your life,' Max said. 'Maybe that's what she was here for. Maybe it was fate that you met her.'

'I don't care about fate,' Katie said. She felt the tears spill over and sniffed to try and stop her nose from running, too. 'I care about Violet.'

Max held her while she cried, stroking her back and saying, gently, 'I know. I'm sorry.'

Katie leaned into Max, feeling safe with his arms around her. The crying left as quickly as it had come and she felt calmer than she had in days. The warm light was still inside her, she could feel it and, looking down at her stomach, she almost expected to be glowing. The image of a shaft of light shining out of her belly button made her laugh.

'Does she have hysteria?' Zofia said. 'It is shock, I think.'

'I'm fine,' Katie said. The rain was easing off, too. She looked up at the clearing sky and smiled, filled with wonderful knowledge. 'Violet doesn't have to be gone. I can bring her back.'

'What do you mean?'

'I've been bringing them into being, yes? Making them stronger? I can do that. I can feel how to do that, now. I think—' Katie stepped forward and held her hands above the surface of the water.

'I don't think that's a good idea,' Max said. 'She's been released or crossed over to the other side or whatever spirits do once they're not kept here. And we should go inside and sit down. In the dry. Away from the water you just nearly drowned in.'

'I'm fine,' Katie said.

'I'm not talking about you,' Max said. He was gritting his teeth to stop them from chattering, but Katie couldn't stop thinking about the light.

'In a moment.' Katie closed her eyes and reached out. She felt the trace of Violet's soul, a tiny piece of her spirit. Very quiet, very thin. Very hard to catch. Like a tiny scrap of tissue paper blowing in a gale.

'Got her,' Katie said, opening her eyes. She pictured a pinch of light threading out and igniting that scrap of paper, until Violet was standing in front of her. Almost completely transparent, but there.

'I'm the light,' Katie said, reaching out her hands to Violet. 'You don't have to go.'

Violet opened her mouth in a wail.

'It's okay,' Katie said, threading more light to Violet, making her stronger again, watching as her transparent body became more and more solid.

'Please stop,' Violet said, in between horrible gasps. 'You have to let me go.'

'But I'm saving you. You can stay here with us.' Katie gestured. 'You said some life was better than none at all.'

'I'm supposed to go,' Violet said and her voice was so quiet, Katie wasn't sure if she was speaking out loud or just in her mind. 'I don't belong here.'

'But I don't want you to leave me.' Katie felt angry again. What was the point of having bloody power if you couldn't do what you wanted? 'I'll miss you.'

'I shan't miss you,' Violet said, sounding like her old self. 'I'm ready for a new adventure.' Violet was fading again; she was using the force of her own will to give back whatever energy Katie was passing along the golden thread.

'I could make you stay,' Katie said, flexing her fingers and feeling the power within her move. She could feel its texture, its weight. She wondered what would happen if she used it all. Maybe she could make Violet strong enough to play with her doll's house, to eat food, to dance with nice-looking men at weddings, to kiss.

Violet smiled sadly, her face just a suggestion shimmering in the air. 'No, you couldn't. You're not that cruel.'

Katie stopped fighting. She watched as Violet faded away, her soul gone and just a tiny echo of a life once again.

'Good.' Zofia let out a noisy breath and patted Katie's arm. 'Time to go in now, I think.'

Katie nodded and followed Zofia. She was dimly aware of Max's arm around her shoulder and, then, of familiar voices shouting from the driveway.

Gwen and Cam rounded the corner and began crunching across the gravel. Katie pulled away from Max and went to meet them.

'I'm fine,' she said. 'It's over.' She found herself promptly in a Cam and Gwen sandwich, getting hugged to within an inch of her life. Cam broke away first and grabbed Max in a quick hug, too. 'You all right?'

'Sort of,' Max said. 'Henry tried to drown Katie.'

'Shh.' Katie shot him a warning look. 'It wasn't that bad.'

'Oh, my God,' Gwen said. She was shaking. 'I told you not to come back here. I told you—'

'And it wasn't Henry. It was Alexander James.'

Max raised an eyebrow. 'Violet's other suitor?'

Katie nodded. For the benefit of Cam and Gwen, she said, 'He was an archaeologist and a friend of the Beaufort family. He was obsessed with Violet, wrote her loads of love letters, but she didn't feel the same way. He saw her kissing Henry in the garden and drowned her in the ornamental pond.' Katie pointed to the large rectangle of water. Even now the rain had stopped, the sky was grey and the water looked black.

'Bastard,' Max said.

'Is her body down there?' Gwen said, swallowing.

'What's left of it, yes.'

'Do we have to burn her bones?' Max said and Gwen looked surprised.

'No.' Katie patted his arm. 'I'm beyond all of that.'

'What do you mean?' Cam said, but Katie was striding across the wet grass. Violet hadn't wanted her help, but there was something else she could do.

THE ELECTRICITY still wasn't on, but the clouds had parted and light was streaming through the mullioned windows. Barton was standing on the parquet of the reception hall, by the front window. He looked a little shaken. 'What was all that about?'

'A murderous ghost called Alexander James just tried to kill me,' Katie said. 'I like the way you rushed out to help.'

'I didn't know what was happening,' Barton said, indignant.

Katie turned to Max. 'Do you see? He absolutely has no idea. No psychic ability.'

'Now, hang on—' Barton said.

'If you did—' Katie turned back and began advancing on Barton '—you would be running right about now.'

She knew Gwen and Cam and Zofia and Max had come in behind her and she flashed them what she hoped was a reassuring smile.

Barton shrugged. He was trying to pull off his usual, confident pose, but his foot was tapping on the floor, giving him away. 'Magda says there's nothing to be frightened of. Spirits can't hurt us. You should know that.'

'Magda's wrong. Which, given that she's a figment of your imagination, is not a surprise.' She put her face near to Barton's. 'I don't like you, but I don't want you dead. At least, I don't want your death on my conscience. Alexander James is desperate. He'll use anybody he thinks has the least little bit of psychic power. If you don't tell him you don't have any, that you were lying about communicating with the other side, about having a spirit guide called Magda, then he's going to try to use you as a doorway and I don't know what that'll do to you. I don't know if you'd survive.'

'Oh, God,' Barton moaned. 'Help me.'

'Help yourself,' Katie said. 'Can't you feel how cold it is in here?' She reached out and felt the echoes of the hundreds of people who had passed through the space, those who'd lived and died. Like turning up the gas on an antique lamp, she pushed out a little bit of her power, until the echoes got louder and there were voices clamouring, faces appearing out of the walls and the glass and the air. The room was instantly freezing.

'Please,' Barton said, his eyes wide.

Katie looked over his shoulder, as if she could see a ghostly figure rising up ready to smite Barton. His eyes rolled in his head and for moment Katie thought he was just going to faint. 'I'd hurry up if I were you,' she added.

'I was lying. I don't have a spirit guide. I chose the name Magda from a book. I never got a message. Not any kind of message. I can't talk to the other side. I can't see ghosts.'

Katie stepped forward, ready to stop him, but Barton was in full flow. His eyes were wide and terrified, not seeing Katie or Max or Zofia. 'I thought I did, once,' he said, 'when I was a child. It scared me silly but then all the grown ups liked hearing about it. Mummy made me tell the story at her dinner parties and everyone would look at me like I was important and I just started embellishing.' His eyes skimmed Katie's face and then seemed to refocus. 'Please. I never meant for it to go this far. Please help me.'

'It's okay. He's gone.' Katie reached out and patted Barton on the arm. 'You're quite safe.' She pulled the light back, tucked it away. The voices quieted, the faces disappeared and the temperature went back up to normal.

'Oh, thank God.' Barton sank into the nearest armchair. He put his head in his hands and they were shaking.

'Shall I get you a drink?' Zofia said, kindly. 'Scotch?'

Barton lifted his head and, blinking back tears, said, 'Single malt if you've got it. I can't stomach a blend.'

Max shook his head. 'I think he's recovering.'

'What was that?' Gwen touched Katie's arm. 'What did you do? What were all those voices?'

Katie hugged her tight. She hadn't thought about Gwen. Of course she'd be able to hear them. 'Sorry,' she whispered into Gwen's ear. 'Just a party trick. Nothing to worry about.'

'A ghost tried to kill you? Alexander? Is he still here?'

Katie held up the witch's ball and tilted it, so that Gwen could see. 'Oh, my God.'

Katie looked at the image in the reflection of the burnished surface of the ball. Rather than reflecting the hallway and the main staircase, with its ornately carved finials, it was showing the oak panelling of the library. And, standing by the fireplace, his unlit pipe in one hand and a scowl of defeat on his face, was Alexander James. His lips were moving but she couldn't hear a thing. It was brilliant.

'So,' Zofia said, peering over Katie's shoulder. 'He was in there the whole time. When you were scaring Mr Barton.'

'He wasn't in any danger,' Katie said. 'And neither are you. He's going to stay trapped in here and I'll keep it far away from the hotel.'

'How did he get in there?' Gwen said. She looked at Katie, fear in her eyes. 'How did you—?'

'His soul was linked to a brooch we found.' Katie nodded to Max. 'The bronze one. When Violet threw it into the pond, Alexander had to follow it and that's what pulled him out from my body. Once he wasn't linked to me, Zofia uncovered the witch's ball and that trapped him.' She turned to Zofia. 'I don't know how to thank you for that.'

Patrick came through the staff door, his arms full of torches and candles. He stopped when he saw the group, blinked at Gwen and Cam and said, 'What did I miss?'

CHAPTER 31

Katie walked down the driveway with Gwen. Max had volunteered to finish his shift at The Grange before coming back to the house as Anna and Zofia were run off their feet with restless MOPs. Katie couldn't believe that she'd thought he was egotistical. When push came to shove, Max always tried to do the right thing. For an ex-con-man, he was strangely moral. Which was a peculiarly old-fashioned thing to think. Maybe she'd been spending too much time in the nineteen thirties.

'Hannah will be worried,' Gwen said, keeping a brisk pace. 'She came to warn you. About your energy spilling out.'

Katie wasn't sure if she was imagining it, but Gwen didn't seem to be able to look her in the eye.

'It's okay, you know,' she said. 'I know how to control it now.'

Gwen nodded, but she still looked slightly dazed.

Hannah Ash wasn't in the kitchen of End House, but there was a lime-green Post-it note attached to the fridge. It said: 'Glad you're not dead. Hannah.'

'Bloody wise women,' Katie said. She went to the freezer and got out an ice-cube tray. 'Drink?'

'Please,' Gwen said.

Katie stood in front of the fridge. 'What's Pimm's like? That's a summer drink, isn't it?'

'Why are you so calm?' Gwen said. 'You're bringing ghosts to life.'

'I was,' Katie said. 'I'm not any more. Not unless I want to.'

Gwen looked worried. 'I was thinking about Lily. She died a violent death. She might have hung around.'

'And she was psychotic,' Katie said. 'Don't forget that. Perfect ghost material.'

'That's not good,' Gwen said, sitting down.

'I told you. Not going to happen. I can feel the energy now. I'm not going to let it leak out. I'm not going to bring Lily or anybody else back. Not by accident, at any rate.'

'You're scaring me a little right now,' Gwen said.

'You just need a drink.' Katie stopped mixing and passed the glass to Gwen, who grabbed it like a drowning woman and took a long sip.

Katie tried some as well. It was nice. Refreshing. Sweet without being sickly. She took a longer drink.

'Hannah said it wasn't like a tap, though, that you could run out. You must be careful—'

'I know. I'm giving away chunks of my own life. You can't make energy. That's basic physics.'

Gwen shook her head. 'I think it might be best if we don't tell Ruby and David.'

Katie laughed. 'You think?' She drank some more of her Pimm's, picturing her mum and dad lying on matching sun loungers on the deck of a cruise ship in the middle of the ocean. 'I'm so glad they missed this.'

'I'll drink to that,' Gwen said and they clinked glasses. Gwen was still worrying; Katie could see the line between her eyebrows getting deeper and deeper.

'I promise I'll be careful. You know me.'

Gwen yawned and covered her mouth quickly. 'Sorry.'

'You're exhausted,' Cam said from the doorway. 'Come on.' He led Gwen into the living room and made her lie on the sofa. He took her drink and passed it to Katie to hold. 'We'll be right next door.'

In the kitchen he dumped Gwen's glass on the side and said, 'She's been so worried and we didn't get much sleep last night—'

'Ew, too much information,' Katie said. She was only joking but Cam blushed deep red and Katie wished she hadn't said anything. Instead she downed her drink and enjoyed the warm glow it spread through her. Finally, she could see the appeal of alcohol. She leaned against the counter, looking around Gwen's kitchen and feeling so relaxed and sleepy that her eyes slipped out of focus. In that instant, it was like seeing a slightly different scene. Or, the same scene but with an overlay. She could see a spark of yellow light inside Cam and a grey mass of past life moving gently through the air around them. It was like doing a magic eye picture when it suddenly flipped from a two-dimensional pattern to a three-dimensional image. She blinked and her vision returned to normal.She went to the living room to check on Gwen.

Gwen was still asleep on the sofa and Katie pulled the crochet blanket from the back and draped it over her. Gwen didn't so much as flutter an eyelid. She really must be exhausted.

Katie waited for the stab of guilt, but it didn't come.

She hadn't done anything wrong. She hadn't fucked up. Things might not have gone perfectly but she hadn't been a silly kid; she hadn't been a victim.

Cam was in the doorway. 'Tea?' he whispered, making a tipping gesture with his hand, as if drinking from a mug.

Katie nodded. 'Just a sec.' She pulled the blanket, straightening it over Gwen's legs. She checked that Cam had gone, listened for sounds of him in the kitchen. She put her hand lightly on the blanket, approximately in the middle of Gwen's sleeping form, and closed her eyes.

She could feel it. Now that she'd done it once, she could sense it there, curled up inside. She liked to picture it as a ball of light, something positive, but in truth it didn't feel positive or negative. It just was. A raw, primeval thing. The thing that people meant when they talked about 'life force' or 'will to live' or 'grit'. The thing that kept the elderly breathing long after they'd prefer to call it a day. The thing that made babies, so tiny they could fit into the palm of your hand, swallow a droplet of milk.

Katie pictured a piece of light breaking away from that glowing sphere, pictured it as a tiny spark of light that travelled down her arm, into her hand and out through her fingers into Gwen. She pictured it nesting somewhere inside Gwen, somewhere it could take root.

Katie opened her eyes. Gwen was still breathing deeply. Still fast asleep. There was no way to know whether it had worked, or how many years of her own life Katie had just given up, but Katie knew it didn't matter. Either way, it was worth it. Besides, she was a Harper. She had to help if she could.

. . .

THE NEXT DAY, Katie met Max at the hotel. The day was grey and cool, the grass wet and muddy from the storm.

They walked through the winding paths of the lower garden, along the beech-tree-lined 'lady's walk' and into the maze-like layout of thick hedges and rambling flower beds. Every so often, the hedges opened up to reveal a little circle of lawn with crumbling statuary or a broken fountain. Max was telling her about Laura. They'd been together for five months and things had been going badly for four of those.

'You don't have to tell me,' Katie said. 'It's in the past.'

'I want to,' Max said. 'I don't want you to think it was some great love story or anything. I just felt so guilty. I walked away from that accident with barely a scratch. It wasn't fair.'

'It was an accident.'

'She was screaming in my ear. It was dark. The road was slippery,' Max said, his voice flat. 'They're just excuses. She still died.'

'You know Barton was lying, though, right?'

'I know he didn't get a message.' Max squeezed Katie's hand. 'And I'm glad I got the new perspective on conning. I mean, it was what I was brought up to do. I was running scams in primary school, but I always thought I was a good guy. That if I stuck to the rules, I wasn't truly bad, but getting caught by Barton...' He trailed off and shrugged. 'It didn't feel good.'

'I know.' Katie reached out and hugged him close. After a moment, they broke apart and carried on walking.

'How are you doing now? About Laura?' Katie was wondering whether she should offer to try a seance or a spell or whether a real message from Laura might make Max feel worse, not better.

'You don't have to worry about me,' Max said. 'I'm always all right.'

'You are such a liar,' Katie said, smiling to soften the words.

Max shrugged. 'I thought I'd feel better. Relieved or something, but I don't.'

'Give it time.'

'I'm going to feel guilty for a while longer, I think.' Max put his hands on Katie's waist and pulled her closer. He was smiling now, looking like his old self. 'You could always distract me. You know, if you wanted to help.'

'I think a bit of guilt won't do you any harm at all.'

'Harsh,' Max said, and kissed her.

BY THE WEEKEND, everything had calmed down. Anna had stopped asking Katie whether there were any ghosts in the room and Gwen had stopped looking at her as if she were about to sprout horns.

Cam and Max had even been out for a bonding drink at The Red Lion and Cam had pronounced Max 'suitable-ish'.

Katie took Max to meet Fred Byres and on the way back they called into End House.

'How was he?' Gwen said.

'Gardening. He says his roses have never looked better.' Katie didn't mention that Fred was no longer even using his bifocals; Gwen would only worry.

'Did you see the Haunted Hotels website?'

'What did Patrick do?'

'Got The Grange listed. The town council is going nuts.' Gwen nudged Cam. 'I've never seen Elaine so angry and that's saying something.'

'I know,' Cam said. 'I give Patrick a week before he takes it down.'

'Still,' Gwen said, 'it might be a good time to take a little time off.'

'I could do with a holiday,' Katie said. That picture of her parents lying in the sun had stayed with her. She could fancy some of that. And maybe a drink with one of those paper umbrellas.

'You deserve one,' Gwen said.

'Shall we show her?' Cam said. 'Come outside.'

'Ta-da!' Gwen spread her arms wide with a flourish. 'Bob gave her a complete overhaul.'

'Bob the barman?' Katie said. 'At The Red Lion?'

'Bob the camper-van-obsessed barman, yes,' Gwen said. 'The man's a genius with engines. Nanette has never sounded so good.'

'Nanette?' Max said, looking nonplussed.

'You're going to let me drive Nanette?' Katie felt tears threaten.

'She's all yours, honeybunch,' Gwen said. 'I don't use her any more and she's getting all bored and lonely.'

'But—'

Cam put an arm around Gwen and kissed the top of her head. He smiled at Katie and said, 'Take some time off. Have a gap year.'

Katie felt her throat close up. It was so nice of them, but... 'I can't take a year. I've signed a contract to live with Anna. I've got to work out what I'm doing next. I might do a course, or something. I can't—'

'I knew you'd say that,' Cam said. 'Just for for a few

weeks. Take a trip, have some fun. Or use the time to work out whatever it is you feel you need to work out. Everything will still be here when you get back.'

Katie let out a breath. 'That is amazing.' She threw her arms around Cam and Gwen. 'Thank you, thank you.'

'Where will you go?' Gwen said.

'Paris, Barcelona, Prague, Rome, Venice,' Katie said. 'Everywhere.'

'Maybe avoid the catacombs, though,' Gwen said.

Katie wanted to tell her that the dead were everywhere. Graveyards and catacombs were no busier than the average high street, but maybe that was information she didn't really need.

Cam hugged her and then stepped away, towards Max. 'You're going with her, yes?'

'Um,' Max said.

'You don't have to,' Katie said, trying not to feel as if she'd been punched.

'He is,' Cam said. He stuck out his hand. 'Best of luck.'

'Hey!' Katie said as Max warily shook Cam's hand.

Gwen smiled. 'I'm relying on you to make sure she has some fun, okay?'

'No problem,' Max said. He put an arm around Katie's shoulders.

Cam opened his mouth, but Max said, 'I know, I know. If I hurt her you'll have me killed.'

'Oh, son.' Cam shook his head. 'Not only is that girl clever and beautiful and twenty-one years old, she's the latest in a very long line of witches and it appears she has power over life and death. I reckon I'm the least of your worries.' And then he smiled. Widely.

ONCE GWEN and Cam had gone back into the house, Katie gave Max the guided tour of the van. Gwen had reupholstered the bed settee and had fitted beautiful wooden drawers and cupboards along one wall. 'I can't believe she's given me Nanette,' Katie said.

'Me neither,' Max said, not looking quite as thrilled as Katie thought Nanette deserved.

'Where do you want to go?' Katie said. 'How about France? Or Italy?'

'If you think this rust bucket will get us that far,' Max said.

'Don't be rude,' Katie said, patting the van. 'You'll hurt her feelings.'

'Weirdo,' Max said, with affection. Then, 'I suppose we've got enough cash for repairs, anyway. Even after I've paid off my debts, I've still got plenty of cash from my dad's watch.'

Katie felt cold. She'd forgotten about poor Oliver Cole. 'That's something I don't understand. Why is he at peace? I never gave him his watch back.'

'Maybe it was just the thought that he'd left ten grand's worth of jewellery in his wash bag. Maybe he knew what his wife would do and he couldn't stand the thought of it being chucked out. I mean, if I'd left ten grand lying around, it'd prey on my mind, too.' Max pulled Katie to him. 'Or, it wasn't really the watch he wanted. Maybe he just wanted someone to know how he died.'

'You mean, he was just saying "watch".' Katie thought about the dreams, how she had repeatedly watched Oliver Cole die without understanding what had happened. Now it felt obvious: it had been

Alexander trying out his first possession. A practice-run. She could imagine him drifting into Oliver Cole and just staying there to see what happened. She sat down. 'You know I brought the ghosts into life? Does that mean I killed Mr Cole?'

'What do you mean?'

'I think it was Alexander testing out his powers. I think that's what gave Oliver Cole his heart attack.'

'You don't know that.'

Katie shook her head. 'He was so cold. Like he'd been in a freezer. You know what that means. If I hadn't been at The Grange, Mr Cole would never have died.'

'Doesn't make it your fault.'

Katie leaned against Max and rested her head on his shoulder. She'd always thought you needed to have all the information, all the knowledge, and that way you could protect yourself from ever making a mistake. Now she knew that wasn't possible. Didn't matter how hard you tried, you could never be sure you knew everything. Instead, she took comfort from the feel of Max's arm around her shoulders, the diesel-and-herb smell of Nanette and the warm light of her power, curled up inside.

'So,' she said, after a moment, 'you got your watch back?'

'Don't worry. I paid for it,' Max said. 'They only had it marked up at two fifty, so I made a donation, too.' He looked at her, anxious for approval.

Katie touched his cheek, wanted to wipe away the uncertainty. 'You did good.'

'I don't want you getting the wrong idea of my reformed character. It was still only a fraction of what it was worth,' Max said. 'If I was being truly good, I would've told them so they could've made full whack.'

'It's a grey area,' Katie said. 'It did belong to you in the first place.'

'I'm sick of the grey area,' Max said, turning so that his face was close to hers. 'I've lived my whole life swimming in it, but I want that to change. I want to be with you and being with you makes me want to be a better person.'

'That's good, but I'm glad you kept some of the money.'

Max put his hands on her waist and looked into her eyes. 'Really?'

'Really,' Katie said, enjoying the sensation of his hands holding her. 'You can use it for university fees if you decide you want to study maths or to start a business or go travelling or whatever you want. Fresh start. And, if there's enough left over, you can take me out for that dinner.'

'I did ask you out about a hundred years ago, didn't I?'

'You did,' Katie said, moving closer. 'But I forgive you. You've been busy.'

'I really like you,' Max said. He looked so uncertain. 'A lot.'

'I know.' Katie smiled up at him, drinking in the sight of his upturned mouth, the warmth in his eyes. So what if he had a dodgy past? No one was perfect.

'And if we still like each other after four months in this tin can, I reckon I should stick around.'

'Is that right?' Katie said, happiness spreading through her like sunshine.

Max smiled. 'Trust me.'

ACKNOWLEDGMENTS

This book put up a bit of a fight and it truly wouldn't
exist without the encouragement and editorial support
of Sally and Victoria at Carina UK.
Thank you, also, to my wonderful agent, Sallyanne
Sweeney, for her continuing enthusiasm and guidance.
I'm so grateful to all my friends and family for their
understanding while I wrestled with this book, and to
Holly and James for putting up with 'Deadline Mum'
with love and good grace.
Finally, thank you to my brother, Matthew, for the pep
talks and delicious beer.

ABOUT THE AUTHOR

Sarah lives in rural Scotland with her children and husband. She drinks too much tea, loves the work of Joss Whedon, and is the proud owner of a writing shed.

Sign up to the Sarah Painter Books Readers' Club at the address below. It's absolutely free and you'll get book release news, giveaways and exclusive FREE stuff!

www.sarah-painter.com

www.ingramcontent.com/pod-product-compliance
Lightning Source LLC
Chambersburg PA
CBHW030358200726